SHUNNED HOUSES

SHUNNED HOUSES

An Anthology of Weird Stories, Unspeakable Poems, and Impious Essays

edited by

KATHERINE KERESTMAN AND S. T. JOSHI

WordCrafts

*"What terrified me will terrify others;
and I need only describe the spectre which had haunted
my midnight pillow."*

~Mary Shelley

Contents

Introduction
Katherine Kerestman and S. T. Joshi

A man's home is his castle—but what if his castle is the *Castle of Otranto*? Suzie's a good homemaker, but what if all the Fuller Brush Man's cleaning solutions cannot get the luminous mold from her basement floor? And what if the answer to the draftiness of your ancestral mansion is double-walled insulation consisting of an internment vault between two stone walls? Some say home is where the heart is, but what if the heart is the "Tell-Tale Heart"?

In the best weird fiction, and in mainstream literature, too, houses are often key players. Not merely backdrops contributing to atmosphere and setting, houses often carry the burdens of past hopes and dread, death and misdeeds. In general—whether or not the supernatural plays a role in its biography—a house is haunted. Sometimes it is the uncertainty (whether a house is haunted merely by its history or by ghosts) that is the crux of the matter, as in Henry James's *The Turn of the Screw* (1898) or Shirley Jackson's *The Haunting of Hill House* (1959).

We face these qualms in real life, too. For example, people often find the elderly houses of Gettysburg, whose wooden frames are aerated with bullet holes, every bit as disturbing as the spirits that are said to haunt them: when contemplating the bores in the planks of the old walls, one is hard pressed to avoid picturing a dust storm raised by blue-coated soldiers on horseback—as they thread their way through a terrified citizenry fleeing on foot or in wagons along the dirt roads—or hearing the booming of cannons and feeling the shuddering of the earth, as the awful battle is being waged in the meadows and rolling hills just out of eyesight. Visitors (and overnight guests) at Lizzie Borden's house in Fall River, Massachusetts, are shown the precise place on the stairs people were standing when they first glimpsed Mrs. Borden's axe-slain body lying on the floor betwixt the bed and the dresser, and even the stove in the kitchen where Lizzie burned her stained dress. Visitors to the Tower of London gravitate to the beheading site of Anne Boleyn.

Indeed, accounts of "real" haunted houses have an ancient lineage, if the letter of Pliny the Younger (1st century c.e.) included here is any guide. This account is the ultimate ancestor of countless others that followed in its wake. The American poet John Greenleaf Whittier, in his first book, *Legends of New-England* (1831), found occasion to write a quasi-fictional account of a haunted house he had read about in the work of Cotton Mather. The Society of Psychical Research, founded in England in 1882 (an American branch was established in 1885), made a specialty of investigating purported haunted houses. Jessie Adelaide Middleton wrote dozens of accounts in the early twentieth century, one of which we have included. The great weird writer Algernon Blackwood recounts one such venture in which he participated in his contribution to this volume.

Houses, and other places, can be reservoirs of joy or misery. When this affective power endures, a place is said to be "haunted." When this energy for good or evil (or any other manner of energy) continues—especially when it touches people who were not involved in the primary circumstance which occurred in that location—then a place is considered alive. Places, then, may serve as portals through which a person can enter into the past, both psychically and physically; moreover, the effects of a place upon a person may influence what happens going forward. Places are causes, and they are effects.

Among places, one's home is special, and yet the word "home" may be infused with doubtful associations. At the end of a stressful day at work, a person may want to run home—to the house that functions as his harbor, shelter, or castle (as in "king of one's castle"); on the other hand, a person's home is sometimes a place to run away from, a cage or a trap. A house may be a homeowner's medium for self-expression, a blank canvas or parchment upon which a decorator may realize her artistic vision—except when the artist is entangled in the crawling vines within the "Yellow Wallpaper," the imperishable 1892 tale by Charlotte Perkins Gilman.

The Gothic novel of the late eighteenth and early nineteenth centuries specialized in the "haunted castle," in such novels as the aforementioned *Castle of Otranto* (1764) by Horace Walpole, Ann Radcliffe's *The Mysteries of Udolpho* (1794), and many others. The late Gothic writer G. P. R. James produced a compelling account in "A Night in an Old Castle" (1854), included here.

With thick stone walls and narrow windows, Wuthering Heights (in the 1848 novel by Emily Brontë) is a fortress with endless, barren moors that serve as an earthen moat, built to withstand a siege. Its owner, Heathcliff, too, has built a suit of emotional armor around himself, for he is determined to brook no further abuse or deprivation—and to launch the first strike in any fray. Heathcliff's bedroom has

> a carpet—a good one, but the pattern was obliterated by dust; a fireplace hung with cut-paper, dropping to pieces; a handsome oak-bedstead with ample crimson curtains of rather expensive material and modern make; but they had evidently experienced rough usage: the vallances hung in festoons, wrenched from their rings, and the iron rod supporting them was bent in an arc on one side, causing the drapery to trail upon the floor. The chairs were also damaged, many of them severely; and deep indentations deformed the panels of the walls.

Heathcliff has made his house over in his own image.

In Nathaniel Hawthorne's *The House of the Seven Gables* (1851), the house rests upon land stolen from the Maules by the Pyncheons. The description of its "seven acutely peaked gables, facing towards various points of the compass" is suggestive of circumspection, as if the house holds many secrets; indeed, within its walls an ancestral portrait conceals an ill-gotten land deed. Just as the family home has fallen into disrepair, the Pyncheons have come down in the world to such an extent that Hepzibah has added a cent shop to the manse and taken in a boarder to supplement her income. At the resolution of their lifelong ordeal (living under a Maule curse), the blameless descendants of their larcenous forebear move out of the blood-soaked mansion.

But it was Edgar Allan Poe who, as in so many other ways, refashioned the haunted house in the course of revolutionizing the weird tale. The repetition of the phrase "vacant eye-like windows" at the opening of "The Fall of the House of Usher" (1839) cues the reader that this gloomy edifice is more alive than inanimate wood and brick. The narrator, upon first viewing the house, experiences a deep depression: "I looked upon the scene before me—upon the mere house, and the simple landscape features of the domain—upon the bleak walls . . . with an utter depression of soul which I can compare to no earthly sensation more properly than to the after-dream of the reveller upon opium." He puzzles over his reaction: "what was it that so unnerved me in the contemplation of the House of Usher?" and concludes that "there *are* combinations of very simple natural objects which have the power of thus affecting us . . . a mere different arrangement of the particulars of the scene, of the details of the picture, would be sufficient to modify, or perhaps to annihilate its capacity for sorrowful impression." At length, he comes to understand that the house and the Usher siblings, Roderick and Madeline, are one and the same: the lack of issue to inherit either the *patronymic* or the *house* of Usher "so identified the two as to merge . . . both the family and the mansion."

Among Poe's many successors, Guy de Maupassant and

Ambrose Bierce hold a high place. Maupassant's "The Inn" (1886) is a grim tale of psychological terror that closely approaches the *conte cruel* (cruel tale) mastered by Villiers de l'Isle-Adam, Maurice Level, and other French writers. Bierce's "Whither?" (1889) is an early version of the well-known tale "The Spook House"—and this version suggests that he was crafting a pseudo-"real" account, possibly as a parody of the actions of the Society for Psychical Research, toward which he cast a skeptical eye.

The residence in William Hope Hodgson's *The House on the Borderland* (1908) is far more than merely a "haunted house," and the extract from an early chapter that we present here attests to the author's power in creating a powerful atmosphere of the weird by means of telling details and a focus on the protagonist's disturbed reactions as he ventures through the cavernous house in a remote corner of Ireland. A. E. W. Mason abandoned his usual practice of detective-story writing to pen an unforgettable haunted house tale on a novel premise, "The House of Terror" (1917). And the obscure English writer M. A. Manhood, in "Misery Cottage" (1928), evokes both terror and a grisly personal tragedy.[1]

H. P. Lovecraft's "The Shunned House" (1924) features a deadly domicile (based on an actual house in the author's native city of Providence, Rhode Island—one that he earlier dramatized in the poem "The House," included here) possessed by a natural, rather than a supernatural, entity that "insidiously sap[s]" the "vitality" of its occupants, unnaturally hastening a natural death for most of its victims, although "those who did not die displayed in varying degree a type of anemia or consumption, and sometimes a decline of the mental faculties, which spoke ill for the salubriousness of the building."

The danger in "The Shunned House" is not merely a sanitary problem for the Providence Department of Health, but a weird enigma waiting to be unraveled by a physician with a penchant for

---

1   We are grateful to Debra K. Every for providing us with the text of this story.

occult detective work. Dr. Elihu Whipple, who has always been fascinated by the house with a bad reputation, with his nephew, the narrator, conducts a scientific investigation of the moldy, shunned house and discovers an anthropomorphic form in the basement mold, "a sort of cloudy whitish pattern on the dirt floor—a vague, shifting deposit of mold or nitre which we sometimes thought we could trace amidst the sparse fungous growths near the huge fireplace of the basement kitchen. Once in a while it struck us that this patch bore an uncanny resemblance to a doubled-up human figure, though generally no such kinship existed, and often there was no whitish deposit whatever."

While science saves the day on this occasion (although Dr. Whipple dies in the process), the fatal experiment has exposed the malicious properties of nature to the horrified narrator. Thus, a house, whose purpose is the protection of its inhabitants, may be invaded by enemies (ghosts, other people, curses, or more nameless entities), and, once breached, may become the enemy, sucking the life force of its occupants or falling down and crushing the life out of them. But what alternative is possible? Wide-open spaces, no roof to keep out the rain, no walls to keep out foes and animals, no walls to contain secrets and information?

Contemporary writers have not failed to draw upon the venerable trope of the haunted house and made it their own by novelties of approach, tone, and theme; and we are proud to present here a representative sample of recent and original tales and poems. Ramsey Campbell's "Napier Court" (1971) is simultaneously a weird tale about the supernatural properties of a house and a psychological portrait of the disturbed young woman who occupies it. Campbell went on to write the outstanding *The House on Nazareth Hill* (1996), which may challenge *The Haunting of Hill House* as the best haunted house novel ever written.

Anna Taborska, in "Endless," tells of the weird goings-on in a rental house. A decrepit hotel is the source of horror in Michael Aronovitz's "Share Your Bounty," where even social media posts contribute to the atmosphere of terror. Tony LaMalfa's "The Red Ensign" takes us to a baleful farmhouse in New England, while Katherine Kerestman's "Haunted House" is a stream-of-consciousness narrative of a sinister house that kids on Halloween approach at their peril. The residence in Stephen Mark Rainey's "The House at Black Tooth Pond" is the locus of a poignant domestic trauma, while the seedy residence in John Shirley's "Empty Bottles" houses terrors uniquely associated with our own technology-engulfed world. Jacob Moon's "The Space" is a rumination on the gruesome Victorian tradition of photographing the recently dead.

It is unsurprising that weird houses have entered poetry over the centuries. Whether it is the "stately pleasure-dome" that Samuel Taylor Coleridge saw in a dream, or the "haunted palace" that Poe envisioned, or the mysterious abodes found in the poems of Edwin Arlington Robinson, Robert Frost, and others, or the "home of Poe" that Frank Belknap Long speaks of in a haunting prose poem, the spectral house stalks through poetry at the highest levels. The pulp magazine *Weird Tales* seemed particularly receptive to such work, as the poems of Cristel Hastings and Lilla Price Savino in this volume attest. We are grateful that such leading contemporary poets and prose-poets as Adam Bolivar, Frank Coffman, Margaret Curtis, Rebecca Fraser, Ian Futter, Maxwell I. Gold, Lori R. Lopez, D. L. Myers, Ngo Binh Anh Khoa, Michael Potts, Ann K. Schwader, DJ Tyrer, and Kyla Lee Ward have offered their distinctive riffs on this age-old motif.

The haunted house is not only the preserve of literature. The theme is particularly amenable to such visual media as film, television, and the graphic novel. Five afternoons a week for five years, millions of devotees ran home from school or work to watch television's *Dark Shadows*. Fans regarded Collinwood—the brooding, decaying, sinister, secretive, ancestral hall of the Collins family—as their own ancestral mansion, and love of the mansion inculcated a fondness for the brooding, decaying, sinister, secretive, ancestral personality as well. The architecture of Collinwood mirrors the character of those who live within its walls—to wit, the secret panels, closed-off wings, cellar cells with iron bars, and disused towers of Collinwood. Barnabas, Tom Jennings, Burke Devlin, and assorted family members are haunted people whose tragic memories and experiences plague them every bit as much as the ghosts of Josette, Quentin, Beth, and Bill Malloy haunt the chambers of Collinwood. The house has a crenellated roof for falling off of, a dirt floor in the basement for digging up bodies under, false walls for hiding doors behind, and great Gothic stone fireplaces in every room; the Old House on the estate, restored to its 1795 condition and intentionally lacking all the modern conveniences, is an appropriate setting for its 175-year-old vampire inmate; and the children on the estate play in a cemetery and a mausoleum, as well as on Widows' Hill, a favorite place for suicides and murderers.

The best we can do is hope that we live in a benevolent house. Exorcise often. Perhaps propitiate the Lares and Penates. And scrub our walls and floors regularly.

Perhaps you're thinking now that "home" sounds rather a nasty thing you would rather do without.

Kubla Khan
Or, a Vision in a Dream. A Fragment
Samuel Taylor Coleridge

In Xanadu did Kubla Khan
A stately pleasure-dome decree:
Where Alph, the sacred river, ran
Through caverns measureless to man
    Down to a sunless sea.
So twice five miles of fertile ground
With walls and towers were girdled round;
And there were gardens bright with sinuous rills,
Where blossomed many an incense-bearing tree;
And here were forests ancient as the hills,
Enfolding sunny spots of greenery.

But oh! that deep romantic chasm which slanted
Down the green hill athwart a cedarn cover!
A savage place! as holy and enchanted
As e'er beneath a waning moon was haunted
By woman wailing for her demon-lover!
And from this chasm, with ceaseless turmoil seething,
As if this earth in fast thick pants were breathing,
A mighty fountain momently was forced:
Amid whose swift half-intermitted burst
Huge fragments vaulted like rebounding hail,
Or chaffy grain beneath the thresher's flail:
And mid these dancing rocks at once and ever
It flung up momently the sacred river.

Five miles meandering with a mazy motion
Through wood and dale the sacred river ran,
Then reached the caverns measureless to man,
And sank in tumult to a lifeless ocean;
And 'mid this tumult Kubla heard from far
Ancestral voices prophesying war!
   The shadow of the dome of pleasure
   Floated midway on the waves;
   Where was heard the mingled measure
   From the fountain and the caves.
It was a miracle of rare device,
A sunny pleasure-dome with caves of ice!

   A damsel with a dulcimer
   In a vision once I saw:
   It was an Abyssinian maid
   And on her dulcimer she played,
   Singing of Mount Abora.
   Could I revive within me
   Her symphony and song,
   To such a deep delight 'twould win me,
That with music loud and long,
I would build that dome in air,
That sunny dome! those caves of ice!
And all who heard should see them there,
And all should cry, Beware! Beware!
His flashing eyes, his floating hair!
Weave a circle round him thrice,
And close your eyes with holy dread
For he on honey-dew hath fed,
And drunk the milk of Paradise.

The House in the Arena
William Hope Hodgson

A minute came and went, and I was at the exit of the chasm, staring out upon an enormous amphitheatre of mountains. Yet, of the mountains, and the terrible grandeur of the place, I recked nothing; for I was confounded with amazement, to behold, at a distance of several miles, and occupying the centre of the arena, a stupendous structure, built apparently of green jade. Yet, in itself, it was not the discovery of the building that had so astonished me; but the fact, which became every moment more apparent, that in no particular, save in colour and its enormous size, did the lonely structure vary from this house in which I live.

For awhile, I continued to stare, fixedly. Even then, I could scarcely believe that I saw aright. In my mind, a question formed, reiterating incessantly: "What does it mean?" "What does it mean?" and I was unable to make answer, even out of the depths of my imagination. I seemed capable only of wonder and fear. For a time longer, I gazed, noting, continually, some fresh point of resemblance that attracted me. At last, wearied and sorely puzzled, I turned from it, to view the rest of the strange place on to which I had intruded.

Hitherto, I had been so engrossed in my scrutiny of the House, that I had given only a cursory glance round. Now, as I looked, I began to realise upon what sort of a place I had come. The arena, for so I have termed it, appeared a perfect circle of about ten to twelve miles in diameter, the House, as I have mentioned before, standing in the centre. The surface of the place, like to that of the Plain, had a peculiar, misty appearance, that was yet not mist.

From a rapid survey, my glance passed quickly upwards, along the slopes of the circling mountains. How silent they were. I think that this same abominable stillness was more trying to me, than anything that I had, so far, seen or imagined. I was looking up, now, at the great crags, towering so loftily. Up there, the impalpable redness gave a blurred appearance to everything.

And then, as I peered, curiously, a new terror came to me; for, away up among the dim peaks to my right, I had descried a vast shape of blackness, giant-like. It grew upon my sight. It had an enormous equine head, with gigantic ears, and seemed to peer steadfastly down into the arena. There was that about the pose, that gave me the impression of an eternal watchfulness—of having warded that dismal place, through unknown eternities. Slowly, the monster became plainer to me; and then, suddenly, my gaze sprang from it to something further off and higher among the crags. For a long minute, I gazed, fearfully. I was strangely conscious of something not altogether unfamiliar—as though something stirred in the back of my mind. The thing was black, and had four grotesque arms. The features showed, indistinctly. Round the neck, I made out several light-coloured objects. Slowly, the details came to me, and I realised, coldly, that they were skulls. Further down the body was another circling belt, showing less dark against the black trunk. Then, even as I puzzled to know what the thing was, a memory slid into my mind, and straightway, I knew that I was looking at a monstrous representation of Kali, the Hindu goddess of death.

Other remembrances of my old student days drifted into my thoughts. My glance fell back upon the huge beast-headed Thing. Simultaneously, I recognised it for the ancient Egyptian god Set, or Seth, the Destroyer of Souls. With the knowledge, there came a great sweep of questioning—"Two of the—!" I stopped, and endeavoured to think. Things beyond my imagination, peered into my frightened mind. I saw, obscurely. "The old gods of mythology!" I tried to comprehend to what it was all pointing. My gaze dwelt, flickeringly, between the two. "If—"

An idea came swiftly, and I turned, and glanced rapidly upwards, searching the gloomy crags, away to my left. Something loomed out under a great peak, a shape of greyness. I wondered I had not seen it earlier, and then remembered I had not yet viewed that portion. I saw it more plainly now. It was, as I have said, grey. It had a tremendous head; but no eyes. That part of its face was blank.

Now, I saw that there were other things up among the mountains. Further off, reclining on a lofty ledge, I made out a livid mass, irregular and ghoulish. It seemed without form, save for an unclean, half-animal face, that looked out, vilely, from somewhere about its middle. And then, I saw others—there were hundreds of them. They seemed to grow out of the shadows. Several, I recognised, almost immediately, as mythological deities; others were strange to me, utterly strange, beyond the power of a human mind to conceive.

On each side, I looked, and saw more, continually. The mountains were full of strange things—Beast-gods, and Horrors, so atrocious and bestial that possibility and decency deny any further attempt to describe them. And I—I was filled with a terrible sense of overwhelming horror and fear and repugnance; yet, spite of these, I wondered exceedingly. Was there then, after all, something in the old heathen worship, something more than the mere deifying of men, animals and elements? The thought gripped me—was there?

Later, a question repeated itself. What were they, those Beast-gods, and the others? At first, they had appeared to me, just sculptured Monsters, placed indiscriminately among the inaccessible peaks and precipices of the surrounding mountains. Now, as I scrutinised them with greater intentness, my mind began to reach out to fresh conclusions. There was something about them, an indescribable sort of silent vitality, that suggested, to my broadening consciousness, a state of life-in-death—a something that was by no means life, as we understand it; but rather an inhuman form of existence, that well might be likened to a deathless trance—a condition in which it was possible to imagine their continuing, eternally. "Immortal!" the word rose in my thoughts unbidden;

and, straightway, I grew to wondering whether this might be the immortality of the gods.

And then, in the midst of my wondering and musing, something happened. Until then, I had been staying, just within the shadow of the exit of the great rift. Now, without volition on my part, I drifted out of the semi-darkness, and began to move slowly across the arena—towards the House. At this, I gave up all thoughts of those prodigious Shapes above me—and could only stare, frightenedly, at the tremendous structure, towards which I was being conveyed so remorselessly. Yet, though I searched earnestly, I could discover nothing that I had not already seen, and so became gradually calmer.

Presently, I had reached a point more than half-way between the House and the gorge. All around, was spread the stark loneliness of the place, and the unbroken silence. Steadily, I neared the great building. Then, all at once, something caught my vision, something that came round one of the huge buttresses of the House, and so into full view. It was a gigantic thing, and moved with a curious lope, going almost upright, after the manner of a man. It was quite unclothed, and had a remarkable luminous appearance. Yet it was the face that attracted and frightened me the most. It was the face of a swine.

Silently, intently, I watched this horrible creature, and forgot my fear, momentarily, in my interest in its movements. It was making its way, cumbrously, round the building, stopping, as it came to each window, to peer in, and shake at the bars, with which—as in this house—they were protected; and whenever it came to a door, it would push at it, fingering the fastening stealthily. Evidently, it was searching for an ingress into the House.

I had come now to within less than a quarter of a mile of the great structure, and still I was compelled forward. Abruptly, the Thing turned, and gazed, hideously, in my direction. It opened its mouth, and, for the first time, the stillness of that abominable place was broken, by a deep, booming note, that sent an added thrill of apprehension through me. Then, immediately, I became aware that it was coming towards me, swiftly and silently. In an instant, it had covered half the distance that lay between. And still, I was borne helplessly to meet it. Only a hundred yards, and the brutish ferocity of the giant face numbed me with a feeling of unmitigated horror. I could have screamed, in the supremeness of my fear; and then, in the very moment of my extremity and despair, I became conscious that I was looking down upon the arena, from a rapidly-increasing height. I was rising, rising. In an inconceivably short while, I had reached an altitude of many hundred feet. Beneath me, the spot that I had just left, was occupied by the foul Swine-creature. It had gone down on all fours, and was snuffing and rooting, like a veritable hog, at the surface of the arena. A moment, and it rose to its feet, clutching upwards, with an expression of desire upon its face, such as I have never seen in this world.

Continually, I mounted higher. A few minutes, it seemed, and I had risen above the great mountains—floating, alone, afar in the redness. At a tremendous distance below, the arena showed, dimly; with the mighty House looking no larger than a tiny spot of green. The Swine-thing was no longer visible.

Presently, I passed over the mountains, out above the huge breadth of the plain. Far away, on its surface, in the direction of the ring-shaped sun, there showed a confused blur. I looked towards it, indifferently. It reminded me, somewhat, of the first glimpse I had caught of the mountain-amphitheatre.

With a sense of weariness, I glanced upwards at the immense ring of fire. What a strange thing it was! Then, as I stared, out from the dark centre, there spurted a sudden flare of extraordinary vivid fire. Compared with the size of the black centre, it was as naught; yet, in itself, stupendous. With awakened interest, I watched it carefully, noting its strange boiling and glowing. Then, in a moment, the whole thing grew dim and unreal, and so passed out of sight. Much amazed, I glanced down to the Plain from which I was still rising. Thus, I received a fresh surprise. The Plain—everything, had vanished, and only a sea of red mist was spread, far below me. Gradually, as I stared, this grew remote, and died away into a dim, far mystery of red, against an unfathomable night. Awhile, and even this had gone, and I was wrapped in an impalpable, lightless gloom.

The Haunted House

Cristel Hastings

It stands deserted through the mildewed years;
Its only friends the wind and evening star
And the gray mist that rains its dripping tears
And wonders who its ghostly tenants are.

They say it's best to take the upper trail
Where sunshine floods the flowered, perfumed way,
Avoiding an old road where thistles sail
And blank-eyed windows stare back, gaunt and gray.

They say the wails have bullet-tunneled holes,
And that the rats run screeching through the night;
They say queer shapes slip out and Avalk the knolls,
Seeking the souls that long ago took flight.

Queer lights glow where the zero hour sounds,
And winds moan through the empty, aching halls;
And as they bend the trees, a shadow bounds
From room to room, and sends its shrieking calls.

Forgotten with each dawn the moaning croon,
The screeching rats, the shadow shapes that strode;
But if I must go by, even at noon,
It's just as well to take the upper road.

A Haven for the Homeless

Frank Coffman

(An Interlocking Rubaiyat, with a definite nod to Robert Frost)

Whose house this was I think I know—
He died these many years ago.
Vacant, but less cold than outdoors.
Burr! It must be ten below!

Outside these walls, a blizzard roars;
Through tattered coat the wind just bores.
These walls stop that, and now I will
Set down my bedroll on these floors.

In this tight corner, safe until
I face tomorrow's Winter chill,
I hope this pile of rags will keep
What warmth my body clings to still.

* * *

I startle from a fitful sleep.
It's not the cold makes my flesh creep!
For there, beside me, is the man!
The Owner sits in darkness deep.

And softly—softly as he can—
He tells me that he has a plan:
"Just let your woes all drift away;
Remember the good race you ran.

"There is no further debt to pay,
No better day than *this* Today."
  And so, I think that I will stay.
  And now, I know that I shall stay.

The House of Terror

A. E. W. Mason

There are eager spirits who enter upon each morning like adventurers upon an unknown sea. Mr. Rupert Glynn, however, was not of that company. He had been christened "Rupert" in an ironical moment, for he preferred the day to be humdrum. Possessed of an easy independence, which he had never done a stroke of work to enlarge, he remained a bachelor, not from lark of opportunity to become a husband, but in order that his comfort might not be disarranged.

"A hunting-box in the Midlands," he used to say, "a set of chambers in the Albany, the season in town, a cure in the autumn at some French spa where a modest game of baccarat can be enjoyed, and a five-pound note in my pocket at the service of a friend—these conditions satisfy my simple wants, and I can rub along."

Contentment had rounded his figure, and he was a little thicker in the jaw and redder in the face than he used to be. But his eye was clear, and he had many friends, a fact for which it was easy to account. For there was a pleasant earthliness about him which made him restful company. It seemed impossible that strange startling things could happen in his presence; he had so stolid and comfortable a look, his life was so customary and sane. "When I am frightened by queer shuffling sounds in the dead of night," said a nervous friend of his, "I think of Rupert Glynn and I am comforted." Yet just because of this atmosphere of security which he diffused about him, Mr. Glynn was dragged into mysteries, and made acquainted with terrors.

In the first days of February Mr. Glynn found upon his breakfast-table at Melton a letter which he read through with an increasing gravity. Mr. Glynn being a man of method, kept a file of the *Morning Post*. He rang the bell for his servant, and fetched to the table his pocket diary. He turned back the pages until he read in the space reserved for November 15th, "My first run of the year."

Then he spoke to his servant, who was now waiting in the room:

"Thompson, bring me the *Morning Post* of November 16th."

Mr. Glynn remembered that he had read a particular announcement in the paper on the morning after his first run, when he was very stiff. Thompson brought him the copy for which he had asked, and, turning over the pages, he soon lighted upon the paragraph.

"Mr. James Thresk has recovered from his recent breakdown, and left London yesterday with Mrs. Thresk for North Uist."

Glynn laid down his newspaper and contemplated the immediate future with gloom. It was a very long way to the Outer Hebrides, and, moreover, he had eight horses in his stable. Yet he could hardly refuse to take the journey in the face of that paragraph. It was not, indeed, in his nature to refuse. For the letter written by Linda Thresk claimed his presence urgently. He took it up again. There was no reason expressed as to why he was needed. And there were instructions, besides, which puzzled him, very explicit instructions. He was to bring his guns, he was to send a telegram from Loch Boisdale, the last harbour into which the steamer from Oban put before it reached North Uist, and from no other place. He was, in a word, to pretend that he had been shooting in a neighbouring island to North Uist, and that, since he was so near, he ventured to trespass for a night or two on Mrs. Thresk's hospitality. All these precautions seemed to Glynn ominous, but still more ominous was the style of the letter. A word here, a sentence there—nay, the very agitation of the handwriting, filled Glynn with uneasiness. The appeal was almost pitiful. He seemed to see Linda Thresk bending over the pages of the letter which he now held in his hand, writing hurriedly, with a twitching, terrified face, and every now and then looking up, and to this side and to that, with the eyes of a hunted animal. He remembered Linda's appearance very well as he held her letter in his hand, although three years had passed since he had seen her—a fragile, slender woman with a pale, delicate face, big dark eyes, and masses of dark hair—a woman with the look of a girl and an almost hot-house air of refinement.

Mr. Glynn laid the letter down again, and again rang for his servant.

"Pack for a fortnight," he said. "And get my guns out. I am going away."

Thompson was as surprised as his self-respect allowed him to be.

"Your guns, sir?" he asked. "I think they are in town, but we have not used them for so long."

"I know," said Mr. Glynn impatiently. "But we are going to use them now."

Thompson knew very well that Mr. Glynn could not hit a haystack twenty yards away, and had altogether abandoned a sport in which he was so lamentably deficient. But a still greater shock was to be inflicted upon him.

"Thompson," said Mr. Glynn, "I shall not take you with me. I shall go alone."

And go alone he did. Here was the five-pound note, in a word, at the service of a friend. But he was not without perplexities, to keep his thoughts busy upon his journey.

Why had Linda Thresk sent for him out of all her friends?

For since her marriage three years before, he had clean lost sight of her, and even before her marriage he had, after all, been only one of many. He found no answer to that question. On the other hand, he faithfully fulfilled Mrs. Thresk's instructions. He took his guns with him, and when the steamer stopped beside the little quay at Loch Boisdale he went ashore and sent off his telegram. Two hours later he disembarked at Lochmaddy in North

21

Uist, and, hiring a trap at the inn, set off on his long drive across that flat and melancholy island. The sun set, the swift darkness followed, and the moon had risen before he heard the murmurous thunder of the sea upon the western shore. It was about ten minutes later when, beyond a turn of the road, he saw the house and lights shining brightly in its windows. It was a small white house with a few out-buildings at the back, set in a flat peat country on the edge of a great marsh. Ten yards from the house a great brake of reeds marked the beginning of the marsh, and beyond the reeds the bog stretched away glistening with pools to the low sand-hills. Beyond the sand-hills the Atlantic ran out to meet the darkness, a shimmering plain of silver. One sapling stood up from the middle of the marsh, and laid a finger across the moon. But except that sapling, there were not any trees.

To Glynn, fresh from the meadowlands of Leicestershire with their neat patterns of hedges, white gates and trees, this corner of the Outer Hebrides upon the edge of the Atlantic had the wildest and most desolate look. The seagulls and curlews cried perpetually above the marsh, and the quiet sea broke upon the sand with a haunting and mournful sound. Glynn looked at the little house set so far away in solitude, and was glad that he had come. To his southern way of thinking, trouble was best met and terrors most easily endured in the lighted ways of cities, where companionship was to be had by the mere stepping across the threshold.

When the trap drove up to the door, there was some delay in answering Glynn's summons. A middle-aged man-servant came at last to the door, and peered out from the doorway in surprise.

"I sent a telegram," said Glynn, "from Loch Bois-dale. I am Mr. Glynn."

"A telegram?" said the man. "It will not come up until the morning, sir."

Then the voice of the driver broke in.

"I brought up a telegram from Lochmaddy. It's from a gentleman who is coming to visit Mrs. Thresk from South Uist."

In the outer islands, where all are curious, news is not always to be had, and the privacy of the telegraph system is not recognised. Glynn laughed, and the same moment the man-servant opened an inner door of the tiny hall. Glynn stepped into a low-roofed parlour which was obviously the one living-room of the house. On his right hand there was a great fireplace with a peat fire burning in the grate, and a high-backed horsehair sofa in front of it. On his left at a small round table Thresk and his wife were dining.

Both Thresk and his wife sprang up as he entered. Linda advanced to him with every mark of surprise upon her face.

"You!" she cried, holding out her hand. "Where have you sprung from?"

"South Uist," said Glynn, repeating his lesson.

"And you have come on to us That is kind of you! Martin, you must take Mr. Glynn's bag up to the guest-room. I expect you will be wanting your dinner."

"I sent you a telegram asking you whether you would mind if I trespassed upon your hospitality for a night or so."

He saw Linda's eyes fixed upon him with some anxiety, and he continued at once:

"I sent it from Loch Boisdale."

A wave of relief passed over Linda's face.

"It will not come up until the morning," she said with a smile.

"As a matter of fact, the driver brought it up with him," said Glynn. And Martin handed to Mrs. Thresk the telegram. Over his shoulder, Glynn saw Thresk raise his head. He had been standing by the table listening to what was said. Now he advanced. He was a tall man, powerfully built, with a strongly-marked, broad face, which was only saved from coarseness by its look of power. They made a strange contrast, the husband and wife, as they stood side by side—she slight and exquisitely delicate in her colour, dainty in her movements, he clumsy and big and masterful. Glynn suddenly recalled gossip which had run through the town about the time of their marriage. Linda had been engaged to another—a man whose name Glynn did not remember, but on whom, so the story ran, her heart was set.

"Of course you are very welcome," said Thresk, as he held out his hand, and Glynn noticed with something of a shock that his throat was bandaged. He looked towards Linda. Her eyes were resting upon him with a look of agonised appeal. He was not to remark upon that wounded throat. He took Thresk's hand.

"We shall be delighted if you will stay with us as long as you can," said Thresk. "We have been up here for more than three months. You come to us from another world, and visitors from another world are always interesting, aren't they, Linda?"

He spoke his question with a quiet smile, like a man secretly amused. But on Linda's face fear flashed out suddenly and was gone. It seemed to Glynn that she was at pains to repress a shiver.

"Martin will show you your room," said Thresk. "What's the matter?"

Glynn was staring at the table in consternation. Where had been the use of all the pretence that he had come unexpectedly on an unpremeditated visit? His telegram had only this minute arrived—and yet there was the table laid for three people. Thresk followed the direction of his visitor's eyes.

"Oh, I see," he said with a laugh.

Glynn flushed. No wonder Thresk was amused. He had been sitting at the table; and between himself and his wife the third place was laid.

"I will go up and change," said Glynn awkwardly.

"Well, don't be long!" replied Thresk.

Glynn followed Martin to the guest-room. But he was annoyed. He did not, under any circumstances, like to look a fool. But he had the strongest possible objection to travelling three hundred miles in order to look it. If he wanted to look a fool, he grumbled, he could have managed it just as well in the Midlands.

But he was to be more deeply offended. For when he came

down into the dining-room he walked to the table and drew out the vacant chair. At once Thresk shot out his hand and stopped him.

"You mustn't sit there!" he cried violently. Then his face changed. Slowly the smile of amusement reappeared upon it. "After all, why not?" he said. "Try, yes, try," and he watched Glynn with a strange intentness.

Glynn sat down slowly. A trick was being played upon him—of that he was sure. He was still more sure when Thresk's face relaxed and he broke into a laugh.

"Well, that's funny!" he cried, and Glynn, in exasperation, asked indignantly:

"What's funny?"

But Thresk was no longer listening. He was staring across the room towards the front door, as though he heard outside yet another visitor. Glynn turned angrily towards Linda. At once his anger died away. Her face was white as paper, and her eyes full of fear. Her need was real, whatever it might be. Thresk turned sharply back again.

"It's a long journey from London to North Uist," he said pleasantly.

"No doubt," replied Glynn, as he set himself to his dinner. "But I have come from South Uist. However, I am just as hungry as if I had come from London."

He laughed, and Thresk joined in the laugh.

"I am glad of that," he said, "for it's quite a long time since we have seen you."

"Yes, it is," replied Glynn carelessly. "A year, I should think."

"Three years," said Thresk. "For I don't think that you have ever come to see us in London."

"We are so seldom there," interrupted Linda.

"Three months a year, my dear," said Thresk. "But I know very well that a man will take a day's journey in the Outer Islands to see his friends, whereas he wouldn't cross the street in London. And, in any case, we are very glad to see you. By the way," and he reached out his hand carelessly for the salt, "isn't this rather a new departure for you, Glynn? You were always a sociable fellow. A hunting-box in the Midlands, and all the lighted candles in the season. The Outer Islands were hardly in your line." And he turned quickly towards him. "You have brought your guns?"

"Of course," said Glynn, laughing as easily as he could under a cross-examination which he began to find anything but comfortable. "But I won't guarantee that I can shoot any better than I used to."

"Never mind," said Thresk. "We'll shoot the bog to-morrow, and it will be strange if you don't bring down something. It's full of duck. You don't mind getting wet, I suppose? There was once a man named Charming—" he broke off upon the name, and laughed again with that air of secret amusement. "Did you ever hear of him?" he asked of Glynn.

"Yes," replied Glynn slowly. "I knew him."

At the mention of the name he had seen Linda flinch, and he knew why she flinched.

"Did you?" exclaimed Thresk, with a keen interest. "Then you will appreciate the story. He came up here on a visit."

Glynn started.

"He came here!" he cried, and could have bitten out his tongue for uttering the cry.

"Oh, yes," said Thresk easily, "I asked him," and Glynn looked from Thresk to Thresk's wife in amazement. Linda for once did not meet Glynn's eyes. Her own were fixed upon the tablecloth. She was sitting in her chair rather rigidly. One hand rested upon the tablecloth, and it was tightly clenched. Alone of the three James Thresk appeared at ease.

"I took him out to shoot that bog," he continued with a laugh. "He loathed getting wet. He was always so very well dressed, wasn't he, Linda? The reeds begin twenty yards from the front door, and within the first five minutes he was up to the waist!" Thresk suddenly checked his laughter. "However, it ceased to be a laughing matter. Charming got a little too near the sapling in the middle."

"Is it dangerous there?" asked Glynn.

"Yes, it's dangerous." Thresk rose from his chair and walked across the room to the window. He pulled up the blind and, curving his hands about his eyes to shut out the light of the room, leaned his face against the window-frame and looked out. "It's more than dangerous," he said in a low voice. "Just round that sapling, it's swift and certain death. You would sink to the waist," and he spoke still more slowly, as though he were measuring by the utterance of the syllables the time it would take for the disaster to be complete—"from the waist to the shoulders, from the shoulders dean out of sight, before any help could reach you."

He stopped abruptly, and Glynn, watching him from the table, saw his attitude change. He dropped his head, he hunched his back, and made a strange hissing sound with his breath.

"Linda!" he cried, in a low, startling voice, "Linda!"

Glynn, unimpressionable man that he was, started to his feet. The long journey, the loneliness of the little house set in this wild, flat country, the terror which hung over it and was heavy in the very atmosphere of the rooms, were working already upon his nerves.

"Who is it?" he cried.

Linda laid a hand upon his arm.

"There's no one," she said in a whisper. "Take no notice."

And, looking at her quivering face, Glynn was inspired to ask a question, was wrought up to believe that the answer would explain to him why Thresk leaned his forehead against the window-pane and called upon his wife in so strange a voice.

"Did Channing sink—by the sapling?"

"No," said Linda hurriedly, and as hurriedly she drew away in her chair. Glynn turned and saw Thresk himself standing just behind his shoulder. He had crept down noiselessly behind them.

"No," Thresk repeated. "But he is dead. Didn't you know that? Oh, yes, he is dead," and suddenly he broke out with a passionate violence. "A clever fellow—an infernally clever fellow. You are surprised to hear me say that, Glynn. You underrated him like the rest of us. We thought him a milksop, a tame cat, a poor, weak, interloping, unprofitable creature who would sidle obsequiously into your house, and make his home there. But we were wrong—all except Linda there."

Linda sat with her head bowed, and said not a word. She was sitting so that Glynn could see her profile, and though she said nothing, her lips were trembling.

"Linda was right," and Thresk turned carelessly to Glynn. "Did you know that Linda was at one time engaged to Channing?"

"Yes, I knew," said Glynn awkwardly.

"It was difficult for most of us to understand," said Thresk. "There seemed no sort of reason why a girl like Linda should select a man like Channing to fix her heart upon. But she was right. Channing was a clever fellow—oh, a very clever fellow," and he leaned over and touched Glynn upon the sleeve, "for he died."

Glynn started back.

"What are you saying?" he cried.

Thresk burst into a laugh.

"That my throat hurts me to-night," he said.

Glynn recovered himself with an effort. "Oh, yes," he said, as though now for the first time he had noticed the bandage. "Yes, I see you have hurt your throat. How did you do it?"

Thresk chuckled.

"Not very well done, Glynn. Will you smoke?"

The plates had been cleared from the table, and the coffee brought in. Thresk rose from his seat and crossed to the mantelshelf on which a box of cigars was laid. As he took up the box and turned again towards the table, a parchment scroll which hung on a nail at the side of the fireplace caught his eye.

"Do you see this?" he said, and he unrolled it. "It's my landlord's family tree. All the ancestors of Mr. Robert Donald McCullough right back to the days of Bruce. McCullough's prouder of that scroll than of anything else in the world. He is more interested in it than in anything else in the world."

For a moment he fingered it, and in the tone of a man communing with himself, he added:

"Now, isn't that curious?"

Glynn rose from his chair, and moved down the table so that he could see the scroll unimpeded by Thresk's bulky figure. Thresk, however, was not speaking any longer to his guest. Glynn sat down again. But he sat down now in the chair which Thresk had used; the chair in which he himself had been sitting between Thresk and Linda was empty.

"What interests me," Thresk continued, hie a man in a dream, "is what is happening now—and very strange, queer, interesting things are happening now—for those who have eyes to see. Yes, through centuries and centuries, McCulloughs have succeeded McCulloughs, and lived in this distant, little corner of the Outer Islands through forays and wars and rebellions, and the oversetting of kings, and yet nothing has ever happened in this house to any one of them half so interesting and half so strange as what is happening now to us, the shooting tenants of a year."

Thresk dropped the scroll, and, coming out of his dream, brought the cigar-box to the table.

"You have changed your seat!" he said with a smile, as he offered the box to Glynn. Glynn took out of it a cigar, and leaning back, cut off the end. As he stooped forward to light it, he saw the cigar-box still held out to him. Thresk had not moved. He seemed to have forgotten Glynn's presence in the room. His eyes were fixed upon the empty chair. He stood strangely rigid, and then he suddenly cried out:

"Take care, Linda!"

There was so sharp a note of warning in his voice that Linda sprang to her feet, with her hand pressed upon her heart. Glynn was startled too, and because he was startled he turned angrily to Thresk.

"Of what should Mrs. Thresk take care?"

Thresk took his eyes for a moment, and only for a moment, from the empty chair.

"Do you see nothing?" he asked, in a whisper, and his glance went back again. "Not a shadow which leans across the table there towards Linda, darkening the candle-light?"

"No; for there's nothing to cast a shadow."

"Is there not?" said Thresk, with a queer smile. "That's where you make your mistake. Aren't you conscious of something very strange, very insidious, close by us in this room?"

"I am aware that you are frightening Mrs. Thresk," said Glynn roughly; and, indeed, standing by the table, with her white face and her bosom heaving under her hand, she looked the very embodiment of terror. Thresk turned at once to her. A look of solicitude made his gross face quite tender. He took her by the arm, and in a chiding, affectionate tone he said very gently:

"You are not frightened, Linda, are you? Interested—yes, just as I am. But not frightened. There's nothing to be frightened at. We are not children."

"Oh, rim," she said, and she leaned upon his arm. He led her across to the sofa, and sat down beside her.

"That's right. Now we are comfortable." But the last word was not completed. It seemed that it froze upon his lips. He stopped, looked for a second into space, and then, dropping his arm from about his wife's waist, he deliberately moved aside from her, and made a space between them.

"Now we are in our proper places—the four of us," he said bitterly.

"The three of us," Glynn corrected, as he walked round the table. "Where's the fourth?"

And then there came to him this extraordinary answer given in the quietest voice imaginable.

"Between my wife and me. Where should he be?"

Glynn stared. There was no one in the room but Linda, Thresk, and himself—no one. But—but—it was the loneliness of the spot, and its silence, and its great distance from his world, no doubt, which troubled him. Thresk's manner, too, and his words were having their effect. That was all, Glynn declared stoutly to himself. But—but—he did not wonder that Linda had written so urgently for him to come to her. His back went cold, and the hair stirred upon his scalp.

"Who is it, then?" he cried violently.

Linda rose from the sofa, and took a quick step towards him. Her eyes implored him to silence.

"There is no one," she protested in a low voice.

"No," cried Glynn loudly. "Let us understand what wild fancy he has! Who is the fourth?"

Upon Thresk's face came a look of sullenness.

"Who should he be?"

"Who is he?" Glynn insisted.

"Channing," said Thresk. "Mildmay Channing." He sat for a while, brooding with his head sunk upon his breast. And Glynn started back. Some vague recollection was stirring in his memory. There had been a story current amongst Linda's friends at the time of her marriage. She had been in love with Channing, desperately in love with him. The marriage with Thresk had been forced on her by her parents—yes, and by Thresk's persistency. It had been a civilised imitation of the Rape of the Sabine Women. That was how the story ran, Glynn remembered. He waited to hear more from James Thresk, and in a moment the words came, but in a thoroughly injured tone.

"It's strange that you can't see either."

"There is some one else, then, as blind as I am?" said Glynn.

"There was. Yes, yes, the dog," replied Thresk, gazing into the fire. "You and the dog," he repeated uneasily, "you and the dog. But the dog saw in the end, Glynn, and so will you—even you."

Linda turned quickly, but before she could speak, Glynn made a sign to her. He went over to her side. A glance at Thresk showed him that he was lost in his thoughts.

"If you want me to help you, you must leave us alone," he said.

She hesitated for a moment, and then swiftly crossed the room and went out at the door. Glynn, who had let his cigar go out, lit it again at the flame of one of the candles on the dining-table. Then he planted himself in front of Thresk.

"You are terrifying your wife," he said. "You are frightening her to death."

Thresk did not reply to the accusation directly. He smiled quietly at Glynn.

"She sent for you."

Glynn looked uncomfortable, and Thresk went on: "You haven't come from South Uist. You have come from London."

"No," said Glynn.

"From Melton, then. You came because Linda sent for you."

"If it were so," stammered Glynn, "it would only be another proof that you are frightening her." Thresk shook his head.

"It wasn't because Linda was afraid that she sent for you," he said stubbornly. "I know Linda. I'll tell you the truth," and he fixed his burning eyes on Glynn's face. "She sent for you because she hates being here with me."

"Hates being with you!" cried Glynn, and Thresk nodded his head. Glynn could hardly even so believe that he had heard aright. "Why, you must be mad!" he protested. "Mad or blind. There's just one person of whom your wife is thinking, for whom she is caring, for whose health she is troubled. It has been evident to me ever since I have been in this house—in spite of her fears. Every time she looks at you her eyes are tender with solicitude. That one person is yourself."

"No," said Thresk. "It's Channing."

"But he's dead, man!" cried Glynn in exasperation. "You told me so yourself not half an hour ago. He is dead."

"Yes," answered Thresk. "He's dead. That's where he beat me. You don't understand that?"

"No, I don't," replied Glynn.

He was speaking aggressively; he stood with his legs apart

in an aggressive attitude. Thresk looked him over from head to foot and agreed.

"No," he said, "and I don't see why you should. You are rather like me, comfortable and commonplace, and of the earth earthy. Before men of our gross stamp could believe and understand what I am going to tell you, they would have to reach—do you mind if I say a refinement?—by passing through the same fires which have tempered me."

Glynn made no reply. He shifted his position so that the firelight might fall upon Thresk's face with its full strength. Thresk leaned forward with his hands upon his knees, and very quietly, though now and then a note of scorn rang in his voice, he told his story.

"You tell me my wife cares for me. I reply that she would have cared, if Charming had not died. When I first met Linda she was engaged to him. You know that. She was devoted to him. You know that too. I knew it and I didn't mind. I wasn't afraid of Channing. A poor, feeble creature—heaps of opportunities, not one of them foreseen, not one of them grasped when it came his way. A grumbler, a bag of envy, a beggar for sympathy at any woman's lap! Why should I have worried my head about Channing? And I didn't. Linda's people were all for breaking off their engagement. After all, I was some good. I had made my way. I had roughed it in South America; and I had come home a rich man—not such a very easy thing, as the superior people who haven't the heart even to try to be rich men are inclined to think. Well, the engagement was broken off, Channing hadn't a penny to marry on, and nobody would give him a job. Look here!" And he suddenly swung round upon Glynn.

"I gave Channing his chance. I knew he couldn't make any use of it. I wanted to prove he wasn't any good. So I put a bit of a railway in Chili into his hands, and he brought the thing to the edge of bankruptcy within twelve months. So the engagement was broken off. Linda clung to the fellow. I knew it, and I didn't mind. She didn't want to marry me. I knew it, and I didn't mind. Her parents broke her down to it. She sobbed through the night before we were married. I knew it, and I didn't mind. You think me a beast, of course," he added, with a look at Glynn. "But just consider the case from my point of view. Channing was no match for Linda. I was. I wanted time, that was all. Give me only time, and I knew that I could win her."

Boastful as the words sounded, there was nothing aggressive in Thresk's voice. He was speaking with a quiet simplicity which robbed them quite of offence. He was unassumingly certain.

"Why?" asked Glynn. "Why, given time, were you sure that you could win her?"

"Because I wanted enough. That's my creed, Glynn. If you want enough, want with every thought, and nerve, and pulse, the thing you want comes along all right. There was the difference between Channing and me. He hadn't the heart to want enough. I wanted enough to go to school again. I set myself to learn the small attentions which mean so much to women. They weren't in my line naturally. I pay so little heed to things of that kind myself that it did not easily occur to me that women might think differently. But I learnt my lesson, and I got my reward. Just simple little precautions, like having a cloak ready for her, almost before she was aware that she was cold. And I would see a look of surprise on her face, and the surprise flush into a smile of pleasure. Oh, I was holding her, Glynn, I can tell you. I went about it so very warily," and Thresk laughed with a knowing air. "I didn't shut my door on Channing either. Not I! I wasn't going to make a martyr of him. I let him sidle in and out of the house, and I laughed. For I was holding her. Every day she came a step or two nearer to me."

He broke off suddenly, and his voice, which had taken on a tender and wistful note, incongruous in so big a creature, rose in a gust of anger.

"But he died! He died and caught her back again."

Glynn raised his hands in despair.

"That memory has long since faded," he argued, and Thresk burst out in a bitter laugh.

"Memory," he cried, flinging himself into a chair. "You are one of the imaginative people after all, Glynn." And Glynn stared in round-eyed surprise. Here to him was conclusive proof that there was something seriously wrong with Thresk's mind. Never had Mr. Glynn been called imaginative before, and his soul revolted against the aspersion. "Yes," said Thresk, pointing an accusing finger. "Imaginative! I am one of the practical people. I don't worry about memories. Actual real things interest me—such as Channing's presence now—in this house." And he spoke suddenly, leaning forward with so burning a fire in his eyes and voice that Glynn, in spite of himself, looked nervously across his shoulder. He rose hastily from the sofa, and rather in order to speak than with any thought of what he was saying, he asked:

"When did he die?"

"Four months ago. I was ill at the time."

The exclamation sprang from Glynn's lips before he could check it. Here to him was the explanation of Thresk's illusions. But he was sorry that he had not kept silent. For he saw Thresk staring angrily at him.

"What did you mean by your 'Ah'?" Thresk asked roughly.

"Merely that I had seen a line about your illness in a news-paper," Glynn explained hastily.

Thresk leaned back satisfied.

"Yes," he resumed. "I broke down. I had had a hard life, you see, and I was paying for it. I am right enough now, however," and his voice rose in a challenge to Glynn to contradict him.

Nothing was further from Glynn's thoughts.

"Of course," he said quickly.

"I saw Channing's death in the obituary column whilst I was lying in bed, and, to tell you the truth, I was relieved by it."

"But I thought you said you didn't mind about Channing?" Glynn interrupted, and Thresk laughed with a little discomfort.

"Well, perhaps I did mind a little more than I care to admit," Thresk confessed. "At all events, I felt relieved at his death. What a fool I was!" And he stopped for a moment as though he wondered now that his mind was so clear, at the delusion which had beset him.

"I thought that it was all over with Charming. Oh, what a fool I was! Even after he came back and would sidle up to my bedside in his old fawning style, I couldn't bring myself to take him seriously, and I was only amused."

"He came to your bedside!" exclaimed Glynn.

"Yes," replied Thresk, and he laughed at the recollection. "He came with his humble smirk, and pottered about the room as if he were my nurse. I put out my tongue at him, and told him he was dead and done for, and that he had better not meddle with the bottles on my table. Yes, he amused me. What a fool I was! I thought no one else saw him. That was my first mistake. I thought he was helpless. . . . That was my second."

Thresk got up from his chair, and, standing over the fireplace, knocked the ash off his cigar.

"Do you remember a great Danish boar-hound I used to have?" he asked.

"Yes," replied Glynn, puzzled by the sudden change of subject. "But what has the boar-hound to do with your story?"

"A good deal," said Thresk. "I was very fond of that dog."

"The dog was fond of you," said Glynn.

"Yes. Remember that!" Thresk cried suddenly. "For it's true." Then he relapsed again into a quiet, level voice.

"It took me some time to get well. I was moved up-here. It was the one place where I wanted to be. But I wasn't used to sitting round and doing nothing. So the time of my convalescence hung pretty heavily, and, casting about for some way of amusing myself, I wondered whether I could teach the dog to see Channing as I saw him. I tried. Whenever I saw Channing come in at the door, I used to call the dog to my side and point Channing out to him with my finger as Charming moved about the room."

Thresk sat down in a chair opposite to Glynn, and with a singular alertness began to act over again the scenes which had taken place in his sick room upstairs.

"I used to say, 'Hst! Hst!' 'There! Do you see? By the window!' or if Channing moved towards Linda I would turn the dog's head and make his eyes follow him across the room. At first the dog saw nothing. Then he began to avoid me, to slink away with his tail between his legs, to growl. He was frightened. Yes, he was frightened!" And Thresk nodded his head in a quick, interested way.

"He was frightened of you," cried Glynn, "and I don't wonder."

For even to him there was something uncanny and impish in Thresk's quick movements and vivid gestures.

"Wait a bit," said Thresk. "He was frightened, but not of me. He saw Channing. His hair bristled under my fingers as I pointed the fellow out. I had to keep one hand on his neck, you see, to keep him by me. He began to yelp in a queer, panicky way, and tremble—a man in a fever couldn't tremble and shake any more than that dog did. And then one day, when we were alone together, the dog and I and Channing—the dog sprang at my throat."

"That's how you were wounded!" cried Glynn, leaping from his sofa. He stood staring in horror at Thresk. "I wonder the dog didn't kill you."

"He very nearly did," said Thresk. "Oh, very nearly."

"You had frightened him out of his wits."

Thresk laughed contemptuously.

"That's the obvious explanation, of course," he said. "But it's not the true one. I have been living amongst the subtleties of life. I know about things now. The dog sprang at me because—" He stopped and glanced uneasily about the room. When he raised his face again, there was a look upon it which Glynn had not seen there before—a look of sudden terror. He leaned forward that he might be the nearer to Glynn, and his voice sank to a whisper—"well, because Channing set him on to me."

It was no doubt less the statement itself than the crafty look which accompanied it, and the whisper which uttered it, that shocked Glynn. But he was shocked. There came upon him—yes, even upon him, the sane, prosaic Glynn—a sudden doubt whether, after all, Thresk was mad. It occurred to him as a possibility that Thresk was speaking the mere, bare truth. Suppose that it were the truth Suppose that Channing were here! In this room! Glynn felt the flesh creep upon his bones.

"Ah, you are beginning to understand," said Thresk, watching his companion. "You are beginning to get frightened, too." And he nodded his head in comprehension. "I used not to know what fear meant. But I knew the meaning well enough as soon as I had guessed why the dog sprang at my throat. For I realised my helplessness."

Throughout their conversation Glynn had been perpetually puzzled by something unexpected in Thresk's conclusions. He followed his reasoning up to a point, and then came a word which left him at a loss. Thresk's fear he understood. But why the sense of helplessness? And he asked for an explanation.

"Because I had no weapons to fight Channing with," Thresk replied. "I could cope with the living man and win every time. But against the dead man I was helpless. I couldn't hurt him. I couldn't even come to grips with him. I had just to sit by and make room. And that's what I have been doing ever since. I have been sitting by and watching—without a single resource, without a single opportunity of a counterstroke. Oh, I had my time—when Channing was alive. But upon my word, he has the best of it. Here I sit without raising a hand while he recaptures Linda."

"There you are wrong," cried Glynn, seizing gladly, in the midst of these subtleties, upon some fact of which he felt sure. "Your wife is yours. There has been no recapture. Besides, she doesn't believe that Channing is here."

Thresk laughed.

"Do you think she would tell me if she did?" he asked. "No."

He rose from his chair and, walking to the window, thrust

back the curtains and looked out. So he stood for the space of a minute. Then he came back and, looking fixedly at Glynn, said with an air of extraordinary cunning:

"But I have a plan. Yes, I have a plan. I shall get on level terms with Mr. Channing again one of these fine days, and then I'll prove to him for a second time which of us two is the better man."

He made a sign to Glynn, and looked towards the door. It was already opening. He advanced to it as Linda came into the room.

"You have come back, Linda! I have been talking to Glynn at such a rate that he hasn't been able to get a word in edgeways," he said, with a swift change to a gaiety of voice and manner. "However, I'll show him a good day's sport to-morrow, Linda. We will shoot the bog, and perhaps you'll come out with the luncheon to the sand-hills?"

Linda Thresk smiled.

"Of course I will," she said. She showed to Glynn a face of gratitude. "It has done you good, Jim, to have a man to talk to," and she laid a hand upon her husband's arm and laughed quite happily. Glynn turned his back upon them and walked up to the window, leaving them standing side by side in the firelight. Outside, the moon shone from a clear sky upon the pools and the reeds of the marsh and the low white sand-hills, chequered with their tufts of grass. But upon the sea beyond, a white mist lay thick and low.

"There's a sea-fog," said Glynn; and Thresk, at the fire, suddenly lifted his head, and looked towards the window with a strange intensity. One might have thought that a sea-fog was a strange, unusual thing among the Outer Islands.

"Watch it!" he said, and there was a vibration in his voice which matched the intensity of his look. "You will see it suddenly creep through the gaps in the sand-hills and pass over the marsh like an army that obeys a command. I have watched it by the hour, time and time again. It gathers on the level of the sea and waits and waits until it seems that the word is given. Then it comes swirling through the gaps of the sand-hills and eats up the marsh in a minute."

Even as he spoke Glynn cried out:

"That's extraordinary!"

The fog had crept out through the gaps. Only the summits of the sand-hills rose in the moonlight like little peaks above clouds; and over the marsh the fog burst like cannon smoke and lay curling and writhing up to the very reeds twenty yards from the house. The sapling alone stood high above it, like the mast of a wreck in the sea.

"How high is it?" asked Thresk.

"Breast high," replied Glynn.

"Only breast high," said Thresk, and there seemed to be a note of disappointment in his voice. However, in the next moment he shook it off. "The fog will be gone before morning," he said. "I'll go and tell Donald to bring the dogs round at nine to-morrow, and have your guns ready. Nine is not too early for you, I suppose?"

"Not a bit," said Glynn; and Thresk, going up to the door which led from the house, opened it, went out, and closed it again behind him.

Glynn turned at once towards Linda Thresk. But she held up a warning hand, and waited for the outer door to slam. No sound, however, broke the silence. Glynn went to the inner door and opened it. A bank of white fog, upon which he saw his own shadow most brightly limned by the light behind him, filled the outer passage and crept by him into the room. Glynn closed the latch quickly.

"He has left the outer door open," he said, and, coming back into the room he stood beside the fire looking down into Linda's face.

"He has been talking to me," said Glynn.

Linda looked at him curiously.

"How much did he tell you?"

"There can be little he left unsaid. He told me of the dog, of Channing's death——"

"Yes?"

"Of Channing's return."

"Yes?"

"And of you."

With each sentence Glynn's embarrassment had increased. Linda, however, held him to his story. "What did he say of me?"

"That but for Channing's death he would have held you. That since Channing died—and came back—he had lost you."

Linda nodded her head. Nothing in Glynn's words surprised her—that was clear. It was a story already familiar to her which he was repeating.

"Is that all?" she said.

"I think so. Yes," replied Glynn, glad to get the business over. Yet he had omitted the most important part of Thresk's confession—the one part which Linda did not already know. He omitted it because he had forgotten it. There was something else which he had in his mind to say.

"When Thresk told me that Channing had won you back, I ventured to say that no one watching you and Thresk, even with the most indifferent eyes, could doubt that it was always and only of him that you were thinking."

"Thank you," said Linda, quietly. "That is true."

"And now," said Glynn, "I want, in my turn, to ask you a question. I have been a little curious. I want, too, to do what I can. Therefore, I ask you, why did you send for me? What is it that you think I can do? That other friends of yours can't?"

A slight colour came into Linda's cheeks; and for a moment she lowered her eyes. She spoke with an accent of apology.

"It is quite true that there are friends whom I see more constantly than you, Mr. Glynn, and upon whom I have, perhaps, greater claims."

"Oh, I did not mean you to think that I was reluctant to come," Glynn exclaimed, and Linda smiled, lifting her eyes to his.

"No," she said. "I remembered your kindness. It was that recollection which helped me to appeal to you," and she resumed her explanation as though he had never interrupted her.

"Nor was there any particular thing which I thought you could do. But—well, here's the truth—I have been living in terror. This house has become a house of terror. I am frightened, and I have come almost to believe—" and she looked about her with a shiver of her shoulders, sinking her voice to a whisper as she spoke—"that Jim was right—that he is here after all."

And Glynn recoiled. Just for a moment the same fancy had occurred to him.

"You don't believe that—really!" he cried.

"No—no," she answered. "Once I think calmly. But it is so difficult to think calmly and reasonably here. Oh—" and she threw up her arms suddenly, and her whole face and eyes were alight with terror—

"the very air is to me heavy with fear in this house. It is Jim's quiet certainty."

"Yes, that's it!" exclaimed Glynn, catching eagerly at that explanation because it absolved him to his own common sense for the inexplicable fear which he had felt invade himself. "Yes, Jim's quiet, certain, commonplace way in which he speaks of Channing's presence here. That's what makes his illusion so convincing."

"Well, I thought that if I could get you here, you who—" and she hesitated in order to make her description polite—"are not afflicted by fancies, who are pleasantly sensible"—thus did Linda express her faith that Mr. Glynn was of the earth, earthy—"I myself should lose my terror, and Jim, too, might lose his illusion. But now," she looked at him keenly, "I think that Jim is affecting you—that you, too—yes"—she sprang up suddenly and stood before him, with her dark, terror-haunted eyes fixed upon him—"that you, too, believe Mildmay Channing is here."

"No," he protested violently—too violently unless the accusation were true.

"Yes," she repeated, nodding her head quietly. "You, too, believe that Mildmay Channing is here."

And before her horror-stricken face the protest which was

on the tip of his tongue remained unuttered. His eyes sought the floor. With a sudden movement of despair Linda turned aside. Even the earthliness of Mr. Glynn had brought her no comfort or security. He had fallen under the spell, as she had done. It seemed that they had no more words to speak to one another. They stood and waited helplessly until Thresk should return.

But that return was delayed.

"He has been a long time speaking to the keeper," said Linda listlessly, and rather to break a silence which was becoming intolerable, than with any intention in the words. But they struck a chord of terror in Glynn's thoughts. He walked quickly to the window, and hastily tore the curtain aside.

The flurry of his movements aroused Linda's attention. She followed him with her eyes. She saw him curve his hands about his forehead and press his face against the pane, even as Thresk had done an hour before. She started forward from the fireplace and Glynn swung round with his arms extended, barring the window. His face was white, his lips shook. The one important statement of Thresk's he now recalled.

"Don't look!" he cried, and as he spoke, Linda pushed past him. She flung up the window. Outside the fog curled and smoked upon the marsh breast high. The moonlight played upon it; above it the air was clear and pure, and in the sky stars shone faintly. Above the mist the bare sapling stood like a pointing finger, and halfway between the sapling and the house Thresk's head and shoulders showed plain to see. But they were turned away from the house.

"Jim! Jim!" cried Linda, shaking the windowframe with her hand. Her voice rang loudly out on the still air. But Thresk never so much as turned his head. He moved slowly towards the sapling, feeling the unstable ground beneath him with his feet.

"Jim! Jim!" again she cried. And behind her she heard a strange, unsteady whispering voice.

"'On equal terms!' That's what he said—I did not understand. He said, 'On equal terms.'"

And even as Glynn spoke, both Linda and he saw Thresk throw up his arms and sink suddenly beneath the bog. Linda ran to the door, stumbling as she ran, and with a queer, sobbing noise in her throat.

Glynn caught her by the arm.

"It is of no use. You know. Round the sapling—there is no chance of rescue. It is my fault, I should have understood: He had no fear of Channing—if only he could meet him on equal terms."

Linda stared at Glynn. For a little while the meaning of the words did not sink into her mind.

"He said that!" she cried. "And you did not tell me." She crept back to the fireplace and cowered in front of it, shivering.

"But he said he would come back to me," she said in the voice of a child who has been deceived. "Yes, Jim said he would come back to me."

Of course it was a chance, accident, coincidence, a breath of wind—call it what you will, except what Linda Thresk and Glynn called it. But even as she uttered her complaint, "He said he would come back to me," the latch of the door clicked loudly. There was a rush of cold air into the room. The door swung slowly inwards and stood wide open.

Linda sprang to her feet. Both she and Glynn turned to the open door. The white fog billowed into the room. Glynn felt the hair stir and move upon his scalp. He stood transfixed. Was it possible? he asked himself. Had Thresk indeed come back to fight for Linda once more, and to fight now as he had fought the first time—on equal terms? He stood expecting the white fog to shape itself into the likeness of a man. And then he heard a wild scream of laughter behind him. He turned in time to catch Linda as she fell.

The Haunted Palace

Edgar Allan Poe

In the greenest of our valleys
By good angels tenanted,
Once a fair and stately palace—
Radiant palace—reared its head.
In the monarch Thought's dominion,
It stood there!
Never seraph spread a pinion
Over fabric half so fair!

Banners yellow, glorious, golden,
On its roof did float and flow
(This—all this—was in the olden
Time long ago)
And every gentle air that dallied,
In that sweet day,
Along the ramparts plumed and pallid,
A wingèd odor went away.

Wanderers in that happy valley,
Through two luminous windows, saw
Spirits moving musically
To a lute's well-tunèd law,
Round about a throne where, sitting,
Porphyrogene!
In state his glory well befitting,
The ruler of the realm was seen.

And all with pearl and ruby glowing
Was the fair palace door,
Through which came flowing, flowing, flowing
And sparkling evermore,
A troop of Echoes, whose sweet duty
Was but to sing,
In voices of surpassing beauty,
The wit and wisdom of their king.

But evil things, in robes of sorrow,
Assailed the monarch's high estate;
(Ah, let us mourn!—for never morrow
Shall dawn upon him, desolate!)
And round about his home the glory
That blushed and bloomed
Is but a dim-remembered story
Of the old time entombed.

And travellers, now, within that valley,
Through the red-litten windows see
Vast forms that move fantastically
To a discordant melody;
While, like a ghastly rapid river,
Through the pale door
A hideous throng rush out forever,
And laugh—but smile no more.

Empty Bottles

John Shirley

They should have been expecting me.

They'd received a letter, posted a month earlier. It contained a note from Mom and a short letter from me. Mom's note referenced a meeting she'd had when they'd signed the new agreement about my college fund: *"You said he could come and visit you any time, Karl, long as I informed you a few weeks ahead, and I'm doing so. You don't answer phone calls, you neglected to give me your email, and I use a landline, so I don't text. Yes, there are still people with landlines. I hope you remember that invitation. You were looking at your phone when we were talking and I couldn't tell if we were on the same page or not."*

I almost didn't go to Dad's house. I was only in San Jose for a few days, to do some post-graduate research, and I thought I should see him, but he hadn't written back to Mom or called. I wasn't sure I'd be welcome. But since having the dream—an acutely bad dream—I was troubled by the feeling that I really ought to go see him. At least once. Yes, he had pretty much abandoned me when I was a little kid. But why not get some closure?

On a summer day just before sunset, with the crickets starting to stridulate, I got out of the taxi next to the mailbox, suitcase in hand. The taxi drove away before I could tell the guy to wait. Because I was suddenly not sure that my dad still lived here. The house had peeling white paint and the hasty look of houses built way back in the 1960s. The lawn had become knee-high weeds. There was a Tesla parked in the driveway, but it was missing a wheel and grass grew up around its axles.

The house's window blinds were all closed. This was the address, all right. Dad had moved here after the divorce from my mother about sixteen years earlier—but was he *still* here? I glanced at the open mailbox—saw it was overflowing. Several pieces were moldering on the sidewalk. Mostly junk mail. I noticed a rain-browned envelope sticking out from the rest in the mailbox. It showed my mother's return address.

"Christ!" I took the letter out and looked it over. Addressed to my dad. The date confirmed it was definitely the letter. It had been in the mailbox about six weeks.

I looked at the house again. It seemed very, very still. But the sun chose that moment to dip behind the horizon, and the evening darkened all at once, so I could see light glowing around the edges of the blinds.

Carrying the envelope, I went to the door, put down my bag, and knocked. I waited. No response. I looked for a doorbell. Where the doorbell should be, not quite fitting in the gap, was a thimble-sized receded disk of glass. One of those front-door security cameras. There was a tiny little speaker under the lens.

I waved at the camera. "Hi! It's Cedric! Your son, Dad! Anyone home?"

I waited. No response.

"We sent a letter a long time ago! Look!" I held it in front of the camera. "More than a month ago!"

I waited a full minute, then knocked again, harder.

The door clicked, and I figured it was unlocked now. I picked up my bag, opened the door, and called, "Dad?"

I stepped through into an empty dining room, musty, and smelling of decaying old food. A Roomba was bumbling around the old amber-yellow carpet. Beyond a food-prep counter was a small kitchen, with dirty dishes piled in the sink, cabinets with their doors wide open, an avocado green refrigerator, and a clean tile floor.

"Dad?" I called again. I could hear electronics humming. The carpet ran through a doorway into a living room, cluttered with entertainment systems and devices I didn't recognize. I walked in, saw my eleven-year-old half-brother sprawled on the sofa. I'd never met him, but I'd found a couple of his selfies online.

He'd been plump in the photos; now he was bloated. He was wearing his underpants and a T-shirt that was much too small for his pink belly. His hair was matted and thick with grease.

"Leroy?" I said.

He didn't look up at me. His focus was on a screen of some kind, propped on his raised knees. I could see the Bluetooth pods in his ears, making it hard for him to hear me. He had a phone in his left hand and every so often he thumbed it. It looked like a game, something of the Candy Crush variety.

I dropped my bag on the floor, tapped him on the shoulder—and he startled. "Whuh!"

I raised my voice. "Leroy, it's me, Cedric. Your half-brother. Dad said I could visit." I waved the letter at him. "We sent him a letter, but it's been stuck in your mailbox for over a month."

"Whuh?"

I smiled at him. "Do pardon me . . ." I reached down and took a Bluetooth pod out of one of his ears.

"Hey!"

"I'm Cedric, dude."

"Whuh?" He absently touched the screen in front of him.

"You already said that, bro. Here I am, your half-brother. It's a fait accompli—I just showed up. You don't remember hearing about a Cedric in your family? As in, we've got half our DNA in common?"

He squinched his already squinched up eyes even more. "Yuh . . ."

I bent over and looked at the screen on his lap. It appeared to be a transparent pane of glass in a gray plastic frame and nothing more—except images that came and went when he touched it. "How do you talk to that thing? I don't see a keyboard."

"Voice," he said.

The image currently on the screen was of an athletic-looking young dude of about twelve, very handsome, his eyes glittering with intelligence. "Who's that?"

"'S me," Leroy said, frowning.

"Oh, like an avatar?"

"'S me."

"Whatever you say, little brother." I set his Bluetooth pod on his chest and went to find Dad.

I walked down a short hallway. And something darted in front of me. It looked like a shrunken, translucent, hollow-eyed version of my half-brother—glimpsed as it slid into a crack in the wall. It was as if the crack vacuumed the thing in. And it was gone.

"Leroy!" I blurted, stopping in my tracks.

I shook my head. Either it was my imagination going loopy or it was some kind of projected electronic image. Maybe the kid was pranking me somehow.

I walked on, feeling . . . odd. Faintly nauseated. As if there was a high-pitched sound bothering my ears, but it was so high-pitched it was inaudible—just beyond the range of hearing. Yet I could feel it vibrating against my ear drums.

To the right was a bedroom or a den, I couldn't tell which because it was jammed with a jumble of mismatched items: electronics, some plugged in on little metal tables, some in wobbly, dust-coated stacks in the corner. There was a sofa, covered with other gear, and tilted back in a Lay-Z-Boy easy chair was my dad, looking like a larger version of Leroy, but with a beard. He was shaped like a bowling pin, with his narrow shoulders and bulbous middle—a bowling pin wearing a sweat-stained bathrobe. His eyes were trapped in pouchy swollen skin around the sockets.

Dad's hands were busy, one tapping at the transparent screen held on his lap by a mechanical arm extending from the wall, the other on the keyboard under another screen set up on little metal table beside the chair. A strong smell of sweat and piss came off him. He was flicking his eyes between me and the screens, his lips moving. There was a cooler beside him filled with generic packages of food and crumpled wrappers. I stepped into the room, stepping over old interlinked PCs, a linked system all in one room, and caught his reluctant gaze.

"Dad"—I waved the envelope at him—"this letter from me and my mom, confirming your invitation and my plan to come today. It's been turning yellow in your mailbox for a month. You want to read it?"

Dad muttered something. Glanced at me, looked back at the screens, kept tapping and typing as he said. "Not a good time. Should've checked. I've almost got this done."

"Almost got what done, Dad?"

"A new kind of WiFi. Revolutionary. Can't talk about it."

That wasn't implausible. He had a successful WiFi boosting start-up some years back. Lost control to investors but retained a decent income from some tech spin-off. "So this is not a good time—when do you want me to come back?"

"Another week, maybe two. Maybe a month."

I noticed pill bottles on his metal table. One of them was Adderall. Nettled at his dismissal of me after I'd made the trek here, I said, "Hitting the stealth meth, dad?" I pointed at the Adderall bottle.

"Not meth."

"It's the gradual kind of meth, but it'll get you. I don't know why I'm talking to you like I'm the adult here."

He didn't respond to that. Kept tapping and typing, his mouth loose and very red in his gray-black beard.

I went on, "Hey—you want me to leave, fine, but I don't have anyplace else to stay in this town tonight and I'm on a tight budget. Okay if I just stay here tonight? Leave in the morning. Maybe you'll get a chance to unhook, and in the morning we'll have a chinwag, as Mom likes to say. Does anyone say chinwag in this country besides Mom? Anyhow—"

"The garage." Tap tap, type type.

"What about it?"

"Stay in there. Electric heater, a cot. Some packaged food. Spare PC you can hook up. Games."

"You know how Mom is, she's kind of a Luddite. Or machine minimalist or whatever. So I never got into it. I do have a cell phone here, and I have a laptop at home, but that's it."

Tap. Type. Tap. Type.

"Uh—how about upstairs? Looks like there's an attic room."

"Filled with servers."

"Servers? Like rows of big computers? Really! The garage it is." I shrugged, tossed the water-stained envelope onto the corner of the little metal table, and turned away, deciding I should see if Leroy's mother was here. Best say hello so she didn't think I was a home invader.

Marjorie was farther down the hall, in a bedroom, panting in puce yoga tights as she pumped away on an exercise bicycle, tilting on its platform, and turning its handlebars to veer virtually through the digital canyons she was seeing in her VR goggles. She was in early middle age, in good shape, her shoulder-length hair striped pink and neon blue. Her muscular limbs were bronzed from the tanning lamp I could see over the bed in a corner. A vibrant contrast to her housemates.

She couldn't see I was here so I called out, "Marjorie! It's Cedric!"

She yipped in startlement and clawed her VR glasses off.

"Um . . ." She stared at me, mouth open. "Who?"

"Cedric—Leroy's half-brother. We've never actually met, but I'm sure my father complained about having to contribute to my tuition—"

"Oh, god, he used to spew the venom over that all right, ha!" She climbed off the bike, dabbed her forehead with a small towel, and looked me over in the most candid way anyone's ever done. She cocked her head toward a juicer on a table beside her bike. "Want a smoothie? Energy greens."

"Naw, I'm good."

She reached out and patted my upper arm in a way that told me she was checking for muscles. "Look at you! You almost look healthy!"

"Uh—thanks?"

"Did you see that human slug who calls himself my husband?" she asked, in a tone another woman would use to say something pleasant. Her auburn eyebrows bobbed. Her blue eyes were a little too close together; this and her small nose and wide mouth gave her a slightly simian look.

"I saw Dad. He seems really, *really* caught up in something."

She glanced at the ceiling. "Or it's caught him."

I didn't think about that remark until later. I went on, "I'm not a needy guy. Mom's partner Kathy was a wonderful parent. But Dad hasn't seen me since I was little, wouldn't even do a video talk. You'd think he'd have the decency to say, 'Hi, son, how are you, get your degree yet?' Nope. We wrote to him. He didn't answer back to tell me not to come, and I was in town, so—"

"You expected *decency* from Karl?" A small dry laugh at that. "Like expecting a cool drink from a dried-out well. Only reason I stay here is because it's free, and he leaves me alone and lets me order in the food I want, and I've got my gear all set up." She straightened proudly and went on, "I'm training, see."

"For . . . ?"

"The international virtual bike races! I was number three in California women's league last year. I've still got something left." Majorie sighed. "My poor Leroy—Karl got his obsessions into Leroy's head when he was eight. Took him out of school, just brainwashed him with his bullshit. Kid is a crackhead for games and social media. Pretends to be a grown-up online." She cocked her head and looked at me speculatively. "You're staying? Where you going to sleep?"

"The garage, I'm told."

"*Ick!* You don't want to sleep out there. You can bunk with me." She looked affectedly casual.

"I—no, I feel like, you know, some privacy tonight. Got books in my bag to read for my master's."

"Books? Physical books?"

"Yeah. A couple."

"Huh. Well, think about it. If you get restless …" She reached out and stroked my little soul-patch beard with the tip of her finger. "You'll know where I am. There's two bathrooms, by the way—one's mine, you go through that door. The one at the other end of the house is unspeakable. They tend to pour buckets into it, if you know what I mean."

I grimaced and said, "Well, maybe see you in the morning." I went to the door and then turned back to her and asked, "Um, is there some kind of holographic system here, or projection? I saw something. It looked kinda like Leroy, if he were a ghost. I thought maybe the kid was pranking me."

"Oh. That." Her expression went blank. She rubbed her hands slowly together. "Yeah. Maybe. Maybe it's a prank." She went back to her bike, straddled it, and put on her VR goggles again. "Just ignore all that stuff. That's some serious advice, Cedric." She told the system, "Race restart." And she began peddling.

The garage was poorly lit, dusty, stored chockful of outdated tech and mysterious cardboard boxes. There was a folded-up metal-frame cot. Several shelves contained stacks of Eternally Edible packages, a vile-tasting but allegedly nutritious product. There was a large flashlight hanging from a nail on the wall.

The cot smelled of mildew. Setting it up, I caught a glimpse of movement from the corner of my eye. I looked—and saw what looked like my father, but hollow-eyed, his face a bit warped, flitting across the reflective glass panel of the garage door. Then gone.

Just ignore all that stuff, Marjorie had said. *That's some serious advice.*

Probably just a distorted image of myself, trick of the light thing, I decided. Had to be.

I looked around for blankets, found a few folded in a box, made up the cot as best I could, and stretched out on it, trying to sort through my feelings.

Why had I come here? For real—*why?*

It probably wasn't just the nightmare about Dad. The dream of him as a hollow-eyed apparition, a phantom dad screaming to be let out of a cage. The steel cage was coruscating with red sparks with energy, each spark making him cringe in pain. *Please, Cedric—get me out!*

I am not a guy who believes in supernatural dreaming. But I did think maybe my subconscious was trying to tell me something. My therapist thought so too. That's when I told Mom, "Let's write him a letter."

Now I was sorry I'd come. I felt nothing, after my brief encounter with my father, except a painful emptiness.

I took my phone from my pocket and thought dourly, the sad little kid in me needs his mother. But though I pressed speed dial for my mother, I didn't get her on the phone.

"Hello, Cedric," said the man on my phone's screen. A very odd-looking man.

"What the hell," I mumbled, punching a button ending the call. "Fat-fingered Face Timing with some rando?" Maybe all those servers in the attic were messing with my cell.

The man's face vanished from my phone—and reappeared. "Don't do that, please, Cedric," he said. His voice was professorially orotund. "This is the most expedient way for us to talk. I'm here in the house with you. Your father's house on Spruce Street. But I can speak more clearly through this device."

Suppose you removed the skin from a human, head and all, and hung it on a hanger. That's what this looked like. Sort of melting, head stretched out like something from a Modigliani painting. His eyes, I saw now, were sockets—with a light in each one, way to the back.

"You're staring aghast," he said, his lips moving floppily. "Let

me try something." The face shifted, becoming almost normal—almost like a living human being. "Is that better, Cedric?"

"My dad is doing this," I said, my mind flailing for explanation.

"No, Cedric, I'm simply someone wishing to speak to you. This contact is not some hack from your father. But he's *here*. Look around. We can nudge him into the garage."

Another movement caught at the corner of my eye—and there was the ghost of my dad, squeezing out from a crack in a concrete wall: eyes like bruises with little lights in them, mouth gaping, beard streaming, squirming along the top of a row of cardboard boxes, like an undulating caterpillar. The thing looked desperately around—panicky, mouth quivering. I heard it whimpering.

"Got to be a projection," I said.

"No," said the man in the phone screen. "It's a ghost—a lost soul. Go over to it. Put out your hand. You can feel it—subtle though its substance is."

I snorted and said, "Suggestion, placebo effect—that what you're counting on?" But I crossed the dusty space to the thing. It seemed aware of me, its head flapping frantically on its body as I approached.

I didn't want to touch it. But I made myself. I wanted to get to the bottom of this. Prove this was all some trick.

I pressed the fingertips of my left hand into the thing—and I felt a sort of gelatinous substance, which made my hands feel as if they'd touched dry ice. And the dad-thing reacted, cringing, twisting itself, to escape my touch. But just as it pulled away, I got a powerful hit of something I can only describe as the essence of a human mind. A flashing series of memories, faces, situations—all resonating with an ill-defined familiarity.

It was my father's mind. And there was a mutual recognition. I heard his voice say, *I'm sorry, Cedric. I'm really sorry. I should have—*

That's where it cut off. And the squirming subtle-bodied thing wriggled away at great speed toward the door into the house. It squeezed under the door and was gone, but for a dissolving wisp of mist.

"Cedric?" The voice from my phone.

I took a long shivery breath and looked at the cell phone screen. My voice came out a croak. "Who *are* you?"

"In life I went by the name Demetrious Calas."

"In life . . ."

"I died, as you would call it, in 1977. Thereupon I was assigned to the next pneumic plane, but because of my history in computer science I was called back to this cruder level to try to rescue souls trapped in electronically generated fields."

"Souls trapped in . . . what?"

"Souls become trapped on Earth in several ways. One is just a slow giving up on one's soul, as millions of people do every day. They simply fail to nourish their souls—souls are nourished by self-awareness and empathy. Their souls loosen from them, wander the world for a time, and essentially melt away. Another sort of soul becomes emotionally trapped, due to trauma or unspeakable loss. But in modern times many souls are abandoned in favor of fixating on phones, social media, and the addictive madness associated with those devices. Souls shrivel and break away. That's what's happened to poor Leroy."

"He's . . . lost his soul?"

"Yes, Leroy and your father are what we call—empty bottles. Leroy is soulless, poor thing. Yet his soul has its own separate being now—quite undeveloped, but it's there. You saw it wandering the hallway, I believe."

"Look, the soul is a supernatural concept—I don't subscribe to—um . . ."

"The soul is *not* supernatural. That's a common misconception. It's a *material* being, but a very subtle one. It is *biological*—but an unfamiliar biology. It is a consciousness that grows within the body of a healthy person. If we live intelligently and ethically, the soul is cultivated within us. Souls will someday be found to exist within the realm of science."

"Yeah? Science doesn't believe in heaven and hell."

"Such places don't exist. But there are subtle psychic landscapes, low on the scale, which have their own spiritual ecology, their own food chain. And *predators.* Some spirits become trapped in those psychic landscapes because they were predatory in life, or parasitical. Such places are hellish. Higher pneumic planes are more elevated—with a civilization that would be hard to describe."

I snorted. "This is bullshit. I've stumbled into some kind of weird VR video game, right?"

"What did you feel when you touched the soul of your father?"

"Oh, that." I felt a deep pang thinking about it. The fear in him, the loneliness, the regret. "It was—"

"It was *real,* wasn't it? Didn't have the taste of things that are true?"

"It . . ." My gut twisted as I thought of the lost soul of my father. "Yes."

"I wasn't expecting you here, but it may be providential. We're looking for a way to switch off the house's electrical system—shut down everything at once. I hoped to persuade Marjorie to do it. But she refuses to talk to me. She retains her soul, but it's a shriveled little thing that gets smaller every day." Calas sighed. "We haven't got enough telekinetic finesse to throw the circuit breakers. Now that you're here, you can do this yourself. You simply go to the fuse box and shut down the house's power for three minutes."

"The house . . . my dad's soul is trapped in it?"

"Yes, within the strong electromagnetic field he's set up for his experiments. Its energy systems and electrical fields constitute a trap for souls."

"I had a dream about my dad . . ."

He nodded. "So I understand. Now you know what your dream was about."

"So is my dad aware of his—his *soul*—wandering the house?"

"The man you spoke to is no longer your father in any important way. It is *aware* of its separated soul, yes. But its cognition has decided the soul is an illusion."

"Wait." Did I understand Calas right? "Are you saying that my dad and my half-brother . . . *are being haunted by their own souls?*"

"Yes. Depending on what you mean by your father and your brother. Your father's body and brain, your brother's body and brain—they are haunted by their own souls."

"They are their own ghosts?" I was tempted to say, *Aren't we all, in a way?*

"Yes. Their souls can never return to their bodies. They have become 'ghosts.'"

I went through all the obvious reality checks then. *Am I awake?* A pinch confirmed it. *Have I been drugged?* Had a whole period of drug experimentation in the past—this was not that.

It felt as if I'd known about these things on some level, but had to have it shown me in person to believe it.

"How do I know I can trust you?"

"Trust me? To persuade you to turn off the lights for three minutes? What other motive would I have than the one I've described? I have been assigned to set two souls free."

"And once they're free?"

"I'll escort them to the next plane. They'll be sorted out there."

"I don't know . . ."

"I have an idea. I'll try to pull my appearance together a little and come to you in person. Then you'll know I'm what I say I am."

"Actually—please don't do that."

"Oh I insist!"

Someone behind me touched me on the shoulder. I jumped and spun on my heel.

"Sorry," Calas said. "Didn't meant to startle you."

Before me was the ghost of a short, wide-shouldered, dark-eyed man who seemed to droop, his wide face warping and reshaping over and over. A pale fogginess about his body was shaped like a robe.

"I've been in this plane too long," Calas said, his voice coming through distantly, echoing faintly. "Having trouble keeping a human shape. It's hard work being dead in this world. In mine, it's a breeze. Reach out and touch me, now."

"I don't think so, no," I said, starting to back away.

But he reached out and took my hand and I felt my fingertips within the membrane of his being—and was shocked by a flashing of memories; images of a life in this world and in another. First there was a sense of a child gazing up at a smiling man with a black mustache. His father. Then his mother, wearing an ornate shawl, thousands of life images flashing by like shuffling cards, interwoven with warmth and sadness and humor. Then came a gathering darkness—followed by an intelligent beam of light that became a tunnel, leading to a plane on which beings floated in shifting, abstract energy forms. They were symmetrical, like living emblems. I could see Calas's essential spiritual self—and knew instantly I could trust him.

I drew my hand back and found I was gasping. Overwhelmed by having just directly experienced another being's otherness.

Calas turned away—and in the process seemed to go through a doorway, shrinking to a point and vanishing. Yet I sensed him still close by.

His voice came from my phone. "Are you satisfied, Cedric?"

I took a deep breath and said, "I'll turn off the electricity—for three minutes."

"I recommend that you block the house door into the garage, first."

I was afraid to ask why. I blocked the door with the cot, grabbed the flashlight, and went to the fuse box in the corner of the garage. I glanced at my watch, noted the time, and threw the circuit breakers.

The room went pitch black.

"What the hell am I doing?" I muttered. But I clicked on the flashlight, directed on the circuit breakers. I didn't want to look anywhere else, just did not want to see ghosts in that dark room.

I immediately heard my father shout—must have been loud, coming through all those walls. *What the fuck!*

My father's body and brain shouted it, anyway.

I felt a difference in the house—the vague sick feeling was gone. The half-heard buzz had gone silent. Those servers were turned off. But I was still afraid to look around in the dark garage.

I looked at the luminous dial of my watch. I waited.

A minute passed. A second one. Then a rattling and pounding came at the door to the garage—it made me jump. My nerves were raw. Someone was pushing at the door. The metal-framed cot was slowing them down—but a hard shove pushed it back. I saw a flutter of two anxious ghosts around the door, Leroy and Dad, like hysterical toddlers in spectral form.

I looked at my watch.

"Less than a minute remains, Cedric!" came Calas's voice.

"Right." I went to the cot, straddled it, braced it against the door.

Dad started shouting, "Turn those breakers back, *turn 'em back!*"

The ghosts cried out echoingly, "No don't no don't no don't! Don't turn them back—don't—"

And then their voices faded out—and so did the ghosts. More accurately, they were getting smaller, as if in the perspective of distance, then they spun around and went down a kind of glowing drain—and were gone.

And that's when my father heaved himself against the door, and it banged hard on the cot, knocking me aside. I fell, rolled on the concrete, and he stampeded past me, running to the power box, yelling, "Oh God oh God oh God it has to be salvageable!"

The lights came on; the hum returned. My father, what was left of him, rounded on me and said, "Why? Why did you turn off the power?"

"To save your soul," I murmured. Not even loud enough for him to hear.

But he stormed past me and ran through the door and I heard his feet stamping up the stairs as he hurried to the servers in the attic room.

In a few moments he shrieked, "*Nooooo!* It's gone! It's all gone!"

I didn't wait for him to get downstairs. I heard Calas on my phone. "You have succeeded. I took them onward—I came back to say goodbye and thank you." I looked at the phone, saw his face—a proper face, not melting—looking back at me.

"Where are they going?" I asked, sitting up. "Dad's soul—and Leroy's?"

"Neither up nor down but onward. Thank you. I'll see you 'round the mountain." And his face vanished.

"Time for me to vanish too," I muttered, standing up.

I found my baggage, had to dodge past Marjorie on my way to the door. She was gasping, weeping, "What's going on? What happened?"

"You really should get out of here," I told her, backing away, out the front door. "Before you lose your soul too."

Then I strode off, in a feverish hurry to be away from there, calling a cab as I went.

I didn't go back for two years. I tried to talk to a philosophy professor, an existentialist, about what had happened in the house. He suggested I get medication for hallucinations.

I do know that it seemed as if a weight had been lifted from me when I walked away from that house. And it had to do with setting my father and my half-brother free.

But I kept wondering what was left of my half-brother. Just a kid, after all.

The question troubled me. I tried calling my dad's number. It was no longer in service.

Mom's partner is an assistant prosecutor. She called certain police contacts, who talked to Child Protection Services. We got some of the story, off the record. It seems Marjorie took Dad to court, got half of his money and half the house. The house was mostly gutted when she was done. She refused to care for Leroy, called him "a little monster." My father was evicted from the house, which now stood vacant. No more was known.

One drizzly November morning I went back to the vacant house and knocked on the door. I knocked just in case there were squatters in the house.

There were. A man and his little boy. They were eating scraps of Eternally Edibles, wandering from room to room, dragging broken electronics by the wire. Dad and Leroy were filthy and muttering endlessly.

They are quite physically alive. But in their way . . . they are haunting that house.

The Midnight Hour

Algernon Blackwood

In the distant days when I was so eager to see a ghost with my own eyes, I recall a singular example of the strange effects of terror; and I don't mean the terror of meeting a tiger, or a burglar face to face with a pistol raised; I mean spiritual or ghostly terror, whichever you prefer.

I've always felt a psychological interest in these alleged effects of terror: paralysis of movement, speechlessness, hair turning white (apparently quite unsubstantiated) and the rest. With regard to the latter, you may know the delightful tale of the old lady who was so terrified by a ghost that her wig, carefully draped on the dressing-table, was white next morning.

But coming back to my own personal experiences, I once came across a result of terror that was quite new to me. If you don't want to hear about it, just turn over the page to the enchanting pictures you will find. If you care to listen, however, may I add, before my little tale, that it was only years later I came across a reference to this particular effect of ghostly terror in Kipling. It is the only reference I know. Kipling, you must admit, was a prince of accurate observations. He mentions it. All right. If you're still reading, here's what happened.

Eager to see a ghost with my own eyes, I was lucky enough to get advance notice of haunted houses the Psychical Research Society considered worth investigating, cases, that is, with good evidence behind them. Among these was a certain unfurnished house in a Brighton square. The story was horrible. A manservant in the household, crazily in love with a housemaid, had crashed the girl over the banisters to her death. The evidence of the crime, as also the evidence supporting its alleged re-enactment in ghostly terms, was overwhelming.

Rather by subterfuge, I got the keys of the empty house from the Brighton agents, and I well recall the agent's admission, when I pressed him, that the house was said to be haunted. That admission (from a house agent) took some getting, but I got it. And I planned to spend a night in this unfurnished, empty haunted house.

I had arranged to take a sister with me, but at the last moment she got "cold feet." She just couldn't face it. Nor did I blame her. In the daylight of the sunny Brighton front it was easy; when the dusk fell and shadows began to creep, it was different. It so happened that our hostess exclaimed suddenly, "Oh, I'll come, if you want a companion. I don't believe in this ghostly stuff and, anyhow, I don't care a damn!"

We went together. It was about 11.30 p.m. The night was still. No wind. And the sound of the surf fell booming through the deserted square as we made our quiet way, not talking much, I noticed. A moon, almost at the full, silvered the empty square and silent streets. Everybody seemed in bed. My companion, my hostess, whom I knew slightly, was a youngish woman, gay, cheery, chatty. But as we entered the square and approached the house, her chatty volubility, I noticed, died away. It was all so silent, so deserted. The bright moonlight, the booming of the surf, these alone struck our senses. We padded on together then in silence towards the empty house. I recall wishing I had been alone. I didn't quite like her increasing silence.

And then we reached the house in the corner of the square. It looked menacing to me in that blaze of moonlight. I had brought with me a thermos, candles, matches, food, and a rug. First making sure there was no one in sight, above all a wandering bobby, we mounted the steps and I put the key in. Once inside, I closed the front door behind me and took out my matchbox. For this was before the days of electric torches, I must mention. And as I opened the box, there was a sound of someone coughing close beside me. There, standing in the darkness of the entrance hall, someone coughed. It was a man's cough, I swear.

It gave me a nasty turn, I admit. There was someone else in the empty house besides our two selves. There was no possible doubt in my mind about that cough. It was close beside me as I stood in that darkened hall. It was a natural, not a premeditated cough. A shiver ran up my back. Yet, that strange thing, as later interrogation proved, was that my companion had *not* heard it. It came to my ears only. Now, please remember, that of seeing a ghost I had no faintest fear, I was burning to see one. I had no fear of that kind, for my interest was far stronger than any superstitious terror. But that cough, close against my ears in the darkness—well, it gave me a nasty turn as I've said. And, to make things worse, I had opened my matchbox upside-down, so that its contents scattered on to the stone floor—and had to be picked up. A rat, a mouse even, anything might start a fire. Laboriously, while my friend said nothing, I picked them up—and lit my candle.

So, here and now, was the immediate problem. Somebody else besides ourselves was in this empty, unfurnished house. They might he crooks, using a haunted house as their hiding place. A dozen explanations flashed through my mind. But, at any rate, we must first search the house from floor to ceiling.

Persuading my companion with some difficulty that this was first necessary, we carried it out faithfully, from the kitchen and scullery to the servants' rooms on the top floor. A nasty, creepy business, I admit it was, expecting any minute to see a face in the shadows or a figure slinking round a door. I think the servants' attics were the worst. It was here, of course, the murderer had found his victim before he crashed her over the banisters to her death. We found—we saw—nothing: and eventually, we sat up to wait for events in a small room at the top of the stairs leading from the attics to the lower floors. We sat on the bare boards, a lit candle shining through the door of a half-open cupboard . . . waiting, waiting, waiting, and listening, listening, listening. We spoke little, and for some reason in whispers only. The moonlight fell in slantingly across the floor. We just heard the distant booming of the surf at the end of the square. Otherwise there was silence, silence broken only by our rare whispered remarks.

I was expectant, keyed up, hopeful. I admit it. But I had no sense of fear. If, by any lucky chance, as the hours wore on, there came a voice, step, or some evidence, of anybody moving, I was ready, on the instant, to jump up and investigate. I *might*, God knows, see the terrified housemaid in full flight down the stairs, I *might* see the lovecrazed man full tilt at her heels, hunting her down to her terrible death. I *might*, with any luck, see a ghost at last!

For my companion, so eagerly did I sit there waiting as the hours passed, I admit I had little thought; and then—suddenly—it struck me: "Does she feel the same? Is she perhaps a bit scared? Could she jump up and come with me?" I think her prolonged silence made me suddenly ask these questions. And I imagine an unwelcome doubt about her state of mind caused them.

We were sitting, as I said, side by side on the bare boards of the little room at the top of the stairs. The candlelight through the opened door of the cupboard made her face plainly visible. I glanced down at her sideways.

"If we hear a step or a voice," I whispered, "we ought to go out and investigate it at once. Are you all right?"

But the sight of her face froze me stiff. She did not answer. Her face, not uncomely, had somehow gone back to the face of child-hood. It was the face of a girl, lines and wrinkles all ironed out. It was a face masked by utter terror, its youthfulness somehow terrible.

My own reactions were immediate. I must get her out of the house. My mind worked quickly at that moment. If a step or a voice had come outside en the stairs or landing, she could not have moved for terror. I realised that. Her terror had been growing, increasing for hours evidently, but I had not noticed it. Had anything "ghostly" intervened just then, she would simply have passed out. I knew it. I felt sure of it. I must get her out of the house at once. To be caught in an empty house with an unconscious young woman on my hands at 2 a.m., with police and press inquisitive, publicity and the rest, would have been an unenviable situation.

And so it was. Explaining as convincingly as I could that nothing was now likely to happen—it was almost early morning and we had sat waiting for hours—I took her arm and we crawled together, side by side, down the long stairs and so out into the street and the fresh keen air blowing in from the sea. And she told me frankly that for hours she had been too scared to move or speak, not even to whisper.

And, as I mentioned, it was only years later that I came across a ghost story of Kipling's where he mentions this strange effect of real terror that blots out the adult face and masks it with the innocence of childhood. My experience at least can claim this backing from a close observer. An unusual thrill had certainly come my way, though it was not, after all, the thrill I had hoped for, the thrill of seeing a ghost at last.

Soul House

Kyla Lee Ward

*"Fired clay offering tray ('soul-house') in the form an enclo-
sure, with a two-storey building set against the rear wall.
Twelfth Dynasty."*—catalogue entry for BM EA32610

A shabti in my place they should have found,
A servitor whose heart could never ache.
But when my master went below the ground,
The lector priest a model house did make.
My house, in clay. Through processes opaque,
About it the most potent magic wound,
And in his tomb, surprised I was to wake.
Around I walk, and once again around.

This reproduction, although small, is sound.
The lifted floor grants refuge from the snake.
A mudbrick wall, the courtyard does surround,
And to the roof, I may the stairway take.
The house I purchased for my children's sake!
All houses model the primeval mound,
But here the lotus dawn will never break.
Around I walk, and once again around.

I've herbs to pick and barley grain to pound,
I pluck the birds and set them on to bake,
And baste them well, till all are nicely browned.
With dates and honey, I compose a cake,

And of this feast your spirit does partake.
Yet I'm alone: come herdsman and his hound,
I'd crack the finest jar, their thirst to slake!
Around I walk and once again around.

Envoi
Prince, to so address the justified I quake—
Was it by your command that I was bound?
Else lone and lost, a sorcerous mistake,
Around I walk, and once again around.

Endless

Anna Taborska

*Reader beware
as you pass by.
As you are now,
so once was I.
As I am now,
so you will be.
Therefore prepare
to follow me.*

*—Anonymous grave inscription,
Old Southfield Cemetery*

Elizabeth sat in the window, looking out at the street below, sweating and fighting the urge to go to the pub. She didn't drink much—just a couple of units of an evening—but her doctor had been insisting that she cut it out altogether; her liver was struggling as years of anti-inflammatory meds and other over-the-counter painkillers for her arthritis and migraines took their toll.

Elizabeth had been convincing herself that beer didn't really count; that it was a good alternative to "proper" alcohol because it was weak and there was only so much of it you could drink. Now she told herself that she had to go for a walk. The doctor had said she needed to do more exercise. Besides, the stuffiness in her flat was starting to make her head hurt, and fresh air would be much better for her than another round of ibuprofen.

Dusk was coming on apace and if she was to go out, the sooner she did so the better. She swapped her baggy vest for a bra and T-shirt, stuffed her wallet, phone and rape alarm into the pockets of her shorts, and headed out.

Clara woke with a start. She'd been fighting for air and it took her a moment to work out that her throat wasn't hurting anymore and it must have been a dream. Then she realized that she wasn't in bed; wasn't even indoors. Where was she?

Fighting her growing fear, Clara sat up and looked around. It was getting dark, but the dirty urban glow and distant streetlamps provided enough light for her to ascertain her surroundings. Parched grass, trees, bushes and . . . gravestones. A moment's panic, but then Clara was on her feet and getting her bearings. She recognized the grave with the ominous inscription; she was in the local cemetery, about ten minutes' walk from her house.

Then a horrifying thought sliced its way through her confusion like a shard of glass, instantly turning apprehension to a sickening dread: Katie!

Elizabeth finished her pint, said goodbye to the bartender and left The Organ Grinder. Who'd she been kidding? Ever since she'd resolved not to keep any alcohol at home, her walks inevitably led to the local pub.

As she went to cross the road, she was almost knocked off her feet by a red-haired woman, running in the opposite direction. Or, more precisely, she would have been knocked off her feet had she not moved out of the way fast enough. The woman had an intense, focused look on her face, though Elizabeth couldn't fathom how she knew that, given that she hadn't seen the woman's face clearly. And to her dismay, in the brief moment before the woman ran off and disappeared from view, Elizabeth noticed that she wasn't wearing anything on her feet. Then she was gone, and Elizabeth quickened her pace as she walked past the alleyway that led to the side entrance of the Old Southfield Cemetery, and headed home.

Elizabeth had only just finished checking that the front door and all the windows were locked when her phone rang. It was the new tenant from her rental property, located about half a mile from her block of flats. As she answered the phone, Elizabeth hoped the call wasn't about what she thought it was about.

"Hi, Greg."

"Hi, Dr. Simmons."

"You know you can call me Elizabeth."

"Yes. Elizabeth." Greg sounded stressed and nervous. "I'm really sorry to bother you . . ." *Here we go,* thought Elizabeth. "It's just that . . . I was wondering . . . is there anyone else living here?"

"No," Elizabeth tried to sound casual. "Just you."

"Oh," said Greg. "It's just that I thought I heard someone downstairs."

"It's an old house," Elizabeth replied. "It makes funny noises. You'll get used to it."

"Oh," repeated Greg. "Okay." Elizabeth pretended not to notice that he was obviously far from okay. "Well . . . I'm sorry I bothered you."

"It's no bother, Greg," Elizabeth interjected quickly, before the young man had the chance to say anything else. "Goodnight."

Elizabeth wasn't going to lose another tenant. Her first one—an ex-military Scotsman built like a brick outhouse—had disappeared without leaving a forwarding address; cup of tea, tabloid newspaper, and burnt-down cigarette in the ashtray on the coffee table, Mary Celeste–style. Prior to that, he'd called her twice in the middle of the night, scared shitless, claiming that there was someone in the house with him. After he vanished, evidently through the left-open back door of the property, she'd found an enormous kitchen knife under his pillow.

Elizabeth had put the episode down to something (or someone) from the man's past catching up with him. But then she'd had three students staying in the property—nice Asian lads from the University of Westminster, who drove souped-up Ford Fiestas and Toyota Supras, and didn't seem like nervous types. They'd called several times in the middle of the night, saying that someone was rummaging around downstairs and, as soon as they'd found alternative accommodation, they'd left. Elizabeth had checked the house, of course. After all, you heard about incidents of unwanted visitors sneaking in through the cellar or the attic and helping themselves to food or sleeping in a property, but there was no way of getting in or out other than through the windows or doors, and she'd had the locks changed as soon as she took possession of the house. Whatever it was that was going on in there (she didn't believe in ghosts), Elizabeth figured that if everyone ignored it, it would go away.

Clara woke with a jolt in the darkness of the cemetery, her relief at being able to breathe short-lived as she realized she was not at home. Around her the black shapes of trees reached out with gnarly limbs, and gravestones protruded like vast broken teeth. Her shock was starting to subside when a thought so desperate and so dreadful assailed her that she was up and running before she could fathom how she got here and why her throat didn't hurt.

Orienting herself thanks to the anonymous grave with the creepy inscription, Clara bolted out of the cemetery and across the main road. She didn't even notice the taxi that swerved to avoid her, or the thump and crash as headlight shattered against bollard.

"Oi! Come back, you crazy bitch!" resonated somewhere behind her as the shocked cabby got out to survey the damage wrought by the flight of the wild, barefooted redhead, at once furious and relieved at not having run her over.

All Clara could think of was her little girl left alone with Him. If He'd been drinking again (and there was no "if" about it) and Clara wasn't there to bear the brunt of his drunken rage, then there was no telling what he might do. She could see her house at the end of the road, the large dark brown door sucking up all the light from the streetlamp that was struggling to illuminate it. She prayed that she wasn't too late.

Elizabeth had spent the day working from home, marking student essays. It was a boring task at best, and the stuffiness caused by the lack of through-air in her flat had done nothing to aid her powers of concentration. By the time she was done it was evening already, but the temperature—both inside and out—showed no sign of dropping.

Elizabeth set off for The Organ Grinder. This time she didn't even try to pretend that her walk would take her anywhere else. She sat at her usual corner table and tried to relax, but her mind kept returning to her rental property and her less than honest lack of disclosure to her tenant.

Elizabeth had used money inherited from her mother to buy a small, old, cottage-style terraced house as an investment. She'd cleaned it up and fixed what needed fixing, but left the outside, including the disproportionately large, dark brown front door, and much of the characterful interior, as it was. The house was set back a little from the road, with a small garden and large bay window on the ground floor in the front, and a paved yard in the back. It stood in the middle of a row of similar houses, and yet there was something about it that caught the attention of passers-by. Those who paused to look saw nothing unusual, yet shivered and braced themselves against the sudden cold that seemed to settle around their heart and spine before rapidly moving on. Those who hurried past without stopping nevertheless felt their mood suddenly change; their thoughts interrupted by a flood of melancholy and an inexplicable sense of confusion and loss. It was as though long-dead fingers somehow reached from the impenetrable, unforgiving void and brushed the living with an ice-cold touch. Then as soon as it had come, the feeling was gone, leaving people bewildered and struggling to get back to the shopping list, work meeting agenda, or takeaway dinner menu that they'd been mentally preparing a moment ago.

Elizabeth's thoughts turned to her mother. The two of them had always been close, and they'd become even more so when Elizabeth had moved back in with her mother, to care for her in her final years. Elizabeth couldn't stop the tears welling up in her eyes. She downed the rest of her pint and hurried out of the pub.

Back home, Elizabeth decided to have an early night, but the flat was too warm and her room far too stuffy for comfort. Add to that the hot flushes that accompanied her age, and decent sleep had become a distant dream.

Elizabeth pulled off the single sheet covering her and flipped her pillow over in the hope that its underside would be a little cooler—if only for a few seconds. She tossed and turned and tried to distract herself from the gloomy thoughts that always seemed to find her in the dead of night. Finally, after what seemed like hours, and against all odds, Elizabeth fell asleep.

And then her phone rang.

After the initial shock of her rude awakening, Elizabeth reached for the phone, checking the caller before answering. It was Greg—agitated, apologetic, and downright frightened.

"I'm really sorry to bother you again . . ." Elizabeth braced herself. "And I'm sorry to call so late."

"What time is it?" Elizabeth asked.

"It's after midnight." Greg's discomfort at the other end of the phone was almost tangible. "I'm really sorry, but there's definitely someone downstairs." He spoke the last five words quickly, as though to let them linger would be to instill them with a truth too frightening to contemplate. Elizabeth hesitated, disoriented from having been woken up and unsure how to respond.

"What makes you think that?" she finally asked, already knowing the answer all too well.

"I can hear them moving around."

"I'm sure it's just the house settling," said Elizabeth. There was silence at the other end, so she continued, "You know, just the wood expanding or contracting with the changing temperature."

"But I heard footsteps," said Greg. "And doors banging. And things being moved around."

"The walls are really thin." Elizabeth had managed to get her head together. "Sometimes, when the neighbors are walking around, it sounds as if they're in the house with you. I promise you, it's nothing to worry about. Okay?" There was a long pause; Greg was the first to break.

"Yes, Doctor. I mean, Elizabeth."

This time Elizabeth didn't fall asleep. She was still staring at the ceiling as dawn crept in and her room started to lighten.

Another day of sweating, marking essays, and coming up with ideas for a new lecture course in preparation for the next academic year. Elizabeth wondered how many students would bother turning up to her lectures. How many had attended her lectures over the years? Had she actually taught any of them anything useful? Anything at all? Sometimes Elizabeth wondered if there was any point to it. Or was it just a string of endless days turning into endless years?

Her thoughts drifted back to her tenant and the bizarre state of affairs at the rental property. Perhaps she would call Greg. Maybe even go round and search the house with him, put his mind at ease . . . But who was she kidding?

As whatever tormented essence that remained of Clara awoke in the Old Southfield Cemetery and ran home to rescue her infant daughter from the clutches of the husband who'd murdered her (and to wreak havoc with Greg's mental health), Elizabeth sat in The Organ Grinder, nursing a solitary pint.

*

FOR RENT

Bijou terraced house. Two bedrooms.
Small garden. Plenty of period charm.
Price discounted for quick rental.

The House

H. P. Lovecraft

'Tis a grove-circled dwelling
    Set close to a hill,
Where the branches are telling
    Strange legends of ill;
Over timbers so old
    That they breathe of the dead,
Crawl the vines, green and cold,
    By strange nourishment fed;
And no man knows the juices they suck from the depths of
their dank slimy bed.

    In the gardens are growing
        Tall blossoms and fair,
Each pallid bloom throwing
        Perfume on the air;
But the afternoon sun
        With its shining red rays
Makes the picture loom dun
        On the curious gaze,
And above the sweet scent of the blossoms rise odours of num-
berless days.

    The rank grasses are waving
        On terrace and lawn,
Dim memories sav'ring
        Of things that have gone;

The stones of the walks
    Are encrusted and wet,
And a strange spirit stalks
When the red sun has set,
And the soul of the watcher is fill'd with faint pictures he fain
would forget.

    It was in the hot Junetime
      I stood by that scene,
When the gold rays of noontime
      Beat bright on the green.
But I shiver'd with cold,
      Groping feebly for light,
As a picture unroll'd—
And my age-spanning sight
Saw the time I had been there before flash like fulgury out of
the night.

Napier Court

Ramsey Campbell

Alma Napier sat up in bed. Five minutes ago she'd laid down *Victimes de Devoir* to cough, then stared round her bedroom heavy-eyed; the partly open door reflected panels of cold October sunlight, which glanced from the flowered wallpaper, glared from the glass-fronted bookcase, but left the metronome on top in shadow and failed to reach the corner where her music-stand was standing. She'd thought she had heard footsteps on the stairs. Beyond the brilliant panel she could see the darker landing; she waited for someone to appear. Her clock, displayed within its glass tube, showed 11:03. It must be Maureen. Then she thought: could it be her parents? Had they decided to give up their holiday after all? She had looked forward to being left alone for a fortnight when her cold had confined her to the house; she wanted time to prove herself, to make her own way—she felt a stab of misery as she listened. Couldn't they leave her alone for two weeks? Didn't they trust her? The silence thickened; the darkness on the landing seemed to move. "Who's there? Is that you, Maureen?" she called and coughed. The darkness moved again. Of course it didn't, she said, willing her hands to unclench. She held up one; the little finger twitched. Don't be childish, she told herself, where's your strength? She slid out of the cocoon of warmth, slipped on her slippers and dressing-gown, and went downstairs.

The house was empty. "You see?" she said aloud. What else had she expected? She entered the kitchen. On the windowsill sat the medicine her mother had bought. "I don't like to leave you alone," she'd said two hours ago. "Promise you'll take this and stay in bed until you're better. I've asked Maureen to buy anything you need while she's shopping." "Mother," Alma had protested, "I could have asked her. After all, she is my friend." "I know I'm being overprotective, I know I can't expect to be liked for it any more," and oh God, Alma thought, all the strain of calming her down, of parting friends; there was no longer any question of love. As her mother was leaving the bedroom while her father bumped the last case down to the car, she'd said "Alma, I don't want to talk about Peter, as you well know, but you did promise—" "I've told you," Alma had replied somewhat sharply, "I shan't be seeing him again." That was all over. She wished everything were over, all this possessiveness that threatened to erase her completely; she wished she could be left alone with her music. But that wasn't to be, not for two years. There was the medicine bottle, incarnating her mother's continued influence in the house. Taking medicine for a cold was a sign of weakness, in Alma's opinion, but her chest hurt terribly when she coughed; after all, her mother wasn't imposing it on her, if she took it that was her own decision. She measured a spoonful and gulped it down. Then she padded determinedly through the hall, past the living-room (her father's desk reflected in one mirror), the dining-room (her mother's flower arrangements preserved under glass in another), and upstairs, past her mother's Victorian valentines framed above the ornate banister. Now, she ordered herself, to bed, and another chapter of *Victimes de Devoir* before Maureen arrived. She'd never make the Brichester French Circle if she carried on like this.

As soon as she climbed into bed, trying to preserve its bag of warmth, she was troubled by something she remembered having seen. In the hall—what had been wrong? She caught it: as she'd mounted the stairs she'd seen a shape in the hall mirror. Maureen's coat hanging on the coat-stand—but Maureen wasn't here. Certainly something pale had stood against the front-door panes. About to investigate, she addressed herself: the house was empty, there could be nothing there. All right, she'd asked Maureen to check the story of the house in the library's files of the *Brichester Herald*—but that didn't mean she believed the hints she'd heard in the corner shop that day, before her mother had intervened with "Now, Alma, don't upset yourself" and to the shopkeeper "Haunted, indeed. I'm afraid we grew out of that sort of thing in Severnford." If she had seemed to glimpse a figure in the hall it merely meant she was delirious. She'd asked Maureen to check purely because she wanted to face up to the house, to come to terms with it. She was determined to stop thinking of her room as her refuge, where she was protected by her music. Before she left the house she wanted to make it a step towards maturity.

The darkness shifted on the landing. Tired eyes, she explained—yet again her room enfolded her. She reached out and removed her flute from its case; she admired its length, its shine, the perfection of its measurements as they fitted to her fingers. She couldn't play it now—each time she tried she coughed—but it seemed charged with beauty. Her appreciation over, she laid the instrument to rest in its long black box.

"You retreat into your room and your music." Peter had said that, but he'd been speaking of a retreat from Hiroshima, from the conditions in Lower Brichester, from all the horrid things he'd insisted she confront. That was over, she said quickly, and the house was empty. Yet her eyes strayed from *Victimes de Devoir.*

Footsteps on the stairs again. This time she recognised Maureen's. The others—which she hadn't heard, of course—had been indeterminate, even sexless. She thought she'd ask Maureen whether she'd left her coat in the hall; she might have entered while Alma had slept, with the key she'd borrowed. The door opened and the panel of sunlight fled, darkening the room. No, thought Alma; to inquire into possible delusions would be an admission of weakness.

Maureen dropped her carrier and sneezed. "I think I've got your cold," she said indistinctly.

"Oh dear." Alma's mood had darkened with the room, with her decision not to speak. She searched for conversation in which to lose herself. "Have you heard yet when you're going to library school?" she asked.

"It's not settled yet. I don't know, the idea of a spinster career is beginning to depress me. I'm glad you're not faced with that."

"You shouldn't brood," Alma advised, restlessly stacking her books on the bedspread.

Maureen examined the titles. *"Victimes de Devoir, Therese Desqueyroux.* In the original French, good Lord. Why are you grappling with these?"

"So that I'll be an interesting young woman," Alma replied instantly. "I'm sure I've told you I feel guilty doing nothing. I can't practice, not with this cold. I only hope it's past before the Camside concert. Which reminds me, do you think I could borrow your transistor during the day? For the music programme. To give me peace."

"All right. I can't today, I start work at one. Though I think—no, it doesn't matter."

"Go on."

"Well, I agree with Peter, you know that. You can't have peace and beauty without closing your eyes to the world. Didn't he say that to seek peace in music was to seek complete absence of sensation, of awareness?"

"He said that and you know my answer." Alma unwillingly remembered; he had been here in her room, taking in the music in the bookcase, the polished record-player—she'd sensed his disapproval and felt miserable; why couldn't he stay the strong forthright man she'd come to admire and love? "Really, darling, this is an immature attitude," he'd said. "I can't help feeling you want to abdicate from the human race and its suffering." Her eyes embraced the room. This was security, apart from the external chaos, the horrid part of life. "Even you appreciate the beauty of the museum exhibits," she told Maureen.

"I suppose that's why you work there. I admire them, yes, but in many cases by ignoring their history of cruelty."

"Why must you and Peter always look for the horrid things? What about this house? There are beautiful things here. That record-player—you can look at it and imagine all the craftsmanship it took. Doesn't that seem to you fulfilling?"

"You know we leftists have a functional aesthetic. Anyway—" Maureen paused. "If that's your view of the house you'd best not know what I found out about it."

"Go on, I want to hear."

"If you insist. The *Brichester Herald* was useless—they reported the death of the owner and that was all—but I came across a chapter in Pamela Jones' book on local hauntings which gives the details. The last owner of the house lost a fortune in the stock market—I don't know how exactly, of course it's not my field—and he became a recluse in this house. There's worse to come, are you sure you want—? Well, he went mad. Things started disappearing, so he said, and he accused something he thought was living in the house, something that used to stand behind him or mock him from the empty rooms. I can imagine how he started having hallucinations, looking at this view—"

Alma joined her at the window. "Why?" she disagreed. "I think it's beautiful." She admired the court before the house, the stone pillars framing the iron flourish of the gates; then a stooped woman passed across the picture, heaving a pram from which overflowed a huge cloth bag of washing. Alma felt depressed again; the scene was spoiled.

"Sorry, Alma," Maureen said; her cold hand touched Alma's fingers. Alma frowned slightly and insinuated herself between the sheets. ". . . Sorry," Maureen said again. "Do you want to hear the rest? It's conventional, really. He gassed himself. The Jones book has something about a note he wrote—insane, of course: he said he wanted to 'fade into the house, the one possession left to me,' whatever that meant. Afterwards the stories started; people used to see someone very tall and thin standing at the front door on moonlit nights, and one man saw a figure at an upstairs window with its head turning back and forth like clockwork. Yes, and one of the neighbours used to dream that the house was screaming for help—the book explained that, but not to me I'm afraid. I shouldn't be telling you all this, you'll be alone until tonight."

"Don't worry, Maureen. It's just enjoyably creepy."

"A perceptive comment. It blinds you to what really happened. To think of him in this house, possessing the rooms, eating, sleeping—you forget he lived once, he was real. I wonder which room—"

"You don't have to harp on it," Alma said. "You sound like Peter."

"Poor Peter, you are attacking him today. He'll be here to protect you tonight, after all."

"He won't, because we've parted."

"You could have stopped me talking about him, then. But how for God's sake did it happen?"

"Oh, on Friday. I don't want to talk about it." Walking hand in hand to the front door and as always kissing as Peter turned the key; her father waiting in the hall: "Now listen, Peter, this can't go on"—prompted by her mother, Alma knew, her father was too weak to act independently. She'd pulled Peter into the kitchen—"Go, darling, I'll try and calm them down," she'd said desperately—but her mother was waiting, immediately animated, like a fairground puppet by a penny: "You know you've broken my heart, Alma, marrying beneath you." Alma had slumped into a chair, but Peter leaned against the dresser, facing them all, her mother's prepared speech. "Peter, I will not have you marrying Alma—you're uneducated, you'll get nowhere at the library, you're obsessed with politics and you don't care how much they distress Alma—" and on and on. If only he'd come to her instead of standing pugnaciously apart! She'd looked up at him finally, tearful, and he'd said "Well, darling, I'll answer any point of your mother's you feel is not already answered"—and suddenly everything had been too much; she'd run sobbing to her room. Below, the back door had closed. She'd wrenched open the window; Peter was crossing the garden beneath the rain. "Peter," she'd cried out. "Whatever happens I still love you—" but her mother was before her, pushing her away from the window, shouting down "Go back to your kennel." . . . "What?" she asked Maureen, distracted back.

"I said I don't believe it was your decision. It must have been your mother."

"That's irrelevant. I broke it off finally." Her letter: "It would be impossible to continue when my parents refuse to receive you but anyway I don't want to any more, I want to study hard and become a musician"—she'd posted it on Saturday after a sleepless sobbing night, and immediately she'd felt released, at peace. Then the thought disturbed her: it must have reached Peter by now; surely he wouldn't try to see her? He wouldn't be able to get in; she was safe.

"You can't tell me you love your mother more than Peter. You're simply taking refuge again."

"Surely you don't think I love her now. But I still feel I must be loyal. Is there a difference between love and loyalty?"

"Never having had either, I wouldn't know. Good God, Alma, stop barricading yourself with pseudo-philosophy!"

"If you must know, Maureen, I shall be leaving them as soon as I've paid for my flute. They gave it to me for my twenty-first and now they're threatening to take it back. It'll take me two years, but I shall pay."

"And you'll be twenty-five. God Almighty, why? Bowing down to private ownership?"

"You wouldn't understand any more than Peter would."

"You've returned the ring, of course."

"No." Alma shifted *Victimes de Devoir*. "Once I asked Peter if I could keep it if we broke up." Two weeks before their separation; she'd felt the pressures—her parents' crush, his horrors—misshaping her, callous as thumbs on plasticine. And he'd replied that there'd be no question of their breaking up, which she'd taken for assent.

"And Peter's feelings?" Maureen let the question resonate, but it was muffled by the music.

"Maureen, I just want to remember the happy times."

"I don't understand that remark. At least, perhaps I do, but I don't like it."

"You don't approve."

"I do not." Maureen brandished her watch; from her motion she might have been about to slap Alma. "I can't discuss it with you. I'll be late." She buttoned herself into her coat on the landing. "I suppose I'll see Peter later," she said and clumped downstairs.

With the slam Alma was alone. Her hot water bottle chilled her toes; she thrust it to the foot of the bed. The room was darker; rain patted the pane. The metronome stood stolid in the shadow as if stilled forever. Maureen might well see Peter later; they both worked at Brichester Central Library. What if Maureen should attempt to heal the breach, to lend Peter her key? It was the sort of thing Maureen might well do, particularly as she liked Peter. Alma recalled suggesting once that they take Maureen out—"she does seem lonely, Peter"—only to find the two of them ideologically united against her; the most difficult two hours she'd spent with either of them, listening to their agreement on Vietnam and the rest across the cocktail bar table: horrid. Later she'd go down and bolt the door. But now—she turned restlessly and *Victimes de Devoir* toppled to the floor. She felt guilty not to be reading on—but she yearned to fill herself with music.

The shadows weighed on her eyes; she pulled the cord for light. Spray laced the window like cobwebs on a misty morning; outside the world was slate. The needle on her record-player was dulled, but she selected the first record, Britten's *Nocturne* ("Finnegan's Half-Awake" Peter had commented; she'd never understood what he meant). She placed the needle and let the music expand through her, flowing into troubled crevices. The beauty of Peter

Pears' voice. Peter. Suddenly she was listening to the words: sickly light, huge seaworms— She picked off the needle; she didn't want it to wear away the beauty. Usually Britten could transmute all to beauty. Had Peter's pitiless vision thrown the horrid part into such relief? Once she'd taken him to a performance of the *War Requiem* and in the interval he'd commented "I agree with you— Britten succeeds completely in beautifying war, which is precisely my objection." And later he'd admitted that for the last half hour he'd been pitying the poor cymbal player, bobbing up and down on cue as if in church. That was his trouble: he couldn't achieve peace.

Suppose he came to the house? she thought again. Her gaze flew to the bedroom door, the massed dark on the landing. For a moment she was sure that Peter was out there; wasn't someone watching from the stairs? She coughed jaggedly; it recalled her. Deliberately she lifted her flute from its case and rippled a scale before the next cough came. Later she'd practice, no matter how she coughed; her breathing exercises might cure her lungs. "I find all these exercises a little terrifying," said Peter, "a little robotic." She frowned miserably; he seemed to wait wherever she sought peace. But thoughts of him carried her to the dressing-table drawer, to her ring; she didn't have to remember, the diamond itself crystallised beauty. She turned the jewel but it refused to sparkle beneath the heavy sky. Had he been uneducated? Well, he'd known nothing about music, he'd never known what a cadenza was—"what's the point of your academic analysis, where does it touch life?" Enough. She snapped the lid on the ring and restored it to its drawer. From now on she'd allow herself no time for disturbing memories: down-stairs for soup—she must eat—then her flute exercises followed by *Victimes de Devoir* until she needed sleep.

The staircase merged into the hall, vaguely defined beneath her drowsiness; the Victorian valentines looked dusty in the dusk, neglected in the depths of an antique shop. As Alma passed the living-room a stray light was caught in the mirror and a memory was trapped: herself and Peter on the couch, separating instantly, tongues retreating guiltily into mouths, each time the opening door flashed in the mirror: towards the end Peter would clutch her rebelliously, but she couldn't let her parents come on them embracing, not after their own marriage had been drained of love. "We'll be each other's peace," she'd once told Peter, secretly aware as she spoke that she was terrified of sex. Once they were engaged she'd felt a duty to give in—but she'd panted uncontrollably, her mouth gulping over his, shaming her. One dreadful night Peter had rested his head on her shoulder and she'd known that he was consulting his watch behind her back. And suddenly, weeks later, it had come right; she was at peace, soothed, her fears almost engulfed—which was precisely when her parents had shattered the calm, the door thrown open, jarring the mirror: "Peter, this is a respectable house, I won't have you keeping us all up like this until God knows what hour, even if you are used to that sort of thing—" and then that final confrontation— Quickly, Alma told herself, onwards. She thrust the memories back into the darkness of the two dead rooms to be crushed by her father's desk, choked by her mother's flowers.

On the kitchen windowsill the medicine was black against the back garden, the grey grass plastered down by rain: it loomed like a poison bottle in a Hitchcock film. What was Peter doing at this moment? Where would he be tonight? She fumbled sleepily with the tin of tomato soup and watched it gush into the pan. Where would he be tonight? With someone else? If only he would try to contact her, to show her he still cared— Nonsense. She turned up the gas. No doubt he'd be at the cinema; he'd tried to force films on her, past her music. Such as the film they'd seen on the afternoon of their parting, the afternoon they'd taken off work together, *Hurry Sundown*; it hadn't been the theme of racism which had seemed so horrid, but those scenes with Michael Caine sublimating his sex drive through his saxophone—she'd brushed her hair against Peter's cheek, hopefully, desperately, but he was intent on the screen, and she could only guess his thoughts, too accurately. Perhaps he and

Maureen would find each other: Alma hoped so—then she could forget about them both. The soup bubbled, and she poured it into a dish. Gas sweetened the air; she checked the control, but it seemed turned tight. The dresser—there he had stood, pugnaciously apart, watching her. She set the medicine before her on the table; she'd take it upstairs with her—she didn't want to come downstairs again. In her mind she overcame the suffocating shadow of the rooms, thick with years of tobacco smoke in one, with lavender water in another, by her shining flute, the sheets of music brightly turning.

A dim thin figure moved down the hall towards the kitchen; it hadn't entered by the front door—rather it had emerged from the twin vista in the hail mirror. Alma sipped her soup, not tasting it but warmed. The figure fingered the twined flowers, sat at her father's desk. Alma bent her head over the plate. The figure stood outside the kitchen door, one hand on the doorknob. Alma stood; her chair screeched; she saw herself pulled erect by panic in the familiar kitchen like a child in darkness, and willed herself to sit. The figure climbed the stairs, entered her room, padded through the shadows, examining her music, breathing on her flute. Alma's spoon tipped and the soup drained back into its disc. Then, determinedly, she dipped again.

She had to fasten her thoughts on something as she mounted the stairs, medicine in hand; she thought of the Camside orchestral concert next week—thank God she wouldn't be faced with Peter chewing gum amid the ranks of placid tufted eggs. She felt for her bedroom light-switch. Behind the bookcase shadows sprang back into hiding and were defined. She smiled at the room and at herself; then carefully she closed the door. After the soup she felt a little hot, lightheaded. She moved to the window and admired the court set back from the bare street; above the roofs the sky was diluted lime and lemon beneath clouds like wads of stuffing. "Napier Court—I see the point, but don't you think that naming houses is a bit pretentious?" Alma slid her feet through the cold sheets, recoiling from the frigid bottle. She'd fill it later;

now she needed rest. She set aside *Victimes de Devoir* and lay back on the pillow.

Alma awoke. Someone was outside on the landing. At once she knew: Peter had borrowed Maureen's key. He came into the room, and as he did so her mother appeared from behind the door and drove the music-stand into his face. Alma awoke. She was swaddled in blankets, breathing through them. For a moment she lay inert; one hand was limp between her legs, her ear pressed on the pillow; these two parts of her felt miles distant, and something vast throbbed silently against her eardrums. She catalogued herself: slight delirium, a yearning for the toilet. She drifted with the bed; she disliked to emerge, to be oriented by the cold.

Nonsense, don't indulge your weakness, she told herself, and poked her head out. Surely she'd left the light on? Darkness blindfolded her, warm as the blankets. She reached for the cord, and the blue window blackened as the room appeared. The furniture felt padded by delirium. Alma burned. She struggled into her dressing-gown and saw the clock: 12:05. Past midnight and Maureen hadn't come? Then she realised: the clock had stopped—it must have been around the time of Maureen's departure. Of course Maureen wouldn't return; she'd been repelled by disapproval. Which meant that Alma would have no transistor, no means of discovering the time. She felt as if she floated, bodiless, disoriented, robbed of sensation, and went to the window for some indication; the street was deserted, as it might be at any hour soon after dark.

Turning from the pane she pivoted in the mirror; behind her the bed stood at her left. That wasn't right; right was where it stood. Or did it reverse in the reflection? She turned to look but froze; if she faced round she'd meet a figure waiting, hands outstretched, one side of its face incomplete, like those photographs from Vietnam Peter had insisted she confront— The thought released her; she turned to an empty room. So much for her delirium. Deliberately she switched out the light and padded down the landing.

On her way back she passed her mother's room; she felt

compelled to enter. Between the twin beds, shelves displayed the Betjemans, the books on Greece, histories of the Severn Valley. On the beds the sheets were stretched taut as one finds them on first entering a hotel room. When Peter had stayed for weekends her father had moved back into this room. Her father—out every night to the pub with his friends; he hadn't been vindictive to her mother, just unfeeling and unable to adjust to her domestic rhythm. When her mother had accused Alma of marrying beneath her she'd spoken of herself. Deceptively freed by their absence, Alma began to understand her mother's hostility to Peter. "You're a handsome bugger," her mother had once told him; Alma had pinpointed that as the genesis of her hostility—it had preyed on her mother's mind, this lowering herself to say what she thought he'd like only to realise that the potential of this vulgarity lurked within herself. Now Alma saw the truth; once more sleeping in the same room as her husband, she'd had the failure of her marriage forced upon her; she'd projected it on Alma's love for Peter. Alma felt released; she had understood them, perhaps she could even come once more to love them, just as eventually she'd understood that buying Napier Court had fulfilled her father's ambition to own a house in Brichester—her father, trying to talk to Peter who never communicated with him (he might have been unable, but this was no longer important), finally walking away from Peter whistling "Release Me" which he'd reprised the day after the separation, somewhat unfeelingly she thought. Even this she could understand. To seal her understanding, she turned out the light and closed the door.

Immediately a figure rose before her mother's mirror, combing long fingers through its hair. Alma managed not to shudder; she strode to her own door, opened it on blackness and crossed to her bed. She reached out to it and fell on her knees; it was not there.

As she knelt trembling, the house rearranged itself round her; the dark corridors and rooms, perhaps not empty as she prayed, watched pitilessly, came to bear upon her. She staggered to her feet and clutched the cord, almost touching a gaping face, which was not there when the light came on. Her bed was inches from her knees, where it had been when she left it, she insisted. Yet this failed to calm her. There was more than darkness in the house; she was no longer comfortingly alone in her warm and welcoming home. Had Peter borrowed Maureen's key? All at once she hoped he had; then she'd be in his arms, admitting that her promise to her mother had been desperate; she yearned for his protection—strengthened by it she believed she might confront horrors if he demanded them.

She watched for Peter from the window. One night while he was staying Peter had come to her room— She focused on the court; it seemed cut off from the world, imprisoning. Eclipsed by the gatepost, a pedestrian crossing's beacons exchanged signals without meaning; she thought of others flashing far into the night on cold lonely country roads, and shivered. He had come into her room; they'd caressed furtively and whispered so as not to wake her parents, though now she suspected that her mother had lain awake, listening through her father's snores. "Take me," she'd pleaded—but in the end she couldn't; the wall was too attentive. Now she squirmed at her remembered endearments: "my nice Peter"—"my handsome Peter"—"my lovely Peter"—and at last her halting praise of his body, the painful search for new phrases. She no longer cared to recall; she sloughed off the memories with an epileptic shudder.

A man had appeared in the gateway of the court. Alma stiffened. The figure passed; she relaxed, but only for a moment; had there not been something strange about its long loping strides, its trailing shadow? This was childish, she rebuked herself; she'd no more need to become obsessed with someone hastening to a date than with Peter, who was no longer in a position to protect her. She turned from the window before the figure should form behind her, and picked up her flute. Half an hour of exercises, then sleep. She opened the case. It was empty.

It was as if her mother had returned and taken back the

flute; she felt the house again rise up round her. She grasped an explanation; last time she'd fingered her flute—when had that been? Time had slipped away—she hadn't replaced it in its case. She threw the sheets back from the bed; only the dead bottle was exposed. She knelt again and peered beneath the bed. Something bent above her, waiting, grinning. No, the flute hadn't rolled. She stood up and the figure moved behind her. "Don't," she whimpered. At that moment she saw that the dressing-table drawer was open. She took one step towards it, to her ring, but could not look into it, knowing what was there—a face peering up at her from the drawer, its eyes opening, infinitely slowly, the lashes parting stickily— Delirium again? It didn't matter. Alma's lips trembled. She could still escape. She went to the wardrobe—but nothing could have made her open it; instead she caught up her clothes from the chair at the foot of the bed and dressed clumsily, dragging her skirt round to reach the zip. The room was silent; her music had fled, but any minute something else would take its place.

Since she had to face the darkened house, she did so. She trembled only once. The Victorian valentines hung immobile; the mirrors extended the darkness, strengthened its power. The house waited. Alma fell into the court; from the cobblestones, the erect gateposts, the street beyond, she drew courage. Two years and she'd be far from here, a complete person. Freed from fear, she left the front door open, and shivered as the night air knifed through the dangerous warmth of her cold. She must go—where? To Maureen's, she decided; that was not too far, and she knew Maureen to be kind. She'd forget her disapproval if she saw Alma like this. Alma strode towards the orange fan which flared from the beacon behind the gatepost, and stopped.

Resting against the beacon was a white bag, half as high as Alma. She'd seen such bags before, full of laundry. Yet she could not force herself to pull back the gates and pass. Suddenly the gates were her protection against the shapeless mass, for deep within herself she suppressed a horror that the bag might move towards her, flapping. It couldn't be what it appeared, who would have left it there at this time of night? A car hissed past on the glittering tarmac. Alma choked a scream for help. Screaming in the middle of the street—what would her mother have thought? Musicians didn't do that sort of thing. Besides, why shouldn't someone have left a bag of washing at the crossing while she went for help to heft it to the laundry? Alma touched the gates and withdrew, chilled; here she was, risking pneumonia in the night, and for what? The panic of delirium. As a child she'd screamed hoarsely through her cold that a man was bending over her; she was too old for that. Back to bed—no, to find her flute, and then to bed, to purge herself of these horrid visions. Ironically she thought Peter would be proud of her if he knew. Her flute—must the two years any longer be meaningful? Still touched by understanding, she couldn't think that her parents would hold to their threat, made after all before she'd written to Peter. What must have been a night breeze moved the bag. Forcing her footsteps not to drag, Alma left the orange radiance and closed the door behind her; her last test.

In the hall the thing she had thought was Maureen's coat shifted wakefully. Alma ignored it, but her flesh crept hot and cold. At the far end of the hall mirror, a figure approached, arms extended as if blindly. Alma smiled; it was too like a childish fear to frighten her: "enjoyably creepy"—she tried to recapture her mood of the morning, but every organ of her body felt hot and pounding. She broke and ran to her room; the light, oddly, was still on.

In the rooms below, her father's desk creaked; the flower arrangements writhed. Did it matter? Alma argued desperately. There was no lock on her door, but she refused to barricade it; there was nothing solid abroad in the house, nothing to harm her but the lure of her own fears. Her flute—she wouldn't play it once she found it; she'd go to bed with its protection. She moved round the bed and saw the flute, overlaid by *Victimes de Devoir*. The flute was bent in half.

One tear pressed from Alma's eyes before she realised the full horror. As she whirled, completely disoriented, a mirror crashed below. Something shrieked towards her through the corridors. She sank onto the bed, defenceless, wishing all were over. Music blasted from the record player, the *Nocturne;* Alma leapt up and screamed. "In roaring he shall rise," the voice bawled, "and on the surface—" A music stand was hurled to the floor. "—die!" The needle scraped across the record and clicked off. The walls seemed on the point of tearing, bulging inwards. Alma no longer cared. She'd screamed once; she could do no more. Now she waited.

When the figure formed deep in the mirror she knew that all was over. She faced it, drained of feeling. It grew closer, arms stretched out, its face inflated grey by gas. Alma wept; it was horrid. She knew who it was; a shaft of truth had pierced the suffocating warmth of her delirium. The suicide had possessed the house, was the house; he had waited for someone like her. "Go on," she sobbed at him, "take me." The bloated cheeks moved in a swollen grin; the arms stretched out for her and vanished.

The house was empty. Alma was surrounded by a vacuum into which something must rush. She stood up shaking and fell into the vacuum; her sight was torn away. She tried to move; there was no longer any muscle to respond. She felt nothing, but utter horror closed her in. Somewhere she sensed her body, moving happily on her bedroom carpet, picking up her ruined flute, breathing a hideous note into it. She tried to scream. Impossible.

Only in dreams can houses scream for help.

House of the Lost

Ian Futter

Behind an old sign, stuck in clay

a broken gate with battered teeth
protects a garden, dead and grey—
a mocking mouth of rotten heath.

You cannot see the house by day;
You cannot see it in the night,
but all will feel the garden's grip—
an itching in the nether light.

And most ignore the garden's pull,
but some push through the gaping maw,
past leeching leaves and thickets full,
to stand before the house in awe.

And though it's difficult to see,
the shape that shifts, beyond the lea,
six steps toward the meadow's floor
will soon propel you through its door

into the hallway, twisting, vast;
a fading passage to the past,
where flicking forms, their shadows clear,
affirm that there are others here.

Then onward up the absent stair,
which leads to bedrooms, never there,
past piercing portraits' vacant frames—
strange tractate of forgotten names.

Each peaceful plank, on which you tread,
will lead you past a missing bed
toward a window; grand, but small,
which goads the prying, one and all.

For if you peek beyond the frame,
you'll see no street from which you came,
but if you care to gaze below

you'll see yourself, six steps to go.

A Night in an Old Castle

G. P. R. James

It was one of the most awful nights I ever remember having seen. We had set out from St. Goar in a carriage which we had hired at Cologne, drawn by two black horses, which proved as stubborn and strange a pair of brutes as man could undertake to drive. Not that I undertook it, for I wanted to see the Rhine from the land route, and not to weary my arms and occupy my attention with an unprofitable pair of dirty reins; but my friend, Mr. Lawrence, was rather fond of pulling at horses' mouths, and he preferred driving himself, and me too, to being troubled—bored he called it—with coachman. The landlord of the "Adler" knew me well, and had no fear of trusting his horses with me, though, to say sooth, I had some fear of trusting myself with them.

They were assuredly a strange, unaccountable pair of brutes, and when the little baggage we took with us had been put in, and I went down to the carriage, I did not like the appearance of them at all. At first sight they looked merely like a heavy pair of funeral horses, accustomed to nod their heads under heavy black plumes, and walk along at solemn pace with a mute before them; but when I came to examine their eyes, there was a sort of dull, unpleasant fire in them, and the one nearest turned round his head and stared at me out of the corner of his eye with a sort of supercilious, impertinent fun that I shall not easily forget. It seemed as if he were saying, "I'll give you a dance before I've done!" Then suddenly he stamped his foot upon the pavement of the inn yard, as if losing patience at my delay, and opening his fiery nostrils gave a great snort.

99

I got in, however, beside my friend, and away we went. As far as Bonn all was well enough; but there the horses insisted upon stopping to eat. Lawrence tried to persuade them it would be better to go on; but it was of no use: they had been accustomed to stop at the Star, and stop they would. We made the best of it, fed the horses, and got some dinner ourselves, and then we set out again.

The landlord of the Star saw us politely to the carriage, and, addressing my friend as he took the reins in hand, observed, in no very consolatory tone, "You had better take care of that horse, sir; he is the devil himself:" and so, on my word, I believe he was. Where he took us for the first five minutes I really do not know; but I have a remembrance of careering hither and thither about the great square, and having a running view of the University and the Palace of Popplesdorff. He would go any way on earth but up the Rhine. But Lawrence, who was really a very good whip, brought him to his senses at length, and that before he had knocked the little crazy carriage all to pieces. Thus we were at length going along the high and proper road, at a speed dangerous to market men and women, and to our own necks; but even that at length was quieted down, and our further journey only suffered interruption from an occasional dart which both the horses would make at any diverging road that led away from the river, as if they had a presentiment that their course up the stream would lead to something strange and horrible. The instinct of brutes is a very curious subject of study. How far it is inferior, how far superior, to human reason—how much beyond man's keenest perception it goes—how near it approaches to the supernatural, are questions over which I have often pondered for hours.

We set out from St. Goar, then, with that same pair of horses, and the little rickety open carriage, on the 9th of October—a day ever memorable to me. We were somewhat late, for we had been idling away our time in speculations vain enough; but it was a beautiful day. The Rhine was hurry with the vintage; all hearts seemed open as the wine gushed from the glorious clusters, and one could hardly help thinking leniently and sympathetically even of Noah and his first intemperance. Songs were breaking out from the hill-sides; the sun shone upon gay dresses and pleasant faces, and the merry laugh was often in the air. Oh! the Rhine land is a bright and pleasant land, especially in the gay season of the grape.

The horses that day seemed to have lost all their fire. It seemed as if it was their fate to go on whatever lay before them; and forward they dragged us at a slow, heavy trot, with drooping heads and heaving sides. Even the one whom the landlord of the Star had called a devil was as tame as his companion, and minded the whip no more than if he had been tickled with a straw.

About three o'clock we saw a large heavy cloud begin to rise before us, overtopping the mountains, overshadowing the Rhine. It was only in hue that it bore the look of a thundercloud. It had no knobs, or pillars, or writhing twists about it; but it was inky black, and kept advancing like a wall of marble, dark as night at the lower part, and leaden-gray at the superior edge. The wind had lulled away to a perfect calm, but still that cloud kept marching on over the sky, absorbing into itself some light vapors that had been floating above over the blue, and gradually hiding the more distant hills, where we had caught a sight of them, in its own dim vail.

A light wind at length fluttered in our faces, hot and unrefreshing, like the breath of fever. "Put up the hood!" said Lawrence, "we are going to have it!"

Hardly had he spoken when a bright flash burst from the cloud, and I could see a serpent-like line of fire dart across the Rhine. It nearly blinded one, but it had no effect upon the horses; they did not even start. Then came a clap of thunder which I thought would bring the rocks and mountains on our heads. There were two or three more such flashes, and two or three other roars, and then the giant began to weep. Down came the rain like fury: it seemed as if we had got into the middle of a water-spout; and the sky, too, grew so dark that an unnatural shadow filled the whole valley of the Rhine, late so bright and smiling. I thought that we

101

were going to have two of the plagues of Egypt at once—darkness that could be felt, and fire mingled with hail. Indeed they did come upon us at last. But no one can describe how that storm worked itself up. It was like one of those concerted pieces of music, beginning with a few instruments, and bringing in more and more, and louder and louder, till all seems one universal crash. Nor can one easily picture to imagination the change which came over the scene while all this went on. The rocks, the mountains, the castles, the towers— except those that were close by—were either shut out from sight completely, or appeared like dim spectres through the descending rain. The vineyards, with their gay population scattered, looked dank and dismal; the hills, in a thousand directions, were channeled by red turbid cascades; and the black rocks seemed slimy and foul, with the oozing waters that trickled over their dark faces amidst the lichens and the weeds.

We were wet to the skin in five minutes; but as the thunder and lightning diminished—which they did toward sunset—the wind rose and blew with terrific violence, threatening to overset the carriage. The horses would hardly drag it on; and I am sure we did not go more than three miles an hour, while the rain, which continued harder than ever, was dashed furiously in our faces, nearly blinding both man and beast. At length, to complete our discomforts, night fell; and one so black and murky I have never seen. It was in vain whipping; neither horse would go the least out of his determined pace; and, besides, the whip had become so soaked and limp that it was of little service, moving as unwillingly as the brutes themselves, and curling itself up into a thousand knots.

I got as far back in the carriage as I could, and said nothing. As for my companion he seemed at his wits' end, and I could hear mattered curses which might have well been spared, but which I was in no mood to reprove.

At length he said, "This will never do! I can not see a step before me. We shall meet with some accident. Let us get into the

first place of shelter we can find. Any cottage, any roadside pub-
lic-house or beer-house, is better than this."

"I do not think you will find any thing of the kind," I answered
gloomily; "if you do, I can be contented with any place to get out
of this pelting—a cave in the rock if nothing better."

He drove on nearly at a walk for about two miles further, and
then suddenly pulled up. I could hardly see any thing but a great
black point of rock sticking out, as it seemed to me, right across
the road. But Lawrence declared that he perceived a shed under
the rock, and a building on the top of it, and asked me to get out
and reconnoitre. I was as glad to catch at straws as he could be,
and I alighted as well as I could, stumbling upon a large stone over
which he had nearly driven us, and sinking deep in mud and seemed
to block the way was only one of those many little points round
which the river turns in its course through the mountains, and on
approaching near it I discovered the shed he had seen. It was an
old dilapidated timber-built hut, which might have belonged at
some former period to a boatman, or perhaps a vine-dresser; but
it was open at two sides, and we might as well have been in the
carriage as there. By the side, however, I found a path with a step
or two cut in the rock, and I judged rightly that it must lead to
the building Lawrence had seen above. On returning to the side
of the carriage, I clearly perceived the building too, and made it
out to be one of the old castles of which such multitudes stud the
banks of the frontier river. Some of these, as we all know, are in
a very ruinous, some in a more perfect state; and I proposed to
my companion to draw the horses and carriage under the shed,
climb the path, and take our chance of what we should find above.
Phaëthon himself could not have been more sick of charioteering
than Lawrence was: he jumped at the proposal. We secured our
vehicle and its brutes as well as we could, and I began to climb.
Lawrence staid a minute behind to get the portmanteau out from
under the seat where we had stowed it to keep it dry; and then
came hallooing after me with it upon his shoulder.

"Do you think there is a chance of finding any one up there?" he asked, as he overtook me.

"A chance, certainly; but a poor one," I answered. "Marzburg and one or two other old castles are inhabited; but not many. However, we shall soon know; for this one is low down, thank Heaven! and here we are at some gate or barbican."

I can not say that it was very promising to the feel—for sight aided us but little—and the multitude of stones we tumbled over gave no idea of the castle itself being in a high state of repair. Lawrence thought fit to give a loud halloo; but the whistling wind drowned it—and would have drowned it, if he had shouted like Achilles from the trenches.

We next had to pick our way across what had probably been a court of the castle; that was an easy matter, for the stones in the open space were few, and the inequalities not many. The moon, I suppose, had risen by this time, for there seemed more light, though the rain ceased not; but we could now perceive several towers and walls quite plainly; and at length I found myself under a deep archway, on one side of which the drifting deluge did not reach me. Lawrence was by my side in a minute, and, thanks to what he was accustomed to jeer me for, as one of my old bachelor habits; I was soon enabled to afford both him and myself some light. There are three things I always carry with me in traveling: a box of wax-wick matches—these are in my pocket well wrapped up in oil silk; a ball of string, and a couple of wax candles: the wax candles, I believe, once saved my life.

As soon as I got under shelter, I extracted my large box of matches and lighted one easily enough. It burned while one might count twenty, but that sufficed to show us that we were under a great gateway between two high towers. A second which I lighted Lawrence carried out into an inner court, but it was extinguished in a moment. I had perceived, however, a doorway on either side of this arch, and the spikes of a portcullis protruding through the arch above, which showed that the castle had some woodwork left about it; and as soon as he came back we lighted another match, and set out to explore what was behind the two doorways, which we managed easily by getting a new light as soon as the old one was burned out. On the right there was nothing but one small room, with no exit but the entrance, and with a roof broken in and fink weeds rising from the encumbered floor. On the left was a room of the same size, equally dilapidated, but with a second door and two steps leading to a larger room or hall, the roof of which was perfect except at one end. There were two old lozenge-shaped windows likewise, minus a few panes; but the sills were raised nearly a man's height from the floor, and thus, when one was seated on the ground, one's head was out of the draught. Comparison is a wonderful thing, and the place looked quite comfortable. Lawrence threw down the portmanteau, and while he held a lighted match, I undid it and got out a wax candle. We had now the means of light till morning, and it remained to get some dry clothing, if it could be found. We had each a dress-suit and a couple of shirts in the portmanteau; and though the rain in one spot had contrived to penetrate the solid leather and wet the shoulder of my coat and the knee of his pantaloons, it was certainly better to have but one damp place of a few inches about one than to be wet all over. We therefore dressed ourselves in what the apprentice boys would call our best clothes, and a little brandy from the flask made us feel still more comfortable. The taste for luxuries increases with marvelous rapidity under indulgence. An hour before, we should have thought a dry coat and a place of shelter formed the height of human felicity, but now we began to long for a fire on the broad stone hearth at the end of the room. Lawrence was fertile in resources and keen-sighted enough. He had remarked a quantity of fallen rafters in the first little room we had entered, and he now made sundry pilgrimages thither in the dark—for we dared not take out the candle—till he had accumulated enough wood to keep us dry all night. Some of it was wet and would not burn, but other pieces were quite dry, and we soon had a roaring fire, by which we sat down on the ground, hoping to make ourselves comfortable.

Oh the vanity of human expectations! As long as we had been busy in repairing our previous disasters we had been well enough; but as soon as we were still—no, not quite so soon as that, but by the time we had stared into the fire for ten minutes, and made out half a dozen pictures on the firebrands, miseries began to press upon us.

"I wish to heaven I had something to sit upon!" said Lawrence, "if it were but a three-legged stool. My knees get quite cramped."

"How the wind howls and mourns," said I, listening. "It would not surprise me if one half of this old crazy place were to come down upon our heads."

"The rain is pouring on as heavily as ever," said Lawrence. "I should not wonder if that puddle at the other end were to swell into a lake and wash us out at the door."

"Those poor brutes of horses," said I, "must have a bad time of it, and the chaise will be like a full sponge."

"Come, come!" said Lawrence, "this will never do. We shall croak ourselves into a fit of the horrors. Let us forget the storm, and the horses, and the old tumble-down place, and fancy ourselves in a middling sort of inn, with a good fire, but little to eat. It is the best policy to laugh at petty evils. Come, can not you tell us a story beginning 'Once upon a time'?"

I was in no fit mood for story-telling, but there was some philosophy in his plan, and I accordingly agreed, upon the condition that when I had concluded my narrative he would tell another story.

"Once upon a time," I said, "when the late Duke of Hamilton was a young man, and traveling in Italy—making the grand tour, as it was called in those days—he came one night to a solitary inn in the mountains, where he was forced to take refuge from a storm like that which we have met with to-day—"

"Oh, I know that story," cried Lawrence, interrupting me; "I have heard it a hundred times; and besides, you do not tell it right— My God, what is that?"

As he spoke, he sprang up on his feet with a look of consternation and a face turning suddenly pale.

"What! What?" I cried, "I heard nothing."

"Listen!" he said, "it was certainly a shriek."

We were silent as death for the next minute, and then again, rising above the moaning wind and pattering rain, came one of the most piercing, agonizing shrieks I ever heard. It seemed quite close to where we sat—driven in, as it were, through the broken panes of the casement.

"There must have been some accident," I said, anxiously. "Let us go down and see."

We had contrived to fix our candle between two pieces of firewood, and, leaving it burning, we hurried out through the little ante-room to the old dark archway. The night seemed blacker than ever, and the storm no less severe.

"Stay, stay!" said Lawrence; "let us listen. We hear nothing to direct us where to search."

I stopped, and we bent our ears in vain for another sound. We heard the wind sigh, and the rustling patter of the rain, and the roaring of the mighty river as, swollen tremendously, it went roaring along through its rocky channel, but nothing like a human voice made itself heard. At length, without giving me any warning, and making me start like a guilty spirit at the crow of cock, Lawrence shouted with the full force of his powerful lungs, inquiring if there was any one there and in distress. No answer was returned, and again and again he called without obtaining a reply. It was evident that the lips which had uttered those sounds of pain or terror were either far away or still in death; and having nothing to guide us further, we returned to our place of shelter. It was long, however, ere we could shake off the impression those two shrieks had made. We had neither of us become hardened, like Macbeth, to sounds of woe, and for some time we went on speculating on the occurrence, and supposing many things, with very little to guide us to a right judgment. There was the rushing Rhine and the slippery road, on which many an accident might happen, and there were almost as many perils imminent as those which St. Paul recapitulates as having overtaken himself. But there was nothing certain. After we had tired ourselves with such fancies Lawrence proposed a little more brandy. I did not object; and then we told tales of screams and shrieks which had been heard at different times and places by various credible witnesses—ourselves among the rest—for which no natural cause had ever been assigned.

At length, quite tired out, I proposed that we should try to sleep. Lawrence ensconced himself behind the door; I took up a position in the other corner, sitting on the floor with my back supported by the two walls, and at a sufficient distance from the window. I should have said we had piled more wood on the fire, in such a way as we hoped would keep it in at least till we woke; and it flickered and flared and cast strange lights upon the walls and old windows, and upon a door at the other end of the room which we had never particularly examined, on account of the wet and decayed state of the floor in that part. It was a very common door—a mass of planks placed perpendicularly and bound together by two great horizontal bars—but as the fire-light played upon it, there was something unpleasant to me in its aspect. I kept my eyes fixed upon it, and wondered what was beyond; and, in the sort of unpleasant fancifulness which besets one sometimes when dreary, I began to imagine all sorts of things. It seemed to me to move as if about to be opened; but it was only the shaking of the wind. It looked like a prison door, I thought—the entrance to some unhappy wretch's cell; and when I was half asleep, I asked myself if there could be any one there still—could the shrieks we heard issue thence—or could the spirit of the tortured captive still come back to mourn over the sorrows endured in life? I shut my eyes to get rid of the sight of it; but when I opened them again, there it was staring me full in the face. Sometimes when the flame subsided indeed, I lost sight of it; but that was as bad or worse than the full view, for then I could not tell whether it was open or shut. But at length, calling myself a fool, I turned away from it, and soon after dozed off to sleep.

I could not have been really in slumber more than an hour, and was dreaming that I had been carried off a road into a river, and just heard all the roaring and rushing of a torrent in my ears, when Lawrence woke me by shaking me violently by the shoulder, and exclaiming: "Listen, listen! What in the fiend's name can all that be?"

I started up bewildered; but in a moment I heard sounds such as I never heard before in my life; frantic yells and cries, and groans even—all very different from the shrieks we had heard before. Then, suddenly, there was a wild peal of laughter ringing all through the room, more terrible than the rest. I can not bear to be woke suddenly out of my sleep; but to be woke by such sounds as that quite overcame me, and I shook like a leaf. Still, my eyes turned toward the door at the other end of the room. The fire had sunk low; the rays of our solitary candle did not reach it, but there was now another light upon it, fitful as the flickering of the flame, but paler and colder. It seemed blue almost to me. But as soon as I could recall my senses I perceived that the moon was breaking the clouds, and from time to time shining through the casement as the scattered vapors were hurried over her by the wind.

"What in Heaven's name can it be?" I exclaimed, quite aghast.

"I don't know, but we must see," answered my companion, who had been awake longer and recovered his presence of mind. "Light the other candle, and bring the one that is alight. We must find out what this is. Some poor creature may be wanting help."

"The sound comes from beyond that door," I said: "let us see what is behind it."

I acknowledge I had some trepidation in making the proposal, but my peculiar temperament urged me forward in spite of myself toward scenes which I could not doubt were fearful; and I can boldly say that if Lawrence had hesitated to go I would have gone alone. It would seem as if Fate, in giving me this impulse toward sights painful to other men and to myself also, had prearranged the combinations which continually brought them in my way; and at this time of life I had learned to look upon it as a part of my destiny to find somewhere or other in my path at almost every step some of those events which make the heart sicken and the blood freeze.

Taking the candle in my hand, then, I advanced at once toward the door. Lawrence stopped a moment to examine by the light I had left behind a pair of pistols which he had brought in his pockets, and to put on fresh caps, although I believe they had escaped the rain. Thus I had reached the door before he came up, and had opened it, for all the iron-work but a latch had been carried off. The moment it was thrown back, the cries and groans were heard more distinctly than before; but I could see nothing before me but darkness, and it required a moment or two for the light to penetrate the darkness beyond. I had not taken two steps beyond the threshold ere Lawrence was by my side, and we found ourselves in a stone passage without windows, appearing to lead round the building. Ten paces on, however, we came to the top of a flight of steps, broken and mouldy, with grass and weeds growing up between the crevices. Part of the wall had fallen there, but it was on the side away from the wind; and although the fluttering air, diverted by some obstacles from its course, caused the flame of the candle to waver, I carried it still lighted past the aperture. It was a work of some danger to descend those steps, for they rocked and tottered under the foot, and they seemed interminable; but after the first twenty had been passed we had no more to fear from wind. The masonry ceased; the walls became the solid rock, rudely hewn out for a passage for the stairs; and the steps themselves were of the native stone, squared and flattened at one time probably, but worn by many feet, and in some places broken, by what influences I do not know.

When we were about half way down, the sounds, which had been growing louder and louder, suddenly ceased, and a deathlike stillness succeeded.

"Stay a bit," said my companion: "let us reconnoitre. We may as well look before we leap. Hold up the light."

I did as he asked, but the faint rays of the candle showed us nothing but the black irregular faces of the rock on either side, a small rill of water percolating through a crevice, and flowing over, down upon the steps, along which it poured in miniature cascades, and beyond, a black chasm where we could see nothing.

"Come on," said Lawrence, advancing; "we must see the end of it."

Forward we went—down, down, some two-and-thirty steps more, without hearing another sound; but just as we reached the bottom step something gave a wild sort of yell, and I could hear a scrambling and tumbling at a good distance in advance.

My heart beat terribly, and Lawrence stopped short. I was far more agitated than he was, but he showed what he felt more, and any one who had seen us would have said that he was frightened, I perfectly cool. He had passed me on the stairs; I now passed him, and holding the light high up gazed around.

It was very difficult to see any thing distinctly, but here and there the beams caught upon rough points of rock, and low arches rudely hewn in the dark stone, and I made out that we were in a series of vaults excavated below the castle, with massive partitions between them, and here and there a doorway or passage from one to the other. It seemed a perfect labyrinth at first sight, and now that all was silent again, we had nothing to guide us. I listened, but all was still as death; and I was advancing again, when my companion asked me to stop, and proposed that we should examine the ground on each side as we went on, marking the spot from which we started. It seemed a good plan, and I was stooping down to pile up some of the loose stones with which the ground or floor was plentifully encumbered, when a large black snake glided away, and at the same moment a bat or a small owl flitted by, and extinguished the light with its wings.

"Good Heaven, how unlucky!" cried Lawrence; "have you got the match-box?"

"No," I answered; "I left it on the floor near where I was sleeping. Feel your way up the steps, my good friend, and bring it and the other candle. I will remain here till you come. Be quick!"

"You go; let me stay," said Lawrence. But I was ashamed to accept his offer; and there was a something, I knew not what, that urged me to remain. "No, no," I said, "go quickly; but give me one of your pistols," and I repeated the last words in German, lest any one who understood that language should be within ear-shot.

We were so near the foot of the steps that Lawrence could make no mistake, and I soon heard his feet ascending at a rapid rate, tripping and stumbling, it is true, but still going on. As I listened, I thought I heard a light sound also from the other side, but I concluded that it was but the echo of his steps through the hollow passages, and I stood quite still, hardly breathing. I could hear my heart beat, and the arteries of the throat were very unpleasant—throb, throb, throbbing.

After a moment or two I heard Lawrence's feet as it seemed to me almost above me, and I know not what impression of having some other being near me, made me resolve to cock the pistol. I tried to do it with my thumb as I held it in my right hand, but the lock went hard, and I found it would be necessary to lay down the candle to effect it. Just as I was stooping to do so, I became suddenly conscious of having some living creature close by me; and the next instant I felt cold fingers at my throat, and an arm thrown round me. Not a word was spoken, but the grasp became tight upon my neck, and I struggled violently for breath and life. But the strength of the being that grasped me seemed gigantic, and his hand felt like a hand of iron.

Oh what a moment was that! Never, except in a terrible dream, have I felt any thing like it. I tried to cry, to shout, but I could not, his hold of my throat was so tight; power of muscle seemed to fail me; my head turned giddy; my heart felt as if stopping; flashes of light shone from my eyes.

My right hand, however, was free, and by a violent effort I

forced back the cock of the pistol nearly to the click; but then I lost all power. The hammer fell; the weapon went off with a loud echoing report, and for an instant, by the flash, I saw a hideous face with a gray beard close gazing into mine.

The sound of Lawrence's footsteps running rapidly overhead were the most joyful I had ever heard; but the next instant I felt myself cast violently backward, and I fell half stunned and bewildered to the ground.

Before I could rise the light of the candle began to appear, as Lawrence came down the stairs, first faint, and then brighter; and I heard his voice exclaiming, "What has happened? What has happened?"

"Take care!" I cried faintly; "there is some man or some devil here, and he has half killed me!"

Looking carefully around, Lawrence helped me to rise, and then we picked up the candle I had let fall and lighted it again, he gazing in my face from time to time, but seeming hardly to like to take his eyes off the vaults, or to enter into any conversation, for fear of some sudden attack. Nothing was to be seen, however; my savage assailant was gone, leaving no trace behind him but a cut upon the back of my head, received as he cast me backward.

"What has happened?" said Lawrence at length, in a very low voice. "Why, your face looks quite blue, and you are bleeding!"

"No wonder," I answered; "for I have been half strangled, and have nearly had my brains dashed out. Have you got powder and ball? If so, load the pistol;" and giving it to him, I sat down on the last step of the stairs to recover myself a little, keeping a wary eye upon the gloom beyond him while he re-charged the weapon.

From time to time he asked a question, and I answered, till he had heard all that had happened, and then, after a minute's thought, he said, "Do you know, I think we had better give this up, and barricade ourselves into the room up stairs. There may be more of these ruffians than one."

"No, no," I answered; "I am resolved to see the end of it. There is only one, depend upon it, or I should have had both upon me. We are two, and can deal with him at all events. I have a great notion that some crime has been committed here this night, and we ought to ascertain the facts. Those first shrieks were from a woman's voice."

"Well, well," answered my companion, "I am with you, if you are ready. Here, take one light and one pistol, and you examine the right-hand vaults: while I take the left. We are now on our guard, and can help each other."

We walked on accordingly, very slowly and carefully, taking care to look round us at every step, for the vaults were very rugged and irregular, and there was many a point and angle which might have concealed an assailant, but we met with no living creature. At length I thought I perceived a glimmer of light before me, but a little to the left, and calling up Lawrence, who was at some yards' distance, I pointed it out to him.

"To be sure I see it," he answered; "it is the moon shining. We must be near the entrance of the vaults. But what is that? There seems to be some one lying down there."

He laid his hand upon my arm as he spoke, and we both stood still and gazed forward. The object toward which his eyes were directed certainly looked like a human figure, but it moved not in the least, and I slowly advanced toward it. Gradually I discerned what it was. There was the dress of a woman, gay colored and considerably ornamented, and a neat little foot and shoe, with a small buckle in it, resting on a piece of fallen rock. The head was away from us, and she lay perfectly still.

My spirit felt chilled; but I went on, quickening my pace, and Lawrence and I soon stood beside her, holding the lights over her. She was a young girl of nineteen or twenty, dressed in gala costume, with some touch of the city garb, some of the peasant attire. Her hair, which was all loose, wet, and disheveled, was exceedingly rich and beautiful, and her face must have been very pretty in the sweet happy coloring of health and life. Now it was deathly pale, and the windows of the soul were closed. It was a sad, sad sight to see! Her garments were all wet, and there was some froth about the mouth, but the fingers of the hands were limp and natural, as if there had been no struggle, and the features of the face were not distorted. There was, however, a wound upon her temple, from which some blood had flowed, and some scratches upon her cheek, and upon the small fair ears.

She looked very sweet as she lay there, and Lawrence and I stood and gazed at her long. Her dress was somewhat discomposed, and I straightened it over her ankles, though the sense of modesty and maiden shame had gone out with all the other gentle harmonies in that young heart. How came she by her death? How came she there? Was she slain by accident, or had she met with violence? were questions that pressed upon our thoughts. But we said little then, and after a time left her where we found her. It mattered not to her that the bed was hard or the air cold.

We searched every corner of the vaults, however, for him I could not help believing her murderer, but without success; and on going to the mouth of the vault, where there had once been a door, long gone to warm some peasant's winter hearth, we found that it led out upon the road close by the side of the Rhine, and hardly a dozen paces from the river.

It was clear how he had escaped; and we sadly took our way back to the chamber above, where we passed the rest of the night in melancholy talk over the sad events that must have happened.

We slept no more, nor tried to sleep; but as soon as the east was gray went down to the shed where we had left the horses, and resumed our journey, to give information at the next village of what we had discovered.

The horses were very stiff, and at first could hardly drag us along, for the road was in a horrible state, but they soon warmed to the work, and in little more than three quarters of an hour we reached a small village, where we got some refreshment, while the landlord of the little Gasthaus ran at my request for the Polizei.

When the only officer in the place came, I told him every thing that had happened in the best German I could muster, and willingly agreed to go back with him to the spot, and show him where the body lay. The rumor spread like wildfire in the village; a crowd of the good peasantry collected round the door; and when we set out, taking a torch or two with us, as I described the vaults as very dark, we had at least a hundred persons in our train, among whom were a number of youths and young girls. As nothing but one old chaise was to be procured in the village, and it did not look as if it would rain, we pursued our way on foot, but we certainly accomplished the distance faster than we had done with two horses in the morning. All the way the officer—I really do not know his right German title—continued conversing with Lawrence, who did not understand a word of German, and with myself, for whom his German was a warld too fast. I gave him, however, all the information I could, and as his language has the strange peculiarity of being easier to speak than to understand, I made him master, I believe, of every little incident of the last eventful night.

My description of the face of the man who had first nearly strangled me and then nearly dashed my brains out, and of whom I had caught a glimpse by the flash of the pistol, seemed to interest him more than all the rest. He stopped when I gave it to him, called several of the girls and young men about him, and conversed with them for a moment or two with a good deal of eagerness. The greater part of what they said escaped me, but I heard a proper name frequently repeated, sounding like Herr Katzenberger, and the whole ended with a sad and gloomy shake of the head.

Soon after we resumed our advance we came to the mouth of the vault. It required no torches, however, to let us see what we sought for. The sun, still low, was shining slantingly beneath the heavy brows of the rocky arch, and the rays receded to the spot where the body of the poor girl lay.

All steps were hurried as we came near; and boys and girls, men and women, crowded round. It was evident that every one present recognized a friend in that lifeless form. *"Ach, die Carlina!"*—*"Ach, die arme Carlina!"* arose from a hundred voices; and some eyes were seen to shed bitter tears.

They made a little bier of vine poles and branches, and laid the fair corpse upon it. Then they sought for various green leaves and some of the long-lingering autumn flowers, and strewed them tastefully over the body; and then four stout men raised the death-litter on their shoulders and bore it away toward the village. The men and women, without noise or bustle, formed themselves into a little procession, with a native sense of reverent decorum which is more strongly felt among the German peasantry than among any other people I ever met with, and followed the corpse, two and two.

I had the policeman for my companion; and beseeching him to speak slowly, I asked if he could give me any explanation of the strange and terrible events which must have happened.

"We know very little as yet," he answered; "but we shall probably know more soon. This young lady, poor thing! was the only daughter of a rich but cross-grained man, living at a village a short way further down the Rhine, on the other side. Her mother, who died three years ago, was from our own village. She was dancing away gayly last evening with our young folks, just before the storm came on; for her father had brought her up in his boat, and left her at her aunt's. When it came on with thunder and lightning, they all went into the house, and, as misfortune would have it, that young lad who is carrying the head of the bier sat down by her in a comer, and they could not part soon enough. He was a lover of hers, every one knew; but her father was hard against the match, and before they had been in the house an hour the old man came in and found them chatting in their corner. Perhaps he would have staid all night had it not been for that; but he got very angry, and made her go away with him in his boat in the very midst of the storm. He said he had been on the Rhine many a worse night than that—though few of us have ever seen one. But he was obstinate as a bull, and away they went, though she cried terribly, both from fear and vexation. What happened after, none of us can tell; but old Herr Katzenberger has a gray beard, just such as you speak of."

They carried the body to the little old church, and laid it in the aisle; and then they sent for the village doctor to examine into the mode of her death. I was not present when he came, but I heard afterward that he pronounced her to have died from drowning, and declared that the wound on the temple must have occurred by a blow against some rock when life was quite or nearly extinct. "Otherwise," he said, "it would have bled much more, for the artery itself was torn."

For my part, I was marched up with Lawrence to the Ampthaus, and there subjected to manifold interrogatories, the answers to which were all carefully taken down.

In the midst of these we were interrupted by the inroad of a dozen of peasants, dragging along a man who struggled violently with them, but in whom every one present recognized the father of the poor girl whose body we had found. The peasants said they had found him some six miles off, tearing his flesh with his teeth, and evidently in a state of furious insanity. They had found it very difficult to master him, they declared, for his strength was prodigious.

He was the only witness of what had taken place during that terrible night upon the river, and he could give no sane account. He often accused himself of murdering his child; but the good people charitably concluded that he merely meant he had been the cause of her death by taking her upon the treacherous waters in such a night as that; and the fact of his boat having drifted ashore some miles further down, broken and bottom upward, seemed to confirm that opinion. I made some inquiries regarding the unfortunate man during a subsequent tour; but I only learned that he continued hopelessly insane, without a glimmer of returning reason.

House

Rebecca Fraser

Where roof meets frame on windburned peak
Ancient bones extend and creak
Now woken from tormented dreams
The house pulls the threads of dying screams
And weaves them into every stud
To fill her veins with rotten blood
And all who tread her tainted halls
Hear wretched whispers from her walls
From corners dark where light can't breach
Skeletal arms from shadows reach
To clutch in anguish those who pass
Release us from the house's grasp
But those who enter never leave
Absorbed into each board and eave
They're drawn into the house's soul
And coalesce to make her whole.

Two Haunted Houses
Some Strange Narratives from the Note-Book of an Investigator

Ambrose Bierce

I.

John Easton Lord, of Coopertown, Pennsylvania, sold his house and lot in that town to William Burrill and moved with his family to the suburbs of Pittsburg. The Burrill family occupied the Coopertown house for nearly four years, then abandoned it—being unable to resell it—and occupied another, a half-mile away, which at first they rented and afterward bought. Here the widow of William Burrill and one maiden daughter were living as lately as 1884, which was the date of the writer's last knowledge of him.

At that time the old Lord dwelling, which had stood tenantless for years, had just been demolished, with many others, to make room for a new street. It had long had an uncanny reputation as a "haunted house," and although the skeptics were many, and repeated investigations had been made of the supernatural phenomena said to occur nightly within its walls, it was noticeable that even the most incredulous always spoke of them with gravity and no one in Coopertown attempted to discredit them by ridicule. The subject was universally regarded as worthy of serious discussion. There was reason enough, for one of the dismal traditions of the house—namely that no one could remain alone in it over night and keep both life and reason—had been twice confirmed in the most authenticating way. One hardy investigator had been found in the morning dead without a wound or assignable cause, and another person—a tramp who in all unconsciousness of the dwelling's history had stolen a lodging there—had rushed out at the gray of the morning incurably mad. That the house was haunted was open to honest doubt, but these somber passages in its annals had at least invested that proposition with a certain dignity which made it inaccessible to ridicule.

The manifestations, it appears, began on the 20th day of June, 1872, somewhat more than three years after the Burrill family moved into the house. On the evening of that day, at about 7 o'clock, while the family were sitting on the veranda after dinner, John Easton Lord, the former owner, came in at the gate, ascended the steps of the veranda, passed directly between Mr. and Mrs. Burrill and entered the house by the hall door. Mr. Burrill had risen to greet him, but the proffered hand had remained unheeded. By not so much as a look had Lord recognized any member of the family, to all of whom he was well known. He was immediately followed into the house by Burrill and his son, Parker Burrill, whose astonishment was great indeed at not finding their visitor. The only door by which he could have left the house was found securely locked, with the key inside, and all the windows were fastened excepting those opening on to the veranda. A search of the entire house resulted in nothing. Lord had not been seen by anybody else in town, and the incident was simply without an explanation. A letter to Pittsburg brought out the fact in reply that on the day of its occurrence John Easton Lord had been seven weeks dead.

From this time forward, until they left the house months afterward, the Burrill family appear to have suffered great annoyance and alarm from what were affirmed to be supernatural manifestations. The character of these is inexactly known; with a view to damaging their property as little as possible, all the members of the family preserved a discreet silence; but the most extravagant tales were bruited about, orally and through the local newspapers. It is needless to repeat them here: they were of the kind usually related of houses said to be "haunted." By the time the property had been condemned for a public use, appraised and paid for Mr. Burrill was dead, and the family scattered in distant parts of the country—all except the widow, who was in her dotage, and one elderly maiden daughter, whose austere silence on this subject was infrangible. There is ample and credible testimony, popular and professional, that when the family moved out of the house all were suffering acutely from insomnia and nervous prostration—from which, indeed, the youngest, a girl of seventeen, eventually died.

From voluminous notes of an investigation made by a competent inquirer in 1884 it is found that all, or nearly all, of the least incredible accounts of supernatural occurrences in and about the Lord house relate to the visible apparition of the late John Easton Lord. Most of the testimony as to that element has in it something approaching trustworthiness. If anything at all "out of the common" ever took place there, something which many cool-headed witnesses took to be the ghost of Lord habitually showed itself about the premises by night and sometimes by day. It was considered a malign spirit although in life Lord had been of a singularly amiable disposition.

When the house was pulled down and its site excavated for a new street a workman, beginning a trench from the cellar, uncovered a plain board box which appeared to have been thrust through an opening in the cellar wall into a hole behind it. The opening in the wall had been carefully bricked up so that the place was indistinguishable. The box contained the remains of a human being—a man. The body was little affected by decay, although the appearance of the box and the mould on the clothing indicated that a considerable period must have elapsed since the date of interment; several years, those said whose opinion had most weight. The face of the corpse had apparently undergone very little alteration, and on seeing it every acquaintance of the late Mr. Lord instantly pronounced the body his; but two reputable citizens of Coopertown went to Pittsburg and there found and identified the body of Lord in a cemetery at that city, the family having consented to the exhumation and an adult son of the deceased being present.

Despite the efforts of the officers of the law, assisted by many amateur detectives, working con amore, not the slightest clew to the identity of the dead, the manner of his taking off nor the mystery of his interment has ever been discovered. "Theories" were abundant enough while anybody cared to entertain them, but none were consonant with all the facts, nor even with the main ones here set down. The body was reburied in a public cemetery, and a stone without name or date marks the spot.

II.

On the road leading north from Manchester, in eastern Kentucky, to Booneville, twenty miles away, stood, in 1862, a wooden plantation-house of a somewhat better quality than most of the dwellings in that region. The house was destroyed by fire in the year following—probably by some stragglers from the retreating column of General George W. Morgan, when he was driven from Cumberland Gap to the Ohio river by General Kirby Smith. At the time of its destruction it had for four or five years been vacant. The fields about it were overgrown with brambles, the fences gone, even the few negro quarters, and outhouses generally, fallen partly into ruin by neglect and pillage; for the negroes and poor whites of the vicinity found in the building and fences an abundant supply of fuel, of which they availed themselves without hesitation, openly and by daylight. By daylight alone; after nightfall no human being except passing strangers ever went near the place.

It was known as the "Spook House." That it was tenanted by evil spirits, visible, audible and active, no one in all that region doubted, any more than he doubted what he was told of Sundays by the traveling preacher. Its owner's opinion of the matter was unknown; he and his family had disappeared one night and no trace of them had ever been found. They left everything—household goods, clothing, provisions, the horses in the stable, the cows in the field, the negroes in the quarters—all as it stood; nothing was missing—except a man, a woman, three girls, a boy and a babe! It was not altogether surprising that a plantation where seven human beings could be simultaneously effaced and nobody the wiser should be thought to be under some monstrous curse and teeming with possibilities of evil.

One night in June, 1859, two citizens of Frankfort, Col. J. C. McArdle, a lawyer, and Judge Myron Veigh, of the State Militia, were driving from Booneville to Manchester. Their business was so important that they decided to push on despite the darkness and the mutterings of an approaching storm, which eventually broke upon them just as they arrived opposite the "Spook House." The lightning was so incessant that they easily found their way through the gateway and into a shed, where they unhitched their team, which they conducted into an adjacent stable and unharnessed by no other light than that of the heavens. They then went to the house, through the scourging rain, and knocked at all the doors without, however, eliciting any response. Attributing this to the continuous uproar of the thunder, they pushed at one of the doors, which yielded. They entered without further ceremony. That instant they were in darkness and silence absolute. Not a gleam of the lightning's unceasing blaze penetrated the windows or crevices; not a whisper of the awful tumult without reached them there. It was as if they had suddenly been stricken blind and deaf, and McArdle afterward said that for a moment he believed himself to have been killed by a stroke of lightning as he crossed the threshold. The rest of this adventure can as well be related in that gentleman's words, from the Frankfort Gazette of August 6, 1876:

"When I had somewhat recovered from the dazing effect of the transition from uproar to silence, my first impulse was to reopen the door which I had closed, and from the knob of which I was not conscious of having removed my hand; I felt it distinctly, still in the clasp of my fingers. My notion was to ascertain by stepping again into the storm whether I had been deprived of sight and hearing. I turned the door-knob and pulled open the door. It led into another room! This apartment was suffused with a faint greenish light, the source of which I could not determine, making everything distinctly visible, though nothing was sharply defined. Everything, I say, but in truth the only objects within the blank stone walls of that room were human dead bodies. In number they were perhaps eight or ten—it may well be understood that I did not coolly count them. They were of various ages, or rather sizes, from infancy up, and of both sexes. All were prostrate on the floor in all kinds of attitudes, excepting one, the body, apparently, of a young woman, which sat up, her back supported by an angle of the wall. The babe was clasped in the arms of another and older woman. A half-grown lad lay face downward across the legs of a full-bearded man. One or two were nearly naked, and the hand of a young girl held the fragment of a gown which she had torn open at the breast. The bodies were in various stages of decay, all greatly shrunken in face and figure. Some were but little more than skeletons.

"While I stood stupefied with horror by this ghastly spectacle and still holding open the door by some unaccountable perversity my attention was diverted from the shocking scene and concerned itself with trifles and details. Perhaps my mind, with an instinct of self-preservation, sought relief in matters which would relax its dangerous tension. Among other things I observed that the door which I was holding open was of heavy iron plates riveted. Equidistant from each other and from the top and bottom three strong bolts protruded from the beveled edge. I turned the knob and they were retracted flush with the edge, released it, and they shot out. It was a spring lock. On the inside there was no knob, nor any kind of projection—all was a smooth surface of iron.

"While noting these things with an interest and attention which it now astonishes me to recall I felt myself thrust aside, and Judge Veigh, whom in the intensity and vicissitudes of my

125

feelings I had altogether forgotten, pushed by me into the room. 'For God's sake,' I cried, 'do not go in there! Let us get out of this dreadful place!'

"He gave no heed to my entreaties, but (as fearless a gentleman as lived in all the South) walked quickly to the center of the room, knelt beside one of the bodies for a closer examination and tenderly raised its blackened and shriveled head in his hands. A strong sickening odor came through the doorway, completely overpowering me. My senses reeled; I felt myself falling, and in clutching at the edge of the door for support closed it with a sharp click!

"I remember no more: six weeks later I recovered my reason in a hotel at Manchester, whither I had been taken by strangers the next day. For all these weeks I had suffered from a nervous fever, attended with constant delirium. I had been found lying in the road several miles away from the house; but how I had escaped from it to get there I never knew. On recovery, or as soon as my physicians permitted me to talk, I inquired the fate of Judge Veigh, whom (to humor me, as I now know) they represented as well and at home. No one believed a word of my story, and who can wonder? And who can imagine my grief when, arriving at my home in Frankfort two months later, I learned that Judge Veigh had never been heard of since that night? I then regretted bitterly the pride which since the first few days after the recovery of my reason had forbidden me to repeat my discredited story and insist upon its truth. With all that subsequently occurred—the examination of the house; the failure to find any rooms corresponding to those which I have described; the attempt to have me adjudged insane, and my triumph over my accusers—the readers of the Gazette are entirely familiar. After all these years I am still confident that excavations which I have neither the legal right to undertake nor the wealth to make would disclose the secret of the disappearance of my unhappy friend, and possibly of the Butlers, former occupants and owners of the deserted and now destroyed house. I do not despair of yet bringing about such a research, and it is a source of deep grief to me that it has been delayed by the undeserved hostility and unwise incredulity of the family and friends of the late Judge Veigh."

Colonel J. C. McArdle died in Lexington, Kentucky, on the 15th day of September, 1882.

Dark House of Hunger

D. L. Myers

The dark window and dark door appear black
Beneath twisted cedars bent like tortured men
That twitch and dance in the growing dusk.
In a pool of lurking shadow, the shack
Squats and waits like a silent toad,
While glints of light shimmer in the liquid jet
Beyond its window panes and broken door.
Upon the sagging porch, piles of bones erode
Into pale grey dust the wind pushes away.
The breeze whispers balefully in the trees,
While the house, crouching like a vulture, groans
And with rabid hunger awaits its prey.

All Hallows Harvest

Michael Potts

October time, All Hallows Eve,
Old Man Gleaner wafts the wheat—
A boy next door chills to the bone,
about the harvest of the dead—
lead them to the damp of dark
bereft of life, of love, of grace.
that Mr. Gleaner still looked old
the cursed house where dead souls live.
aware of only drops of cold
the dirt space storing all the dead—
Old Man Gleaner does not care—
to knock on doors that open wide
those children from the neighborhood
with parents asking where they are,
shielding them from ghastly truth
to live on nihilistic bliss—
their vigor in the Old Ones' guts
especially on All Hallows Eve
on dares that form their final fate

grain and chaff are flying high.
gusty winds drive out the dross.
considers what his Grandpa said
how summoners of souls from flesh
walls in claustrophobic space,
The boy—John—knows all the tales
past sixty years when Grandpa saw
In spectral black their minds are dim,
dark water from the basement wall,
root cellar stuffed with long-lost souls.
he laughs at all the kids who come
like rictus mouths that feed on them,
who join the others down below
their ignorance an unknown bliss
that Old Ones, eager, feed on souls
human remains that fade away,
until more come to join the feed
when children reach the haunted house
to serve as supper to the beasts.

The Haunted House

John Greenleaf Whittier

The beautiful river, which retains its Indian name of Merrimack, winds through a country of almost romantic beauty. The last twenty miles of its course in particular, are unsurpassed in quiet and rich scenery, by any river in the United States. There are indeed, no bold and ragged cliffs, like the Highlands of the Hudson, to cast their grim shadows on the water—no blue and lofty mountains, piercing into the thin atmosphere, and wrapping about their rocky proportions the mists of valley and river—but there are luxuriant fields and pleasant villages, and white churchspires, gleaming through the green foliage of oak and elm—and wide forests of Nature's richest coloring, and green hills sloping smoothly and gracefully to the margin of the clear, bright stream, which moves onward to the Ocean, as lightly and gracefully as the moving of a cloud at sunset, when the light wind which propels the aerial voyager is unfelt on earth.

It was on the margin of this stream, during the early times of Massachusetts, that a stranger—a foreigner of considerable fortune—took up his residence. He had a house, constructed from a model of his own which, for elegance and convenience, far surpassed the rude and simple tenements of his neighbors; and he had a small farm, or rather garden, which he seemed to cultivate for amusement, rather than from any absolute necessity of labor. He had no family, save a daughter—an interesting girl of sixteen.

Near the dwelling of Adam McOrne—for such was the stranger's name—lived old Alice Knight—a woman, known throughout the whole valley of the river, from Plum Island to the residence of the Sachem Passaconaway, on the Nashua,—as one under an evil influence—an ill-tempered and malignant old woman—who was seriously suspected of dealing with the Prince of Darkness. Many of her neighbors were ready to make oath that they had been haunted by old Alice, in the shape of a black cat—that she had taken off the wheels of their hay-carts and frozen down their sled-runners, when the team was in full motion—that she had bewitched their swine, and rendered their cattle unruly—nay, more than one good wife averred, that she had bewitched their churns and prevented the butter from forming; and that they could expel her in no other way, than by heating a horse-nail and casting it into the cream. Moreover, they asserted that when this method of exorcism was resorted to, they invariably learned, soon after, that goodwife Alice was suffering under some unknown indisposition. In short, it would be idle to attempt a description of the almost innumerable feats of witchcraft ascribed to the withered and decrepid Alice.

Her exterior was indeed well calculated to favor the idea of her supernatural qualifications. She had the long, blue and skinny finger—the elvish locks of gray and straggling hair—the hooked nose, and the long, upturned chin, which seemed perpetually to threaten its nasal neighbor—the blue lips drawn around a mouth, garnished with two or three unearthly-looking fangs—the bleared and sunken eye—the bowed and attenuated form—and the limping gait, as if the invisible fetters of the Evil One were actually clogging the footsteps of his servant. Then, too, she was poor—poor as the genius of poverty itself—she had no relatives about her—no friends—her hand was against every man, and every man's hand was against her.

Setting the question of her powers of witchcraft aside, Alice Knight was actually an evil-hearted woman. Whether the suspicions and the taunts of her neighbors had aroused into action those evil passions which slumber in the seldom-visited depths of the human heart—or, whether the mortifications of poverty and dependence had changed and perverted her proud spirit—certain it was, that she took advantage of the credulity and fears of her neighbors. When they in the least offended her, she turned upon them with the fierce malison of an enraged Pythoness, and prophesied darkly of some unknown and indescribable evil about to befall them. And, consequently, if any evil did befall them in the space of a twelve-month afterward, another mark was added to the already black list of iniquities, which was accredited to the ill-favored Alice.

With all her fierce and deep-rooted hatred of the human species—one solitary affection—one feeling of kindness, yet lingered in the bosom of Alice Knight. Her son—a young man of twenty-five—her only child—seemed to form the sole and last link of the chain which had once bound her to humanity. Her love of him partook of the fierce passions of her nature—it was wild, ungovernable, and strong as her hate itself.

Gilbert Knight inherited little from his mother, save a portion of her indomitable pride and fierce temperament. He had been a seaman—had visited many of the old lands, and had returned again to his birth-place—a grown up man—with a sun-burned cheek—a fine and noble figure, and a countenance rude and forbidding, yet marked with a character of intellect and conscious power. He had little intercourse with his mother—he refused even to reside in the same dwelling with her—and yet, when in her presence, he was respectful, and even indulgent to her singular disposition and unsocial habits. He had no communion with the inhabitants of his native town—but, stern, unsocial and gloomy, he held himself apart from the sympathies and fellowship of men, with whom indeed, he had few feelings in common.

Mary, the daughter of Adam McOrne, seemed alone to engage the attention of Gilbert Knight. She was young, beautiful, and, considering the condition of the country, well-educated. She naturally felt herself superior to the rude and hard-featured youth around her—she had tasted enough of the sentiment, and received enough of the polish of education, to raise her ideas, at least, above the ignorant and unlettered rustics, who sought her favor.

Despised and spurned at, as the mother of Gilbert Knight was, still her son always commanded respect. There was something in the dignity of his manner, and the fierce flash of his dark eye, which had a powerful influence on all in his presence. Then, too, it was remembered that his father was a man of intellect and family—that he was once wealthy—and had suddenly met with reverses of fortune. These considerations gave Gilbert Knight no little consequence in his native village; and Adam McOrne, who ridiculed the idea of witches and witchcraft, received the occasional visits of Gilbert with as much cordiality as if his mother had never been suspected of evil doings. He was pleased with the frank, bold bearing of the sailor; and with his evident preference of his dwelling, above that of his neighbors—never so much as dreaming, that the visits of Gilbert were paid to any other than himself.

It was a cold, dark night of Autumn, that Gilbert, after leaving the hospitable fire-side of McOrne, directed his steps to the rude and lonely dwelling of his mother. He found the old woman alone;—a few sticks of ignited wood cast a faint light upon the dismal apartment—and an old and blear-eyed cat was at her side, gazing earnestly at her unseemly countenance.

"Mother," said Gilbert, seating himself, "'tis idle—'tis worse than folly to dream of executing our project. Mary McOrne will never be my wife."

"Ha!" exclaimed Alice, fixing her hollow eye upon her son— "Have I not told you that it should be so, and must be? You have lost your courage; you have become weaker than a woman, Gilbert. I tell you that Mary McOrne loves you, as deeply, as passionately as ever man was loved by woman!"

Gilbert started. "I do believe she loves me," he said at length, "but she will never be my wife. She dreads an alliance with our family. She has said so—she has this night solemnly averred that she had rather die at once, than become the daughter-in-law of—of"—Gilbert hesitated.

"Of a witch!" shrieked Alice, in a voice so loud and shrill that it even startled the practiced ear of Gilbert. "'Tis well—I will not be stigmatised as a witch with impunity. That haughty Scotchman and his impudent brat of a daughter shall learn that Alice Knight is not to be insulted in this manner! Gilbert, you shall marry her, or she shall die accursed!"

"Mother!" said Gilbert, rising and fixing his dark eye keenly on that of his mother—"I understand your threat; and I warn you to beware. Practice your infernal tricks upon others as you please—but Mary McOrne is too pure and sacred for such unhallowed dealing; and as you dread the curses of your son, let her not be molested."

He turned away as he ceased speaking, and instantly left the dwelling. He had seen little of his mother for many years—he knew her disposition but imperfectly; and, while in public he ridiculed the idea of her supernatural powers, he yet felt an awe—a fear in her presence—a certainty that she was not like those around her. He knew that the breath of her displeasure operated to appearance like a curse—that she did, either by natural cunning, or supernatural power, mysteriously distress and perplex her neighbors. He saw that her proud spirit had been touched; and that she meditated evil against McOrne and his daughter. The latter, Gilbert really loved—as deeply and devotedly as such a rude spirit could love; and he shuddered at the idea of her subjection to the arts of his mother. He therefore resolved to press his suit once more, and endeavor to overcome the objections which the girl had raised; and, in the event of his failure to do so, to protect her from the wrath of his mother.

But Mary McOrne—much as she loved the dark-eyed stranger, and his tales of peril and shipwreck in other climes—could not associate herself with the son of a witch—the only surviving offspring of a woman, whom she verily believed to be the bond slave of the Tempter. And so she strove with the strong feeling of affection within her—and Gilbert Knight was rejected.

A short time after, the tenants of the dwelling of McOrne were alarmed by strange sounds and unusual appearances. In the dead of the night they would hear heavy footsteps ascending the stair-case, with the clank of a chain—and groans issued from the unoccupied rooms of the building. The doors were mysteriously opened, after having been carefully secured—the curtains of the beds of McOrne and his daughter were drawn aside by an unseen hand; and low whispers of blasphemy and licentiousness, which a spirit of evil, could only have suggested, were breathed, as it were, into their very ears. The servants—a male and female—alike complained of preternatural visitations and unseemly visions. They were disturbed in their daily avocations—the implements of household labor were snatched away by an invisible hand—they saw strange lights in the neighborhood of the dwelling. They heard an unearthly music in the chimney; and saw the furniture of the room dancing about, as if moving to the infernal melody. In short, the fact was soon established, beyond the interposition of a doubt, that the house was haunted.

The days of faery are over. The tale of enchantment—the legend of ghostly power—of unearthly warning and supernatural visitation, have lost their hold on the minds of the great multitude. People sleep quietly where they are placed—no matter by what means they have reached the end of their journey—and there is an end to the church-yard rambles of discontented ghosts—

> ——"That creep
> From out the places where they sleep—
> To publish forth some hidden sin,
> Or drink the ghastly moonshine in,"—

And as for witches, the race is extinct—or, if a few yet remain, they are a miserable libel upon the diabolical reputation of those who figured in the days of Paris and Mather. Haunted houses are getting to be novelties—and corpse-lights and apparitions and unearthly noises, and signs and omens and wonders, are no longer troublesome. Ours is a matter-of-fact age—an age of steam and railway and McAdamization and labor-saving machinery—the poetry of Time has gone by forever, and we have only the sober prose left us.

Among the superstitions of our ancestors, that of Haunted Houses is not the least remarkable. There is scarcely a town or village in New-England which has not, at some period or other of its history, had one or more of these ill-fated mansions. They were generally old, decayed buildings—untenanted, save by the imaginary demons, who there held their midnight revels. But there are many instances of "prestigious spirits" who were impudent enough to locate themselves in houses, where the hearth-stone had not yet grown cold—where the big bible yet lay on the parlor-table; and where, over Indian-pudding and pumpkin-pie, the good man of the mansion always craved a blessing; where the big arm chair was always officiously placed for the minister of the parish, whenever he favored the family with the light of his countenance; and where the good lady taught her children the Catechism every Saturday evening. This was indeed, a bold act of effrontery on the part of the Powers of Evil, yet it was accounted for on the ground, that good men and true were sometimes given over to the buffetings of the enemy, of which fact, the case of Job was considered ample proof.

The visitations to the house of McOrne became more frequent and more terrific. The unfortunate Mary suffered severely. She fully believed in the supernatural character of the sights and sounds which alarmed her; and she looked upon old Alice Knight as the author: especially after hearing a whisper in her ear, in the darkness of midnight, that, unless she married Gilbert Knight she should be haunted as long as she lived. As for the father, he battled long and manfully with the fears which were strengthened day by day—he laughed at the strange noises which filled his mansion, and ridiculed the fears of his daughter—but it was easy to see that his strong mind was shaken by the controlling superstitions of the time; and he yielded slowly to the belief, which had now extended itself through the neighborhood, that his dwelling was under the immediate influence of demoniac agency.

Many were the experiments tried throughout the neighborhood for the discovery of the witch. The old, experienced grand-mothers gathered together almost every evening for consultation, and divers and multiform were the plans devised for counteracting the designs of Satan. All admitted that Alice Knight must be the witch, but unfortunately there was no positive proof of the fact. All the charms and forms of exorcism which were then believed to be potent weapons for the overthrowing of the powers of Wickedness having failed, it was finally settled among the good ladies that the minister of the parish could alone drive the evil spirits from the dwelling of their neighbor. But Adam McOrne was a sinful man; and his oaths had been louder than his prayers on this trying occasion: and, when it was proposed to him to invite the godly parson to his house, for the purpose of laying the spirits that troubled it, he swore fiercely, that rather than have his threshold darkened by the puritan priest, he would see his dwelling converted into the Devil's ball-room, and thronged with all the evil spirits on the face of the earth or beneath it. And, with shaking heads and prophetic visages, the good women left the perverse Scotchman to his fate.

Notwithstanding his bold exterior, the heart of Adam McOrne was daily failing within him. The wild, nursery tales of his childhood came back to him with painful distinctness—and the bogie and kelpie and dwarfish Brownie of his native land, rose fearfully before his imagination. His evenings were lonely and long; and he resolved to invite Gilbert Knight—the fierce sailor, who feared neither man nor fiend—to take up his residence with him: in the firm belief that no power, human or super-human, could shake the nerves of a man, who had wrestled with the tempest upon every sea; and who had braved death in the red battle, when his shattered deck was slippery with blood and piled with human corpses.

Gilbert obeyed the summons of McOrne with pleasure. He had heard the strange stories of the haunted mansion, which were upon every lip in the vicinity; and he felt perfectly convinced that his mother was employed in disturbing the domestic quiet of the Scotchman and his daughter—whether by natural means, or otherwise, he knew not. But he knew her revengeful disposition, and he feared, that unless her schemes were boldly interfered with, she would succeed in irreparably injuring the health and minds of her victims. Besides, he trusted that, should he succeed in accomplishing his purpose and laying the evil spirits of the mansion, he should effectually secure to himself the gratitude of both father and daughter.

Gilbert was received with much cordiality by Adam McOrne. "Ye may weel ken," said the old gentleman, "that I all no the least afeared o' a' this clishmaclaver, o' evil speerits, or deils or witch-bags; but my daughter, puir lassie, she's in an awsome way—a' the time shakin' wi' fear o' wraiths and witches and sic like ill-faured cattle." And Adam McOrne made an endeavor to look unconcerned and resolute in the presence of his guest, as he thus disclaimed any feeling of alarm on his own part. He could not bear that the bold sailor should look upon his weakness.

Even Mary McOrne welcomed the presence of her discarded lover. Yet, while she clung to him as to her only protector, she shuddered at the thought that Gilbert was the son of her evil tormentor—nay more, the horrible suspicion would at times steal over her that he had himself prompted his wicked parent to haunt her and terrify her into an acquiescence with his wishes. But, when she heard his frank and manly proposal to watch all night in a chamber, where the strange sights and sounds were most frequent, she could not but trust that her suspicion was ill-founded, and that in Gilbert Knight she should find a friend and a protector.

Adam McOrne, secretly overjoyed at the idea of having a sentinel in his dwelling, ordered a fire to be kindled in the suspected chamber; and placing a decanter of spirits on the table, he bade his guest good night, and left him to the loneliness of the haunted apartment.

It matters not now what thoughts passed through the mind of Gilbert, as he sat silent and alone, gazing on the glowing embers before him. That his mother was engaged in a strange and dark purpose, in regard to the family of McOrne, he was fully convinced—and he resolved to unravel the mystery of her midnight adventures, and relieve the feelings of the Scotchman and his daughter—even, although in so doing he should implicate his own mother, in guilty and malicious designs.

The old family clock struck one. At that moment a deep groan sounded fearfully through the room.—Gilbert rose to his feet and listened earnestly. It seemed to proceed from the room beneath him; and it was repeated several times, until it died away, like the last murmurs of one in the agonies of death. In a few moments he heard footsteps on the stair case ascending to a long, narrow passage at its head, which communicated with his apartment.

"I will know the cause of this," said Gilbert, mentally, as he threw open the door, and sprang into the passage. A figure attempted to glide past him, appareled in white, uttering, as it did so, a deep and hollow groan.

"Mortal or devil!" shouted Gilbert, springing forward and grasping the figure by the arm—"you go no further. Speak, witch, ghost, whatever you are—declare your errand!"

The figure struggled violently, but the iron grasp of Gilbert remained unshaken. At that moment the hurried voice of the old Scotchman sounded through the passage.

"Haud weel, haud week my braw lad; dinna let go your grip— in God's name haud weel!"

"Let me go," said the figure in a hoarse whisper—"Let me go, or you are a dead man!" Gilbert retained his hold, and endeavored to discover by the dim light which streamed from his apartment, the countenance of the speaker.

"Die, then, unnatural wretch!" shrieked the detected Alice,

snatching a knife from her bosom, and aiming a furious stab at her son. Gilbert pressed his hand to his side, and staggered backward, exclaiming, as the features of his mother, now fully revealed, glared madly upon him—

"Woman, you have murdered your son!"

The knife dropped from the hand of Alice, and with a loud and almost demoniac shriek, she sprang down the stair-case and vanished like a spectre.

Adam McOrne hurried forward, the moment he saw the white figure disappear, and followed Gilbert into his apartment. "Are ye hurt?—are ye wraith-smitten?" asked the Scotchman; and then, as his eye fell on the bloodied dress of Gilbert, he exclaimed— "Waes me—ye are a' streakit wi' bluid—ye are a dead man!"

Gilbert felt that his wound was severe, but with his usual presence of mind, he gave such directions to McOrne and his daughter, as to enable them to prevent the rapid effusion of blood, while a servant was despatched for the nearest physician. Mary McOrne seemed to forget the weakness of her sex, while she ministered to her wounded lover with a quick eye and a skillful hand. It is on occasions like this—when even the strong nerves of manhood are shaken—that the feeble hand of woman is often most efficient. In the hour of excitement and turmoil, the spirit of manly daring may blaze out, with sudden and terrible power—but in the deep trials of suffering humanity—in the watchings by the bed of affliction—then it is that the courage of woman predominates—the very excess of her sympathy sustains her.

The arrival of the physician dissipated in some degree the fears of McOrne and his daughter. The wound of Gilbert was not considered as dangerous; and he was assured that a few days of confinement would be the only ill consequence resulting from it. The kind hearted Scotchman and his kinder hearted daughter watched by his bed until morning, at which time Gilbert was enabled to explain the singular circumstances of the night; and at the same time he expressed a wish that McOrne should visit the dwelling of his mother, who, he feared would resort to some violence upon herself, in the belief that she had, in her frantic passion, murdered her son.

Adam McOrne, convinced by the narration of Gilbert that human ingenuity and malice, instead of demoniac agency, had disturbed his dwelling, sallied out early in the morning to the rude and crazy dwelling of his tormentor.

He found the door open—and on entering, the first object that met his view was the form of Alice Knight, lying on the floor, insensible and motionless. He spoke to her, but she answered not—he lifted her arm, and it fell back with a dead weight upon her side.—She was dead—whether by terror or suicide, he knew not. "Ugh!" said Adam McOrne, in relating the discovery—"there she was—an ill-faured creature—a' cauld and ghuistly, lookin' for a' the world as if she wad hac thankit any Christian soul to hue gie'n her a decent burial."

She was buried the next day in the small garden adjoining her dwelling, for the good people of the neighborhood could not endure the idea of her reposing in their own quiet grave-yard. The minister of the parish indeed attended her funeral, and made a few general remarks upon the enormity of witchcraft and the exceeding craftiness of the great necromancer and magician, who had ensnared the soul of the ill-fated Alice—but when he ventured to pray for the repose of the unhappy woman, more than one of his hearers shook their heads, in the belief that even their own goodly minister had no right to interfere with the acknowledged property of the Enemy.

It is said that Alice did not sleep peaceably, nathless the prayers of the minister. Her house was often lighted up in the dead of the night, until

"Through ilka bore the flames were glancing,"

and the wild and unearthly figure of the old woman herself, crossed more than once the paths of the good people of the neighborhood. At least, such is the story, and it is not our present purpose to dispute it.

The manner in which old Alice contrived to perplex the Scotchman and his daughter, was at length revealed by the disclosures of the servants of the family. They had been persuaded by the old woman to aid her in the strange transactions—partly from an innate love of mischief, and partly from a pique against the worthy Scotchman, whose irritable temperament had more than once discovered itself in the unceremonious collision of his cane with the heads and shoulders of his domestics.

Gilbert recovered rapidly of his wound: and a few months after, the house, which had been given over to the evil powers, as the revelling-place of demons, was brilliantly illuminated for a merry bridal. And the rough, bold sailor, as the husband of Mary McOrne, settled down into a quiet, industrious and sober-minded citizen. Adam McOrne lived to a good old age, stoutly denying to the last that he had ever admitted the idea of witchcraft, and laughing, heartily as before, at the superstitions and credulity of his neighbors.

Note.—The preceding story in founded on a passage in the writings of Dr. Mather. "In 1679 a house," says the Doctor, "in Newbury, (on the Merrimack,) was infested with demons in a most horrid manner." Here follows a long and curious recital of the infernal doings of the ill-natured spirits. The same story is recorded on the records of the court at Salem, where a seaman, by the name of Powell, was tried for witchcraft, on the ground that he had been able to put to flight the demons of the haunted house, by means of the black art—or astrology.

The Scarlet Room

Adam Bolivar

There was a man named Mister Fox
    Whose house was grand and old;
He kept a room of bloody frocks
    Quite ghastly to behold.

He courted Lady Mary Drake,
    This charming gallant squire,
A handsome suitor did he make,
    Whom any would admire.

A wedding day was set, of course,
    That coming Eve of May,
Upon the moor amongst the gorse
    Picked for the bride's bouquet.

The House of Fox lay in the wood,
    Though she had seen it not,
And for as long as it had stood
    Black rumors had it brought.

When her betrothed had gone away,
She ventured to the wood
To learn if what she'd heard folk say
    Had been misunderstood.

The House of Fox at length she found,
    A mansion very old,
Which ancient forest did surround
    And legendry enfold.

Above the gate were writ the words:
    "Be bold, my dear, be bold."
And on the walls were bloodstained swords,
    A horror to behold.

She went into this beastly lair
    And struggled to be bold,
For what she saw inside of there
    Would make her blood run cold.

A scarlet chamber lay within
    With piles of bones a-filled,
A place the Foxes hid their sin,
    The many they had killed.

Now Mary heard a piercing shriek
    And hid behind a cask;
She raised her head to take a peek
    And trembled from the task.

The gallant man betrothed to her
    Held captive here a maid,
Who flailed and made a frightful stir,
    Recoiling from his blade.

The blackguard cut a hand from her
    To steal a ruby ring;
In Mary's lap it landed, sir,
    A most abhorrent thing!

Quick Mary fled that wicked room
    And on her frock a stain;
She fled him who would be her groom,
    His deed etched in her brain.

Then at the breakfast feast she said
    Last night she'd had a dream
That she had found a room of red
    Where blood flowed in a stream.

"Alas, it is not so, my dear,"
    Quoth Mister Fox, her groom.
"It was a dream, so have no fear
    Of any scarlet room."

"Into that room you dragged a maid,
    A ruby ring she had;
To have it you withdrew your blade
    And cropped her hand, you cad!"

"A dream, a dream, that's all it was,"
    The skittish Fox demurred.
"To spread such tales there is no cause;
    I say they are absurd!"

"And here's the ring, the ruby ring,
    And here's that poor maid's hand;
The House of Fox must surely bring
    A blight upon our land."

Then Lady Mary's kindred all
    The wicked Fox struck down;
That Eve of May his house would fall,
    And burned was Mary's gown.

A Life in Rocks

Jonathan Thomas

Sometimes in midstride Tarrier reflected on how lucky he was. A receptive eye to the ground, delicate leverage with a screwdriver, and he had in hand his nigh-daily portion of wonder as he trod Olmsted Boulevard and adjacent terrain. He was used to the faux blindness and grudging nods of joggers, dogwalkers, cellphone prattlers when he said good morning. The cold shoulder just because he was walking around with a rock! Hell, if he cared about the bourgeois judgments of the incurious, the indifferent, the snobby, how much weaker a person would he be?

Today he'd traversed the bulldozed flats of former sylvan tract one block west, more goddamn McMansions coming soon, and the topsoil had yielded a pretty definite hammerstone: granite, ovoid, mango-sized, clustered peck-marks at one end, several polished wear-planes elsewhere. Child's play to scare up impeccable matches for it in Smithsonian, Peabody, other museums' website archives—everyman's artifact-identification resource!

Always exciting to be the first to hold, appreciate, understand Native handiwork in at least four hundred years. How could anyone not be enthralled? Inscrutably, people weren't. But where others saw a random, beat-up rock, Tarrier admired a thing of beauty, an elegantly simple, versatile, precision tool to procure the necessaries of life.

Flicking clay off his trésor-du-jour with a thumbnail, rotating it in search of further confirmatory details, he strode to the Boulevard and crossed paths with a sourpuss millennial in shades, walking a labradoodle. "Hello!" chirped Tarrier affably, and on being snubbed, muttered "Fucking zombie," hoping it carried, but eschewing the rookie mistake of turning to check.

Home was a modest bungalow on a cul-de-sac of renters and other isolationists. Nonetheless it was the ritzy side of town, and he'd only become a homeowner on freelance-copyeditor wages because his elderly landlord of twenty-plus years had balked at the hassle and expense of remodeling the place into marketable shape. Tarrier's for a song, the last of this tax-district's affordable housing!

Today, as often happened upon reentry, second thoughts assailed him at the multitude of artifacts on tabletops, under furniture, in curio cabinets, all meticulously annotated by find-spot, dimensions in centimeters, diagnostic features. There couldn't be so many in his few square miles of stomping grounds, could there? But self-doubt receded once his eyes lit upon slate, argillite, or basalt that had obviously been worked into pestles, adzes, celts. People had been here circa 13,000 years, after all; that had to leave a significant mark. If there was a ton of artifacts, fine, there was a ton of artifacts. It said something about the Native population this locale supported, not about him.

Haply, he mused while surveying his collection, he'd none to please save himself. His self-image was never of an "incel," though he'd handily qualify from an outside perspective. The right girl had simply never come along, and with advancing age and ebbing hormones he was resigned to the strong likelihood she never would. More room for rocks!

When he first noticed lithics sticking out of an eroded Boulevard embankment, the pandemic was making solitary hobbies the order of everyone's day; and before his gleanings had outgrown two Falstaff beer trays, he'd weathered a phase of going to bed jittery. He wasn't positive yet his finds weren't coming from a mortuary context, not till he concluded the overwhelming bulk of busted, battered implements indicated a midden, maybe a worksite. Who'd okay such crummy specimens as grave goods?

Those early nights were fretful, though, partly due to the ethical minefield he might have blundered into, partly at the possibility of aggrieving long-dormant spirits. Often enough, giving his prizes the once-over set him on tenterhooks, inflicted an unfounded, unhealthy sensation of being watched, of flickering movements out the corner of an eye (eventually he tossed most of the trays' contents as wishful-thinking geofacts). Two uneventful weeks convinced him to banish angst, be reassured: any spirits clinging to their erstwhile possessions had nothing against him.

No big leap for tacit approval from the Hereafter to morph into tacit approval from the artifacts themselves. He'd chanced upon (and unfortunately hadn't bookmarked) an online essay mentioning how some Native languages (he'd also, unfortunately, forgotten whether his own region's were included) classified rocks grammatically, and perhaps literally, as animate objects. The "living rock" indeed! Soon his fancy went the extra mile of contending he pocketed no artifacts that didn't want to be pocketed; his best finds, in fact, mutely yoohooed at him from unprepossessing dirt. If that made him an animist, so be it!

Attached as he was to many of his primo gleanings, he absolutely intended donating them to the tribal museum at the state university, somewhat because the collection was nearing hoarder density, mostly because they, like the land, belonged, on a plane of ideal justice, to the heirs of previous owners—and the few dozen items of which he was fondest he'd draw up the papers to bequeath. But first, to ensure he didn't waste museum staff time and embarrass himself (assuming they'd want what amounted to antiquity's trash), he needed to have a goodly sample vetted by a patient, open-minded archaeologist.

Out and about, he did sometimes bump into anthropologists for whom he'd copyedited. Maybe it was his impulsive bad to unbag fresh, uncleaned finds for spot-appraisal that mightn't be his finest, but professors' brusque, kneejerk "No" smacked of elitist snap judgment and never preceded "Why not." Once he'd even incurred a screed against rescuing his hometown's heritage on the grounds that anything bereft of stratigraphy and context was a useless "orphan." Tarrier listened politely rather than foment no-win debate by citing Olmsted Boulevard's environs as the context, wherein artifacts' typology, frequency, and distribution could sub for stratigraphy. In the meantime, yay, he was running an orphanage.

Too bad the state had no institutions, leastwise none according to his online research, hosting regular hours for the public to have their finds assayed as something or nothing. Almost as if the powers-that-be would as lief wash their hands of the precolonial truth! What more to do for now beyond salvaging away, hoping for validation someday? With that quixotic resolve, he washed his treasures from dawn ramble and perched them on a cinderblock out back to dry: a discoid hammerstone and a trapezoidal nutting stone, the round depression on its broadest face perfect for holding acorns and butternuts to crack.

September sunshine had dried his finds by the time he came out to bring them in. He did a double-take, half-seriously wondered if they were haunted, and in broad daylight yet. Well, if so, one ghost anyhow had retained a sense of humor. Hammer and nutting stone were exactly where he'd put them, or were they? Whether or not the nutting stone's divot had been facing upward, it was now. And it contained fragments of acorn kernel, pieces of shell littering the cinderblock. Reason dictated a squirrel must have made a fortuitous pitstop here, but ultimately he could know that no more than he could know it wasn't supernatural whimsy. Something to enshrine in memory among "unsolved mysteries!"

The sense of humor, domestic routines, beliefs, mores of tools' previous owners he often contemplated, on undereducated spec, of course. Still, a dimension of the sacred informed every artifact. Each was all that remained of someone's personality, skillset, and aesthetic judgment. There was nothing else to remember that soul by, and who wouldn't want to be remembered? In that light, disrespect and dishonor would consist in destroying, dumpstering, ignoring relics that restored to centuried individuals figurative snippets of existence, let them speak a few syllables again through their handiwork. Oblivion wouldn't entirely have its way with them.

Doubtless he was on the side of the angels, but had to own up about the realpolitik behind waiting for a simpatico archaeologist to drop out of the sky. The sad fact of it: the good stuff was on private, public, or posted property. On building sites and wooded cemetery fringes he was trespassing, in riverside park and on the Boulevard he was technically pilfering. In his defense, he was of the school that apologies were less problematic than permission. Consequently he'd racked up evidence abounding about his locale's Indigenous past.

Would he have had any of it had he approached developers, cemetery superintendents, Parks Department management? Why should they expose themselves to prospects of disruptive excavations (on their dimes), repatriation issues with tribal authorities, nighthawk depredations? At heart Tarrier needed a professional who agreed that trespassing was the lesser evil next to forfeiting lithic heritage, and who, as a humungous bonus, would run interference or at minimum advise him on dealing with landowners and such. Meanwhile, he'd plug along at job one, prying the maximum ancient heritage from the jaws of obliteration.

Another sad fact dawned on him as he plugged along: the outlooks of artifacts or their associated spirits were nowise monolithic. Instances were mounting of assorted tools, a whetstone, an abrader, a chisel, downright leaping from his fingers to bounce off the street. He was forced to acknowledge some artifacts didn't want to trade the cold, acidic dirt for his airy, warm home. Usually these refuseniks sustained a tiny nick or scrape, nothing like the shattering fate they'd have tempted at their findspots.

But a hefty nine-inch cylindrical pestle, unearthed hours before a cement-mixer would have crushed and buried it under a new sidewalk, would always be a sore point. He set it atop his recycling bin and fetched dish soap and a basin of water. It could have stayed put, yet criminally, it had to roll off the really shallow pitch of the lid, unlike myriad other items. He came out, livid, aghast at the pestle's jagged pieces in the driveway. Artefactual suicide! He was too embarrassed by this casualty on his watch to keep its fragments around as reminders; he chucked them into the weeds under the Norway maple by his garage.

Never had his address exuded the iffiest whiff of the supernatural, not till he'd embarked on his pandemic pastime. And now he couldn't rummage through a shoebox of lithics without flinching at the negative vibes a portion of it projected, despite the voice of reason objecting those vibes originated in his head. Mayhap the living make a place haunted! As with poltergeists, a house abides devoid of the occult till a teen comes along and the furniture starts flying. Nor does everyone overnighting at notoriously haunted mansions report incidents; were some brains wired to generate so-called supernaturalism in certain settings? Was there comfort or quite the opposite in positing that ghosts were mere figments made manifest by a fluke unconscious agency? Where'd that leave the afterlife?

Compunctions about holding lithics against their will slowed down his urban beachcombing not a whit. Out gallivanting, his were a different Tarrier's priorities: foremost, to augment the story of his home turf, of its rightful stewards, one indispensable clue after another. At-home qualms over storage room for new finds, and how he'd ever vet them, stewed on the back burner. Easier to think positive when those finds figuratively hallooed at him, implicitly soliciting rescue. True, he wondered if some rocks just wanted him to carry them around, a sunny change from dreary soil, only to recant on getting airsick after quiescent ages. Animism was great for posing surreal riddles, many more than rationalism could derive from a rock.

Come October, though, those constitutionals had the insouciance knocked out of them, became subject to the same shadows sporadically darkening his indoor life. All because of one find that wasn't stone! He was strolling the footpath alongside the Victorian-era wall of boulders bounding Cygnet Cove Cemetery, and stopped short on impulse to climb some fortuitous rock steps over the wall. Here was territory he hadn't patrolled in months, presently in its golden hour after ticks and poison ivy had subsided, before autumn leaves carpeted everything.

From a Boulevard perspective, forest seemed to loom beyond, but it was a belt of deceptively finite width buffering the graveyard proper; a mulchy service road bisected its length. On the far side of that road were tree-screened cairns and earthen ridges, where yesteryear's gravediggers had dumped the dirt displaced by burials. These spoilheaps had yielded perforated-slate canoe anchors and a cigar-shaped clubhead. Was he qualmish about poking through grave dirt? Of course not; tombs and tumuli were the bread-and-butter of professionals. Not like the loam Tarrier probed had ever been in contact with a corpse!

But today he pawed detritus from a glimpse of smooth, black shaft. A pestle? A steatite pipe? No, qualmish he suddenly was to cradle in hand half a limb bone, stained black, clay-flecked toward the knobbly epiphysis, a blunt break around the eight-inch mark. Was it from an arm or leg? Damn his eyes, he'd copyedited umpteen medical journals. Would that he'd studied up on the anatomical terms he could spell backward and forward, but that was the depth of his knowledge. Decency dictated he couldn't let this pitiful residue molder there. Gingerly fingertips bagged it the while he regarded them askance like double agents of some sticky fate.

The notion of bringing it inside creeped him out. He stashed it, in its barely protective bag, behind the ramshackle chaise lounge on the front porch, and descended into a funk over what to do next. Since the woods were technically off-limits to the public, he'd be foolhardy prancing into the infamously uptight Cygnet Cove offices to announce, "Look what I found!"

That hardly changed the fact: putative human relics didn't belong in a pile of debris. In what passed for an upside, he didn't see how this one relic could be Native, not in soil that dissolved skeletons in a fraction of four hundred years. So at least his cemetery-property finds weren't tainted by association with Native graves, right? But he also couldn't discount that forensic tests might reunite stray bone with the grave whence it had somehow gone AWOL, or otherwise reveal historic insights, or lead to cracking a cold case.

On yet another hand, online research produced no exact match for his specimen among human long bones. Ergo he couldn't really swear he had a part from a person. No point getting into a kerfuffle with his conscience yet, not over possible banquet rubbish! Or was he grasping at copouts?

Yes or no, Tarrier at home couldn't see his way clear to one decision or another, kept doing nothing till the bag of bone slipped his mind for days on end, sparked negligible reaction when his sights lit upon it. Out and about, though, his thing on the doorstep exerted a more daunting influence. He'd routinely hearken to it on the Boulevard, where the cemetery wall functioned as a mile-long mnemonic, be he on the footpath within arm's reach of it, or over on the Boulevard's glorified median-strip of a greenway.

Part of him yearned to hop the wall while the tick-free, leaf litter-free season lasted. The rest of him wanted nothing more to do with the potential to stumble across further skeletal remnants. In a patently arbitrary compromise between conflicting urges, he began focusing on the wall itself. Chipmunks, snakes, wrens, a whole ecosystem of critters dwelt among the stones, burrowed behind them into dirt revetment, churned mini-excavations into the light of day. He'd scooped up an intact slate celt that way!

He was treading the footpath beside the wall when he discovered a cavity new to him, at navel level under a gigantic boulder supported by two hunks of shale. The loose soil on the cavity's floor looked promising, and by gum if an oblong outline wasn't poking out of it, beckoning from murky shadow. A pestle? A chisel? Was it ominous that the cairn whence came the bone was in his line of sight, a straight shot through the woods? And why did that crock recur to him now about the willingness of some artifacts, the antipathy of others, to accompany him home?

A moot point whether some supernal agency was fed up with him or the stoutest wall had to start crumbling sometime. Tarrier's reach beyond his wrist into the cavity coincided with the creak and groan of minerals succumbing to chronic stress. A transient rumble, a muffled thud, and the boulder fractured the underlying shale. Dust and pulverized rock billowed into Tarrier's face, though gritty choking hazard failed to register. He was, he freely admitted, someone for whom a paper cut was harrowing; the pain when tons of boulder pulped flesh and bone was off the scale. To primal scream he gave his all, the instant before swooning, slumping against the wall. Intrepid even in oblivion, he clutched fast the morning's bag of construction-site finds in his unmashed fist.

True to aloof form, as cynical Tarrier would have predicted, most passersby within hearing feigned deafness to his caterwaul. One Good Samaritan of a coronary survivor, though, phoned 911 from the greenway, pegging Tarrier as a fellow sufferer, albeit scarcely optimistic he'd pull through. Luckily, Tarrier remained out of it during his extrication. The EMT crew gawked at the woeful tableau, arriving at the consensus that it was bizarre, huh? Scratching their heads at the riddle of what the hell had happened, they hit up the Parks Department for heavy equipment, and hurry please!

At last, as the traffic-blocking, manpower-intensive, strobe-light operation got underway, the citizens who'd paid lone, limp Tarrier no heed stopped to rubberneck. Once he was freed and EMTs were wheeling over the stretcher, a Parks employee took the initiative to unclench Tarrier's intact fist and peek inside the bag, which did nothing to unmuddy the situation.

"What's in there?" a colleague asked.

"Just a bunch of rocks," answered the Parks guy in a tone both mystified and critical. He dumped out the contents to make sure he was right, grunted in bemusement, and let the empty bag roll windborne down the Boulevard.

When next Tarrier knew, he was transfixed by dazzling blue sky out a broad window in a drafty hospital room. A pathologically chipper nurse adjusted his errant blanket and informed him he was lucky—on top of his luck in going through his maiming ordeal unconscious—insofar as ICU surgery saved his hand. Now that morphine euphoria was wearing off, he was hard pressed to describe as "lucky" the resemblance of his tightly bandaged forearm to a shillelagh. Just as well he couldn't see, though he emphatically felt, the bridge plates, pins, Kirschner wires, other doohickeys no sooner listed by officious doctors than forgotten.

To their inquiries about what he was doing at the wall in the first place, Tarrier decided dissembling was best: he remembered strolling the path, same as hundreds of mornings, then everything was a post-traumatic blank. He also, naturally, said nothing about his missing bag of that morning's finds. The more regrettably, after his discharge he wouldn't be halfway out of the surgical woods, since those plates, pins, and fuck-all else had to come out eventually, not to mention physical therapy, soft-tissue repairs. Thank God for Obamacare, minus which the healthcare system might have written him off as a lousy credit risk and simply amputated.

Several friends and friendly neighbors he updated so they wouldn't freak out at nobody home for a fortnight. Wouldn't hurt, either, for them to keep an eye on the place, grab package deliveries lest porch pirates swoop in, or worse, burglars. He especially dreaded intruders messing with his lithics; guests, though, pointedly ignored the hoard, changed the subject when he showed off particularly spectacular finds. He put on a cheerful front for a couple of pro forma drop-ins who, Tarrier inferred, would have suffered guilty consciences otherwise. They brought him some glossy archaeology 'zines from Walgreens "to pass the time."

Before dozing off that evening he did peruse an intriguing tidbit in a *NatGeo* "special issue" riding the latest wave of

Egyptomania: a Cairo museum director related how a roomful of mummies from a single family had been pell-mell separated into different exhibits. Electrical-system, thermostat, smoke-alarm malfunctions plagued those halls till the family was reunited. Maybe that anecdote, along with whatever drugs still combated pain and infection, contributed to strikingly vivid dreams that recurred nightly and conduced to daily reveries serving very capably "to pass the time," thank you.

In upshot, according to his REM epiphanies, he'd unwittingly fostered conditions to convene a home-grown equivalent of that mummified kindred. Nor would he say his were garden-variety dreams. Instead, he ostensibly tuned in some psychic wavelength imparting the immaterial goings-on at home, where his presence no longer generated interference. The ectoplasmic coast was clear! Even discounting those items languishing in his house under protest, he'd amassed such a tonnage of artifacts as to comprise a tipping point, a critical mass of the scintillas of bygone personalities engrained in rock.

They were vague, rare flickers at first, but with a vacant house in which to regroup, individuals seized on more and more tatters of identity, pulled themselves together, coalesced into long-dormant self-images for cloudy-headed moments, then greater and greater wholes. In the fullness of days they regained the selfhood to perceive and greet one another. Somnolent Tarrier hadn't the extrasensory chops to discern them as sharply as they discerned themselves. His third-eye squint, at best, detected variety in how they wore their hair and clothing, telltales of lifetimes centuries, millennia apart.

A few were friends and relatives savoring jubilant reunions, or else mortal foes with nothing to fight over anymore; nor could they recollect mortal grounds for conflict. A passel more found each other's looks and lingo outlandish, amusing, but again, no reason everyone couldn't get along. On one topic agreement was unanimous. This *wetu* wherein they'd inexplicably met was the weirdest anyone had ever seen, with so many walls inside dividing the floor into silly little spaces, still more walls overhead, a root cellar underfoot. No complaints, though; it was warmer, cheerier than the cold, dank earth in which they'd blinked for a confused instant once in a million blue moons.

What's more, they recognized their own tools among the hundreds everywhere, were dumbstruck beholding these discarded, damaged goods again. Why would anyone keep them? Always good for a wry chuckle, whenever their prior owners phased into sentience and looked around. As for that bone out front, no idea whose it was, nothing to do with them! It gave off pretty disgruntled vibes, though. Better steer clear!

Tarrier, meanwhile, recuperated nicely. The docs were tapering off his psychotropic meds; what a novelty to feel levelheaded! His underemployed mind continued defaulting to fantasies of wall-to-wall spirits, but he wistfully demoted them to idle sickbed pastime. And then the day dawned to bid sickbed goodbye. The stern nurse with authority to sign him out was loath to let him go under his own steam. But he had nobody workdays to hit up for a ride, and damned if he'd blow thirty bucks on an Uber. Plus, the hospital had a bus stop out front, and he swore, fingers crossed, one route amounted to doorstep service.

That route did ply Olmsted Boulevard and dropped him within spitting distance of his uncanny accident scene, a mere half-hour's trot home. He gave slightly askew, evil-hearted boulder wide berth, wondering if maybe he weren't off his rocker to regard it blandly, without flashback terror. No matter; rather, bless those kindlier powers for showing him where three of his scattered artifacts lay in roadside grass. Loads of room for them in his "Patient Belonging Bag" amid meds, gripper slippers, non-slip socks. With renewed bounce in his step, he pondered how immersively real those pipe-dreams of Natives redux had first appeared. Alfresco, they faded into creative exercises, remedies for boredom.

Tarrier also had to consider whether picturing a houseful of contented spirits equaled wishful Anglo thinking or guilt abatement, wherein those Indigenous crafters of his artifacts were ultimately happy. They, at least, were reinhabiting their homeland, in unbodily form that afforded space for Native and Anglo alike, as if four hundred years of deceit, oppression, genocide were water under the bridge, for his privileged part anyhow.

As he turned the corner onto his cul-de-sac, however, the movie in his brain was of ghostly dozens in his parlor pricking up mystic ears at his approach. The bone behind the chaise lounge, as usual, rated nary a thought, beyond a vagrant "Long time, no see," a fleeting twinge of misgiving in his gut, a minute release of gastric acid like a raindrop wetting a seed. He climbed the porch steps, under no illusion anyone would be thrilled to see him, since harmony and good humor reigned in his absence. What could he add to the mix? Whoever he was, tromping up like he owned the place, well, maybe this was his crazy *wetu*, but he was categorically on their land.

His bag dangling by its drawstring from his shillelagh arm, Tarrier twisted the key in the lock, positive he heard garbled muttering from inside, like sustained winds tousling fallen leaves. No, a freak of acoustics must have fooled his fragile cognition: foliage was windborne behind him. Hence he was even more dumbfounded, despite anticipating everything a heartbeat before it happened, when the unlocked door swung inward with too much oomph for a draft or his nudging fingertip to be responsible. And he needed no fluency in Native speech to get the message as a concussive torrent of voices, no two using the same words—be they in the air or solely in his head—fiercely challenged his right to be there.

But he, like them, bound to the same artifacts, had nowhere else to abide. Deep breath and into the breach! Here was ironclad proof the living do indeed make a house haunted. How the dickens to unhaunt it, though? Impossible to think with all that racket! Through the decibels cut a metallic twang like a high-tension wire snapping in his skull, his keys fell jingling from nerveless fingers, his bag dropped with a thud from limp bandaged arm. His extremities might well have been miles away, beyond the wall of righteous clamoring.

Nor would legs in retreat serve him well. As real as the throng before him was the animosity springing from the bone outside. Like the bone, no historic or personal details informed that animosity. Like the throng, its actions lent it definition: manically pacing back and forth, back and forth across the porch, unbearably compounding the din of indecipherable voices as it bawled as if no door stood between them, *How is he not dead? What will it take?*

The Dark House

Edwin Arlington Robinson

Where a faint light shines alone,
Dwells a Demon I have known.
Most of you had better say
"The Dark House," and go your way.
Do not wonder if I stay.

For I know the Demon's eyes
And their lure that never dies.
Banish all your fond alarms,
For I know the foiling charms
Of her eyes and of her arms,

And I know that in one room
Burns a lamp as in a tomb;
And I see the shadow glide,
Back and forth, of one denied
Power to find herself outside.

There he is who was my friend,
Damned, he fancies, to the end—
Vanquished, ever since a door
Closed, he thought, for evermore
On the life that was before.

And the friend who knows him best
Sees him as he sees the rest
Who are striving to be wise
While a Demon's arms and eyes
Hold them as a web would flies.

All the words of all the world,
Aimed together, and then hurled,
Would be stiller in his ears
Than a closing of still shears
On a thread made out of years.

But there lives another sound,
More compelling, more profound;
There's a music, so it seems,
That assuages and redeems,
More than reason, more than dreams.

There's a music yet unheard
By the creature of the word,
Though it matters little more
Than a wave-wash on the shore—
Till a Demon shuts a door.

So, if he be very still
With his Demon, and one will,
Murmurs of it may be blown
To my friend who is alone
In a room that I have known.

After that from everywhere
Singing life will find him there;
And my friend, again outside,
Will be living, having died.

Shave Your Bounty

Michael Aronovitz

It didn't look like much, at least not according to the stereotype. Nick Shockley had always pictured some sort of ominous mansion with towering gazebo balcony turrets and dark windows set in Victorian gable dormers. This was what was left of the Sunset Motel with its cheesy nautical theme, parked at the edge of the Interstate, the office building demolished and the back area dug up and blocked off by a ring of steel drums and orange safety fencing. The only part left untouched in the rubble was the "Illustrious Ocean Sleepers," the last of the "Starboard Cuddy Cabins," three floors, nine rooms, the levels connected by an exposed concrete stairway to the left. Nick's daughter Lexi had jumped from the top room, far right, #13. The downward slope of the roof overhung the back balcony by two feet, and when she approached the rail, her image from what was the courtyard area would have been a veiled torrent, a blur, a spirit without a face. It was raining hard with hurricane winds coming over the top, and the roof had no gutter.

"You sure you want to do this?"

Nick looked over, eyes heavy with grief.

"Yes, Officer."

Sergeant Barnes had his thumbs hooked in his utility belt.

"There's nothing up there," he said. "It's literally a bare room, paneled walls, and a mini-bath with cheap off-white subway tiles."

Nick looked down at his muddy Wolverine boots. "I would have to disagree," he said.

The sergeant cleared his throat. "Mr. Shockley, we combed the place top to bottom, C.S.I. Unit, Forensics, the whole circus."

"Right," Nick said. "Always in groups, never alone."

The sergeant remained expressionless. "You can't bring her back," he said.

Nick was already ducking under the caution tape. "No," he said, "but I can damned well find out the way that she went."

Last spring, the demolition had been halted because of zoning issues, and the moment the last generator was shut down the rumors had started. Nick remembered that he was working on revisions to the schematic he had been drawing up for the new graving dock at the Philadelphia Navy Yard, when Lexi came bouncing in with her laptop, giggling, spinning, dancing with it as if doing a waltz. He stood up and walked out from behind the drafting table, pressing his palm into the small of his back. She had been such a nerd in middle school, but when the braces came off and she discovered Revlon, she had suddenly gone "girly-girl," growing up fast and pretty. He was going to have to start worrying about boys soon. Real soon.

"You laugh like a ninth grader," he said.

"I *am* a ninth grader," she said, pouting, taking a long lock of her newly curled hair and fingering it as if it had suddenly distracted her. She put it in front of her nose and stared, almost going cross-eyed. "I want to get this straightened again," she said.

"You were just at the salon yesterday. Give it a chance."

"I don't want to," she said. "I want it straightened and cut shoulder-length before I go back to school Monday."

"For why?"

"I'm a Swiftie," she said, as if that explained everything. "Look!"

She handed over the laptop. It was her Instagram with a picture of the Sunset Motel's last standing building, a few roof shingles missing, the siding weathered and water-stained like the shadowed underbelly of a highway overpass.

The comment section was busy.

"Haunted," said the first entry.

"Crack-house for ghosts," said the second.

And then came a cavalcade of violent shorties, urban legends, scratch marks, graffiti. Nick scrolled down; it seemed endless.

"In 1961, Saltwater Sam lost five thousand dollars in a back-room poker game, and he lured the winner back to his room at the Sunset Motel, #13, top right in the 'Starboard Cuddy Cabins.' That was where he killed the cheater with a double-sided fisherman's meat mallet."

Each entry added a level.

"He killed the three others from the poker game too, impaling them all on heavy-duty whaling harpoons set in flagpole brackets secured to the balcony railing."

"He slaughtered everyone in the speakeasy with a nine-inch boning knife and a serrated bait scissors. He brought back their intestines in a tarpaulin boat bag and hung them off the shower rod tied in sixty-five different fisherman's knots."

Nick looked up, surfacing, blinking.

"This is what you entertain yourself with?"

"It's funny."

"I don't see the humor."

She squinted at him. "You're blunt," she said. "You're always so blunt."

"You want me to beat around the bush?"

She looked away. "You're morose."

"And this isn't?" He was holding out the laptop, and she turned back and snatched it from him, closing it, hugging it in to her chest like a precious child.

"You always criticize."

"Do not."

She stamped her foot at him.

"No stamps," he said. "And no boo-boo lip either."

"You don't like anything I like."

"Not true."

She lifted her chin. "I am not talking about robotics and math club and all the stuff I inherited from you. I am talking about being creative."

His eyes widened. "That garbage on your Instagram is creative?"

"Yes."

"It's gratuitous and grotesque."

She looked at her feet. "You are," she muttered. "I miss Mom."

It had a dull sort of ring to it, like a bell stuffed with sailcloth.

She padded over, stepped in close, and leaned forward slightly, resting her forehead on Nick's breastbone. He settled his chin on the top of her head and put an arm around her shoulders awkwardly, tenderly.

Then she backed off, exit stage right.

Nick sighed. He missed Melanie too, badly, every second. His wife had been a successful architect, confident, regal without trying, tall with good legs, and she loved to laugh, cook, snuggle, drink wine. She had played guitar, only chords, and she made ballroom necklaces she sold on Etsy. She was five months gone now, pancreatic cancer, and he had been left to raise Lexi by himself. He was from a family of boys, three brothers, and this was a new language, new rules that changed with the coming of the tide.

That night Nick propped the pillows behind his back and sat up in bed with his Dell Precision laptop, reading about Saltwater Sam on Lexi's Instagram account. At first he was confused as to why the comments weren't in reverse chronological order, but rather the opposite. He Googled it and saw something about an algorithm arranging posts in reference to the accounts the user followed and the steps to arranging them in order of most recent, but he clicked back to his original tab. Whatever the reason, it was better this way anyway. He could read the developing story from its inception.

The first fourteen posts were similar to what he'd read earlier, containing a line or two of cheap exposition preceding a "creative kill." There were bloody forty-inch shark saws and heavy-duty two-handed fishing tongs, old rusted chum buckets and T-handled rope-chain bone cutters.

Then the more recent stories kicked in, taking on a narrative feel, starting a month ago.

From ancientmariner_223

"Origin Story: Saltwater Sam was born of the mist floating on the ocean in 1829, fully formed, fully grown, landing surf to sand in a patchwork midshipman's frock coat, a ghost in rags with a sailor's hat pulled down low over his eyes. He had a long jaw, thin and bone-colored. When he grimaced, it was like sandpaper on cement, and when he walked in the wind, his long coattails flew behind him like tattered flags."

barnaclebill59

"Not so! Get your story straight. Saltwater Sam was born in the traditional way, in the cold rainy season of 1829, son of Anne and Billy-Boy MacGregor, both from Cork and resituated in Liverpool because of all the openings for dock labor. As a boy, Saltwater Sam was a gateman's aid, and when he turned twenty-one, he got work on a trawling ship named *The Sunset*. Three days out at sea, he got into an argument with boatswain during a midnight poker game in the crew's quarters, claiming the higher-ranked sailor had been palming the ace of diamonds. Sammy stormed out and soon returned to cut the guy's head off with a double-bitted saddle axe."

Captainnoaheyeloveyou

"My dear fellow douchebags, both stories have merit, but the details shook out differently. The dad, Billy-Boy MacGregor, was a blacksmith who specialized in forging ship anchors and rudder stock, and he knew he could not trust his boy with even a trinket, wood nickel, or left-handed smoke-shifter. When his talentless son turned twenty-one, Dad kicked him to the curb, and it was weeks before the loser found work as a lowly wiper and oiler on *The Sunset*. You are right that the fateful poker game was three nights in, but it was Saltwater Sam who palmed a card, the king of spades, and the boatswain ran him through with a Prussian saber that was stored just behind him in the weapons barrel."

captainahab_ou812

"Children, please, this just is not the way it went down, and you are adding too many red herrings. If I may, Saltwater Sam did not die on *The Sunset,* and furthermore, his biggest crime on that ship was committed against himself, getting addicted to gambling, you know, cards, anytime he could find a game, especially in the periods that they were becalmed in the month-long expedition. Frankly, he lost everything, including the advance on his advances that he begged for from the ship's purser. When they finally docked, he was told to never return to *The Sunset,* and he was left to the elements in the freezing rain with winter coming fast on its heels, disowned by his father and left to wander the streets of Liverpool, homeless and destitute. He became a phantom in rags, slinking corner to corner, alley to alley, bone-thin and swimming in his tattered blue frock overcoat with the dirty sailor's hat pulled low over his eyes. Freakishly then, he started surfacing all over town, always at night and only when it rained. Plus, there were people who claimed to have 'Saltwater Sam Sightings' at different parts of the borough simultaneously, as he was thrown out of all kinds of pubs and inns and made to vacate the Salthouse Dock, the Gladstone Dock, the East Waterloo Dock, and various darkened stairwells on Penny Lane. He was regularly ushered out of places like Abercromby Square and was often found lying in the fetal position and shivering on the sitting benches in Otterspool Park. He slept on bridges, at the foot of the waste-mounds in the Bradbury Dust Yard, and was known to hide in the shadows of the stone gateway to the Saint James Cemetery. The bobbies knew him well, and each time they caught him sneaking around, they shook him rough like an old broken lap-puppet and shouted in his face to 'Shake a leg, buck up, and move on!'"

longjohnsilver14

"All true, and when Saltwater Sam died of hypothermia behind a dock warehouse, they put him in a burlap sack tied with a manila rope drawstring, dumping him in a mass unmarked grave crammed with the bodies of ten other vagrants at the back of the Saint James Cemetery."

marcopolosuckaduck

"Righty-o, but people still claimed to see him lurking in the shadows all over Liverpool . . . floating along the Bridgewater Canal . . . drifting near the approach-slab of the Princess Dock Bridge . . . worming his way along the low crease of the river walls."

jacksparrow2ufu

"And you were screwed from then on if you dared find a card game in a basement somewhere, or worse the back room of a bar."

john_paul_jonesnotzeppelinyouwanker

"It's called a pub, and you neglected to develop the most important detail. Card players started going missing, but only the biggest losers, and only when it was raining."

johnbarrythestud

"What did the cops do?"

john_paul_jonesnotzeppelinyouwanker

"Not much. The Dock Watch could never find witnesses, because the card games were illegal in the first place. Everyone kept mum."

johnbarrythestud

"Mum? Do we have a Brit here?"

john_paul_jonesnotzeppelinyoudick

"Piss off. If Saltwater Sam haunted your card game, you would see him for the flash of an instant before the first shuffle, a dash of a silhouette in the cellar doorway, the keg storage room, or the farthest corner at the back of the loo."

jacksparrow2ufu

"And when you lost all your bank, he'd be waiting for you outside in the shadows with the rain pouring through them, waiting for you to put up your collar or open your umbrella, and at that very moment he'd jump from the dark and render you helpless, stuffing you in a burlap sack with a drawstring."

johnbarrythestud

"To throw you over his shoulder like a sack of grain."

jacksparrow2ufu

"And take you home to the Saint James Cemetery."

john_paul_jonesnotzeppelinyoudick

"To the unmarked grave back in the overgrowth."

Jacquescousteaucannotswim

"Burying you forever under the wood sorrel and ground ivy. Then he wouldn't surface for another twenty-three years, his age when he died of exposure."

Captainmorgan

"By the 1900s, though, he started spreading his net, haunting pubs in London, in Newhall, Whitechapel and Enfield and Soho. And sightings in the United States cropped up in the early 2000s at bed and breakfasts and cheap motels with the same name as the ship that corrupted him. To this day, he is looking for a re-do, for another dance with Lady Luck to turn it around and exit *The Sunset* a winner."

Captainhookandhismedicineshowhaha

"And the game has changed."

Captainmorgan

"It certainly has."

Captainhookandhismedicineshowhaha

"It's all about you now and the voids in your life, the holes in your soul."

Captainmorgan

"And the payout is huge."

Captainhookandhismedicineshowhaha

"Yet the cost is quite chilling."

Captainmorgan
"It's the chance of a lifetime."
Captainhookandhismedicineshowhaha
"With flesh and blood as the ante."
Captainmorgan
"So what's the name of the new game?"
Saltwatersamhimselflol
"Shave Your Bounty."
Captainmorgan
"Explain."
Saltwatersamhimselflol
"In time. Lexi Shockley, how badly do you miss your mum?"

Nick's body jerked as if he had just stuck a fork in a socket. He had been lulled into the story, into the weird slow-burn of a plot-line with so many hands taking up the proverbial fountain pen that the name-titles themselves had sort of blurred into one voice. In fact, about halfway through he hadn't even been reading them.

Saltwatersamhimselflol

Nick cast the laptop to the bedspread, threw off the covers, and swung his bare feet to the floor. It probably was one voice, one clever predator, and the bastard knew Lexi by name. He pushed off the bed.

He froze there on the hardwood. His door was coming open, swinging slowly inward, no one pushing the knob from the hall side.

"Hello?" he said, "Lex?"

Something dashed across the doorway out there like a splat of blue paint in the shape of a sailor's torn frock coat. Nick's mouth had gone dry and sour. The receding steps were headed toward Lexi's room.

He took a step to follow, and outside there was a flash and a boom of thunder followed hard by the moan of the wind blowing into the rain and shaping it into driving sheets like mighty sails bloating, swelling, and bursting to the glass of the bedroom window out there in torrents.

Nick raced through the doorway in his undershirt and flannel pajama bottoms, bare feet, stumbling, catching himself, and the hallway seemed slanted, a cheap funhouse effect, and the ceiling light was flickering like a strobe. Lexi's door was closed, and Nick pictured some bone-thin miscreant in rags and tatters, leaning over her, smiling with his teeth.

He leapt forward and stopped short, put his hand on the knob. The hall wasn't tilted, and he simply had to change the damned bulb in the ceiling light. This was not a damned haunting; he had an intruder. He pushed the door open and crossed the threshold.

Cold rain spattered the floor, coming through the open sliding barn door windows that led to the short deck Lexi liked to use in the warmer weather for doing homework and math puzzles on her phone. The long dusty-rose curtains ballooned and billowed on the hard wind.

The comforter was askew, the pillows tossed.

The bed was otherwise empty.

Nick walked across the muddy jobsite with the morning sun at his back, head down, eyes reddened from weeping. Memories from last night were a clutter of horrific images telling the story of his daughter's untimely demise: the 911 call he made from the house while changing clumsily, quickly, too slowly into jeans, a tee, and his Wolverines, and then the second call from the car, this time admitting the supernatural part of this as he sped across town to the Sunset Motel, taking two wrong turns, the second too wide, and he'd bashed into someone's steel trash can, pushing it along for half a block under the fender, grating, screaming, and when he finally arrived there were police barricades and red and blue streaks rotating from the mounted lightbars on the squad cars parked all around the structure.

Out back, they had tackled him fifteen feet away from Lexi's body, rumpled in the mud with her head looking back at him over

171

her shoulder blades. He had identified her officially at the county morgue, her skin chalky blue, lips waxen, hair wet and straggled across her forehead like varicose veins.

At the station during the first of three questioning sessions with a corporal, junior detective, and a sergeant, he discovered on his phone that the Instagram messages about and from Saltwater Sam had vanished. He had asked that one of their techies try to retrieve the information, but first they claimed they couldn't, and second, it changed the tone of the interview to one that felt more like interrogation. By the time they were through with him, it was 4:00 a.m., and he felt guilty that he just wanted an hour of sleep.

The parking lot was filled with cruisers that looked like an ambush of sleeping white Bengal tigers under the grainy glow of the LED's, but the visitors section was vacant for all but Nick's Mercedes EQS 450.

He pressed the button on his key fob, and a call on his cell phone buzzed in his pocket as if the former had triggered the latter. He got out his iPhone and stared at the screen.

It said "Marlene Shockley Mobile" with the Caller ID pic of his wife that they got taken at the mall a few months before she lost all her hair.

He continued looking with his mouth ajar. It went to voice-mail, and he clicked to it, put it to his ear.

"Honey, I just got home," she said. "I took the redeye flight, because they canceled tomorrow's conference, and I have been trying to reach you. Where are you? Where is Lexi, and why did you leave her deck door open in the middle of a rainstorm? I'm worried, please call."

Numbly, Nick got in his car and closed the door. He was aware of two realities now, the first the one more familiar, the one that had Marlene suffering so badly from the chemo last spring that it had shaken Nick's faith in God. The love of his life had been transformed from a tall striking beauty to a crooked, spidery invalid who needed help up the stairs, help eating, help in the bathroom; she had suffered every breath, and she had wanted to die two months before she actually did. Bitterly, Nick had wanted it too, and that was what shook his faith in himself.

He ran his fingers through his hair.

The newer reality, just as potent, contained one horrible consistency with its freakish metaphorical stepsister. Lexi was dead in both. His lovely darling, his precious baby, and now he could look forward to telling Marlene about this, watch it sicken her with loss, worse than working through the six stages of grief, worse than fifteen rounds of chemo and the hemodialysis when her kidneys quit on her.

Analytically, he felt like some cold intellectual observing himself and criticizing the idea that he wasn't already racing home, pedal to the metal to fall into the arms of his soulmate brought back from the dead.

But . . . no.

Not yet.

Maybe there was a chance for a third reality. Maybe the words to cast the magic spell were etched under a strip of cheap paneling in room #13 at the Sunset . . . a message scrawled on a piece of parchment paper in a bottle floating in the toilet tank . . . the code, combination, and secret incantation written in blood across the mirror on the inner lid of a jewelry box hidden in a void behind a loose piece of cheap off-white subway tile.

Or more likely, Saltwater Sam was waiting for him there, to frighten him, toy with him, tell him his options.

Nick turned back, shielding his eyes against the sun blaring across the horizon. It felt as if he was saluting. Sergeant Barnes didn't signal acknowledgment, but kept his position standing on the other side of the caution tape. Nick glanced to the right. Over by the bulldozers, crawlers, pipe layers, and wheel loaders, the construction trailer's light was on, a shadow passing through it. The job was live again, just as they had said it would be back at the station, only they had said it would start up tomorrow. They were wrong, it seemed. Soon the foreman in the trailer would amble over to Sergeant Barnes, and this little party would be over.

He turned back to the "Starboard Cuddy Cabins" and put his foot on the concrete stairway. The whole thing tilted, the funhouse effect, as if he was suddenly wearing fishbowl lenses making things swim through one another and swell. One careful step at a time, he trudged up the first three without falling, but he had to use the paint-chipped handrail. At the midpoint the whole kit and kaboodle dipped left as if trying to pour him out of a carafe, and he had to grip the rail with both hands. There was a moment that he realized Officer Barnes saw nothing more than a regular set of concrete stairs, and poor Nick embroiled in this strange dog and pony show, acting as if the wind was blowing him around like a bad street mime.

He made it to the first landing, and the wind kicked up. When he reached the second, the rain came in, pitter-patter to a steady drumming, and by the time Nick mounted the third it was howling in driving sheets. Here under the overhang the concrete changed, suddenly uneven like bone, the sole, the deck, and the ribs over the keel framed like that of a nineteenth-century trawling ship: pitted and skeletal.

He burst out to the walkway, his arm crooked at the elbow in front of his face, clothes soaked and heavy on him, and he made it to room #13, grabbing the doorknob and pushing inside, falling hard to the floor made of butternut planking.

He struggled to his feet, hair in his eyes, and he was in a cabin under the poop deck across from a figure sitting behind a big barrel, forearms resting against the curve of the croze, the flat surface of the head no doubt, to be used as a poker table. The figure himself was vibrating while sitting still, like stark animation, rough drafts on multiple pages in the corner of a charcoal sketchbook, thumbed up and flipping closed to create the illusion of living. He

174

had on old deck shoes and duck cloth trousers rolled above the knee, a long and tattered blue frock coat and a dirty straw sailor's hat pulled low over his eyes.

A mahogany swivel chair, most probably stolen from the captain's quarters, materialized at the near side of the barrel.

"Please," said Saltwater Sam, voice pale and raw. Nick approached and he sat. The repulsive spirit got right down to business.

"We're cutting it close, mate," he said. "You've got one hand to play before they demolish this building, sealing the rip in the hull."

"Explain," Nick said.

"No time," Sam answered. "This isn't grade school or a court of law, and I don't owe ya nothing. We're going to play 'Shave Your Bounty.'"

"What if I refuse?"

"You won't."

"Why me?"

He grinned, there was dirt in it. "Why not?" he said. "You had a family. I had no family, no home to speak of, no roots."

Nick made fists. Rainwater dripped off his nose.

"Enough of the pity party," he said. "Let's have a game. I want my daughter back and I want the version of my life that includes my wife, healthy as a racehorse, waiting for me at home."

The thing licked his teeth. "Fine," he said, "let's play. In the current reality, Lexi is dead and dear Marlene got a restart, a whole new timetable, her new worth in remaining years hidden of course."

"What do you mean, worth in years?" said Nick.

"Catch up," he said dryly. "The years themselves are currency, each a valuable poker chip. Still, it is not Marlene's bounty to be dealt here on the table and divided like treasure. It is yours." He leaned back and swept his bony hand palm-up across the playing surface of the barrel. Suddenly, a piece of unlined paper was there and a quill and inkwell. "And so," said Saltwater Sam, "how many of the years left in your life will you give to poor Lexi? Just how much of the back end of your remaining years will you shave off, in order to rekindle and fortify hers?"

Nick's eyes blazed. "How many do I have left?" he said softly.

The aberration put the points of his elbows on the chair's armrests and clasped his bone fingers in the church and steeple thing.

"Who can tell?" he said. "You have kept yourself in reasonable shape, but you are fifty-three. People die at fifty-three, fifty-nine, sixty-one, eighty-one, or even one hundred and three. Who can tell?"

"You repeat yourself a lot."

"No rest for the wicked."

"But what if I go over my bounty?" he said.

Saltwater Sam nodded, like *"Okay, now you get it . . ."*

"It means you fold," he said. "You lose. Nothing changes."

"Not fair."

"Not up for discussion. It keeps you in line, keeps you conservative."

"I'm a liberal."

"Not my problem. You want three of a kind, you go short, that's the game. You risk going long, and you very well might go over, getting a guaranteed pair that excludes your daughter."

Unfair.

Not up for discussion.

And then Nick knew . . . the way to get the more winning pair with the highest return. He put his hand over his mouth and closed his eyes. Lexi had figured the same, her own choice of pairs. Hopefully, the cycle would not be able to continue once they had they bashed this shithole to pieces and carted the scrap to the dump. A rip in the hull then fixed, yes indeed, and hopefully this fiend would be sucked in and locked on the other side of it. Forever.

"I have decided," he said.

Saltwater Sam nodded. "Place your bet."

Nick Shockley leaned over the barrel and dipped the fountain pen. He made his mark. It was not a number.

Saltwater Sam leaned in and turned the page toward himself.

"A royal flush," he whispered. "Like father, like daughter." He looked up, mouth twisted, and Nick wished he could have seen the smoldering in his eyes, hidden by the brim of that dirty straw sailor's hat.

"Right then, tick-tock," the ghost said. "You choose this, and you've got to finish it yourself, finish it fast, like now, house rules."

"House rules," Nick muttered, but his mind was already steps ahead, his face hot, his heart pounding.

"There's the door," said the ghost. He scraped back his chair, and he wasn't talking about the main entrance. He was talking about the door to the back deck.

Nick pushed to his feet, and it suddenly felt as if they were at sea, the room rocking back and forth, Nick scrambling, doing zigzags like a drunk, and when he got to the door and burst to the outside, he had four last thoughts before jumping headlong to his death.

Marlene was the better parent. God, it stopped raining. His mark on the paper inside said, "All," and he heard the distinct sound of a crane starting up, the kind that could swing a ten-thousand-pound wrecking ball.

The Ghost House

Robert Frost

I dwell in a lonely house I know
That vanished many a summer ago,
And left no trace but the cellar walls,
And a cellar in which the daylight falls,
And the purple-stemmed wild raspberries grow.

O'er ruined fences the grape-vines shield
The woods come back to the mowing field;
The orchard tree has grown one copse
Of new wood and old where the woodpecker chops;
The footpath down to the well is healed.

I dwell with a strangely aching heart
In that vanished abode there far apart
On that disused and forgotten road
That has no dust-bath now for the toad.
Night comes; the black bats tumble and dart;

The whippoorwill is coming to shout
And hush and cluck and flutter about:
I hear him begin far enough away
Full many a time to say his say
Before he arrives to say it out.

It is under the small, dim, summer star.
I know not who these mute folk are
Who share the unlit place with me—
Those stones out under the low-limbed tree
Doubtless bear names that the mosses mar.

They are tireless folk, but slow and sad,
Though two, close-keeping, are lass and lad,—
With none among them that ever sings,
And yet, in view of how many things,
As sweet companions as might be had.

Misery Cottage

H. A. Manhood

The Ragged Poet drew up his knees and spoke through the darkness:

"It happened but yesterday, as the beads roll," he said. "A spume-coloured horse was sharing my straw, gift of a tinker who had died in my bed. It was an excellent horse as to soul, but weak in body, even after it had been washed twice over. One morning, the roof of its mouth began to swell in horrible manner and I went in search of medicine. Three out of six crofters ran their fingers along their shelves and shook their heads, but the remaining three spoke similar words: "Jordan Sedile is your man," they said. "Misery Cottage is the address, the hardest nut in Johnstrip Forest." I did not wait to ask why the cottage was so sadly named but took the road after a word with the horse.

Shadows were losing their precise noon crispness when I stepped from the forest into a neat buttonhole of sedgeland with a pond in the middle. I was completely lost, no uncommon happening since my eyes have wills of their own. It was an agreeable pond, laced about with willow herb and agrimony, and well disked with lily pads, with here and there a yellow lily placed like a parted orange upon a green-bronzed dish. Moorhens were plying fussily between the stems, their brilliant mounted black heads jerking with amusing regularity. I wondered at their composure, but only until I saw that they were watched by one other beside myself, a child of about ten years, obviously possessed of the gift of animal understanding. She was sitting cross-legged upon the brink, crooning a bright endless song as she rocked a doll made of a wooden ladle and a stuffed coatsleeve in her arms. She had not seen me. Twice she broke off the song to utter an abusive warning to the bullheads of the pond, and once she spat upon the water as if in disgust at some underhanded method of attack. She was thin, but seemingly healthy as a wild animal. Her only garment was a short ragged frock of moreen, once white, but now shot with many stains as if she habitually dined upon it, the bodice bulging like a bird crop by reason of the accumulation of oddments stored within. Her legs and feet were bare, a cinnamon brown in colour, so finely scarred as to have the appearance of being wrapped in ragged red veiling. Her black, grass-powdered hair was drawn hack and tied tightly with an old bootlace, the thick tuft hopping from side to side with her every movement as if protesting against such restriction. Her face, by some God-whim, was only light-touched with brown, thin and small, reminding me of a netsuke in its sharp perfection.

Only the need of a true direction forced me to approach. The break in the harmony was very definite. The song seemed to solidify in her throat and she bounced to her feet, holding the doll protectively behind her, staring with an angry intensity that was almost numbing in its fierceness. Her eyes were a true tortoiseshell in colour.

"What d'you want?" she demanded.

Her voice had the quality of a splinter of wood driven into the flesh. She was trembling on the verge of flight. I came no nearer, but explained hurriedly.

"Misery Cottage . . . Jordan S-E-D-I-L-E? What d'you want him for? You want one of his old horse-cures? Oh!"

Her expression softened to one of detached amusement. She brought the doll to the front and reassured it: "Wants a silly old horse-cure, he does. . . ." She pointed towards me, appeared to listen to the doll's reply and sat down again with the loose ease of a puppy, chewing a windlestraw, no longer interested.

"Well?" The true direction seemed as far away as ever. Thought of that swollen mouth made me impatient.

She turned her head and stared: "Go to hell!"

"Perhaps I will after I've been to the cottage . . ."

Her face rippled and she whispered to the doll: "He may go after he's been to the cottage . . ." And then she chuckled: "Do you want to know the way there too?"

"If it's no trouble."

She laughed long and delightedly, the sound reminding me of a spinning gem. Her eyes became much more friendly. She studied my shoes, creeping forward a little on hands and knees to see them the better: "You've gone two-three miles out of your way, or did you paddle through the bog on purpose?"

"Not on purpose, but I'm not sorry I paddled. I've never seen a marsh warbler before . . ."

"A what?"

"A marsh warbler—little brown bird."

"Oh! the little brown birdies in the basket trees who've toggled the tunes of all the other birds." She pursed her lips and whistled a thin unmistakable mixture of the song of the goldfinch, blackbird, robin and redpoll. And then she laughed, clucked like a hen and forgot the whole performance. With great care she began to scrub the bowl of the ladle with a corner of her frock, scolding the while with mock ferocity.

I came and sat down beside her. She edged away a little, but did not run. I offered a piece of angelica and she refused it with an acid curse, mistaking its quality. For several minutes she watched me munching, plainly puzzled, and then she held out a tarnished hand: "Please," she said. And, after the first hesitant mouthful: "Bloody good!" Hunching her shoulders with pleasure she came a little nearer and laid the doll between us as if in token of trust. I lifted a spider from the coatsleeve skirt and made inquiry:

"What is its name?"

Staring out of the corners of her eyes she replied: "Billy

Bastard," and it was clear that the word held no particular meaning for her.

"A good name," said I, preparatory to suggesting another less vivid.

"Of course it is." Anger flickered and passed. She parodied a lost peewit and suddenly caught at my hand, comparing it with her own, grimacing at the black cusps of her nails:

"You must be a lazy swine to have hands like that," she said. "You should see my father's hands—hard as hoofs and strong!" Her face drooped, quivering with an unexplained sadness, and then she tossed her head: "Why. I've seen him knock nails in with them!"

"A father to be proud of. . . ."

She nodded emphatically, eyes dark and brimming.

"Would you mind telling me his name?"

She shook her head as if to empty it of sadness and tears broke upon my hands like summer rain:

"Depends whether you're buying or selling a horse. *Mister* Sedile most of 'em call him until they get round the corner and then it's 'that bloody rogue Sedile.' Sometimes I spit on them out of a tree as they pass but it doesn't seem to do any good. . . ."

"So Jordan Sedile is your father?"

"Yes, though he doesn't want to be!"

"Doesn't want to be?"

'No! He hates me—hates me like hell, d'you hear?" She pounded her body, tears welling, choking: "Wants to sell me, he does, just like a horse, and I love him so. . . . It hurts . . . it hurts . . ."

I held her close and for a while she imagined I was her father, grown loving by a miracle. She tucked her head inside my jacket, buttoning and unbuttoning my waistcoat with blind fingers, sobbing with painful feeling. Only slowly, as trodden grass revives, did she recover. Lifting a shame-flushed, tear-wet face she sniffed until I begged her not to and suggested in a cold little voice that we should go home:

"You'd better be seeing about that horse-cure." Her tone admitted of no further confidences.

Rising hastily, she shook herself, snatched up the doll, thumped it and marched off, the oddments in the pouch of her frock bumping and chiming together, the tuft of hair swinging jauntily. I followed, at a considered distance, praying for a return of her former mood.

For perhaps ten minutes we walked with bottled tongues, she making her own path through the hassock grass and ferns, avoiding the larger flowers. Grass and fern merged into a gorse-bronzed brake tunnelled with rabbit bores in such a wholehearted way as to suggest that giant fingers had been poked at random through the lattice of stems. Brambles caught and lifted the moreen frock at every step, thrushes and blackbirds bubbling joyful on all sides, as if inspired by the sight of her young body. A bread-soft oak trunk lay across the way. A hop and a jump carried her safely over. I thought to do likewise, unaware of the marsh puddle upon the farther side. I did not overbalance, simply remained standing like a newly planted branch, ankle deep in singularly rich mud. She turned at sound of the splash, lips parted expectantly, sinking slowly to her knees, weakened with laughter, charmed by the word or so that I let fall. Somewhat recovered, I came up with her and ventured to wonder if she would give attention to my mud-freaked face. Very willingly she licked a corner of her frock and caught hold of my head . . . only just in time did I produce a handkerchief. She thought it rather a pity to use clean linen for such a purpose, but did not argue. Under her hand I became more or less wholesome again and possessed of candid information as to my facial peculiarities. She was still laughing when we entered the forest. One after the other she drew up her legs inside her frock and wiped away the cuckoo-spit, looking like a reeling heron as she did so. Sometimes tossing the doll high into the air and catching it as it fell, she proceeded to describe the way.

The forest was cathedral-like in its vaulting at that point, stately beeches supporting a gold-dipped eiderdown of jade green high above. The bunched finger trunks had a dim purple, old marble magnificence. It was very quiet, and but for the birds almost like being inside a great balloon. Here and there spouts of sunshine seemed to break through the crescent drifts of leaves; sometimes a bird clipped off a length and wheeled up into the green, spilling its happiness, causing leaves to flash like parried blades as it settled. Birds were many, not often seen, only heard. Now came to us the trembling cry of a woodwren, in deep despair because none responded to its insistent, double-belling summons; now the murmur of wood pigeons, lazily pumping their bottles full of smooth bubbling liquid. Blackbirds fluted undecidedly, as if puzzled by the echo, a solitary chiffchaff offering placid explanation from a natural bressumer; but, finest of all, was the returning, clear-passioned song of the blackcap, bright and compelling as its watchful eyes. Rhododendrons were in every glade, trusses of warm violet bloom seeming to be listening for an echo of their own sweetness. The child had long ago held a christening over many of the flowers and was not interested in their actual names: marigolds were "sunheads," nettles "devilwhiskers," meadowsweet "milk-froth," and tansy "button-cards," all peculiarly appropriate. An unevenly raked area beneath an oak was nearly explained: "Pheasants, mumping for acorns." She picked up two snails linked in a love embrace, showed them to me, whispered to them and replaced them carefully in the shade of a leaf. At one point she sniffed, pounced forward and held up a green grass snake, caught by the tip of its tail: "Sleepy blasted things, snakes," she said. Give 'em a bellyful of sunshine and they think they're God A'mighty. No good talking to 'em—they're deaf as water. Off with you!" She clapped her hands and the snake rippled away with the ease of quicksilver down a slope, and we went on, passing beyond the beeches, worming our way through thickets of blackthorn and holly, birch and hazel, butterburs flapping their ear-like leaves irritably about our legs. Before a particular elm she halted, climbed ten yards in ten seconds, dipped inside her frock and emptied a twisted leaf full of ant's eggs into the nesting hole of a green woodpecker. Over a rayed bunch of feathers beneath a thorn bush she made brief but accurate comment: "Some old hawky been skinning a thrustboy." The scrub became threadbare and we stepped into a turned seam of road that seemed not to curve in all its length. In a distant chine was Misery Cottage, a brooch securing the cape of forest upon the shoulder of earth. Inquiry elicited the fact that there was no other dwelling within a mile and a half.

Progress down the road was for her a continual shuttling from side to side since she had a fondness for wild strawberries. Whenever the thought occurred to her she skipped up with a spray of berries, dropped it into my hand and was off again. My tentative questioning secured for me a patchwork of information. It seemed that she had attended school in two parishes, but not for long. The children in each, I was informed, had been quite daft, but almost human compared with the teachers. She thought of God as a kind of almighty blacksmith whose word was blasting and whose name was convenient to express surprise. She could cook a little, snare rabbits, ride "any knacker under the sun," and knew where babies came from. To know more was unnecessary. Most of the people she had met "certainly ought to have been drowned when they were hatched." Her friends included a gamekeeper who could shoot straight when he was dead drunk, numerous gypsies and horses, a swan, a rabbit with only three legs, a badger, an adder which lived in the scrub behind the cottage, and several cows, an entirely satisfactory company in her opinion. Useless to point out the danger of friendship with badger or adder; they were her friends, reject them and you yourself were rejected. Her loyalty had a rare shining Christ-colour. In an evil moment I asked her name and her gaiety was quenched:

"Haven't got one," she muttered.

"But surely . . . ?"

"No, I tell you!"

"But doesn't he ever call you anything?"

"Nothing nice or true—only dirty, stringy words. Most of the time he don't take any notice of me at all . . . just as if I was scabby! Names his horses but not me—don't think I'm worth one, damn him!" She regretted the curse at once and reached out a hand as if to snatch it back: "No, no, I don't mean that . . . I don't mind being without a name if he thinks it best—only he don't ever think about it at all. I had to make up one to use at school . . . just like wearing someone else's drawers. . . ."

Her lips came together and her face set into hard unnatural lines, and she would say no more, but ran on ahead, maintaining a distance of a dozen yards between us until we came to the cottage.

A staring eyed, sulking place it was, of flint with brick corners, hung with rags of ivy, a perfect beggar among cottages, well deserving of its name. Looked at from the road it seemed to be bending over to gaze at its own reflection in the muck-clouded pond at its feet. The walls bulged everywhere as if it were with child. A basket had been clapped over the central one of the three chimneys—evidently to discourage nesting birds—giving it the appearance of an erring madam under escort. A brass bed-knob glared shrewishly from a cur-rainless upper window. Upon one side of the crumbling porch was a cracked chamber pot filled with dead ferns, and on the other a twisted snake of piping with a dribbling, blackened tap for head. The skull of a horse lay upon a lower sill, together with an old boot and half a loaf dried to a chalky hardness. The surrounding garden, tenanted only a lonely bullace and vagabond mauve and white mallows and dust-heavy nettles, had a disheartened, trampled appearance, vastly unsettling to the soul. A single smudgy duck floated upon the pond, diving under every minute or so as if determined to commit suicide. You could smell misery even if its presence had not been advertised by the chalked copper-lid nailed to the doddered oak by the gate, surely the most disquieting notice ever displayed. Each letter was as firm as a hoof-print, all except the last, which threatened to slip off the board altogether:

FOR SALE
HEALTHY CHILD
PRICE FIFTY POUNDS

—a tragedy sketched in just seven words.

Adjoining the cottage was an almond-shaped meadow with a surprisingly substantial stabling in a far corner. Evidently Sedile gave more thought to the comfort of his animals than to his own. Three stallions peered over the crippled ox-fence as we drew near, wheeling away with concerted snortings as the child stamped her foot and waved her hands. She watched to see if my eyes would find the chalked lid, nodding mournfully as I read, urging me forward with scowling petulance. The gate almost dropped to pieces under her touch. In angry silence she rewedged it and went on up the broken path. A thin rasping informed her as to her father's whereabouts and she led the way to the back of the cottage. Jordan Sedile was sharpening a knife upon the scullery sill. He glanced up as we approached, staring with antagonistic intentness. The child did not look at him, but at a spot just above his head:

"Horse-cure," she said, flinging a hand towards me, and ran on into the house, holding the doll tightly, as if afraid for its life.

Without a word Sedile continued to work the blade, only straightening when the edge was of a satisfactory keenness. He was all that I had imagined him to be, a massive, scorched-looking man approaching fifty, deliberately truculent in manner and speech, with dark, starved eyes that reminded me of cathedral alcoves, so shadowed were they. He had not shaved for many days. His burnt-earth red hair bristled like a bedeguar, and it was not difficult to conceive the existence of irritating gall-flies within his skull. The fit of his clothes suggested that he had bought them by weight. His shirt was of a greenish serge, unbuttoned to expose a black-haired dough of chest. The cuffs of his tweed jacket were turned back and had worn out in that position. His horse-worn breeches sagged about his thighs as if weighted with horseshoes

188

of lead, a nail replacing the top-most button. His leggings and boots were sweat-darkened and stirrup-bitten. He smelt strongly of horse, his long calloused hands emphasizing his understanding of them. Stropping the knife very deliberately upon his palm he riveted a dozen words:

"Want a horse-cure? What sort?—a cure for lampas? Far gone? H'm!"

He looked me up and down, peered round me as if suspecting that someone was in hiding behind, sniffed, and without further comment strode into the house, his footsteps echoing upon the uncovered floors like stones bounced in a barrel. The child was staring from an upper window, head supported on hands. She affected not to notice me and began repeating the chipped notes of a sparrow performing upon the gutter-head, dipping from sight as Sedile reappeared with a screw of paper in his hand:

"Try that," he grunted, and pulling the knife from his lapel, returned to the makeshift whetstone, muttering angrily to himself.

I watched him for several minutes, puzzled, reminded, oddly enough, of a sundial in a cellar. He had been badly hurt at some time and was not yet recovered, perhaps never would he whole again unless he could empty himself of rancour. An unhappy marriage, perhaps, with the child remaining as a constant reminder. I wondered whether it would be possible to startle him into speaking his mind. Crossing to the board. I studied it, hoping for revelation: "Healthy child . . . fifty pounds." A grey business . . . I had money enough. I felt eyes upon me, and, turning quickly, saw both Sedile and the child staring, the one with bitter amusement, the other with large-eyed misery. Thrusting his hands deep into his pockets, Sedile slouched across, trampling mallows underfoot heedlessly, dust rising from the nettles as if he had scorched them in passing.

"Thinking of buying?" he asked.

"I might, if it were only to provide her with a name. On what did you base the price of fifty pounds?"

Had he still held the knife he probably would have used it.

His hands crept from his pockets, strangely white, as with nettle rash, his face tightening, the bristles suddenly seeming unreal:

"I'd bloody you for that . . . only . . . only . . . Christ Almighty, man! it's not fifty pounds I'm wanting, only a fifty-pound affection. Are you blind, all of you? Haven't any of you suffered—can't you see? If I give money with her there's plenty who'll have her for the sake of the money, and if I give her away for nothing there's plenty who'll make bad use of her—but if I ask fifty pounds, only those who want her will take her. . . . Why man, I *want* her to he happy, but I, I can't feel anything but hatred for her. I've tried. God knows. . . ." His voice blurred: "But why should I explain—you wouldn't understand . . . all blind, every damned one!"

He limped away, wrapping his soul, straightening as the mask slipped into place again, taking up the knife, driving it along the sill, but without method.

I sat down upon an upturned trough near him, picking out words that would bring us to a common level:

"Not all blind, Sedile, or without understanding. It is only that those with understanding are so few that they have become cautious, hiding feeling to escape gibes. Loneliness breeds only bitterness . . ."

"Loneliness?" he tossed the knife aside and stared tiredly: "Ay, loneliness, 'tis the making and breaking of a man."

"Not the breaking of a man unless he be willing, or incomplete. Loneliness is but a state of mind. Without experiencing it we should not understand it. Once understood it can do no harm. One passes beyond it."

He caught the thought in his hands and turned it about: "You think then"—he spoke as in a rediscovered language: "You think we breed our own sorrows, that we feel hatred and loneliness simply because we don't think far enough ahead? A man is what he wants to be, is that your meaning?"

"Yes."

He shook his head: "You're wrong, that I do know. There are

some things a man can't stomach, times when it would be easier to die than be loving or charitable."

"Whoever feels that is incomplete. People have become like clocks, regulating themselves by each other. Perhaps one in every ten thousand has an original hardness, has the will to live by his own thoughts—no more."

"Easy to talk. You wouldn't be loving a man who'd hooked your wife, for instance, would you now?"

"No, but neither should I hate him. Hatred would only wear me out and amuse him. Better to ignore him altogether. If my wife found contentment with him I should feel some sort of respect for him. If her contentment endured I should be much better employed in assessing my own deficiencies than in raging at his success ..."

His eyes expressed his dubiousness: "You've the knack of argument, but I'm thinking a picture postcard of hell is mighty different from the real thing."

"Perhaps not so vastly different, since both are born of imagination."

He rasped his cheek: "H'm! You seem sound in theory, but I know of a case that'll rock you. I haven't spoken of it before...."

"That's been the trouble."

"Maybe, but I wasn't aching to collect any of those gibes you were mentioning. Perhaps I have kept it corked away too long, become cankered.... I don't know. If all the world was like you and me there wouldn't have been any need to chalk that board by the gate. They'd have had the understanding to be knowing why the sight of *her*,"—he pointed to the porch where the child was busy with her doll, pretending to feed it with pieces of bread sprinkled with sugar—"would brangle what's left of my soul. They'd have taken her from my sight, gladly. Christ, man! it's unbearable. I've tried and tried—she's mine, but I can't forget the way she came to be mine. Between ten and eleven years ago it happened, but the gall is still soft. They think I'm crazed, most of 'em hereabouts. Times I've wished I was ... a madman only thinks in patches, not all the time. I've been sliced about, that's all. I'll tell you.

"I was sixteen when I bolted from home. My mother was sound enough, but she was between the legs of the old man and didn't dare cross him. There were few who did. 'Tweazer' Sedile they called him through the town. He ran a pub called *The Pot of Jam*, down by the racecourse, and a pretty pot it was too! They used to say he was licensed to the Devil, so many souls per annum, and at times it seemed that there was more than a speck of truth in it. My mother died of cancer—she wasn't sorry . . . she seemed to dry up all at once. I remember towards the end she asked for some biscuits, something dainty to tempt her fancy, and my father sent her up half a dozen cartwheel arrowroots from the urn in the taproom. They remained on the bedside chair until she died and then he put them back into the urn. . . . That finished me. I shot the hoof one fine morning, sorning myself on a parcel of travelling copers, never giving a second thought to the two brothers and the kid sister Jennie I was leaving behind. All three took after my father, more or less, and mud can't hurt mud. I thought.

"For eighteen years after that I spun my own wheel, keeping to the horse line, roosting where I fancied—Russia, America, Nigeria . . . picking an easy living. Horses must be the religion of about a third of the folk of the world, the third that can't read. There's something about a horse, a clean, simple, beautiful something that works on you deep down. I wouldn't give much for a man who wasn't a bit hurt by the sight of a thoroughbred in action, who didn't ache to touch and possess. . . . The truest man I've ever known was a half-breed horse-thief. He couldn't help stealing horses. It scarred his soul to see one being worked like a machine. Just to see him handling a man-sick horse was like watching a plant reviving under your eyes, something you couldn't forget, something that made you want to scrub and scrub away at yourself until you were as clean as the horse. You could feel the exchange of understanding; horse and man knew something that you can't buy, can't guess at, can't share unless you give and give and give, unless you are willing to suffer the nails in your palm for your friend, for any man. . . . I know all that, just as I know there's fish in the river, but I can't feel it—that's my curse. Understanding comes like bits of music at night, but not the full, lasting understanding, or I'd not be wanting her out of my sight. . . ."

He nodded towards the child, a sickness in his eyes. She had crept close, had been listening. Sedile's glance hurt her like a thrown flint. She shook her head with pitiful anger, whispered something to the doll and, jumping to her feet, ran round the corner of the house, reappearing a moment later, stepping stealthily, keeping close to the hedge, thinking herself unobserved. Before the doddered oak she paused, raised herself on tiptoe and spat at the lid, and then, abandoning caution, scrambled into the road and ran from sight.

"Just like her mother!" husked Sedile. "If she weren't . . . O Christ ! why should it have happened to me?" Pulling a thread from his sleeve, he twisted it aimlessly round a finger, tightening it until the finger was rigid and inflamed, staring, ripping it off with vicious suddenness as if it reminded him of the root of his tragedy. When he spoke again his voice had an almost brutal, sodden force:

"I came back to the home town for no particular reason, heavy with money. A new name was painted under *The Pot of Jam*. I went inside, had a drink and made inquiry: 'Dead!' they said: 'Amen!' said I, and out I went to have a look at the racecourse. A meeting was billed for that afternoon. Within the hour I'd had a few more drinks, bought a racer that had been entered and backed her to the sky. 'Nightlight' she was called—a warning, I've thought since. The rest of the day was like one of those Punch and Judy reels, a coloured nightmare. My racer pulled off the event and my money was ten times doubled. I felt a perfect Solomon. I'd collected a few friends of a sort, and *The Pot of Jam* being the nearest pub to the course, we presently turned into it for supper and beds. The food was wasted, but the rummers fitted our hands to a nicety. We sang, played quoits with pretzels, chalked filth upon the benches, yawned and inquired about beds and women. Both were available. Drunk though I was I was still fastidious and insisted upon being provided with a virgin, convincing the old bitch of a landlady that I knew the difference. The need was met without any difficulty. I climbed into bed, and presently, through the darkness, came a naked woman. Without a word she crept in beside me.

"I awoke about dawn, feeling inside and out as if I'd lain in a midden. I drank water, flung open the window and presently crossed to have a look at the woman. She was still sleeping. I looked and looked and laughed, and she awoke, shivered, pulled the bedding over her and after a minute spoke my name as I hope never to hear it spoken again. We'd both come home. . . ."

"Good God! you don't mean . . . ?"

"Ay, that I do. It was my own sister Jennie. She'd touched bottom, come home for help, ignorant of the old man's death. In desperation she'd accepted the sin-money offered by the landlady. She hadn't taken the usual trade precautions. The child was hers— ours . . . she died bearing it. Now you will understand."

His hands dropped, dug into the earth as if they wanted to bury themselves from sight.

Sitting there by his side I cursed the imagination that I had thought was my salvation. Beauty is, after all, only a reflection of the inner mind. Trees became simply bits of wood, flowers stains and rents in a great bedsheet, birds mechanical lime producers. . . . I thought of the child and knew not which of the two was most deserving of pity. As if in response to my thought she appeared through the hedge at that moment, and came towards us, smiling queerly, one hand held behind her. Sedile did not move, only stared. She stood before us, swaying, speaking slowly, gazing at Sedile:

"I heard . . . you are going to sell me to him. You won't be able to now . . . you won't be bothered any more. I did love you so."

Her hand dropped into sight and in it was a twenty inch adder, a twisting, tawny, black scarred ribbon of horror with blue enamelled belly and an electric thread of tongue that pierced her flesh twice before I reached her. Her fingers were pinched about the tricorn head, forcing the venom into the fangs. There were more than a dozen punctures in her body. Dropping the snake, she held my legs, crying:

"You mustn't kill him . . . I made him bite . . . he didn't want to."

I lifted her. Sedile was still staring, his hands still held a scoop of dust. I was on the threshold before he awoke. Leaping forward, he tore at my arms, caught the child:

"Leave her alone! She's mine . . . mine! Take the skewbald— ride like hell . . . doctor lives by the church." He turned to the child, smiling in a naked way: "We've been pulling different ways, Jennie, you and me . . . I didn't think . . ."

The child raised a swollen hand and laid it over his mouth.

Two hours later the doctor and I entered the cottage. Sedile was sitting in a barrel chair, the child quiet and hideous in his arms. A medicine chest had been emptied on the floor beside him. There was a little fern of spilt white powder on his jacket. His lips were white and spongy. He shook his head at the doctor, speaking with choking difficulty: "Too late, she'd eaten nightshade and toadies as well. . . ." Lifting his head towards me, he nodded: "You were right—we mix our own happiness and sorrow." He brushed away the doctor, smiling down at the child, jerking a fly from the bunched frock: "Couldn't let her go all that way alone," he muttered, and so saying, died.

Papered Over

Ann K. Schwader

Delivered of her child, & from all work
unsuited to her nervous state, she rests
sequestered in this bright & airy room
with nothing to complain of—save the paper
whose tortured arabesques in sickly yellow
entice her mind. Conspire to hold it captive.

She is his wife & patient. Or his captive?
Deprived of books, of company, of work
beyond the light domestic, her thoughts yellow
& curl upon themselves when her gaze rests
against the rude impertinence of paper
with bulbous eyes that track her through the room.

At least there is a window in this room
that lets her gaze escape. No longer captive
to every senseless twisting of the paper's
conspicuous design, her fancy works
to people paths outside. Yet if it rests
in idleness too long, it fades to yellow.

Is there a hidden space behind the yellow
pattern yet unfaded—even room
enough for creeping through? The question rests
on her imagination like a captive
warning, kept suppressed too long to work
against the optic horrors of this paper.

196

Now moonlight shows a shaking in the paper,
as though some prisoner has gripped its yellow
bars in desperation at the work
to free herself. The quiet of this room
is nothing but deception. Daylight's captive
creeps out come midnight, roaming without rest.

At last she understands the secret. Rests
at ease now, plotting how to strip off paper
that twists in prison patterns, keeping captive
women from their creeping. Scented yellow
with her exertion, she secures the room,
disposes of its key, & sets to work.

Her shoulder soon rests deeply in its yellow
track worn through the paper in this room,
another captive trapped within strange works.

—After Charlotte Perkins Gilman's "The Yellow Wallpaper"

The Space

Jacob Moon

It finally happened! I'd been hoping on all my lucky stars that it would have happened before Ben left for his business trip last week. Three days in California—not forever, but it is when the only child you'll both have is sure to take her first steps at any moment. Sure enough, about an hour after he left, I was reading in the nook when Ellie stood up in the center of the room, wobbled a bit, then took six steps to where I sat. Six, my new favorite number! When she got to me, I scooped her up and twirled her around the room, both of us shrieking with excitement. Tears were streaming down my face too, partly because it meant my child was no longer an infant in my eyes, and partly because Ben had missed it. I Face Timed him once he made it to the airport, but of course she didn't walk for him. The little bugger.

Oh, exciting news—the renovations are almost done. The master bathroom looks fantastic, and although the kitchen is a definite improvement I'm not overjoyed with the glittery backsplash. It looked more subdued in the showroom. I considered asking Ben to have it ripped out, since I think it clashes with the rest of the house; these late nineteenth-century Tudors are charming, and I love that ours turned a hundred and fifty the year after we bought it. But I knew that we couldn't justify that expense, and certainly not my main wish of installing central heating. The existing radiators and the living room fireplace will have to suffice come winter. Oh, well. The nursery is last on the list. Then finally a stop to all this banging and dust. I can't wait. It's is the smallest room in the house—basically a closet, and even though it's fine for Ellie now, I know that she'll appreciate the added thirty square feet once she gets older. That's what the blueprints say we'll gain by knocking out the plaster wall that one of the former owners installed, probably to insulate the room from the north facing brick wall.

Ellie is walking everywhere now. It's amazing how fast babies adapt to their newfound independence. I'm glad I put up both baby gates, because while I was folding laundry in our bedroom the other day Ellie walked off without my realizing it. She was only gone for five seconds, but when I ran out to find where she was I saw her standing at the gate blocking the staircase leading to the main floor. I shuddered at the thought of what might have happened if the gate hadn't been there. Speaking of negative thoughts, that reminds me that Dad is going in for another procedure next week. His heart again. It makes me sad to see him so feeble these days, after he's worked so hard his whole life. As they say—youth is wasted on the young.

Another migraine yesterday. Spent the whole day in bed with the shades drawn. Thank goodness Ellie was an angel and slept most of the day. Woke up today feeling fine, a blessing because I knew Ben was coming home today and I didn't want to miss Ellie walking for him. When I heard his car pull into the driveway, I sat in the family room balancing Ellie in a standing position, my intention being to have her walk to him as he came in. A memorable homecoming! But when she saw him walk through the front door, she plopped down on all fours and *crawled* to him! I cried out in frustration, but Ben just laughed as he picked her up and kissed her. Thankfully, she did finally walk for him later on. I guess Mom was right about my stubbornness being passed on to my children as God's punishment for the trials I'd put her through as a kid.

Ben and I discussed the last renovation plans over dinner. The workers were set to arrive tomorrow. A one-day job, two at the most. I told him I wanted to do the painting and finally put up the Winnie-the-Pooh border I've been meaning to add for months.

It'll be fun to decorate the new brick accent wall, too. I've been needing to occupy myself with something other than my weekly in-person book club and caring for Ellie. Maybe another year and I'll go back to work, although if Ben had it his way I'd stay home with Ellie until she starts school. Um, no.

Once the work began, I stayed in the living room with Ellie while Ben was upstairs with the workers to help coordinate things. For an hour I listened to them bang and rip away what sounded like large chunks of wall, until a minute-long pause came, followed by Ben poking his head around the staircase opening and yelling down for me to come take a look at something they'd found. Putting Ellie in her playpen so she wouldn't be exposed to the dust, I went upstairs and found Ben and the workers discussing something as they faced the newly exposed brick wall. When they stepped aside I realized it wasn't the wall itself he'd called me upstairs to see, but a dozen large black-and-white portraits—each eighteen by twenty-four inches in size and encased in bronze-colored frames—leaning against the wall. Most of the subjects were children between about three and fifteen years of age, with two being infants cradled by their seated parents. All the subjects appeared to be from the Victorian era, evidenced by their clothing, the old-world tapestries hung behind them, and the antique furniture staged beneath or around them. Most of them had been photographed while standing, with the exception of the infants and several of the younger children. Ben picked up a standing, unsmiling child's portrait for us to view it better.

"Why does no one from back then smile?" I asked.

"No one did in those days. It took too long for the photograph to take," he said. Studying it, I was amazed at how the child—a handsome dark-haired boy of about seven and dressed in a suit—still held such youthful exuberance in his eyes after what had probably been more than a century.

That's when the head contractor stepped forward and pointed to something I hadn't seen before—a partially obscured metal stand at the boy's feet. "He's dead."

I frowned. "What?"

The contractor pointed out the ends of two metal braces extending up from the stand—one holding the boy's head in place and the other clamped firmly around his waist. "Memento Mori," he said, nodding to himself. "Photographing the recently dead in Victorian times, as commemoration. My aunt ran a studio once and told me about it." Ben and I both studied the portrait more closely. He was right. Looking through the other portraits, not only were the other children observed with similar brace-like devices holding them upright, but each of their limbs (including those of the cradled infants) were positioned unnaturally. The contractor explained that their eyelids had either been glued open or the closed lids painted to look like eyes. A closer inspection of the photos found a familiar section of exposed brick wall and window behind the hanging tapestries, one matching a section of wall and window in our living room.

Ben and I laughed it off, but later on over dinner we revisited the idea, agreeing that whoever had taken the photos had pobably once used the home as a photography studio. The apparent fact that they'd also photographed children's corpses and made them look lifelike weighed heavily on me, especially since, if true, it meant that they or someone else had intentionally sealed them behind one of the walls where my daughter slept. It was such a morbid notion that soon after I asked Ben to get rid of them. He did, and took them to an antique dealer. The man studied them and authenticated their age as being late Victorian. As for the children truly being dead or not, he couldn't be sure. Either way, I was glad they were gone, the bonus being that the frames had been worth a combined five hundred dollars. A nice offset to the work we'd just done.

About a week later something strange happened while Ben was at work that I'm not sure how to explain. I had just walked into our bedroom with a basket of laundry when I noticed our wedding photo facing backward atop the dresser. Sometimes I'll move it and the other photos beside it when I'm dusting. But I'd just dusted two days ago, and I've never once turned it around backward, out of my belief that it's bad luck. I was sure it had been facing properly several minutes before, since it's my habit to glance at our smiling faces in it every time I come or go. It probably shouldn't have bothered me enough to bring it up to Ben over dinner, but that's what I did. Deciding that he'd done it for some reason and that I must have missed noticing it before, I asked him never to turn it backward in the future, since I considered it a bad omen. He laughed and said I must have turned it, because he never touches it. That angered me, because I'd basically just told him it wasn't me, that he should know that if I asked him why he'd done something it wasn't because I'd done it and forgotten. He apologized, but still insisted he wasn't responsible. We finished dinner in silence, as I picked at my food and tried to get Ellie to finish hers, stealing little glances up at Ben to see if he had changed his mind. If he had, he didn't let on.

Something similar happened a few days later. While Ben was putting Ellie down for bed and I was getting out of the shower, I heard something fall onto the bedroom's wood floor. I turned and saw our wedding photo lying on the floor, face down. I assumed that Ben had moved it closer to the dresser's edge, and that the weight of me walking across the floor had caused it to shift slightly and fall. But as I picked it up, I remembered having been bothered enough by the first incident to put a strip of grip tape beneath both of the frame's corners and the stand itself. Replacing it in that position, annoyed that the glass had cracked, I tested it by attempting to slide it across the dresser surface. It wouldn't budge. When it still didn't move after I stomped back and forth across the bedroom floor several times, I stood staring at it, my arms crossed as a disturbing thought entered my mind. While I'd been in the shower, Ben had knocked the portrait onto the floor without bothering to replace it. Accidents happened, but I considered it a grossly insensitive thing for him not to care enough to replace it.

I took care of nearly everything else in the house, after all. But I chose to forget it for the one-off thing I hoped it was. He's been stressed at work lately, and with my postpartum causing me mood swings, I didn't want the argument for either of our sakes.

Two days later I went into our bedroom closet for something and found one of my favorite dresses missing. I'd assumed that Ben had taken it to the cleaners, since I'd asked him to take a different dress, and that he'd gotten them confused. But later that day, after I'd come back from a walk with Ellie and was making lunch, I found it in the kitchen trash can, ripped to shreds. I stared at it dumbly for several moments before bursting into tears. Ben has always hated it because he thinks it's too short to be worn in public. The last time I wore it to his colleague's cocktail party he complained all evening that the other men he worked with were ogling me. I remember giving him a half-hearted promise on the way home that I'd donate it with some other things the following day, opting to appease his sometimes overly jealous streak in lieu of my own desire to wear whatever the hell I wanted. But that had been more than a month ago, and I'd never donated it. Surely he would have been upset to see it still hanging there. But could his jealousy possibly have been severe enough to warrant him ripping it (not cutting it) into shreds and disposing it like so much trash?

I stewed all day, picking up my phone a dozen times and beginning to dial his work extension before hanging up. I felt silly bothering him at the office over something he probably meant no ill will over. I *had* promised to get rid of it, after all. Still, I found myself anxious all day, unable to concentrate and staring out the bay window at the leafless trees. When he finally walked through the front door at five thirty, I was already a wreck. He sensed something was wrong right away and asked me about it. I told him. When I'd finished, he stood with a perplexed expression on his face before denying it and asking if I was joking.

"Why would I joke about something like that?" I asked him, bitterness tinging my voice. When I showed him the torn-up dress, he gave me a look I haven't seen since our early dating life when he'd caught me lying about another man. I was twenty at the time, and regretted it so much that I never lied to him about a man after that. Now, I wasn't sure what bothered me more, him thinking that I was lying and blaming him for the dress, or his silent insinuation that someone else had been over. I was still so angry later that night that I beat him to the punch and slept on the living room couch, with Ellie in her Pack 'N Play beside me. I slept better than I thought I would, only waking once to go to the bathroom and another time due to a weird dream where Ellie was whispering in my ear. Dream-Ellie had used more advanced vocabulary than the occasional 'mama' and 'dada' she actually knows. I remember waking and rolling over to find her sleeping peacefully, a smile on my lips because it had seemed so real, and sweet to hear how she might sound as a slightly older child.

Make-up sex is only as good as the extended afterglow it produces, I think. Ben and I have always been good that way—quick to fight but quicker to forgive. I woke to the smell of bacon and pancakes, and shuffled into the kitchen with Ellie on my hip to find Ben standing at the stove wearing the *Want My Meat?* apron I'd given him last Christmas as a gag. "Yes, please," I said, letting him see my eyes linger over the apron's words. I put Ellie upstairs in her crib before we made fast love in the bedroom, then ate breakfast with Ellie stuffing pancakes into her mouth. We didn't speak about the dress, concentrating instead on his new account at work and our upcoming trip to the coast. I can't speak for Ben, but for my sake I chalked the dress incident up to one of those things in life that are either simply inexplicable or are of such minor consequence that it doesn't pay to overthink them. Mom taught me that.

Life went on uneventfully until a week or so later, when something odd happened while I was putting Ellie down for bed. She'd been sleeping with us the past few nights, since I'd felt the nursery had seemed much colder and darker with the newly added space. Sophie, our cat, is more human than animal at times, and began displaying an immediate overprotectiveness toward Ellie from the time we brought her home from the hospital. Ever since, she's shown the deep maternal instinct to Ellie that I have no doubt she would have shown to her own litter had we not had her spayed, going so far as to sleep in her room whenever Ellie does. No doubt sensing a normal bedtime routine, Sophie followed me up the stairs into the nursery. Moments after I'd entered the darkened room and laid Ellie in the crib, Sophie emitted a loud hiss from behind me.

The hairs on the back of my neck immediately stood on end, and my exposed skin turned to gooseflesh. I knew what she'd hissed at before I'd spun around: a mouse. I'd seen them occasionally in the house, including the nursery. Now, as I clutched my face with both hands and stared wide-eyed into the strip of darkness of the room's newly opened space, I imagined some long-fanged rodent with tufts of matted hair crouching there. Ben has laid traps after we've seen them scurry from behind the refrigerator or heard them scratching behind the baseboards. But this wasn't me hearing a sudden "snap" of a sprung trap in the middle of the night, Ben snoring beside me in bed. It was here, a very present danger. I wanted to step forward to slap on the light, afraid of what I'd see but not wishing to confront it in the dark. Ever the protector, Sophie sprang in front of me and stood between me and the darkened space, her back arched and tail straightened, with claws extended. I called her name, but she refused to move. She hissed into the darkness again, a long, primal sound I've never heard from her before, until she finally heeded my call of her name. Even then, she kept a keen eye on the rectangle of blackness the hallway light wouldn't penetrate, and only seemed to relax once I steeled myself to turn the light switch on to find nothing there.

Maybe the fright was a good thing. Ben and I had sex again before going to sleep. Twice in one day for the first time since I can remember. Afterward, lying sweating beside each other in bed, he joked that maybe we should demolish the archway in the kitchen next. We both laughed.

The laughter was short-lived, because Dad died the next day. It was sudden. He'd been over at the house the day before to see Ellie's remodeled room, and he'd seemed fine climbing the staircase. A heart attack at home. Nothing anyone could have done, even if they'd been standing there with a phone in their hand, the doctors said. I'm crushed and feel empty. We gave him a beautiful service the following Saturday, sans flowers and dirges, since Dad never wanted those. It gave me a strange comfort knowing he didn't have to go through life without Mom anymore. People always comment how peaceful the dead seem lying in their caskets. Seeing him like that at the funeral made me think about those dead children propped up in braces, their heads and bodies supported, their eyes glued open or the lids painted. Even the infants' chubby cheeks, probably from cotton the embalmer had stuffed into their mouths. As creepy as those thoughts seemed to me, I couldn't help but understand that to those children's families the act of posing them dead like that had been one of reverence. Who was I to say what was macabre? Maybe in a hundred years people will be aghast at me keeping Mom and Dad's ashes on the mantle as I've chosen to do.

Ben took a few days off work but finally went back the Monday after the funeral. I've gone back to having Ellie sleep in her own room again, even though there's still something about the nursery I don't like: its coldness. And the darkness that even her lamp and hallway light don't seem to reach. Ben says that the exposed brick wall might be causing the temperature to drop a few degrees, but it seems colder than that. I haven't seen or heard any mice recently, but as a precaution I asked him to set more traps in the crawlspaces and attic. He just nodded.

Then, a few nights later in the middle of the night, something happened that even my faintest sensibilities could not attribute to mice: the sound of footsteps in the upstairs hallway. I'd assumed

Ben had woken to get a drink from downstairs or to use the bathroom with the light off, but when I rolled over he was there beside me, asleep. My next thought was that somehow Ellie had gotten out of her crib and was sleepwalking up and down the upstairs hallway. But that was ridiculous. The crib was certified childproof, and even if she'd somehow gotten out there was no way she could have produced the quickly paced, heavy footsteps I'd heard. I propped myself up onto one elbow and turned my ear toward the open bedroom door to listen for the noise again. When it didn't come for another minute, I lay back down—but then I heard the footsteps again, this time moving in the direction of the nursery.

I should have woken Ben. Ours is a relatively safe neighborhood, but a house down the street was burglarized one night last year while the family was asleep. No one was hurt, and the burglar ran from the home when confronted by the husband. Despite the rarity of such a thing happening again, it wasn't out of the question. Stupidly, I eased out of bed and crept to the doorway, peeking in the direction I'd heard the footsteps and tiptoeing down the bare floorboards. Ellie's room is at the end of the hall nearest the staircase. In the hallway nightlight's glow I detected what I thought to be slight inward movement from her bedroom door, and a barely audible creak from the rusty hinge. My heart began to pound, and all my senses heightened as motherly instinct overcame my body. I was certain that an intruder was now entering the room where my baby daughter slept.

I threw the door open and flipped the light on. Nothing, except Ellie lying asleep in her crib and Sophie curled up on the floor nearby. I picked Ellie up and hugged her warm form close to my chest. She stirred awake, but I shushed her and she fell immediately back to sleep. As I left the room with her still clutched to me, I glanced back at the darkened space where those portraits had been hidden away in the wall for a century or more. Thinking of them made me shiver. I know it's irrational, but as I closed her door behind me and hurried back into our bedroom—loyal Sophie on my heels—I decided to have a serious talk with Ben about it in the morning.

When I brought up the strange things that have happened since our renovation, adding the footsteps I'd heard the night before, he rolled his eyes. "Footsteps?" he asked, giving me that look a parent gives an over-imaginative child. "Yes," I said, annoyed he wasn't taking me seriously. When he laughed, I lost it, slamming the glass I'd been holding onto the counter harder than I'd intended. It shattered, and a shard cut my finger. Holding my bleeding finger beneath the running tap, I told him in no uncertain terms that I was not imagining it, going so far to say that I now believed that by selling those portraits we'd somehow displaced entities in the house we shouldn't have.

"What do you want me to do, hire a priest to come sprinkle holy water?" he asked.

"No. I was thinking of buying back the portraits, then burning them," I said.

His jaw dropped. "You can't be serious."

"I am. What's the name of the place you sold them to?"

He shook his head. "This is crazy. Knocking down that wall has caused more trouble than it's been worth."

I considered something, then came to lay a hand on his chest. "Agreed. We'll burn them and let those children's spirits go where they're supposed to. Then we'll close the space back up to set things right."

He gave me a stern look. "Look, I know you're still reeling from—"

"You have no idea what I'm reeling from," I said, incensed that he'd tried to feel for me. "Please don't ever do that."

We went back and forth for the next hour, until finally Ben threw up his hands and told me he was tired of hearing about it, that if that's what I really wanted to do, he'd go buy them back in the morning and call the contractor to redo the job. Ben may not be an overly prideful man, but he's still a man. Another thing my mother taught me was always to allow a man to save face whenever possible. If made sense to me that he'd be embarrassed to undo the work we'd just paid to have done. I'd come up with a way to prevent that, if I could.

We were in luck, sort of. All the portraits were still there, save for one. An antique collector had bought one of them the day before, he said, but privacy laws prohibited him from disclosing the man's name. When Ben asked the dealer how much it would cost to buy back the ones that were available, he almost choked at the answer—double! Still, we accepted; it was worth it to set things right again, I felt. As we drove home in silence, all but one of the portraits in the truck's bed, my heart pounded like a drum. Thoughts swirled in my mind, ones I can't properly attribute to just this thing that was happening. Was I still sad about the miscarriage? Yes. I'd gone to counseling, but it hadn't helped. Maybe, just maybe, this new idea would make me feel better. Make everyone feel better.

Later on, instead of watching him mope around about the additional lost money and him watching me compulsively clean the house, I told him that I needed a break from it all—from him, from the house, even from Ellie. As an escape, I went to my book club after taking the last few weeks off after Dad. The girls were all super-supportive of me, since they knew what had happened, and a few of them took me out to coffee afterward. In confidence, I asked my closest friend of the bunch, a very nice East Indian woman named Gita, if she believed in spirits that inhabit homes. She said that Hindus like her generally believe that to be the case, adding that more often than not the spirits offer comfort and should be embraced. I'm sure she assumed I was speaking of Dad's spirit and not a different one. Just what that spirit was, I couldn't be sure. Either way, I didn't correct her.

Not only did I heed Mom's advice about protecting a man's ego, I did her one better. I took the initiative by hiring a different contractor to do the work. When I told Ben that I'd already taken care of it and had even taken a loan from my 401k so as to protect our cash emergency fund, he began to argue the point before I told him that I'd heard the footsteps again the night before, several of them, in fact, like children running in the hallway. I'd heard their echoing whispers, too. He looked at me oddly when I'd said that, as if I were a stranger telling him an obvious lie instead of his wife. Then he said that once the work was finished, he didn't want to hear another word about footsteps or disturbed wedding portraits, that this whole affair had gone on long enough. I agreed, kissing him on the cheek before turning to take Ellie with me to our bed. Ben just stood there rubbing his head in silence.

The new contractor began the today, just as the first snow flurries of the season began to fall from the gray November sky. Winter was here. While the workers hauled studs and sheets of drywall upstairs, I sat reading in the nook with Ellie playing beside me on the floor. Ben had offered to take the day off to oversee the project again, but I told him that he'd already missed enough work because of this, and Dad too. Besides, I was more than capable of handling it, and it gave me a sense of satisfaction knowing that for the first time since losing the baby I was fully taking charge of my happiness. Per my instructions, before the last section of drywall had yet to be placed in the same spot the old wall had been, the contractor set his tools down and walked out to his truck. A private moment of commemoration just for me, I'd told him. I set Ellie in her Pack 'N Play, then went out to the garage to get the wrapped item I'd kept hidden in the rafters for the past several days. A gift not just for myself, but our entire family, one I'd paid an antique dealer a thousand dollars to buy for me on condition of anonymity. A Victorian portrait of a seven-year-old boy, handsome even in death as he stood unsmiling and propped by an almost-hidden stand, and me kissing his cheek before placing the portrait behind the wall, because deep down I know the baby was a boy.

Now I'll have one.

Letter to Licinius Sura

Pliny the Younger

Our leisure furnishes me with the opportunity of learning from you, and you with that of instructing me. Accordingly, I particularly wish to know whether you think there exist such things as phantoms, possessing an appearance peculiar to themselves, and a certain supernatural power, or that mere empty delusions receive a shape from our fears. For my part, I am led to believe in their existence, especially by what I hear happened to Curtius Rufus. While still in humble circumstances and obscure, he was a hanger-on in the suit of the Governor of Africa. While pacing LI le colonnade one afternoon, there appeared to him a female form of superhuman size and beauty. She informed the terrified man that she was "Africa," and had come to foretell future events; for that he would go to Rome, would fill offices of state there, and would even return to that same province with the highest powers, and die in it. All which things were fulfilled. Moreover, as he touched at Carthage, and was disembarking from his ship, the same form is said to have presented itself to him on the shore. It is certain that, being seized with illness, and auguring the future from the past and misfortune from his previous prosperity, he himself abandoned all hope of life, though none of those about him despaired.

Is not the following story again still more appalling and not less marvellous? I will relate it as it was received by me:

There was at Athens a mansion, spacious and commodious, but of evil repute and dangerous to health. In the dead of night there was a noise as of iron, and, if you listened more closely, a clanking of chains was heard, first of all from a distance, and afterward hard by. Presently a spectre used to appear, an ancient man sinking with emaciation and squalor, with a long beard and bristly hair, wearing shackles on his legs and fetters on his hands, and shaking them. Hence the inmates, by reason of their fears, passed miserable and horrible nights in sleeplessness. This want of sleep was followed by disease, and, their terrors increasing, by death. For in the daytime as well, though the apparition had departed, yet a reminiscence of it flitted before their eyes, and their dread outlived its cause. The mansion was accordingly deserted, and condemned to solitude, was entirely abandoned to the dreadful ghost. However, it was advertised, on the chance of someone, ignorant of the fearful curse attached to it, being willing to buy or to rent it. Athenodorus, the philosopher, came to Athens, and read the advertisement. When he had been informed of the terms, which were so low as to appear suspicious, he made inquiries, and learned the whole of the particulars. Yet none the less on that account, nay, all the more readily, did he rent the house. As evening began to draw on, he ordered a sofa to be set for himself in the front part of the house, and called for his notebooks, writing implements, and a light. The whole of his servants he dismissed to the interior apartments, and for himself applied his soul, eyes, and hand to composition, that his mind might not, from want of occupation, picture to itself the phantoms of which he had heard, or any empty terrors. At the commencement there was the universal silence of night. Soon the shaking of irons and the clanking of chains was heard, yet he never raised his eyes nor slackened his pen, but hardened his soul and deadened his ears by its help. The noise grew and approached: now it seemed to be heard at the door, and next inside the door. He looked round, beheld and recognized the figure he had been told of. It was standing and signalling to him with its finger, as though inviting him He, in reply, made a sign with his hand that it should wait a moment, and applied himself afresh to his tablets and pen. Upon this the figure kept rattling its chains over his head as he wrote. On looking round again, he saw it making the same signal as before, and without delay took up a light and followed it. It moved with a slow step, as though oppressed by its chains, and, after turning into the courtyard of the house, vanished suddenly and left his company. On being thus left to himself, he marked the spot with some grass and leaves which he plucked. Nekt day he applied to the magistrates, and urged them to have the spot in question dug up. There were found there some bones attached to and intermingled with fetters; the body to which they had belonged, rotted away by time and the soil, had abandoned them thus naked and corroded to the chains. They were collected and interred at the public expense, and the house was ever afterward free from the spirit, which had obtained due sepulture.

The above story I believe on the strength of those who affirm it. What follows I am myself in a position to affirm to others. I have a freedman, who is not without some knowledge of letters. A younger brother of his was sleeping with him in the same bed. The latter dreamed he saw someone sitting on the couch, who approached a pair of scissors to his head, and even cut the hair from the crown of it. When day dawned he was found to be cropped round the crown, and his locks were discovered lying about. A very short time afterward a fresh occurrence of the same kind confirmed the truth of the former one. A lad of mine was sleeping, in company with several others, in the pages' apartment. There came through the windows (so he tells the story) two figures in white tunics, who cut his hair as he lay, and departed the way they came. In his case, too, daylight exhibited him shorn, and his locks scattered around. Nothing remarkable followed, except, perhaps, this, that I was not brought under accusation, as I should have been, if Domitian (in whose reign these events happened) had lived longer. For in his desk was found an information against me which had been presented by Carus; from which circumstance may be conjectured—inasmuch as it is the custom of accused persons to let their hair grow—that the cutting off of my slaves' hair was a sign of the danger which threatened me being averted.

I beg, then, that you will apply your great learning to this subject. The matter is one deserves long and deep consideration on your part; nor am I, for my part, undeserving of having the fruits of your wisdom imparted to me. You may even argue on both sides (as your way is), provided you argue more forcibly on one side than the other, so as not to dismiss me in suspense and anxiety, when the very cause of my consulting you has been to have my doubts put an end to.

Beach Shanty

Katherine Kerestman

The old house on the beach,
Where gales scrape the paint from the wood before it is dried,
Its skeletal boards bleach,
And its warped shingles fling out at the red, roiling tide,

Crouches under two dunes,
Watching the waves thrashing themselves up into typhoons,
Launching wat'ry harpoons,
Growing strong and upsurging with the pull of two moons,

Watches the scaled sea-beast,
The indigo, twenty-legged, seven-headed mer-beast,
Swim from dark realms due East,
Devour schooners and sailors in grisly blood feast,

Spit out their gnawed-on bones,
Swim south, stirring black whirlpools that suck down the freighters.
Dark night echoes their moans,
As carnivorous eels race grotesque alligators.

The Inn

Guy de Maupassant
Translated by Storm Jameson

Looking just like all the other wooden hostelries set down amid the High Alps, at the foot of the glaciers, in the bare and rocky corridors that cleave the white peaks of the mountains, the Schwarenback Inn serves as a refuge for travelers over the Gemmi pass.

For six months in the year it remains open, inhabited by Jean Hauser's family; then, as soon as the snow lies in deep drifts, filling the valley and making the descent to Loëche impassable, the women, the father, and the three sons depart, leaving the old guide, Gaspard Hari, to look after the house, with the young guide, Ulrich Kunsi, and Sam, the big St. Bernard dog.

The two men and the beast remain till the spring in this prison of snow, with nothing before their eyes save the immense white slope of the Balmhorn; they are surrounded by pale, gleaming peaks, shut in, blockaded, and buried under the snow that rises round them, enveloping, embracing, and crushing the little house, heaping itself high upon the roof, reaching to the windows, and walling up the door.

It was the day on which the Hauser family was to return to Loëche, for winter was approaching and the descent becoming perilous.

Three mules went in front, loaded with clothes and luggage, and led by the three sons. Then the mother, Jeanne Hauser, and her daughter Louise mounted a fourth mule and set off in their turn.

The father followed them, accompanied by the two guides, who were to escort the family as far as the summit of the actual descent.

First they rounded the little lake, frozen now, at the bottom of the great cavity in the rocks that lay in front of the inn, then they pursued their way along the valley, featureless as a sheet and dominated by snow peaks on every side.

The sun poured down on this dazzling white frozen desert, illuminating it with a cold, blinding glare. No life stirred in this sea of hills; there was no movement in the limitless solitude; no sound disturbed the profound silence.

Little by little the young guide, Ulrich Kunsi, a tall, long-legged Swiss, drew away from Hauser and old Gaspard Hari, and overtook the mule that bore the two women.

The younger of them watched him coming and seemed to call him with her sad eyes. She was a small, fair peasant girl, whose milky cheeks and pale hair seemed bleached by her long sojourn amid the ice.

When he had caught up with the animal that carried her, he put his hand on its buttock and slowed his pace. Old Madame Hauser began to speak to him, enumerating with infinite detail all her recommendations for the winter. It was the first time that he was staying up, whereas old Hari had already spent fourteen winters under the snow at the Schwarenbach Inn.

Ulrich Kunsi listened, but did not appear to understand; he never took his eyes off the young girl. From time to time he would answer, "Yes, Madame Hauser," but his thoughts seemed far away, and his calm face remained impassive.

They reached the Lake of Daube, whose long frozen surface stretched, perfectly motionless, at the bottom of the valley. To their right, the Daubenhorn thrust up its black rocks, rising to a peak, near the enormous moraines of the Loemmern glacier, dominated by the Wildstrubel.

As they drew near the Gemmi pass, where the descent to Loëche begins, they came suddenly upon the vast rim of the Alps of the Valais, from which they were separated by the deep broad valley of the Rhone.

It was a distant host of white, uneven summits, some sharp, others flattened at the top, and all gleaming in the sun: the Mischabel with its two horns, the powerful bulk of the Wissehorn, the weighty Brunnegghorn, the high and formidable pyramid of the murderous Matterhorn, and that monstrous jade, the Dent-Blanche.

Then, right below them, in an enormous cavity at the bottom of a fearful abyss, they caught sight of Loëche, whose houses were like grains of sand thrown into that huge crevice, ended and enclosed by the Gemmi and opening out, below, on to the Rhône.

The mule halted at the edge of the path that runs, twisting, turning endlessly, and coiling back in fantastic and marvelous fashion, down the mountains on the right, as far as to the almost invisible little village at their feet. The women jumped down into the snow.

The two old men had caught them up.

"We must be off," said Hauser. "Goodbye, and keep your spirits up, friends; see you next year."

"Next year," repeated old Hari.

They embraced. Then Madame Hauser in her turn offered her cheeks, and the girl did the same. When it was Ulrich Kunsi's turn, he murmured into Louise's ear, "Don't forget the men up above."

"No, I won't," she replied, so softly that he guessed it without hearing.

"Well, goodbye," repeated Jean Hauser, "and good health to you."

And, passing in front of the women, he began the descent.

Soon all three vanished at the first bend in the road.

And the two men turned back toward the Schwarenbach Inn.

They walked slowly, side by side, without speaking. It was over; they would be shut up alone to gether, for four or five months.

Then Gaspard Hari began to talk about his life there the previous winter. He had stayed up with Michel Canol, who was now too old to try it again, for an accident may easily happen during the long period of solitude. They had not been bored; it was all a matter of playing your proper part from the very first day; and you always succeeded in inventing various distractions, games, and other ways of passing the time.

Ulrich Kunsi listened with lowered eyes, following in thought the friends descending to the village down the winding ways of the Gemmi pass.

Soon they caught sight of the inn, scarcely visible, so small was it, a black speck at the foot of the monstrous wave of snow.

When they opened the door, Sam, the big curly-haired dog, began to gambol round them.

"Come, my son," said old Gaspard, "we have no woman here now; we must get dinner ready, and you will peel the potatoes."

They both sat down on wooden stools and began to dip their bread in the soup.

The next morning seemed a long one to Ulrich Kunsi. Old Hari smoked and spat into the fireplace, while the young man stared through the window at the dazzling mountain opposite the house.

He went out in the afternoon and followed the route of the day before, searching on the ground for the shoe prints of the mule that had borne the two women. When he was at the summit of the pass, he lay down on his face at the edge of the abyss and gazed at Loëche.

The village in its well of rock was not yet drowned in snow, although the snow had drawn very near it, to be halted abruptly by the pine forests that protected the outlying houses. From above, the houses looked like paving-stones in a meadow.

Louise Hauser was there now, in one of those grey buildings. In which? Ulrich Kunsi was too far away to tell them apart. How he longed to go down while it was still possible!

But the sun had disappeared behind the great crest of Wildstrubel, and the young man returned. Old Hari was smoking. At sight of his companion, he proposed a game of cards, and they sat down face to face on either side of the table.

They played for a long time, a simple game called *brisque,* and after supper they went to bed.

The days that followed were like the first, bright and cold, with no fresh snow. Old Gaspard spent the afternoons watching the eagles and rare birds that ventured on the frozen heights, while Ulrich returned regularly to the summit of the Gemmi to gaze at the village. Then they would play cards, dice, or dominoes, winning or losing trifling objects to give an interest to their game.

One morning Hari, the first to get up, called his companion. A moving, deep, light cloud of white foam was falling silently on them and around them, burying them little by little under a thick, frothy coverlet that deadened all sound. It lasted four days and four nights. They had to clear the door and the windows, hollow out a passage, and cut steps in order to walk out over the surface of this powdered ice that twelve hours of frost had made harder than the granite of the moraines.

Thenceforward they lived the life of prisoners, hardly venturing outside their dwelling-place. They had divided up the housework, and each regularly performed his share. Ulrich Kunsi made himself responsible for the washing and cleaning—in fact, for all the labor of keeping the house neat. It was he also who split the wood, while Gaspard Hari cooked and tended the fire. Their tasks, regular and monotonous, were interrupted by long games of cards or dice. They never quarreled, both being of calm and peaceful temper. They never even indulged in moments of impatience, ill humor, or sharp words, for they had determined to possess their souls in patience throughout their winter on the heights.

Sometimes old Gaspard would take his gun and go off after chamois; occasionally he killed one. Then there would be rejoicings at the Schwarenbach Inn, and a great feast of fresh meat.

One morning he went out for this purpose. The outside thermometer had dropped to zero. The sun had not yet risen, and so the hunter hoped to catch the animals on the lower slopes of the Wildstrubel.

Ulrich, left by himself, stayed in bed till ten. He was by nature a heavy sleeper, but had never dared to abandon himself to his weakness in the presence of the old guide, who was always energetic and early out of bed.

He lunched slowly with Sam, who also spent his days and nights sleeping in front of the fire; then he felt sad, frightened by the solitude: he was suffering from his need of their daily game of cards, as a man does suffer under the prick of a powerful habit.

So he went out to meet his companion, who was due back at four o'clock.

The snow had leveled the whole deep valley, filling the crevasses and quilting the rocks; it formed, between the immense peaks, nothing but an immense white bowl, smooth, blinding, and frozen.

It was three weeks since Ulrich had last gone to the edge of the abyss and gazed down at the village. He was anxious to pay a visit thither before climbing the slopes that led to Wildstrubel. Loëche was now also covered by the snow, and it was scarcely possible to distinguish the houses buried under its pale cloak.

He turned to the right and reached the glacier of Loemmem. He walked with his long, mountaineer's stride, striking his iron-tipped stick upon the snow, itself as hard as stone. With his keen eyes he sought for the little moving black speck, far away on that enormous table-cloth.

When he was at the edge of the glacier, he stopped, wondering if the old man really had gone that way. Then he set off again, skirting the moraines at a swifter, more uneasy pace.

The light was fading; the snows were turning pink; a dry icy wind ran in hurried gusts over their crystal surface. Ulrich uttered a shrill cry, quivering and prolonged. His voice fled abroad in the silence that covered the steeping mountains; it ran far away over the deep, motionless billows of icy foam, like the cry of a bird over the waves of the sea; then it died out, and there was no reply.

He resumed his march. The sun had sunk below the far horizon, behind the peaks still reddened by the glow in the sky; but the hollows of the valley were growing gray. And suddenly the young man was afraid. He felt as though the silence, the cold, the solitude, the winter death of the mountains were flowing into his own body, would stop and freeze his blood, stiffen his limbs, and turn him into a still, frozen creature. He began to run, fleeing toward his dwelling-place. The old man, he thought, would have returned during his absence. He must have taken another route; he would be sitting before the fire, with a dead chamois at his feet.

Soon he came in sight of the inn. No smoke was coming from it. Ulrich ran faster, and opened the door. Sam dashed up to greet him, but Gaspard Hari had not returned.

Frightened, Kunzi turned around, as though expecting to find his companion hiding in a corner. Then he re-lit the fire and made the soup, still hoping to see the old man come in.

From time to time he would go out to see if he was in sight. Darkness had fallen, the wan darkness of the mountains, a pale, livid darkness, illumined on the sky's rim by a slender yellow crescent that hovered on the verge of sinking behind the peaks.

Then the young man would return, sit down, warm his feet and hands, and turn over in his mind various possible accidents.

Gaspard might have broken his leg, fallen into a hole, or made a false step and sprained his ankle. And he must be lying in the snow, overcome and stiffened by the cold, in agony of mind, screaming, lost, shouting for help, perhaps, shouting with all the strength of his voice through the silence of the night.

But where? The mountains were so vast, so cruel, and their lower slopes so perilous, especially at that time of year, that it needed ten or twenty guides, walking for a week in every direction, to find a man lost in their immensity.

But Ulrich Kunzi resolved to go out with Sam if Gaspard Hari did not return between midnight and one o'clock in the morning.

He made his arrangements.

He put provisions for two days into a bag, took his steel climbing-irons, wound a long, thin, strong cord about his waist, and made sure that his iron-tipped stick and the ax he used for cutting steps in the ice were in order. Then he waited. The fire blazed in the hearth; the big dog snored in the light of the flames; in its sonorous wooden case the clock sounded its regular tick, like the beating of a heart.

He waited, his ear attuned for distant sounds, shivering when the light breeze swept along the roof and the walls.

Midnight struck; he shuddered. Then, feeling shaky and frightened, he set water on the fire, so as to have a drink of good hot coffee before he set out.

When the clock struck one, he rose, woke Sam, opened the door, and set off in the direction of the Wildstrubel.

For five hours he ascended, scaling the rocks by means of his climbing-irons, cutting steps in the ice, always pressing forward, and sometimes using the rope in order to haul up the dog from the bottom of a wall of rock too steep for him. It was about six o'clock when he reached one of the peaks to which old Gaspard often went in search of chamois.

He waited for daybreak.

The sky paled overhead, and suddenly a fantastic glow, lit none knows whence, came at one stride over the immense sea of pale crests that extended all around him for a hundred leagues. This vague fight seemed to pour from the snow and spread itself abroad. Little by little the loftiest summits in the distance were all tinged with a pink soft as flesh, and the red sun rose behind the massive giants of the Bernese Alps.

Ulrich Kunzi set off again. He walked like a hunter, stooping, searching for traces, and bidding the dog, "Rout him out, boy; rout him out."

He was now going back down the mountain, examining the crevasses, and sometimes calling, sending forth a prolonged shout that died very swiftly in the mute immensities of space. Then he would set his ear to the ground to listen; he fancied he could discern a voice, would begin to run, shouting again, would hear nothing more and would sit down, exhausted and despairing. At about midday he had lunch and gave food to Sam, who was as weary as himself. Then he recommenced his search.

When evening came on he was still walking, having scoured over fifty kilometres of the mountains. Finding himself too far from the house to return to it and too tired to drag himself any further, he dug a hole in the snow and huddled inside it, with the dog, under a blanket he had brought. There they lay, one against the other, the man and the beast, warming each other's bodies, but, even so, frozen to the marrow.

Ulrich scarcely slept at all; his mind was haunted by visions, and his limbs racked by shivering fits.

Day was breaking when he rose. His legs were as stiff as iron bars, his spirit so weak that he was ready to scream with anguish, and his heart so wildly pulsing that he grew dizzy with excitement whenever he thought he heard a noise.

Suddenly he thought that he too was doomed to die of cold out in the solitude, and his terror of such a death whipped up his energy and revived his strength.

He was descending now toward the inn, stumbling and recovering himself, followed in the distance by Sam, who was limping along on three legs.

They did not reach Schwarenbach until about four in the afternoon. The house was empty. The young man lit the fire, ate some food, and went to sleep, too stupefied with exhaustion to think of anything.

He slept for a long, a very long time, in a slumber like death. But suddenly a voice, a cry, a name, "Ulrich," broke through to the depths of his unconsciousness and made him start up. Had he been dreaming? Was this one of the fantastic calls that pierce the dreams of an uneasy mind? No, he heard that quivering cry still, piercing his ears and still present in his body's being, in the tips of his muscular fingers. Assuredly someone had shouted, someone had called "Ulrich!" Someone was there, near the house. He could not doubt it. So he opened the door and yelled, "Is that you, Gaspard?" with all the strength in his throat.

Nothing answered; no sound, no murmur, no groan, nothing. It was dark. The snow was ghostly.

The wind had risen, the icy wind that cracks stones and leaves nothing alive upon these deserted heights. It swept by in sharp gusts, more parching and more deadly than the fiery wind of the desert. Again Ulrich shouted, "Gaspard!—Gaspard!—Gaspard!"

Then he waited. All was silent in the mountains! Then a wave of terror shook him to the bone. With one bound he got back inside the inn, shut the door, and thrust home the bolts; then he fell shivering into a chair, certain that he had just been called by his companion at the moment when he rendered up his soul.

Of that he was sure, as a man is sure of being alive or of eating bread. Old Gaspard Hari had been dying for two days and three nights, somewhere out there, in a hole, in one of those deep untrodden ravines whose whiteness is more sinister than the darkness of a subterranean dungeon. He had been dying for two days and three nights, and a moment ago had succumbed, thinking of his companion. And his soul, scarce freed, had flitted to the inn where Ulrich lay sleeping, and had called him by the mysterious and awful power that the souls of the dead have to haunt the living. It had cried aloud, that voiceless soul, in the afflicted soul of the sleeper; had cried its last farewell, or its reproach, or its curse upon the man who had given up the search too soon.

And Ulrich felt it there, quite close, behind the wall, behind the door he had just shut. It was wandering, like a night bird brushing against a lighted window with its feathers; the frenzied youth was on the point of screaming with horror. He wanted to run away and dared not go out, for there the phantom would remain, day and night, around the inn, so long as the old guide's body remained undiscovered and unburied in the hallowed ground of a cemetery.

Dawn came, and Kunzi recovered some measure of confidence at the sun's shining return. He prepared his meal and made broth for the dog, then sat motionless in a chair, in agony of soul, thinking of the old man lying under the snow.

Then, as soon as night covered the mountains again, new terrors began to assail him. He was walking now around the dark kitchen, poorly lit by the flame of a single candle. He walked from one end of the room to the other, in long strides, listening, listening for that terrifying scream of the other night to come again across the melancholy silence outside. The poor wretch felt lonelier than any man had ever been! He was alone in that immense desert of snow, alone, two thousand meters above the inhabited earth, above human dwellings, above the roaring, palpitating stir of life, alone in the frozen sky! He was tortured by a mad desire to escape, anywhere, anyhow, to get down to Loëche by flinging himself into the abyss; but he dared not even open the door, certain that the other man, the dead man, would bar his way, that he too might not be left alone in the heights.

Toward midnight, weary of walking, overcome with anguish and terror, he drowsed at last in his chair, for he dreaded his bed as a man dreads a haunted place.

And suddenly the piercing cry of the previous night tore at his ears, so loud and shrill that Ulrich stretched out his arms to repel the ghost, and, chair and all, fell over on to his back.

Sam, awakened by the noise, began to bark as frightened dogs will bark, and prowled round the room, seeking the spot whence came the danger. Coming to the door, he sniffed beneath it, panting, sniffling, and whining, with hair on end and tail erect.

Kunzi had risen in terror and, holding his chair by one of its legs, cried out, "Don't come in, don't come in, or I'll kill you!" And the dog, excited by his threats, barked furiously at the invisible foe against whom his master was shouting defiance.

Little by little, Sam calmed down and went back and lay down on the hearth, but he remained uneasy, with head erect and shining eyes, and snarled through his teeth.

Ulrich too recovered his composure, but, feeling that his fear was sapping his strength, he went to get a bottle of brandy from the cupboard, and drank several glasses of it, one after another. His thoughts became vague; his courage was strengthened; a burning fever glided into his veins.

He ate practically nothing next day, limiting his diet to alcohol. And for several days on end he lived in a state of bestial drunkenness. As soon as thoughts of Gaspard Hari returned to him, he started drinking again and continued till he fell to the ground, completely intoxicated. There he would lie, face downwards, dead drunk, his limbs twisted, snoring, with his forehead to the floor. But no sooner had he digested the maddening, burning liquor than the same cry, "Ulrich!" woke him like a bullet piercing his skull; and he rose, still tottering, stretching out his hands to keep from falling, and calling Sam to his aid. And the dog, who seemed to be going mad like his master, would rush at the door, scratching it with his claws and gnawing it with his long white teeth, while the young man, with upturned face and neck straining backwards, swallowed the brandy in great gulps, like cold water drunk after a race; and presently the spirit dulled his thoughts again, and his memory, and his frantic terror.

In three weeks he got through his entire stock of alcohol. But this perpetual drunkenness merely dulled his terror; and it arose with renewed fury as soon as he could no longer assuage it. Then his obsession, made worse by a month of drunkenness and constantly growing in that utter solitude, pierced his brain like a gimlet. He had now taken to striding up and down his dwelling like a caged animal, setting his ear to the door to listen if the thing were there and defying it through the wall.

And each time he dozed, overcome by fatigue, he heard the voice that made him leap to his feet.

At last, one night, he rushed to the door, like a coward pushed to the last extremity, and opened it, to see the thing that called him and force it to be silent.

A gust of cold air struck him full in the face, freezing him to the bone, and he shut the door and thrust home the bolts, without noticing that Sam had rushed out. Then, shuddering, he piled wood on the fire and sat down to warm himself; but suddenly he started. Something was scratching the wall and weeping.

"Go away," he cried frantically. He was answered by a long-drawn melancholy wail.

At that, all that was left of his reason succumbed to abject terror. "Go away," he said again, turning round and round to find a corner to hide in. But the thing outside, still weeping, went all along the side of the house, rubbing against the wall. Ulrich dashed to the oaken sideboard, full of plates and provisions, and, lifting it with superhuman strength, dragged it to the door, to secure himself with a barricade. Then, heaping up all the remaining furniture, bedsteads, mattresses, and chairs, he blocked up the window as though he were preparing for a siege.

But the thing outside was now uttering great mournful moans, and the young man began to answer in like moans.

Whole days and nights went by, and neither ceased to howl. One ran constantly about the house, scratching at the wall with its nails with such violence that it seemed eager to pull it down; the other, inside, followed its every movement, all huddled up, his ear glued to the stone wall, answering its cries with horrible screams.

One evening Ulrich heard no more noises, and sat down, so worn out with fatigue that he fell asleep immediately.

He woke without memory, without thought, as though his head had been emptied during his sunken slumber. He was hungry; he ate.

The winter was over. The Gemmi pass became practicable again, and the Hauser family set off on their way back to the inn.

As soon as they had reached the summit of the ascent, the women clambered on to their mule and began to talk of the two men whom they would shortly see again.

They were surprised that neither of them had descended a few days earlier, as soon as the road was open, to bring news of their long wintering.

At last they caught sight of the inn, still covered and quilted with snow. The door and the window were closed; a little smoke issued from the roof, a fact that reassured old Hauser. But, drawing nearer, he perceived on the threshold the skeleton of an animal picked clean by the eagles, a large skeleton lying on its side.

They all examined it. "It must be Sam," said Mrs. Hauser, and she shouted, "Hey, Gaspard!"

A cry answered from within, a shrill cry, that sounded like the cry of some animal. "Hey, Gaspard!" repeated old Hauser. Another cry like the first was heard.

Then the three men, the father and the two sons, tried to open the door. It stood fast.

They took from the empty cowshed a long beam to use as a battering-ram, and swung it with all their strength. The wood rang and yielded, the planks flew to pieces; then a great crash shook the house and they saw a man standing inside behind the fallen sideboard, with hair falling to the shoulders, a beard on his chest, gleaming eyes, and rags of cloth upon his body.

They could not recognize him, but Louise Hauser exclaimed, "It's Ulrich, Mother!" And her mother saw that it was indeed Ulrich, although his hair was white.

He let them come up to him; he let them touch him; but he made no answer to their questions, and had to be taken to Loëche, where the doctors decided that he was mad.

And no one ever knew what had become of his companion.

Louise Hauser nearly died that summer of a decline attributed to the mountain cold.

Haunted Houses

Im Bang
Translated by James S. Gale

There once lived a man in Seoul called Yi Chang, who frequently told as an experience of his own the following story: He was poor and had no home of his own, so he lived much in quarters loaned him by others. When hard pressed he even went into haunted houses and lived there. Once, after failing to find a place, he heard of one such house in Ink Town (one of the wards of Seoul), at the foot of South Mountain, which had been haunted for generations and was now left vacant. Chang investigated the matter, and finally decided to take possession.

First, to find whether it was really haunted or not, he called his elder brothers, Hugh and Haw, and five or six of his relatives, and had them help clean it out and sleep there. The house had one upper room that was fast locked. Looking through a chink, there was seen to be in the room a tablet chair and a stand for it ; also there was an old harp without any strings, a pair of worn shoes, and some sticks and bits of wood. Nothing else was in the room. Dust lay thick, as though it had gathered through long years of time.

The company, after drinking wine, sat round the table and played at games, watching the night through. When it was late, towards midnight, they suddenly heard the sound of harps and a great multitude of voices, though the words were mixed and unintelligible. It was as though many people were gathered and carousing at a feast. The company then consulted as to what they should do. One drew a sword and struck a hole through the partition that looked into the tower. Instantly there appeared from the other side a sharp blade thrust out towards them. It was blue in colour. In fear and consternation they desisted from further interference with the place. But the sound of the harp and the revelry kept up till the morning. The company broke up at daylight, withdrew from the place, and never again dared to enter.

In the South Ward there was another haunted house, of which Chang desired possession, so he called his friends and brothers once more to make the experiment and see whether it was really haunted or not. On entering, they found two dogs within the enclosure, one black and one tan, lying upon the open verandah, one at each end. Their eyes were fiery red, and though the company shouted at them they did not move. They neither barked nor bit. But when midnight came these two animals got up and went down into the court, and began baying at the inky sky in a way most ominous. They went jumping back and forth. At that time, too, there came some one round the corner of the house dressed in ceremonial robes. The two dogs met him with great delight, jumping up before and behind in their joy at his coming. He ascended to the verandah, and sat down. Immediately five or six multi-coloured demons appeared and bowed before him, in front of the open space. The man then led the demons and the dogs two or three times round the house. They rushed up into the verandah and jumped down again into the court; backwards and forwards they came and went, till at last all of them mysteriously disappeared. The devils went into a hole underneath the floor, while the dogs went up to their quarters and lay down.

The company from the inner room had seen this. When daylight came they examined the place, looked through the chinks of the floor, but saw only an old, worn-out sieve and a few discarded brooms. They went behind the house and found another old broom poked into the chimney. They ordered a servant to gather them up and have them burned. The dogs lay as they were all day long, and neither ate nor moved. Some of the party wished to kill the brutes, but were afraid, so fearsome was their appearance.

This night again they remained, desiring to see if the same phenomena would appear. Again at midnight the two dogs got down into the court and began barking up at the sky. The man in ceremonial robes again came, and the devils, just as the day before.

The company, in fear and disgust, left the following morning, and did not try it again.

A friend, hearing this of Chang, went and asked about it from Hugh and Haw, and they confirmed the story.

There is still another tale of a graduate who was out of house and home and went into a haunted dwelling in Ink Town, which was said to have had the tower where the mysterious sounds were heard. They opened the door, broke out the window, took out the old harp, the spirit chair, the shoes and sticks, and had them burned. Before the fire had finished its work, one of the servants fell down and died. The graduate, seeing this, in fear and dismay put out the fire, restored the things and left the house.

Again there was another homeless man who tried it. In the night a woman in a blue skirt came down from the loft, and acted in a peculiar and uncanny way. The man, seeing this, picked up his belongings and left.

Again, in South Kettle Town, there were a number of woodmen who in the early morning were passing behind the haunted house, when they found an old woman sitting weeping under a tree. They thinking her an evil bogey, one man came up behind and gave her a thrust with his sickle. The witch rushed off into the house, her height appearing to be only about one cubit and a span.

The Woman in the Wall

DJ Tyrer

Family moves into new home, an old house
Strange sounds, sights, disturbing
Lead to hidden room off cellar
Tiny compartment hidden in wall
Discover mummified corpse of woman
Left to die, trapped within the wall
Slow, horrific way to die
Removed, buried, freed from the wall
Assumption the haunting is over
Only, a misapprehension, in fact
Something far older, beneath the house
Demands a sacrifice to sleep quiet
Compels new occupants down into cellar
Where mother pushes daughter into that space
Helps father rebuild the wall
Trapping their girl in the wall
Screaming as slowly, horribly, she dies
A new sacrifice, quieting the horror
That lurks far below the foundations
Of the house its will permeates
Another woman in the wall
Trapped till next time . . .

Three at Table

W. W. Jacobs

The talk in the coffee-room had been of ghosts and apparitions, and nearly everybody present had contributed his mite to
the stock of information upon a hazy and somewhat threadbare
subject. Opinions ranged from rank incredulity to childlike faith,
one believer going so far as to denounce unbelief as impious, with
a reference to the Witch of Endor, which was somewhat marred
by being complicated in an inexplicable fashion with the story of
Jonah.

"Talking of Jonah," he said solemnly, with a happy disregard
of the fact that he had declined to answer several eager questions
put to him on the subject, "look at the strange tales sailors tell us."

"I wouldn't advise you to believe all those," said a bluff, clean-
shaven man, who had been listening without speaking much. "You
see when a sailor gets ashore he's expected to have something to
tell, and his friends would be rather disappointed if he had not."

"It's a well-known fact," interrupted the first speaker firmly,
"that sailors are very prone to see visions."

"They are," said the other dryly, "they generally see them
in pairs, and the shock to the nervous system frequently causes
headache next morning."

"You never saw anything yourself?" suggested an unbeliever.

"Man and boy," said the other, "I've been at sea thirty years,
and the only unpleasant incident of that kind occurred in a quiet
English countryside."

"And that?" said another man.

"I was a young man at the time," said the narrator, drawing at his pipe and glancing good-humouredly at the company. "I had just come back from China, and my own people being away I went down into the country to invite myself to stay with an uncle. When I got down to the place I found it closed and the family in the South of France; but as they were due back in a couple of days I decided to put up at the Royal George, a very decent inn, and await their return.

"The first day I passed well enough; but in the evening the dulness of the rambling old place, in which I was the only visitor, began to weigh upon my spirits, and the next morning after a late breakfast I set out with the intention of having a brisk day's walk.

"I started off in excellent spirits, for the day was bright and frosty, with a powdering of snow on the iron-bound roads and nipped hedges, and the country had to me all the charm of novelty. It was certainly flat, but there was plenty of timber, and the villages through which I passed were old and picturesque.

"I lunched luxuriously on bread and cheese and beer in the bar of a small inn, and resolved to go a little further before turning back. When at length I found I had gone far enough, I turned up a lane at right angles to the road I was passing, and resolved to find my way back by another route. It is a long lane that has no turning, but this had several, each of which had turnings of its own, which generally led, as I found by trying two or three of them, into the open marshes. Then, tired of lanes, I resolved to rely upon the small compass which hung from my watch chain and go across country home.

"I had got well into the marshes when a white fog, which had been for some time hovering round the edge of the ditches, began gradually to spread. There was no escaping it, but by aid of my compass I was saved from making a circular tour and fell instead into frozen ditches or stumbled over roots in the grass. I kept my course, however, until at four o'clock, when night was coming rapidly up to lend a hand to the fog, I was fain to confess myself lost.

"The compass was now no good to me, and I wandered about miserably, occasionally giving a shout on the chance of being heard by some passing shepherd or farmhand. At length by great good luck I found my feet on a rough road driven through the marshes, and by walking slowly and tapping with my stick managed to keep to it. I had followed it for some distance when I heard footsteps approaching me.

"We stopped as we met, and the new arrival, a sturdy-looking countryman, hearing of my plight, walked back with me for nearly a mile, and putting me on to a road gave me minute instructions how to reach a village some three miles distant.

"I was so tired that three miles sounded like ten, and besides that, a little way off from the road I saw dimly a lighted window. I pointed it out, but my companion shuddered and looked round him uneasily.

"'You won't get no good there,' he said, hastily.

"'Why not?' I asked.

"'There's a something there, sir,' he replied, 'what 'tis I dunno, but the little 'un belonging to a gamekeeper as used to live in these parts see it, and it was never much good afterward. Some say as it's a poor mad thing, others says as it's a kind of animal; but whatever it is, it ain't good to see.'

"'Well, I'll keep on, then,' I said. 'Good-night.'

"He went back whistling cheerily until his footsteps died away in the distance, and I followed the road he had indicated until it divided into three, any one of which to a stranger might be said to lead straight on. I was now cold and tired, and having half made up my mind, walked slowly back towards the house.

"At first all I could see of it was the little patch of light at the window. I made for that until it disappeared suddenly, and I found myself walking into a tall hedge. I felt my way round this until I came to a small gate, and opening it cautiously, walked, not without some little nervousness, up a long path which led to the door. There was no light and no sound from within. Half repenting of my temerity I shortened my stick and knocked lightly upon the door.

"I waited a couple of minutes and then knocked again, and my stick was still beating the door when it opened suddenly and a tall bony old woman, holding a candle, confronted me.

"'What do you want?' she demanded gruffly.

"'I've lost my way,' I said, civilly; 'I want to get to Ashville.'

"'Don't know it,' said the old woman.

"She was about to close the door when a man emerged from a room at the side of the hall and came towards us. An old man of great height and breadth of shoulder.

"'Ashville is fifteen miles distant,' he said slowly.

"'If you will direct me to the nearest village, I shall be grateful,' I remarked.

"He made no reply, but exchanged a quick, furtive glance with the woman. She made a gesture of dissent.

"'The nearest place is three miles off,' he said, turning to me and apparently trying to soften a naturally harsh voice; 'if you will give me the pleasure of your company, I will make you as comfortable as I can.'

"I hesitated. They were certainly a queer-looking couple, and the gloomy hall with the shadows thrown by the candle looked hardly more inviting than the darkness outside.

"'You are very kind,' I murmured, irresolutely, 'but—'

"'Come in,' he said quickly; 'shut the door, Anne.'

"Almost before I knew it I was standing inside and the old woman, muttering to herself, had closed the door behind me. With a queer sensation of being trapped I followed my host into the room, and taking the proffered chair warmed my frozen fingers at the fire.

"'Dinner will soon be ready,' said the old man, regarding me closely. 'If you will excuse me—'

"I bowed and he left the room. A minute afterward I heard voices; his and the old woman's, and, I fancied, a third. Before I had finished my inspection of the room he returned, and regarded me with the same strange look I had noticed before.

"'There will be three of us at dinner,' he said, at length. 'We two and my son.'

"I bowed again, and secretly hoped that that look didn't run in the family.

"'I suppose you don't mind dining in the dark,' he said, abruptly.

"'Not at all,' I replied, hiding my surprise as well as I could, 'but really I'm afraid I'm intruding. If you'll allow me'—

"He waved his huge gaunt hands. 'We're not going to lose you now we've got you,' he said, with a dry laugh. 'It's seldom we have company, and now we've got you we'll keep you. My son's eyes are bad, and he can't stand the light. Ah, here is Anne.'

"As he spoke the old woman entered, and, eyeing me stealthily, began to lay the cloth, while my host, taking a chair the other side of the hearth, sat looking silently into the fire. The table set, the old woman brought in a pair of fowls ready carved in a dish, and placing three chairs, left the room. The old man hesitated a moment, and then, rising from his chair, placed a large screen in front of the fire and slowly extinguished the candles.

"'Blind man's holiday,' he said, with clumsy jocosity, and groping his way to the door opened it. Somebody came back into the room with him, and in a slow, uncertain fashion took a seat at the table, and the strangest voice I have ever heard broke a silence which was fast becoming oppressive.

"'A cold night,' it said slowly.

"I replied in the affirmative, and light or no light, fell to with an appetite which had only been sharpened by the snack in the middle of the day. It was somewhat difficult eating in the dark, and it was evident from the behaviour of my invisible companions that they were as unused to dining under such circumstances as I was. We ate in silence until the old woman blundered into the room with some sweets and put them with a crash upon the table.

"'Are you a stranger about here?' inquired the curious voice again.

"I replied in the affirmative, and murmured something about my luck in stumbling upon such a good dinner.

"'Stumbling is a very good word for it,' said the voice grimly. 'You have forgotten the port, father.'

"'So I have,' said the old man, rising. 'It's a bottle of the "Celebrated" to-day; I will get it myself.'

"He felt his way to the door, and closing it behind him, left me alone with my unseen neighbour. There was something so strange about the whole business that I must confess to more than a slight feeling of uneasiness.

"My host seemed to be absent a long time. I heard the man opposite lay down his fork and spoon, and half fancied I could seen a pair of wild eyes shining through the gloom like a cat's.

"With a growing sense of uneasiness I pushed my chair back. It caught the hearthrug, and in my efforts to disentangle it the screen fell over with a crash and in the flickering light of the fire I saw the face of the creature opposite. With a sharp catch of my breath I left my chair and stood with clenched fists beside it. Man or beast, which was it? The flame leaped up and then went out, and in the mere red glow of the fire it looked more devilish than before.

"For a few moments we regarded each other in silence; then the door opened and the old man returned. He stood aghast as he saw the warm firelight, and then approaching the table mechanically put down a couple of bottles.

"'I beg your pardon,' said I, reassured by his presence, 'but I have accidentally overturned the screen. Allow me to replace it.'

"'No,' said the other man, gently, 'let it be. We have had enough of the dark. I'll give you a light.'

"He struck a match and slowly lit the candles. Then I saw that the man opposite had but the remnant of a face, a gaunt wolfish face in which one unquenched eye, the sole remaining feature, still glittered. I was greatly moved, some suspicion of the truth occurring to me.

"'My son was injured some years ago in a burning house,' said the old man. 'Since then we have lived a very retired life. When you came to the door we—' his voice trembled, 'that is—my son—'

"'I thought,' said the son simply, 'that it would be better for me not to come to the dinner-table. But it happens to be my birthday, and my father would not hear of my dining alone, so we hit upon this foolish plan of dining in the dark. I'm sorry I startled you.'

"'I am sorry,' said I, as I reached across the table and gripped his hand, 'that I am such a fool; but it was only in the dark that you startled me.'

"From a faint tinge in the old man's cheek and a certain pleasant softening of the poor solitary eye in front of me I secretly congratulated myself upon this last remark.

"'We never see a friend,' said the old man, apologetically, 'and the temptation to have company was too much for us. Besides, I don't know what else you could have done.'

"'Nothing else half so good, I'm sure,' said I.

"'Come,' said my host, with almost a sprightly air. 'Now we know each other, draw your chairs to the fire and let's keep this birthday in a proper fashion.'

"He drew a small table to the fire for the glasses and produced a box of cigars, and placing a chair for the old servant, sternly bade her to sit down and drink. If the talk was not sparkling, it did not lack for vivacity, and we were soon as merry a party as I have ever seen. The night wore on so rapidly that we could hardly believe our ears when in a lull in the conversation a clock in the hall struck twelve.

"'A last toast before we retire,' said my host, pitching the end of his cigar into the fire and turning to the small table.

"We had drunk several before this, but there was something impressive in the old man's manner as he rose and took up his glass. His tall figure seemed to get taller, and his voice rang as he gazed proudly at his disfigured son.

"'The health of the children my boy saved!' he said, and drained his glass at a draught."

The Witches' House

Margaret Curtis

About the open gateway and the door
A herbal tangle grows, both sweet and fell:
Rosemary for remembrance of the war,
Wild lavender and jasmine by the bell—
And lilies bloom, whose pollen held in store
Might send unwelcome visitors to hell.
To knock or ring: how many strikes in time?
No matter! This door opens with a rhyme.
You hear a thud, perhaps a soft footfall,
But no one comes to greet you as you pause.
Instead, a faint call echoes down the hall,
A whiff of fluff, the scratch of sharpened claws
Convinces you a cat has climbed a wall,
Escaping hunting hounds with snapping jaws.
Whose fate hangs in the balance: theirs or yours?
Who dares invite you in? And for what cause?
A plume of incense drives your cares away,
Scent of an Eastern mystic lingers here,
'Mid dusty shelves of books that line the way,
Containing answers to both hope and fear.
Beyond these toppling towers shines the day,
A promise of Pan's garden at the rear;
And in between two bookends of bright light:
Dim passages and realms of restless night.
You strike a match and pray the wick will burn;

Swear oaths profane—and welcome candle flame.
You hold your ancient torch the more to learn
Of title, publisher, or author's name,
But none are in a tongue you can discern:
A thousand spells of fate—no one the same.
You might waste all your life here—die alone.
You glimpse yourself trapped here, a skeleton.
So through a battered door, your way to wend,
You feel the air suck in and heat turns chill.
The stair calls; you reluctantly descend;
A wavering flame reflects your weakening will.
You break resisting web, prepare to fend
Off bat or beast—no menu to fulfil.
Your eyes adjust and in this gathering gloom,
You wonder—is this dungeon or bedroom?

Your first impression is of comfort, rest,
With scattered cushions cast about the space.
Then turning sunwise—north, south, east, or west—
Altars surround you any way you face:
You do not dare to touch an object lest
You might disturb some ritual in place.
Dense frankincense and sage smoke fill the air;
You sense a presence though the stage is bare.
Then here rise visions, queer and "swift and sweet"[2]
The moon entrapped in crystal amethyst,
A cauldron full of apples, merry meet,
As shadows leap and merge in lover's tryst.
A chant sings through your blood arousing heat.
Magic enfolds you: you are fivefold kissed.
You dance as if possessed and yet you know
No demon dares to follow where you go!
A drop of blood is all of you they ask,

2 Percy Bysshe Shelley, "The Lovely Witch's Cave."

And all your lifelong toil will turn to ease.
You hesitate. It seems a simple task—
Doctors take more when testing for disease—
Yet you withhold, refuse to drop your mask.
There are no gods, or goddess, to appease.
You hear your name, a mirror traps your gaze.
Terror's blind rapture leaves you in a daze.
Moments pass. Vision clears. Shadows retreat.
An empty circle greets those that remain.
The drums are still and only your heart's beat
Completes this ritual. "We wax and wane.
You are our guest no more, so merry meet,
And merry part, and merry meet again!"
Two gleaming eyes of cat, or bat, or fey,
Propel you from this dark into the day.

At the Home of Poe

Frank Belknap Long, Jr.

To H. P. Lovecraft

The home of Poe! It is like a fairy dwelling, a gnomic palace built of the aether of dreams. It is tiny and delicate and lovely, and replete with memories of sere leaves in November and of lilies in April. It is a castle of vanished hopes, of dimly-remembered dreams, of sad memories older than the deluge. The dead years circle slowly and solemnly around its low white walls, and clothe it in a mystic veil of unseen tears. And many marvellous stories could this quaint little old house tell, many weird and cryptic stories of him of the Raven hair, and high, pallid brow, and sad, sweet face, and melancholy mien; and of the beloved Virginia, that sweet child of a thousand magic visions, child of the lonesome, pale-gray latter years, child of the soft and happy South. And how the dreamer of the spheres must have loved this strange little house. Every night the hollow boards of its porch must have echoed to his footfall, and every morn the great rising sun must have sent its rays through the little window, and bathed the lovely tresses of the dream-child in mystical yellow. And perhaps there was laughter within the walls of that house—laughter and merriment and singing. But we know that the Evil One came at last, the grim humourless spectre who loves not beauty, and is not of this world. And we know that the house of youth and of love became a house of death, and that memories bitter as the tears of a beautiful woman assailed the dreamer within. And at last he himself left that house of mourning and sought solace among the stars. But the house remains a vision out of a magical book; a thing seen darkly as in a looking-glass; but lovely beyond the dreams of mortals, and ineffably sad.

The Darkness of Building 727

Ngo Binh Anh Khoa

The symbol of past decades' decadence,
The building's now a tomb of rust and rot,
Devoured by Time's tormenting maw, and not
A glimmer of its former opulence
Remains. These halls now rarely hear the sounds
From living feet or breathing mouths—there is
But silence festering in this cold abyss
Where callous winds on fractured windows pound.
But should one reach the half-built thirteenth floor,
Where many builders met untimely ends,
One can hear echoes of the past again
Through marching footsteps, muffled screams, and more
Till shadowy figures beckon that brave soul
To sit at the steep edge and just let go.

Author's Note: This poem is inspired by the urban legend in my hometown, which revolves around the titular building, more commonly known as Building 727 Tran Hung Dao, where many mysterious deaths and paranormal activities ranging from mildly mischievous to downright lethal were rumored to have taken place due to the ill-advised construction of the unlucky 13th floor. The building was demolished in 2016, but it still remains one of the most famous haunted houses in Ho Chi Minh City. The poem heavily draws inspiration from the urban legend but with certain elements of my own making.

The Haunted House in Kensington
Jessie Adelaide Middleton

About six months ago, a literary friend of mine, who, like myself, is immensely interested in psychic phenomena, told me of a well-authenticated case of haunting in Kensington, and asked me if I would care to visit the house with her and investigate the matter.

Naturally I said yes, and one rainy day in November we called at the house, which is in a quiet road. My friend's brother, who is a doctor, has a surgery there.

The house is a tall, four-storied one, with a small plot of ground at the back, gloomy-looking, but quite ordinary, and not fallen to decay. The upper rooms are used as waiting-rooms, surgeries, and doctor's dispensary. In the basement, the windows of which are more than half underground, live the caretaker, a Naval Reserve man, and his wife.

My friend's brother suggested that we should interview them both, and hear for ourselves the extraordinary things that had been taking place, for which he and the other inmates of the house were absolutely unable to account.

As I have no authority for using the real name of the caretaker and his wife, I will call them Mr. and Mrs. Lee. When we entered the sitting-room, Mrs. Lee—a young and very pretty woman—was leaning over a cradle containing a beautiful baby of a few weeks old. The kettle was singing on the hob, and everything seemed bright and as homely and unghostlike as possible.

I approached the subject of the ghost very delicately, and Mrs. Lee grew serious at once. Her attitude in the matter was that she was "fed up" with it. However, learning that I was very much interested, she kindly told me all she knew, and bit by bit I extracted details of one of the most eerie cases of up-to-date haunting I have ever come across.

To make the story clear, I must first describe the position of the apartments. The rooms Mrs. Lee and her husband occupy are one in the basement and one at the very top of the house. Their living-room is the large kitchen I have spoken of, in front, and it is approached by a long flight of broad stone steps which run down from the entrance hall. On the ground floor above the basement are one waiting-room and the rooms occupied by Dr. G— and my friend's brother. Above these, on the first floor, is another doctor's room, and also a large dispensary in which bottles and stores are kept.

Mrs. Lee and her husband are worried by constant weird and uncanny noises. In the dead of night they hear distinctly people moving about the house. Somebody walks heavily and firmly down the stone steps. They get up, open the door, and search the house thoroughly from roof to basement, but find nothing. The noises generally occur between the hours of one and three o'clock, and are so frequent that the Lees have now got quite used to them.

One night, when they had only been a short time in the house, and had no idea there was anything wrong with it, these noises began.

Mr. and Mrs. Lee were in bed, but were both wakened simultaneously by the sound of loud footsteps coming down the stone stairs leading to the basement. They lay quiet and listened. Nearer and nearer came the footsteps, tramp, tramp, down the stairs, and into the room where they were. They were slow and heavy, and they came forward into the room and stopped near the table in the centre.

There was a pause, and the next moment there was a noise which Lee and his wife describe as the sound of heavy wet swabs being thrown down on the kitchen floor. Lee sprang out of bed and lighted the gas. The kitchen was absolutely empty.

He searched hurriedly, and went into the scullery opposite, but with no result. There was no way of egress from the basement except by the stone stairs again, and the visitor—if there was one—must have therefore been still hidden in the basement. But a thorough search brought no result, and, agreeing that it was "very strange indeed," they returned to bed.

Presently a terrific crash of glass in the dispensary woke the Lees again with a shock. Terrified lest the acids in the bottles should run into one another and cause an explosion, they tore upstairs with all speed.

When they got to the dispensary everything was perfectly still. Not a bottle was broken, and nothing was out of place or disarranged. Nobody was in the room, and as the big bottles do not touch, no vibration could possibly have caused the noises.

Lee and his wife went downstairs, after thoroughly searching the house again in vain, and the rest of the night passed quietly.

One evening not long after, Mrs. Lee's eldest little girl came to her mother, and said, "Mother, there's a man in the scullery."

Wondering how any man could possibly have got there without her hearing him come down the stone steps, Mrs. Lee went to see who it was. As she approached the scullery—which faces the kitchen door—she saw and *heard the key, which was on the outside of the door, turn in the lock.* Steps then passed her down the passage, and she felt what she described as a rush of cold air. She opened the door and looked boldly in. There was no one there. On questioning her little girl, the child told her that she saw a dark man walk into the scullery and shut the door after him.[3]

3   Another evening a man had called to look at Mrs. Lee's sewing-machine which was standing in the kitchen. As she and the man were bending over it they heard the kitchen door open and steps come in. Forgetting that her husband was out at a reserve meeting and would not be back till much later, she said, "Is that you, Bill?" without however turning round. There was no answer. Both Mrs. Lee and the man then turned. There was no one in the room. They had both heard the door open, and someone enter, and they both had felt again the "rush of cold air."

These manifestations were constantly repeated, More or less in the same way, and none of them could be accounted for.

Christmas Eve came, and brought a new development. Mrs. Lee, who was busy in the kitchen, was disturbed by frequent knocking at the back window, which looks out into the piece of ground at the back of the house. This window is at the top of the flight of stone stairs leading down into the basement, and Mrs. Lee was astonished to hear anyone knocking at it, because the piece of garden was quite closed and walled in, and there is no path on either side of the house. Therefore whoever knocked at the window must have been either inside the house or else out in the closed and walled-in garden, unable to escape.

Mrs. Lee went several times to see who was knocking, and finally opened the window, to look into the garden, but seeing nobody there she went on with her work.

Presently one of her neighbours came in, saying, "Someone keeps knocking at your windows. I thought I would come and tell you."

Mrs. Lee explained that she had answered the knocks, but that nobody was there.

"Well," said her neighbour, "how you can live in the house I can't think. *I* wouldn't, if you gave it to me rent free." And off she went.

The knocks and footsteps were still continually heard, and so uncanny were the noises that Mrs. Lee made inquiries about the house, to see if she could find out about the people who had formerly lived in it, without saying what she had heard and seen, for fear of being laughed at.

For some time she was not able to gather any details at all, except that the house had the reputation of being haunted. This she heard from various neighbours, who also told her that the police were well aware of the fact. In confirmation of the latter part of this statement, Mrs. Lee told me that whatever constable happened to be on duty generally watched the house rather carefully, and one or two had asked her somewhat strange questions, without appearing to take much interest, which showed her that the police had heard of some extraordinary goings on there.

One day a hospital nurse living in the district threw some light upon the matter. She said she had heard a story to the effect that, some years ago, one of the doctors in the house had murdered a woman in the kitchen, and had then gone upstairs to the dispensary and shot himself. His body and that of the woman were moved from the house together by the police.

Here, then, was the explanation of the weird noises. The wretched doctor, unable to rest in his grave, visits the scene of his crime nightly and re-acts the ghastly deed. Going down the stone stairs into the kitchen, he kills his victim, and wipes up the blood with the large wet swabs used in surgeries. He then goes into the scullery (locking the door behind him), and washes his hands, evidently with the intention of removing all traces of the crime. When he goes upstairs, however, he is overcome with either fear or remorse, and shoots himself in the dispensary, falling back with a loud crash among the bottles.

His restless footsteps walk at night all about the house—up and down, backwards and forwards. They are heard in rooms at the top of the house as well as down in the basement, and, in fact, everywhere.

So far I have not been able to trace exact details of the crime and suicide. Had the doctor lived to be hanged, it would, of course, have been easy enough to have gathered all particulars. The hospital nurse cannot say exactly when it happened, but she has spoken to old people, since dead, who actually saw the bodies removed.

If any of my readers interested in criminology can throw fresh light on the murder, and will communicate with me, I shall be greatly obliged to them.

The hospital nurse had not heard details of Mr. and Mrs. Lee's ghastly experience. When she volunteered the story, she only knew that the house was said to be haunted, but her information tallied so exactly with what they had heard and seen that it was evidently the explanation.

I have had still further confirmation about the strange manifestations in the house. Dr. G— working there late one night, saw what seemed to him to be a man's leg appearing round the open door. Being busy, he just raised his head, and called out, "Come in." He then saw a dark shape in the doorway, but as he rose to approach it, it vanished instantly. He had the house thoroughly searched, but there was nobody on the premises, neither did he hear anyone go downstairs after the figure had disappeared.

The lady dispenser, I am told, calls one cupboard "the haunted cupboard," on account of the extraordinary noises she hears proceeding from it when she is alone and working late.

Mrs. Lee's statements were corroborated in every detail by her husband, who added several facts, and described, with singular vividness, the way in which the murderer's footsteps came down the stone stairs and crossed the kitchen, and also the horrible effect of the sound of the wet swabs being used to wipe up the blood of his victim after he had done her to death in the silent watches of the night.

The Haunted Castle

Lilla Price Savino

Pale ghosts, with snowy hands and flowing hair,
    Are gliding up and down you stairs and hall;
Tall shapes, in armor clad or fabrics rare,
    Hasten in answer to their loved ones' call.

For this old castle, standing on a hill,
    Has seen twelve generations rise and fall,
And now the last man of its line lies still
    Within the churchyard, near the crumbling wall.

And yet, within its spacious halls and rooms,
    A troop of merrymakers holds full sway—
Spirits of those who here held happy court.
    In wondrous glory of a bygone day.

Mortals who pass see lights and hear strange sounds
    And flee in terror from the fearful place;
They say the castle's haunted by the dead
    Of that ancestral line of noble race.

Play on, pale ghosts, until the cold, gray dawn
    Warns you to seek again your narrow beds,
And, in your tattered grandeur, sink to rest
    Beneath the crumbling stones that mark your heads.

The Red Ensign

Tony LaMalfa

"There are black zones of shadow close to our daily paths, and now and then some evil soul breaks a passage through."

—H. P. Lovecraft, "The Thing on the Doorstep"

The tragedy of Jezebel Rhodes is one I tell sparingly and with a heavy heart. Years ago I was afforded the opportunity to rescue this childhood acquaintance from a life of abject suffering and servitude. As my elementary school classmate, Jezebel was exceptionally ordinary save her crooked smile, which was often mistaken for a scowl. In fact, the entire Rhodes family was itself unremarkable. All I recall of their peripheral impact on the world is the home-made elderberry syrup Jezebel's mother would hawk after school to the other parents for a pittance. Nevertheless, my own mother observed that I was one of the few children to show any kindness to Jezebel, much less take notice of her.

Now that some time has passed, I have attempted to correlate the circumstances of this unpleasant affair with greater clarity. Yet I am not entirely convinced it took place at all, but rather, in my mind, whilst I wrestled with consciousness as the whippoorwills sang on that strange summer's eve of 1919.

Several months prior, as the world spent the winter recovering from war, I elected to take part in a great trek spanning the length of the eastern seaboard, in the company of a dear friend from Atlanta. This southern gentleman, Mr. Uriah Dover Smith, never quite shook his boyhood nickname of "Smitty." Some of his earliest memories included hiking through various regions of the Blue Ridge Mountains with his stalwart father. These exhilarating excursions continued late into Smitty's adolescence until his father died of pneumonia in 1912, leaving my friend with an earnest desire to explore for himself what lay beyond those mountain trails and remote alpine hideaways of Appalachia.

Smitty and I first met in a ditch overseas, somewhere deep in Flanders. My Canadian detachment was besieged alongside his American troop by German artillery. As the situation deteriorated, most of our fellow soldiers perished; but in the end we overcame our aggressors during one final desperate assault on our foes in the dead of night. One thing led to another and, against all odds, Smitty and I survived, though not before I risked my life to save his. In return, he felt he owed me a great debt from the entire ordeal—which I understood but passed off as unnecessary, seeing how I was simply performing my sworn duty.

Thus, as a favor to Smitty—to repay me, as he saw it—I allowed myself to fall in with his ambitious plan to embark on a northward pilgrimage, surrendering to the notion that the natural world might be an appropriate medication for our tour in Europe. I soon learned that this lofty idea was not as far-fetched as I imagined it to be, and our approximate journey would cover parts of what wayfarers later dubbed the "Appalachian Trail."

The genius of Smitty's expedition was that we would depart from a trailhead near Jasper, Georgia, and progress steadily northeast while winter gave way to spring. This would ensure our avoiding the harshest of conditions as we aimed to cross the Potomac by midsummer, with hopes of finally reaching the Catskills before autumn settled in. Furthermore, I proposed to Smitty that, after we took a well-earned rest in Albany, he travel with me westward by rail to Buffalo aboard the Twentieth Century Limited. From there we might visit Niagara Falls before transferring to lesser known lines, all the while gravitating toward my hometown of Toronto. To this he agreed.

Through thickly forested valleys, past placid lakes Smitty and I ventured on foot, never tiring of the clear crisp mountain air and emerald treetops stretching out as far as the eye could see. Upon cresting each six-thousand-foot summit, we consulted his father's weathered maps, updating landmarks along the way with advice from friendly locals or isolated bands of social misfits, whose bright-eyed curiosity was piqued by our daring endeavor.

We welcomed any and all hospitality offered us. The lively banjo-picking of toothy youths, haunting mountain folklore told by crusty grandfathers, and old-time remedies applied by winking widows made quick work of our minor injuries and ailments. Sweet young women with rustic country charm never ceased to catch our eye, rivaling the fancy airs put on by any lovely Southern belle demanding attention. Rural cuisine, which oscillated between crude victuals and culinary virtuosity, was always a welcome treat over our meager trail rations.

For long stretches Smitty and I walked in companionable silence, rarely separating beyond earshot or line of sight and always rendezvousing for lunch or to make camp. Round the warmth of a fire we spent our evening hours swapping stories, playing cards, or cataloguing the day's offerings in our respective journals. My friend even treated us to tunes on his cherished jaw harp, with my feeble harmonica skills augmenting the melody now and again.

Continuing northeast, we kept the Cumberland Plateau on our left and North Carolina's Piedmont region on our right. Days bled into weeks and soon weeks into months. The further we hiked toward our midsummer waypoint, the less serviceable Smitty's maps became and the more we relied upon our compasses and the contours of the landscape or hand-drawn sketches by kindred spirits met along the way. Despite losing our direction once or twice, we made the Potomac ahead of schedule. Because of this, we hooked a train to the nation's capital and basked in the luxuries of city life for nearly a fortnight. As intoxicating as it was, Smitty insisted we press on to save ourselves the discomfort of arriving to Albany in late October.

Now rejuvenated, we quickly returned to our routines on the trail. With the northern end of the Allegheny Mountains to the west and several major Colonial cities to the southeast, we marched on at an excitable pace. Near the border of New Jersey, however, I again longed for the urban comforts and social connections we had tasted back in Washington. Therefore I suggested we make a brief sojourn to New York City. This Smitty unexpectedly rejected. He believed the call of the wild had beckoned us *away* from bustling streets and business districts, back to where silence spoke in whispers to those whose hearts and minds were open. In his reasoning, Smitty also reminded me that our journey's end was less than a month away. Reluctantly, I yielded to his logic but secretly harbored a grudge against this decision—and to some extent, my friend.

By early September we found ourselves traversing the Mohawk Trail toward Greenfield, Massachusetts. I was growing tired and began sulking at having not gotten my way. This only served to dampen our spirits further as we returned to the daily grind of hiking cross country. As if to punctuate the tension that crept into our otherwise amiable relationship, we began to deviate somewhat east of our intended route in order to skirt inclement weather threatening us from the northwest. When the violent storms pushed us eastward further still, we tried to seek shelter together, but it was all for naught. Smitty and I were lost in unfamiliar territory and had become separated on bad terms, having not previously coordinated a rendezvous point should trouble arise. To add insult to injury, my compass stopped working properly.

Exhausted and with no sense of direction, I staggered blindly through a heavy mist that rolled down a densely wooded hillside. As I descended in kind, the swirling mist dissipated with each step, affording me a limited view of my new surroundings. Situated at the bottom of a deep, dark valley, a small group of buildings huddled together in the fading light. My luck, so it seemed, had held out, and I wished the same for Smitty, wherever he had gotten to.

I proceeded toward the humble settlement with little trepidation and was grateful to find relief from the deteriorating weather underneath the awning of what appeared to be a general store, just off the village square. In lieu of proper street lamps, covered sconces of a Gothic nature held wooden torches, the flames of which danced wildly in the wind. The rain clouds let up some, and I found myself staring through bleary eyes at a collection of dilapidated homes encrusted in mold and sporting mismatched windows. Along with the medieval sconces, these neglected buildings gave the vague impression of a broken people, as further evidenced by their unkempt yards—which, to me, bespoke a lack of civic pride. All I could say with absolute certainty was that I had run aground in a rather peculiar place.

In the flickering torchlight I consulted my regional map before gaining entry to the store, which was lit and evidently occupied. Based on the duration of my separation from Smitty and our last known location, I estimated this rural community to be either Orange or Athol. After shaking the water from my clothes, I entered through the main door.

A silent apathy hung about those few denizens loitering around what turned out to be the local inn. Tattered clothes, labor-worn bodies, and poor hygiene suggested poverty and no formal education . . . farmers, perhaps. Weary as I was, my mind entertained the unwholesome practice of inbreeding to have also crept into the ranks of these grim villagers, into whose gullets I imagined they spooned cold porridge or thin vegetable soup, all while neglected children cried innocently to be freed from their desultory upbringing.

True, these projections were not only unfair and unkind but unwarranted. One could not fault these souls for maintaining the conditions in which they were assuredly raised. Why then did I look down upon these particular strangers with disgust? After all, from my many months tramping around the countryside, I may well have passed as their kinsman. But there was something more, a sense of foreboding in that shadowy hamlet which vexed me.

The plump innkeeper stated, rather indifferently, that his establishment could not offer food or lodging—citing a leaky roof over the kitchen and guest rooms, due to the constant battering of storms. He was quick to suggest The Red Ensign, an erstwhile farmhouse down the road which had turned to boarding lodgers. The fact that such an establishment should retain a formal title, whilst the inn remained anonymous to those unaware of its existence, did not pique my curiosity so much as its name, which it shared with the flag of my own beloved nation.

The rain further slackened to a drizzle as the sun sank below a cloudy horizon. I soon came across the boarding house to which I had been directed and found it sat in the same dejected state as its architectural counterparts save the familiar flag flying atop a makeshift pole of rotting timber. My spirits lifted at the sight of this old friend, with its solid red background, Union Jack in the upper left corner, and Canadian coat of arms in the lower right—distinguishing it from other countries of the British Commonwealth. This prompted me to take the uneven porch stairs two at a time, and I rapped on the front door, perhaps a little too enthusiastically.

The faint scent of wood smoke hung in the air as thin bars of warm light spilled out from the slats of shuttered windows on the lower level of The Red Ensign. Yet I remained on that porch for nearly ten minutes, rapping on the door at regular intervals with growing apprehension and no reply. Although nary a noise could be heard there within, the omnipresent sound of whippoorwills striking up their nocturnal chorus emanated from the surrounding forest past fallow fields, beyond a crumbling well set off to one side and a dangerously leaning stack of firewood on the other.

All of a sudden a floorboard creaked softly from behind the door, which I tried and found to be unlocked. Having made it thus far and under such unusual circumstances, I felt obliged to let myself in and announce my presence. But rather than come face to face with a fellow countryman as I had naively hoped, I was hit with a nauseating odor . . . overcooked cabbage. Where the main hallway met the entrance of the house, I was confronted with several choices: follow the trail of candlelight through the open door on my left, allow my nose to guide me forward (presumably toward the kitchen whence the foul stench festered), knock on the closed door to my right, or ascend the stairs.

I exhausted the two former options before resolving to commit to one of the latter. From what I could tell, no one was in the candlelit room. Nor could any soul be found in the messy kitchen, where a hulking cast iron stove belched waves of heat into the food-strewn space while puffing smoke up its fat chimney pipe. What remained most puzzling was that the hallway and both rooms were littered with small clothing covered in crimson stains from an unknown source. I shuddered to think what made those blood-red drips, drops, smears, and spatters.

At first this gave me pause, but fraught with fatigue, I still reasoned that if some dreadful accident *had* occurred, such stains would surely be present on the floors or walls. All this aside, it was safe to assume that any overnight guests were lodged on the second floor. And so I trudged up the stairs as cautiously as I could, unconsciously fearing what my mind still failed to rationalize as the remnants of a simple culinary disaster or unsuccessful dying of the discarded textiles.

On the fifth step, the weight of my left foot provoked an agonizingly loud creak. I drew in a sharp breath, then remembered how foolish it was to keep playing this game, for surely my rapping at the front door would have roused any sleeping residents or fellow travelers. So where was the prowler whose treading prompted me to enter that queer home in the first place?

When nothing came of my singular misstep, I continued both my breathing and my ascent. On the landing I looked down a long and lonely corridor, at the end of which stood an open door. From out of this portal more light spilled, and I was grateful to know I would finally be able to confer with the landlord—or, at the very least, another lodger.

I carefully crept past four other doors, all closed and bearing no signs of activity or occupancy therein. But once more I was disappointed, for I came upon yet another empty room. Inside, a tall, thin candle burned silently in a candlestick, which rested on a wicker nightstand next to a neatly made bed and squat cupboard. Fresh linens welcomed me into their folds of fabric, as if inviting the chaos wrought by the inevitability of becoming wrinkled.

I was far too tired to contest breaching boarding house etiquette, despite not having paid in advance or registered in a ledger. Thus I sloughed off my boots and knapsack, turned the key that lay waiting in the lock, and plunged headlong onto the mattress *without* extinguishing the recently lit candle.

I awoke to a darkened room, illuminated only by slivers of pale moonlight passing through the window shutters. The dim outline of a long-haired individual hunched over my waist, slowly unfastening my belt buckle with practiced skill. The midnight arouser noticed me stir, and my body could not help but respond in kind as a pair of candied lips pressed onto mine, dampening the warning bells ringing in my head until they were subdued to mere vibrations.

We embraced with heated passion until I could feel a woman's bare chest uniting with my own exposed skin, like long-forgotten friends. To augment such a visceral and dreamlike experience, my mind conjured up the image of a horned succubus, her shapely figure and serpentine tail glistening with sweat. On the verge of surrendering myself to the moment, I flinched when a sultry voice spoke words that cut through the drowsiness, as a sharpened scythe would through dry wheat.

"Oh, darling! How the children have missed you. How *I've* missed you!"

At this outlandish sentiment I gave a start, scrambled to my feet, and backed into the corner of the room.

"Who are you?" I asked. "How did you get in?"

Somewhere in the darkness fingers snapped, and the candle on the nightstand sprang to life, as if by its own volition. Judging from what little wick and wax remained in the candlestick, I had been asleep for quite some time, though this did nothing to comfort me, since the flame now burned at the impossible height of several centimeters.

Not a sexual demon but a human temptress perched upon the tangled sheets before me.

"Don't play games, darling," she said. "You've been gone for ages, and we've *so* much catching up to do. Now come back to bed."

As the wanton woman reached out a leathery hand with fingertips stained a rich burgundy, something about her honey-brown hair and baby-blue eyes reached far back into the recesses of my memory and rattled a cage long untouched.

"Jezebel? . . . Is that you?"

I could scarcely believe it, what with having last seen this childhood acquaintance nearly two decades earlier. Her father had taken a job in America when we were only eight, and after the Rhodeses emigrated, no one ever heard from the quiet family again. Most others did not care to know what became of them, but I had always wondered.

From her corded muscles and scarred forearms, it was plain to see that Jezebel's life outside Canada had been one of hardship and hard work. How many countless buckets of water had she hauled or loads of wood had she chopped over the years? Where was the family who whisked her away from the comforts of Toronto in search of better prospects? And why was her destiny tied to this dingy boarding house?

Nevertheless, her circumstances did not seem to deter her from achieving some measure of contentment, which apparently involved the pursuit of physical pleasure as a means of easing her strife. Although it was hard to blame Jezebel for choosing this avenue of expression, I could not hide my embarrassment at the situation. It was far from my intent to take advantage of a woman, especially one whom I had known when we were young.

However, her eyes presently shimmered with desire, and for a moment we stared longingly at each other. Then Jezebel seemed to let down her guard, which afforded me a temporary glimpse at the bygone innocence still lingering beneath.

"Thomas?" she asked, blinking away confusion.

"It's been a while," I said with a weary grin. "What on earth are you doing here?"

"Nothing uplifting," she replied, flashing her own crooked smile, which faded quickly. "I . . . I'm not well."

"I gathered as much. Is there anything I can do?"

All of a sudden her eyes darted around the room and her lip began to quiver.

"He'll be back soon. You need to leave."

"Who? Why?"

"He needs *five* to complete the ritual!"

"Five what? I don't understand."

She gasped before whispering, "He . . . he's here. Thomas! *Thomas!*"

"Wait! Let me help!" I cried.

Then the moment passed, and Jezebel sank back into a lustful stupor, complete with that alluring quality about her voice.

"If you *really* want to help, darling, you'll rescue me from the pain of loneliness. Let's celebrate your return and add another branch to the family tree."

I refused to permit such nonsense but, at the same time, felt compelled to aid that essence of Jezebel still trapped within whatever vixen served the "He" whom she mentioned. Had the poor woman fallen in with a dastardly lover or married some surly husband? And what of the "ritual" requiring some fifth element?

Whoever this enigmatic fellow was, he would arrive shortly. In preparation, I donned my clothing, laced my boots, and made to grab my knapsack. But as I did so, the seductress moved with alarming speed and strength, pinning me against the wall.

"Oh, no! You can't leave. Now that you're here, you'll fulfill your duty," she hissed. To punctuate this statement, the candle's flame burned another four centimeters taller, lighting up the room as if it were broad daylight.

"Jezebel, enough! I'm not staying any longer. If you're in trouble, come with me."

"Shhh. You'll wake the children, darling," she said. Her voice then grew desperate. "The only way either of us will escape is if you submit. He'll finally stop at five."

This was, of course, insanity, and I refused to be coerced.

"I'm going now, Jezebel. I'll send help as soon as I can."

I tried to break free, but her grip did not slacken.

"*Thomas . . .*"

Somehow this alternative personality was taking advantage of Jezebel's familiarity with me and, for the first time, called me by name—as opposed to "darling." I felt the power shift in her favor as we locked eyes once more, for my inclination to assist an old schoolmate actually weakened my psychological defenses. Again, Jezebel's true nature shone through momentarily, but I was unaware of the deceit until it was too late. Her pupils dilated to an unnatural degree and lost their circular shape, becoming pitch-black pentagons as the irises around them shifted from baby blue to bright red.

"You said you wanted to help, didn't you?"

"Yes, I want to help," I said mechanically.

"Well then, you know what to do," she cooed, undoing my belt as before.

"I do."

"So *do it*," she whispered in my ear.

And the deed would have been done had the door to the room not swung open, revealing a young girl in tattered clothes with blonde hair and blue eyes. In her hands she toted a glass bottle filled with dark red liquid.

"Please, Mama, don't finish the ritual!" she cried. "You've no idea how bad it'll be!"

"Back to you room, *you little wench!*" bellowed Jezebel with a guttural harshness made possible only by a man's voice—deep and hollow.

"No, we won't go!" shouted a bronze-skinned boy who popped out from underneath the bed. He wore a pair of heavily patched overalls and a fierce look of determination.

Jezebel—or rather, the being now in possession of her—turned from me to give the boy a swift kick to the head. He deftly evaded the blow just as a burly, red-headed youth burst from the squat cupboard. This older boy was clothed in nothing but a burlap sack.

"You leave him alone!" growled the redhead, who charged Jezebel.

As you can well imagine, I was utterly bewildered by this turn of events. While Jezebel grappled with the angry children, I was free to snatch my knapsack and make for the closest egress: the window. Throwing open its shutters, I reeled back as a fourth child all but *floated* onto the windowsill from somewhere below and proclaimed, "This ends, here and now!"

The graceful girl, more adolescent than the rest, sported a frizzy mane of dark hair. Her olive skin sparkled like the twilit sky behind her. From her perch atop the sill she launched herself at Jezebel, who had nearly escaped the two boys. The shutters snapped together, as if by a sudden gust of wind, and remained closed while a series of curses and threats poured from the pulsating throat of the struggling woman.

I stood stock-still and staring, not wanting to involve myself in this impossibly dramatic and dreamlike affair. Unsure of what to do, I looked down at the youngest child still gripping the blood-red bottle in her hands.

"Elderberry syrup," she said, as if reading my thoughts. "Now go."

But I could not, in good conscience, abandon these young strangers to what appeared to be a proverbial battle between good and evil. All at once the gravity of the situation was made obvious when the four youths turned to me as one and shouted, *"Go!"* Their collective order for me to flee landed with the force of an unexpected punch to the stomach and prompted me, nay, *compelled* me to obey, in a manner similar to how "He" was surely directing Jezebel.

What followed was a simple moment shared between them but a stark realization to me. With their victory close at hand, each youth donned a familiar, crooked smile. These children . . . that expression. The family resemblance was unmistakable: they were Jezebel's progeny. All of them. So what of their father, or rather, *fathers?* Had they, too, been wayward travelers like myself who unwittingly stumbled upon this hellish house? And how, pray tell, had the children of Jezebel come to possess the same supernatural power to command others as "He" did? But wait!—could it be that "He" was also their father, a relationship forged through some unholy trinity of parentage?

As my mind reeled, my body complied with the will of the children to perform one last, singularly disturbing act before departing. To my horror, I witnessed my hands wielding the flaming candlestick. I set ablaze the wicker nightstand, cupboard, and jumble of bedsheets, upon which Jezebel and the three older children were deadlocked.

Howls of fury and throaty protests spewed from the creature inhabiting the beleaguered woman. I attempted to cry out, but my words were choked by an outpouring of emotional turmoil mixed with the noxious plumes of smoke. In the corridor I turned back to the room only to find the door already closing behind me as the young blonde took a long pull of elderberry syrup, a fiery gleam in her eye. . . .

Outside, I leaned against the flagpole, watching the flames lick away this line of the Rhodes lineage. Suddenly a hollow masculine voice roared with rage as its owner succumbed to immolation. When finally I pulled myself from that sorry scene, a small flock of winged creatures emerged from the ruins, passing overhead . . . mourning doves, I believe.

In despair and disbelief, I plodded along and alone in the early morning hours, back through the village square, past the nameless inn and Gothic sconces, the decrepit homes and sleeping families. My only companion during this rather woeful trek was the whippoorwills' reprise before daybreak. And I wondered while I wandered: through my involvement in this unbelievable enterprise, could some malevolent force have possibly been banished from that shadowy hamlet? Were my actions entirely excusable? My conscience redeemable?

Beyond these questions, time stole truth from memory.

Regarding my own rescue, Smitty had employed a hunting party from Athol and discovered my unconscious body in the next valley over, not far from the town of Orange. Evidently I had fallen from an unseen cliff after the sun's glare and morning fog combined to form a blinding force. Furthermore, my friend and fellow soldier thought it quite comical that the Canadian flag stowed in my knapsack yielded more than enough makeshift bandages for my various wounds. But in this I found no humor or irony. I had brought no such flag . . . not to *my* knowledge.

Our time in Albany was spent more on my recovery than our reveling at having completed this arduous journey. Aboard the train to Toronto, I relayed to Smitty my encounter at The Red Ensign, invoking a mixture of curiosity and incredulity. He eventually settled on the following position: I had probably dreamt the entire ordeal whilst unconscious from my fall. As for the inexplicable manifestation of the flag, Smitty reasoned that I must have absentmindedly packed it in advance or somehow acquired it before losing consciousness.

We spent the remainder of our extensive train ride concocting a wildly fantastic theory: that I had actually stumbled into some weird fairy tale wrought from the dark imaginings of starving poets and restless dreamers. This helped to mend the distance put between us before our separation in the wildness, as well as make light of the trauma I had endured.

Of poor Jezebel Rhodes and her children of separate begetters, I can only hope—if these events truly transpired as I remember—that their souls now rest in peace, free from "He" who so aptly borrowed the body and likeness of my old schoolmate for his otherworldly witchcraft.

When I catch the malodorous scent of cooked elderberries or taste their sweet tang in a preserve or fine wine, evermore am I plagued with doubt about the circumstances around this extraordinary occurrence. The village I visited was neither Orange nor Athol, so to which settlement had I then traveled? And what of the mysterious flag in my knapsack? Was it conceivable to retain fragments of reveries in the form of physical objects?

Though my inability to answer these questions may condemn me to lunacy, I fear I shall never again look upon the blessed banner of my homeland with pride or admiration. But even more unspeakable are those stray thoughts regarding the machinations of our unseen adversary—thoughts that bring the greatest unrest to both my waking hours and fitful sleep.

If Jezebel's offspring had not intervened and I indeed fathered a child to complete that supposed occult ritual as "He" so desired, what the devil would have been birthed unto the world? And if "His" reach was acutely adjacent to our reality, was the joint intervention of those valiant children and me enough to thwart "Him"? Had their sacrifice made the all difference? … Or had we merely stalled the inevitable?

Were that the case, may God have mercy on my soul.

An Empty House at Night

Cristel Hastings

Quiet enough at noon among its trees
    And weed-grown paths that slumber in the sun,
The empty house seems settled back at ease
    Watching the gray years drift by, one by one.

Here bees may drone and plunder at their will
    In gardens long forgotten—here a bird
May twitter under eaves where all is still
    And somnolent—where never voice is heard.

But let night come!—the old house is alive
    With sound and motion with each wind that sighs!
An empty house at night becomes a hive
    Of creeping monsters with a thousand eyes.

Each leaf that falls is like a giant's stride
    Across a roof velvet with moss and mold—
Here settling timbers creak—here dragons hide
    To slither from their attics, queerly bold.

The empty rooms are peopled in the gloom
    With hordes of shapeless, voiceless ghosts that roam
Through doors and windows and from room to room
    Of this lone place that once was known as Home.

Winds weep and wail the long nights through—old doors
    Move back and forth propelled by unseen hands
On hinges long unused—along the floors
    Sly forms may stalk the boards in fearsome bands.

Huge spiders spin their curtains, gray and wide,
    On grimy windows shutting out the light
For fear some passer-by may see inside
    The ghostly things that haunt the place at night.

Haunted House

Katherine Kerestman

Cars bouncing to loud music roll tires onto the grass, spill out of its doors cigarette and that other kind of smoke and twos and fours of high school and college kids after thrills. Where's the haunted house, they ask the homeowner, excited already, we want more, creeps and thrills, frights. Things jumping out at you making the girls scream so they hold onto you and who knows where that will lead. This night's electric they say.

Putting away his billfold, the man points down the street. It's a dead end, the haunted house is at the end, have fun. See where the streetlamp is going off and on, flickering like it needs a new bulb, the end of the dead end is around the bend by the streetlamp.

The kids say thanks man and put their arms around their boyfriends/girlfriends, pull out cigarettes and hip flasks, walk down the street. I like haunted houses they say, look at all the cute kids. I used to dress up as a werewolf, I was Superman. My mom was religious and wouldn't let us go trick-or-treating. Look at the Jack-o'-Lanterns, I like pumpkin pie. This is supposed to be the best haunted house in town, everyone's talking about it, vampires ghosts mad scientists. Don't let go of my hand, swear you won't, or I won't go in. I'll hold your hand.

How far is the haunted house? Oh, there, I see the street turning—the old guy said it was around the bend. Trick-or-treating must be over, I don't see any more kids around. Except for the Jack-o'-Lanterns, the houses are all dark. Only the orange eyes, noses, mouths glow in the dark. Did everyone go to bed early?

Even the streetlights are dimmer. Down there—at the end of the street is the flickering one—the man said the house was down there. We're getting closer: see, you can see it now, the old Victorian house—all the windows all lit up! The only lighted house on the street.

Hey, where'd everyone go? Joe, Sandy? Did they find a party, didn't say goodbye, will have to find their own way home. I didn't realize we were out so late, we're the only ones, Barb. At least it doesn't look closed, the house is all lit up. Don't be a scaredycat, Barb, that's why we're here.

Look—there's a graveyard, a little cemetery with a wrought-iron fence. How cool! It's the right night for a cemetery. Do you think it belongs to the people who own the house? The haunted house? See all the mist, the fog, coming out of the ground there, where people are buried six feet under? Bill, did you know that they bury coffins on top of each other, not one per grave? I learned that on a field trip to Sleepy Hollow. The lights are flickering. There's no moon or stars, only Jack-o'-Lanterns, and it's kind of spooky.

Hey, we're here. Let's knock on the door, use the big brass knocker.

"Good evening. It's very late. How can I help you?" the gray-haired woman in the purple dress asks when she opens the paneled front door with the frosted windows. Oh, yes, this is a haunted house, but not the kind that you're thinking of. Would you like to come in, look at it? I can offer you cider and doughnuts. You might as well look at the house, since you came all this way to see it. Oh, yes, that's my cat, Trolly, she and Dolly keep me company, they're spoiled.

This is the parlour—my grandfather was laid out there in his casket—see his funeral wreath in the glass box on the wall, flowers would probably crumble if you touched them now. This is the dining room: I always used to get the feeling that someone was there looking at me. I'll let you look around the upstairs, my knees are weak, be sure you go up to the third floor, the attic, it's

273

full of fun old things, antiques. Oh, don't worry, take your time, I'll wait till you get back.

The house is weird, the lady's not right I don't think but harmless probably lonely. This is a long hallway, look at all the doors. Open one, a bedroom, another and a bathroom they had big families when it was built. Sad to be so empty now. Let's look in the attic real quick and then go. I'd really like to get out of here now there little stairs in the corner, must lead to the attic, trap door in the ceiling, pull on the rope it's opening.

There's the lightswitch, watch your head. What's with the electricity tonight streetlights flickering, houses dark but this one, and now very dim light from the bare bulb hanging from the ceiling. Let me try screwing it in tighter make it a little brighter.

Oh God what is that, the roof is open, purple light coming from the sky, but it is dark out, black not purple sky. Oh no let's go—where's the trap door and the stairs—they can't be gone we just can't see them, let's look.

There is no door no stairs. The room glows purple. The roof is gone, floors, walls too. Nothing but purple light. What are those things—they're coming at us. Yellow, walking on two feet with pointed noses and chins—great big mouths and sharp teeth. Help! Get us out of here! Somebody Help! LADY, HELP! SOME-BODY HELP!

Morning comes a school day, monsters of last night dressed in school clothes, shame the electricity was on the fritz last night Halloween ended too early at least the kids got their trick-or-treating in before the power went out. The man who lives on Felix and Grant wonders when they're coming for the last car left on his lawn or if he'll have to call the police later to get it towed.

the cellar

Lori R. Lopez

It stands to reason,
The demons we battle most
Are already here.
I tell myself this,
Do not go down that stairway—
The evil will hear.
But do I listen?
Why must I ignore the voice
That screams in my ear?
I am such a fool
To cross this threshold of pain.
I might not come back.
The steps always creak
No matter how stealthily
I try to descend.
We all have our foes,
And that root cellar is mine.
Something lurks down there . . .
Eating the carrots,
The beets, garlic and onions.
So far just veggies.
I hear it at night,
Crunching all the potatoes

275

With very large teeth
And worry aloud,
What if it runs out of roots?
Will it climb the stairs?
Might it come for me
In the dark, stomach empty
In search of a snack?
If you lived above
That mysterious beastie,
You would tremble too.
So down I must go
After many second thoughts
And postponed attempts.
You know what I think?
Some people should think again
Before they think twice!

With One Look

Maxwell I. Gold

Dangling o'er the empty, forgotten woods in the far-off nethers of a pitiful nowhere, the tatters of some ancient house waned toward monstrous oblivion. Cradled beneath the hideous and heavy stars, fungi-riddled and brittle stone swayed in the stink of a dark and terrible night. Lumbering rods of steel and timber were the last visions of a place anchored in cosmic derangement where slowly, and certainly, the doomed house of Asher-Fell whispered its final prayers along the hungering abysm where some yellowed, slime-coated evil stirred.

I waited at the edge of the cliff while the tired old shack whose name it bore some thankless aeons ago, rocked in sad dusty winds over a Cyclopean gullet too dark to see, with teeth composed of mud, slime, and bile prepared to swallow the pathetic wooden corpse. I was drawn closer, when all at once my foot, now covered in neon sludge, stuck in the muck of the earth, unable to maintain a firm grasp on both reality and sanity, fumbled toward the cavernous pit. Strangely, the *wind* pushed me back as if something were breathing heavily, pulling, insisting my fate along with the grand home. I couldn't move, unable to displace myself from the grime when pieces of brick and wood began to fall around me.

Below, the breathing intensified, heat and noxious fumes rising with a terrible intensity when I realized the dirt melted away revealing pink, veiny walls dotted by billions of pearl-colored spikes trembling at the touch from every piece of wood and stone as it tumbled against the *walls*.

Dear god, no. All at once I struggled helplessly as the odor from the monstrous creature belched with hungry and primal rhythm. Piece by piece the bones of the broken structure crumbled toward a wanton destruction where I was struck with the cold sensation feeling myself fall into the mouth of a nameless beast, surrounded by the awful loneliness of death.

The House at Black Tooth Pond
Stephen Mark Rainey

By combining a high-pitched vocalization with a shrill, warbling whistle, my brother could mimic the cries of the whippoorwills that lurked in the nighttime woods around Black Tooth Pond, convincingly enough that only a trained ear could discern the difference.

I knew the difference.

The cry, mournful and eerie, now wafted from the darkness outside my bedroom window. I knew that sound, and it made me quail.

It wasn't a whippoorwill's song, but my brother's.

My brother was dead.

One Year Ago

With a heartfelt "Cheers, bro!" I clinked—or, more aptly, clunked—my plastic cup against Phil's, somehow managing to both make contact and avoid a disastrous spill in the near-pitch-darkness of the old ruin. It was good bourbon, and I would have been miffed if a drop had sloshed onto the half-rotting planks beneath our feet. I credit intoxication with our mutual precision. Had either of us been even remotely sober, disaster would have surely followed.

Phil was five years my junior. Most of the civilized world had expected me to be the first to marry and, subsequently, produce a veritable herd of diminutive humans. But no. Although Michela—my "special friend," as my parents called her—and I enjoyed a happy, committed relationship, we preferred maintaining a greater degree of independence, including separate residences.

Children were not on our radar. For us, this arrangement proved ideal. So it was Phil, whom that same civilized world considered Bohemian, leaping with uncharacteristic aplomb into traditionalism. His bride's name was Carli, and I quite liked her, despite her questionable taste in men.

For his own reasons Phil had chosen to celebrate his last unwed night in a crumbling, overgrown house set back from the banks of Black Tooth Pond, a tiny, murky body of water that hid at the end of an ancient lumbering road, five miles or so out of Aiken Mill, our hometown.

I felt no enthusiasm about revisiting this old structure. Yet, for my brother, the setting seemed so fitting that I'd gone along with the idea.

Idiot me.

Bryon Bushnell and Tony Garcia, his best friends from his Beckham College days, had driven down from Georgetown and Baltimore, respectively, for the nuptials.

And this "party."

A dozen years earlier, the three classmates had discovered Black Tooth Pond while exploring the Sylvan County backroads, looking for a place to smoke pot. Since there were no nearby houses and nobody ever seemed to come out here, it became their go-to place to get stoned. The pond was so named, as Phil later discovered, because an array of broken tree trunks, burnt black from some past fire, protruded like rotten teeth from the water at one end.

"You know," came Bryon's half-amused, half-ornery voice from three feet away in the darkness. "We could have just partied out on the banks like we used to."

Nearby, a phone screen flared. Tony's bearded visage appeared and hovered in the abyss like a pale, scruffy ghost. "Yeah, Phil. I'd like to not fall through the floor and die before I've had a chance to kiss your bride. Maybe repeatedly."

"We're all standing at least five feet from the nearest holes in the floor," Phil said. "Don't go wandering, and you'll be fine."

Bryon groaned. "I suppose you're gonna hold the ceremony here too?"

"Nope. Asberry Vineyards, over by Beckham. You'll like it."

"So it's wine rather than moonshine now. This area is coming up in the world."

"Depends on your perspective."

"Funny," Tony said, "all those times we smoked out here, and we never knew this old place existed."

Phil's eyes reflected the phone light as they flicked toward me. "It's damned well hidden. This place was actually Marty's discovery."

Tony's deep voice boomed, "This is your fault, you vile old fuck!"

I sent a wan smile into the darkness. "Nope. All Phil's idea."

My brother raised his cup again. "The more you drink, the better this place looks. What you can see of it." Everyone but me laughed. "Anyway, here's to the best times we ever had back when. And to whatever shit lies ahead."

The cups came up, touched, and tipped. A second later the phone light went out and somebody's breath exploded in the darkness—a clear sign that bourbon had gone down a windpipe.

"Smooth," came Bryon's ragged whisper.

A couple more laughs, and we drank in silence for a minute or so.

That was when we heard it.

The whippoorwill's call. Outside in the night. Soft, melancholy. *Eerie.*

I shivered, remembering that hellish twinge of fear from my first visit here, not so long ago. I had chosen to ignore that incident, pass it off as a case of overwrought nerves, sparked by pre-existing anxiety.

"Listen," my brother said. I heard him step toward the open door, and now I could make out his vague figure, highlighted by a moonbeam that filtered down through the trees. The cry came again, this time loud and clear, from inside the house.

It was Phil. Calling back to the nocturnal bird.

The whippoorwill responded.

Phil called again.

Another response came.

I knew, then and there, it was not from a bird.

Two Years Ago

Phil had never anticipated settling in Aiken Mill, where we'd both grown up, but after college he'd found a good job in town and decided to remain. A small town by any standard, Aiken Mill was still the largest and most prosperous cornerstone of a triad in Sylvan County that included the little communities of Beckham and Barren Creek. Virtually everyone who grew up in our shadowy corner of southwestern Virginia eventually departed for richer hunting grounds, never to return. I had done a four-year stint as an account executive at a bank in Atlanta, but due to both my parents suffering severe health crises, I returned to Aiken Mill to help with their care. There were three banks in town, and I secured a position at one of them. Thus, Phil and I remained at least geographically close as we wended our way through the oftentimes hellish wilds of adulthood.

Phil owned a dog—a perpetually exuberant Golden Retriever named Rufus—whom he loved taking for long walks, usually around Black Tooth Pond. I sometimes joined him. For both of us, these walks provided some much-needed relief from dealing with Mom's leukemia and Dad's Parkinson's.

On this chilly, late fall afternoon, Phil, Rufus, and I were walking the old goat path around the pond. Through the thinning foliage I noticed a break in the trees I hadn't seen before. Beyond it, a narrow, crooked trail led deeper into the woods. I pointed it out to my brother. "Ever been down that way?"

He shook his head. "Never even seen it before. Kinda weird, considering how many times I've been out here."

"Yeah, stoned."

He laughed. "C'mon, I haven't been stoned in years. Wanna check it out?"

I glanced at the deepening blue sky. At most we had an hour before nightfall. "Michela and I are having dinner at seven. Can't go very far."

"It's just now five," he said. "We've got time."

I gave a little shrug. "Okay."

Although the trees were mostly bare, deep shadows fell over us as soon as we set foot on the path. Rufus seemed somewhat more subdued than usual, but he continued to lead as we threaded our way into the woods. A short distance ahead I made out a towering, dark shape, and I realized it was a massive magnolia, at least forty feet tall and thirty in diameter, its lowest branches and boughs spilling onto the ground like scaly green tendrils.

Phil actually gasped. "That is one big motherfucker."

As I proceeded a few steps farther, I saw beyond the tree a dense, tangled network of vines and branches with unnaturally sharp, angular contours. I realized I was seeing the roof of an old structure, draped with mostly dead foliage. From its apex, through a gaping, splintered maw, a giant, ghostly white sycamore had clawed its way *out* of the house and into the sky.

"You really didn't know this was here?" I asked.

Mute with wonder, Phil shook his head. His grip loosened on Rufus's leash, but now the dog showed no inclination to advance farther.

In rural Sylvan County, ancient, abandoned structures were anything but rare, and both Phil and I found such places fascinating. So, taking care to avoid getting snarled in the briers and creepers that surrounded the house, I made my way toward a shadowy rectangle at the nearest end of the structure. From a few feet away I confirmed it was a door, partially opened inward.

"You coming?" I called.

After a long silence Phil said, "Yeah." Then came the slow but chaotic crunch of footsteps as he and Rufus battled their way through the tangled barrier. Near the door a small but sturdy ironwood jutted up from the brambles, so he secured Rufus's leash around its spotty gray trunk. He patted the dog on the head and said, "Okay, buddy, you stand guard, and don't let any marauding groundhogs get us."

Rufus responded with a nonplussed glare.

Carefully mounting a single, weathered concrete stair, I placed a hand on the filthy, peeling door and pushed. With an angry scrape it inched forward and froze. I gave it a more forceful shove and, with what sounded like a sigh of resignation, it swung fully open. A cool, musty odor seeped out of the gloom. I did not find this smell disagreeable, for it reminded me of the earthen cellar of my grandparents' house, where Phil and I played as kids.

Still, as I placed one cautious foot on the interior floorboard, I felt a twinge of revulsion, though not from anything tangible. I shuffled forward, testing my weight, until I felt confident my footing was secure. In the half-light that seeped in through the door and a pair of grimy windows, I discovered that I stood in a small living room, furnished with a disgusting, moldy couch, a few rickety chairs, a wooden coffee table, and the smashed remains of an ancient television set. Trash of all sorts littered the floor: papers, old drink cans, food wrappers, picture frames—some empty, some containing photographs of men, women, and children, their features too smudged and stained to make out—and even some nasty, ragged old clothes. Black mold and strips of disintegrating wallpaper adorned the sagging walls.

"What a treasure trove!" Phil's exclamation was anything but ironic.

I took a few slow steps toward the center of the room. At its farthest end an open door revealed an array of broken branches and the half-visible trunk of the sycamore that had grown up through the roof. To my right, in front of a small brick fireplace, I saw two yawning holes in the floor, their edges jagged and splintered. And in the far left-hand corner a warped staircase with a half-collapsed banister ascended into impenetrable darkness.

I pointed to it. "Your penthouse is waiting. Gonna go up and take a look?"

Phil scoffed. "I'm not entirely stupid." But after a long, thoughtful scan of the stairs he added, "Well, maybe."

I noticed on the coffee table a massive pile of dusty, yellowed envelopes. These turned out to be mail—some unopened—addressed, in various combinations, to Chauncy, Harriet, Maxine, Philbert, and/or Theophilus Cabiness. I thumbed through the lot of them and determined that the postmarks ranged from October 1952 to December 1971.

"The House of Cabiness," I said, barely above a whisper.

"What?"

"This place. Must have belonged to a family named Cabiness." I held up a stack of the envelopes. "Letters, bills, advertisements. Damned peculiar."

It didn't take long to determine, by way of countless late payment and collection notices, that the Cabiness family had accumulated a substantial amount of debt. None of the personal letters bore return addresses, though all their postmarks read Roanoke, Virginia. At random I picked one and carefully withdrew a few sheets of folded, brittle paper. One leaf was a newspaper clipping dated November 17, 1952. A bold headline read, "U.S. Explodes First Hydrogen Bomb in the Pacific," and the article beneath it detailed how the sky above the ocean blazed with the light of 500 suns. Accompanying the clipping, a scrawled note in blood-colored ink read, "Hell is coming. Hell is HERE!" The note was unsigned.

Every anonymous envelope I inspected contained one or more strikingly negative news stories—from the assassinations of John F. Kennedy, Robert F. Kennedy, and Martin Luther King to the 1964 Good Friday earthquake in Alaska to the 1968 My Lai massacre in Vietnam. Inevitably, a terse, unsigned note accompanied each clipping, proclaiming that the torments of hell would soon plague the people of the nation, if not the world.

Phil studied these bleak epistles from over my shoulder.

285

"Looks like they all came from the same sender," he said. He pointed to a stack of unopened envelopes. "I bet the family got fed up with their overwrought compadre and just stopped reading. But why save all this mail—and pile it up here?"

"God knows," I said. "Maybe I'll take the letters with me. They make for a thorough and colorful catalog of very bad news."

"Complete with hysterical personal commentary."

I realized then how difficult seeing the pages had become. Good Lord, it was already getting dark outside.

"This may call for a future visit," Phil said. "Who knows what else we might find?"

Ordinarily, the prospect of further exploration might have excited me, but that earlier sense of foreboding now resurfaced—probably exacerbated by these testaments to everything wrong with the world in the mid-twentieth century. I decided that, whatever their possible historical significance, I didn't care to keep any of these letters. Somehow they felt *poisonous*.

Beyond the open door, opaque shadows draped the brambles and trees. Before we could set foot back outside, a distinctive, warbling trill rang from somewhere nearby. Phil paused and listened.

"Whippoorwill," he said. "I sometimes hear them around my place. Hey, check this out." He shot me a smug smile. Then he drew a long breath, pursed his lips, and unleashed a near-perfect whippoorwill call. With a laugh, he said, "Pretty good, eh?"

"Impressive," I said, not without sincerity, though finding this talent perfectly superfluous.

He called out again and, as if in response, the bird outside sang its mournful song.

"Fun, eh?"

"I'm glad you're enjoying yourself."

With a self-indulgent grin, he stepped through the door and set about untying Rufus's leash. As I made to exit, a low rustling rose behind me.

Then, from *inside* the house, a sharp, shrill whippoorwill cry shattered the silence.

Stung by shock, I spun to face the gloom.

The rustling came again, unmistakably from one of the holes in the floor. In that deep darkness, I glimpsed—or thought I did—a smoky gray smudge, which slid in and out of view like a fast-moving snake. Another trill issued from the opening. This one soft. Almost mocking.

Jolted by surprise—and icy fear—I leaped through the door into daylight's last remnants.

Phil's eyes widened at my abrupt appearance. He must have thought I'd stumbled, because he threw out a steadying hand.

"Careful there! You all right?"

Relief swept over me like a balmy, cleansing breeze, and I waved him away.

I immediately felt stupid. Nerves had gotten the better of me. Some critter had taken up residence inside the crumbling house. Another whippoorwill, outside but nearby, had called out. Their cries could be loud, even disconcerting.

"It's later than I realized," Phil said. "We'd better get you back home. I don't want Michela blaming me for your tardiness when it's clearly your fault."

"Haha."

We headed back toward the pond at a brisk pace. With every step, I felt more and more confident that, inside that house, I'd suffered a simple scrambling of impressions. The barrage of negativity in all those letters and the stress of dealing with my parents' conditions had supercharged my anxiety. This conclusion satisfied me.

Until I chanced a look back.

It wasn't what I saw or even heard, but what I felt. From the huge magnolia, which towered above the surrounding trees like a massive black blob, a low whippoorwill song began to pipe with the same air of mocking purpose I had perceived inside the house.

No, it wasn't a real whippoorwill song. It was mimicry, like my brother's.

Exactly like my brother's.

Rufus picked up his pace, clearly anxious to leave, and Phil hurried to keep up. Though he'd surely heard the same thing I did, he didn't *feel* it. Not the way I had.

Not yet.

I hadn't been home an hour before my dominant, rational mind reassembled my confused impressions from that disturbing experience into a sensible whole.

Anxiety. Stress. Bad lighting.

In the days that followed, Phil continued to invite me to walk with him and Rufus around Black Tooth Pond, and I sometimes did, but I had no desire to return to the House of Cabiness. He, on the other hand, seemed to make intimate friends with the place. After Rufus died, a few months later, Black Tooth Pond and the House of Cabiness became "Phil Things." I didn't know why, but he seemed to resent the fact that I failed to share his enthusiasm.

His increasing affinity—preoccupation, I would say—for whippoorwill songs not only struck me as bewildering, it disturbed the living daylights out of me.

One Year Ago

The day after his "bachelor party," Phil and Carli married as planned. Following their week-long honeymoon in Myrtle Beach, South Carolina, he returned to work in Aiken Mill, did married-people things, and continued to visit Black Tooth Pond and the House of Cabiness with unwavering devotion. He still invited me along, but my days of willingly visiting that place were done.

I never explained my reasons to him. I *couldn't* explain them, not only because I failed to fully understand them but because he refused to abide a word of criticism or advice. His wife had no interest in accompanying him out there, and while she'd liked Rufus well enough, she had no great fondness for dogs, so he never got another one. Thus, his excursions to Black Tooth Pond remained solitary.

It was a gray dawn, a month later, that Carli called me, half hysterical.

"Marty, he's gone. Phil is gone. He's dead."

A wave of shock, disbelief, and *horror* swept over me.

Along with an inexplicable sense of expectations fulfilled.

"When?" I finally managed. "What happened?"

"Last night. He went on one of his walks and didn't come back."

Of course he didn't.

"I kept calling, but he didn't answer his phone. Service is kind of spotty at that place, but I could usually reach him. So, I drove out there. Marty, I . . ."

A very long silence.

Sharp fingers scratching the back of my skull.

"You heard something."

"Birds. Whippoorwills. One was calling from inside that old house. You know how he imitated them, right? This sounded like him. I thought it must *be* him. But it wasn't. It wasn't."

"Where are you?"

"At home. The police just left."

"What else, Carli?"

Her voice caught a few times. "They found him down in that cellar. He'd gone through a hole in the floor."

"But he knew every inch . . ."

"They said he was dragged."

Blood went thundering through my skull, and for a time, I couldn't hear another word.

At last, I said, "I can come over, if you—"

"No. Please. I'm done. I think I'm going to pass out."

"I understand."

"We'll talk later."

"Yes."

And that was it. My brother was gone. Nothing in my life, not even the ever-approaching prospect of my parents dying, had ever felt so awful, so devastating.

So inevitable.

The police questioned me several times. I'm sure they suspected me of murdering Phil, for there was proof aplenty of our excursions to the House of Cabiness together. The only fingerprints in that place—other than some so old as to be meaningless—were ours. In the end, though, their interest in me sputtered and died. In fact, the absence of *any* evidence, other than the obvious brutality of my brother's death, stymied investigators to the point of inaction. *Something* had dragged him alive through the hole in the floor and ripped his body apart. But the only animal tracks in the place were small, mostly from opossums and raccoons. Not a molecule of DNA that might identify some human perpetrator ever came to light.

Eventually, the investigation withered on the vine. On those occasions when either Carli or I pressed the police for information, we found ourselves brushed off, first politely, then with terse aloofness. After a few months, unable to find either closure or hope that the police might discover a meaningful lead, Carli moved to D.C., where she had family—in her words, to seek therapy of a kind that our little town couldn't offer. I feel certain she couldn't cope with living so near the place of her husband's horrific death.

If not for Michela's love and support, I don't know that I could either.

My mother passed away two months after my brother. Three months later I had to commit my father to a specialized care facility. He died there within a matter of weeks. It was a profound, numbing blow to realize that I was now the last living member of the family I'd known and loved my entire life.

For a time I retreated, barely interacted with anyone—other than Michela, who continued to stand by me, though I sensed frustration and the beginnings of depression settling upon her. I went to my job daily, performed nominally, more or less an automaton, though sufficiently aware that I *could not* lose my position and survive. I still wanted to survive. I needed to survive.

I craved answers. However awful they might be.

There was only one place to seek them.

The half-dozen broken trunks protruding from Black Tooth Pond looked more like bony fingers reaching in supplication from the dark water, I thought as I clambered out of my car, which I'd parked just shy of the pond's reed-choked banks. A host of new "No Trespassing" signs leered at me from the nearby trees, but I paid them no heed, for I knew no one would enforce the injunction. The police had put up the signs, but since the demise of the investigation, this place was as dead to them as my brother.

I had learned that, years ago, the Cabiness family indeed owned this land, but once the last of them had either passed or moved away, no deed existed in their name. In accordance with the laws governing abandoned property, Sylvan County had assumed its ownership. At its discretion, the County Board of Supervisors had the authority to sell the Cabiness place at auction. However, as with countless such ancient, ownerless properties in the area, this one had fallen through the cracks.

Much like the afternoon that Phil and I first discovered the House of Cabiness, this one was chilly, breezy, and gray. As I trod the narrow path around the pond, I saw ahead a fluttering yellow ribbon amid the trees—a length of police tape meant to dissuade interlopers. As with the signs, I ignored the tape and made my way through the woods until I reached the grotesque, looming mass of the gigantic magnolia.

I drew to a halt and peered beyond the tree toward the

crooked, angular roof draped with old vines and dead foliage. The huge, ghostly white sycamore that had burst through to claw at the sky. The dark doorway, now gaping wide, through which Phil and I had once entered, never suspecting the events such a thoughtless, trivial act could trigger. Yellow tape formed an "X" over that portal, and another strand hung from the nearby ironwood, clearly the remains of what had been a cordon around the house.

I knew why I was here, but I had no idea what I intended to do. Make my way back inside? To what purpose? Somehow rout a dangerous animal the police could neither find nor identify? Simply stand out here and stare at the structure like a fool, daring it to reveal itself as something other than what it was—a hulking, inanimate object, incapable of perpetuating whatever life, whatever *spirit,* once resided within it?

There were no answers here. What had I been thinking?

I remembered the anonymous letters, piled like a shrine, on the broken coffee table. Chronicles of the twentieth century's grimmest, most inhumane events, accompanied by red-inked forecasts of hell itself rising in their wake. That stack of paper had struck me as being somehow *poisonous.* For an unhinged moment I wondered if the monstrous essence of all that negativity had infected the inhabitants of this place—and somehow lingered after they were long gone.

Was this notion so unhinged?

I felt a resurgence of that sense of darkness and despair, on a level I can only describe as spiritual. Before me the house's walls and windows, the sagging roof, the crumbling chimney all seemed to swell and contract, again and again, as if the structure were *breathing.* A low sliding sound whispered from within. And behind the yellow tape, in the darkness beyond the door, a wispy, gray *smudge* slid quickly in and out of view.

The rapid thudding of my heartbeat rose to deafen me.

Night wouldn't fall for another hour. Still, I expected to hear that shrill, eerie cry ring out above the pounding of my heart. The whippoorwill song that came from a thing *not* a whippoorwill.

Something that mimicked my brother mimicking a whippoorwill.

Something *cruel*.

Finally the thunder in my ears diminished. No further sound came from the house. It was an old, empty structure, a crumbling heap of bricks and boards, no more possessed of life than the pebbles and stones that littered the path.

I would never return to this place. The idea was—and had been—pointless. Foolish. Nothing more than a misconceived attempt to make sense of my brother's death. I turned my back on the House of Cabiness and began to trudge back toward my car.

It wasn't a whippoorwill call. Not even a rustle of leaves. Merely a faint, barely audible whisper behind me. It compelled me to turn and look.

Five half-visible yet somehow distinct little wisps hovered between the house and the giant magnolia. Little more than individual pillars of shimmering heat haze; perhaps dust stirred by tiny cyclones.

One for each of the names I had seen on those letters addressed to members of the Cabiness family.

Yet some flash of intuition convinced me these were not ghosts. Not separate individual *things*, but puzzle pieces, disparate parts of some other, *bigger* whole.

What if *it* had always been here—and *it* attracted human negativity like a magnet?

The little cyclones didn't move toward me but swirled in place, as if watching me, sizing me up. Beyond any question in my mind, they watched me now as they had once watched Phil.

As *it* had watched Phil.

I felt chilled. Terrified. But I whispered, "I won't be back." And I turned away.

I knew my brother had been unable to do this. I also

understood why the police had not returned to complete their investigation.

I walked to my car without looking back. By the time I reached it, darkness had swallowed the woods at the far end of Black Tooth Pond.

Near the streamer of yellow tape that marked the beginning of the path to the House of Cabiness, I noticed a little shimmer, like a wavering heat haze. I ignored it.

I never heard whippoorwills at my house because I lived too close to town. The nocturnal birds favored remote, undeveloped woodland. The call I heard now came from no bird.

The poison from the House of Cabiness had oozed forth and now lurked outside my windows.

I didn't *want* to call Michela, allow the nightmare into which I had stumbled to ensnare her as well, yet I could not refuse the desire—the compulsion—to express my deep feelings for her. I'm certain she knew how I felt, but I was never one to speak too deeply or frequently about such things. I didn't truly believe it, but my intuition, ever faithful, insisted that this might be my last chance.

"I don't like the way you sound," she said, her voice slightly shaky. "Can't you tell me what's wrong?"

"Nothing, really. I just don't feel that well. But I wanted you to know how much I appreciate you. How much I do love you."

She gave a nervous snicker. "Now I know something's wrong with you, Mister I-Don't-Express-My-Feelings-for-Shit."

I hesitated a second too long. "It's really nothing."

"I think I'd better come over there."

"No. Please. Not necessary."

"Marty, I don't think you've ever lied to me. But if you're not lying now, you're not telling me the whole truth. I'll see you in a few minutes."

"Michela, would you not—"

"A few minutes."

She hung up.

How could I not have known? Michela could not have reacted any other way.

I had known she would come. Yet I phoned her anyway.

I tried to call her back, but she wasn't answering.

I crept to my bedroom window, which faced the small but dark stand of woods between my house and the next road over. I couldn't see a thing. Yet, like afterimages on my retinas, I perceived five shimmering little wisps.

My brother's whippoorwill cry rang out. Crashed through my window like a hurled brick. Loud, sharp, and cruel.

Michela would be here within ten minutes.

She would probably find no one home.

Notes on Contributors

The Editors

S.T. Joshi is the author of *The Weird Tale* (1990), *H. P. Lovecraft: The Decline of the West* (1990), and *Unutterable Horror: A History of Supernatural Fiction* (2012). He has prepared corrected editions of H. P. Lovecraft's work for Arkham House and annotated editions of Lovecraft's stories for Penguin Classics. His exhaustive biography, *H. P. Lovecraft: A Life* (1996), was expanded as I *Am Providence: The Life and Times of H. P. Lovecraft* (2010). He has edited the anthologies *American Supernatural Tales* (Penguin, 2007), *A Mountain Walked: Great Tales of the Cthulhu Mythos* (Centipede Press, 2013), *The Madness of Cthulhu* (Titan Books, 2014), and the ongoing *Black Wings* series (PS Publishing, 2010f.). Joshi has won the World Fantasy Award, the British Fantasy Award, the Bram Stoker Award, and the International Horror Guild Award.

Katherine Kerestman is the author of *Lethal* (PsychoToxin Press, 2023), *Creepy Cat's Macabre Travels* (WordCrafts Press, 2020), and *Haunted House and Other Strange Tales* (Hippocampus Press, 2024), as well as the coeditor (with S. T. Joshi) of *The Weird Cat* (WordCrafts Press, 2023). Her Lovecraftian and Gothic works have been featured in *Black Wings VII*, *Penumbra*, *Journ-E*, *Spectral Realms*, *Illumen*, *Retro-Fan*, *Dissections*, *Off-Course*, *Lovecraftiana*, and other discerning publications. Her name is etched among the inscrutable glyphs of the Esoteric Order of Dagon and the Dracula Society.

The Contributors

Michael Aronovitz is the author of the story collections *Seven Deadly Pleasures* (Hippocampus Press, 2009) and *Dancing with Tombstones* (Cemetery Dance, 2021), and the novels *Alice Walks* (Centipede Press, 2013), *The Witch of the Wood* (Hippocampus Press, 2015), *Phantom Effect* (Night Shade, 2016), *The Sculptor* (Night Shade, 2022), and *The Winslow Sisters* (Cemetery Dance, 2024).

Im Bang (1640–1724) was a leading Korean writer of fables, folk tales, poetry, and other matter. He served in the government for many years, including being governor of Seoul.

Ambrose Bierce (1842–1914?) was an American journalist (chiefly for William Randolph Hearst's *San Francisco Examiner*, 1887–1906) and short story writer, best known for his tales of the Civil War (collected in *Tales of Soldiers and Civilians*, 1891) and of supernatural and psychological horror (collected in *Can Such Things Be?*, 1893). His prodigious output also includes essays, poetry, fables, and *The Devil's Dictionary* (1906/1911).

Algernon Blackwood (1869–1951), English short story writer and novelist, worked extensively in the weird, with such volumes as *The Listener and Other Stories* (1907), *John Silence—Physician Extraordinary* (1908), *The Lost Valley and Other Stories* (1910), *Pan's Garden* (1912), and *Incredible Adventures* (1914). Late in life he appeared on radio and television for the BBC, reading horror tales.

Adam Bolivar is a formal poet of dark fantasy, a weird fiction writer and a playwright for marionettes with a particular interest in alliterative verse, balladry, and "Jack" tales. He is the author of *The Lay of Old Hex* (Hippocampus Press, 2017), *The Ettinfell of Beacon Hill* (Jackanapes Press, 2021), *Ballads for the Witching Hour* (Hippocampus Press 2022) and *A Wheel of Ravens* (Jackanapes Press, 2023). A native of Boston, he now resides in Portland, Oregon.

The *Oxford Companion to English Literature* describes Ramsey Campbell as "Britain's most respected living horror writer," and the *Washington Post* sums up his work as "one of the monumental accomplishments of modern popular fiction." He has received the Grand Master Award of the World Horror Convention, the Lifetime Achievement Award of the Horror Writers Association, the Living Legend Award of the International Horror Guild, and the World Fantasy Lifetime Achievement Award. In 2015 he was made an Honorary Fellow of Liverpool John Moores University for outstanding services to literature. The two volumes of *Phantasmagorical Stories* offer a sixty-year retrospective of his short fiction. *The Village Killings* collects his novellas, and *Ramsey's Rambles* his film reviews. His latest novel is *Fellstones* from Flame Tree Press, who have also recently published his *Brichester Mythos* trilogy.

Frank Coffman is a retired professor of English, Creative Writing, and Journalism. Three major collections of speculative verse—*The Coven's Hornbook & Other Poems, Black Flames & Gleaming Shadows,* and *Eclipse of the Moon*—was followed by *What the Night Brings.* His poetry spanning the popular genres has appeared in many magazines, journals, and anthologies. His collection of occult detective stories, *Three Against the Dark,* was published in 2022.

Samuel Taylor Coleridge (1772–1834) was a leading British poet of the early Romantic era. Such poems as *The Rime of the Ancient Mariner* (1798) and *Christabel* (1816) were pioneering ventures into weirdness. His views on the interpretation of literature are embodied in *Biographia Literaria* (1817), where he devised the formula of the "willing suspension of disbelief."

Margaret Curtis, witch, writer, artist, healer, and activist, lives in Wollongong, New South Wales, with her family and a black cat. Published in magazines and anthologies, in print and online, including *Midnight Echo* and *Spectral Realms,* she is the author of four collections of poetry, including *Voice of the Goddess and Other Poems* (1991).

Rebecca Fraser is an Australian author of genre-mashing fiction for children and adults. With a penchant for the dark and speculative, her work has won, been shortlisted for, and honorably mentioned for numerous awards and prizes including the Australian Shadows Awards, Aurealis Awards, and Ditmar Awards.

Robert Frost (1874–1963) was an American poet who gained celebrity with such early volumes as *A Boy's Will* (1913), *North of Boston* (1914), and *New Hampshire* (1923), which celebrated his New England roots. He also wrote plays, and his letters have been extensively published. He was awarded four Pulitzer Prizes for poetry, and in 1960 he received the Congressional Gold Medal.

Born in England, Ian Futter draws on his early fascination with its ancient culture, history, and literature and blends it with his love of the supernatural and the ghosts of its past to create his own particular style of writing. He has had his work published in Jason V Brock's *A Darke Phantastique*, various issues of *Spectral Realms*, *Weird Fiction Review*, and S. T. Joshi's anthology of poetic tributes to Lovecraft, *For the Outsider*. In 2019 his poem "The Visionary" was nominated for a Rhysling Award.

Maxwell I. Gold is an acclaimed Jewish-American cosmic horror poet and editor, with an extensive body of work comprising more than 300 poems since 2017. His writings have earned a place alongside many literary luminaries in the speculative fiction genre. His work has appeared in numerous literary journals, magazines, and anthologies. Maxwell's work has been recognized with multiple nominations including the Rhysling Award, the Pushcart Prize, and the Bram Stoker Awards.

Cristel Hastings (1888–1966) was an American poet who published nearly a score of poems in *Weird Tales* between 1927 and 1940.

William Hope Hodgson (1877–1918) was a British novelist and short story writer best known for the novels *The House on the Borderland* (1908) and *The Night Land* (1912), and for short stories of horror and the supernatural collected in *Carnacki, the Ghost Finder* (1913), *Men of the Deep Waters* (1914), and many posthumous volumes. As a soldier, he died in Belgium during the latter stages of World War I.

W[illiam] W[ymark] Jacobs (1863–1943) was a prolific British author of humorous fiction and tales of the sea; but occasionally he dabbled in the supernatural, as in the celebrated tale "The Monkey's Paw" (1902). These tales can be found in such collections as *The Lady of the Barge* (1902) and *Night Watches* (1914).

G[eorge] P[ayne] R[ainsford] James (1799–1860) was a British writer of Gothic and historical novels, including *Richelieu* (1829), *Attila* (1837), *Agincourt* (1844), and *The Cavalier* (1859). He also wrote several historical treatises, such as *Memoirs of Celebrated Women* (1837) and *Dark Scenes of History* (1849). Among his weird works are the novel *The Castle of Ehrenstein* (1847) and the short story "The Living Apparition" (1846).

Tony LaMalfa is at heart just a big kid from a small town who became a produced playwright a few years before joining the Horror Writers Association in 2020. His theatrical works focus on historical fiction, while his horror stories are inspired by H. P. Lovecraft. He lives in Upper Michigan with his young family and is grateful to S. T. and Katherine for their kindness and professionalism.

Frank Belknap Long (1901–1994), American novelist, short story writer, and poet, was a protégé of H. P. Lovecraft and published many stories in *Weird Tales* and other pulp magazines, as well as the poetry volumes *The Man from Genoa* (1926) and *The Goblin Tower* (1935). Later in his career he wrote several novels of horror, the supernatural, and science fiction, including *Journey into Darkness* (1967) and *The Night of the Wolf* (1972).

Lori R. Lopez is an author-illustrator-poet, hugger of ghosts, and wearer of hats. Verse appears in *Spectral Realms, The Weird Cat, HWA Poetry Showcases, The Sirens Call, The Horror Zine, Space &*

Time, Dreams & Nightmares, JOURN-E, and more. Books include *The Dark Mister Snark,* and *Odds & Ends, Darkverse: The Shadow Hours* (Elgin Nominee; Kindle Book Award Finalist). She has eight Rhysling Nominations and placed Third for Long Form in the 2023 SFPA Poetry Contest.

H. P. Lovecraft (1890–1937), American short story writer, essayist, poet, and epistolarian, has now become recognized as the leading weird writer of the twentieth century. Although he published extensively in *Weird Tales* and other pulp magazines in his lifetime, his book publications were mostly posthumous, beginning with *The Outsider and Others* (1939). His collected stories, poetry, essays, and letters have now been published.

H[arold] A[lfred] Manhood (1904–1991) was a British writer of short stories collected in *Nightseed and Other Tales* (1928), *Apples by Night* (1932), *Crack of Whips* (1934), and *Fierce and Gentle* (1935). He also wrote the novel *Gay Agony* (1930).

A[lfred] E[dward] W[oodley] Mason (1865–1948) was a British author best known for more than thirty novels of mystery and detection, as well as three short story collections: *Ensign Knightley and Other Stories* (1901), *The Four Corners of the World* (1917), and *Dilemmas* (1934). He also wrote plays and articles, and several of his novels were adapted into films.

Jessie Adelaide Middleton (1864–1933) was a British author of a trilogy of purportedly true accounts of ghosts: *The Grey Ghost Book* (1912), *Another Grey Ghost Book* (1914), and *The White Ghost Book* (1916). She also published several volumes of poetry.

An army vet and recently retired member of a large Florida-based Sheriff's Office, Jacob Moon now writes full-time from his home in Clearwater, Florida. He is the father of two adult children. His short fiction has appeared in several magazines, most notably the *Saturday Evening Post,* and he self-published his first two novels, *Furlough* and *Dead Reckoning,* the latter having been a finalist for the 2023 Silver Falchion Award for Best Supernatural Novel. His current projects are a memoir based on his career in Corrections and a horror/thriller novel.

D. L. Myers' work has appeared in *Black Wings VI, A Walk in a Darker Wood, A Walk in a City of Shadows: Tales of Urban Legendry, Spectral Realms, Eye to the Telescope, The Rhysling Anthology,* and other venues. His first collection, *Oracles from the Black Pool,* was published by Hippocampus Press in 2019.

Ngo Binh Anh Khoa is a teacher of English in Ho Chi Minh City, Vietnam. In his free time he enjoys daydreamning, reading, and occasionally writing poetry for personal entertainment. His speculative poems have appeared in *Spectral Realms,* NewMyths. com, *Heroic Fantasy Quarterly, The Audient Void,* and other venues.

Pliny the Younger (C. Plinius Caecilius Secundus, 61–113?) was the nephew of the scientific writer Pliny the Younger. He served as an imperial magistrate in the province of Bithynia and Pontus during the reign of the Emperor Trajan. He is now known for ten books of letters that speal vividly of life in Rome and the provinces.

Edgar Allan Poe (1809–1849), American short story writer

and poet, was a revolutionary figure in weird fiction, detective fiction, and the short story in general. During his lifetime he collected his tales in such volumes as *Tales of the Grotesque and Arabesque* (1840) and *Tales* (1845). His poetry was collected in *The Raven and Other Poems* (1845) and other volumes. His influence upon subsequent literature in English and European literature is incalculable.

Michael Potts is the author of the Southern fiction novel *End of Summer* and the horror novels *Unpardonable Sin* and *Obedience*. He also has published two collections of horror poetry and a book of mainstream poetry as well as stories and poems in literary and horror magazines. He is Professor of Philosophy at Methodist University in Fayetteville, North Carolina. He lives with his wife, Karen, and six cats in Coats, North Carolina.

Stephen Mark Rainey is the author of numerous novels, six short story collections, approximately 200 published works of short fiction, and the scripts to several *Dark Shadows* audio productions (Big Finish), which feature members of the original ABC-TV series cast. For ten years he edited the award-winning *Deathrealm* magazine and has edited the anthologies *Deathrealms* (Delirium Press), *Song of Cthulhu* (Chaosium), *Evermore* (Arkham House), and *Deathrealm: Spirits* (brand-new from Shortwave Publishing).

Edwin Arlington Robinson (1869–1935) was a widely published American poet and playwright. He wrote such poetry volumes as *Children of the Night* (1897), *Merlin* (1917), and *The Man Who Died Twice* (1924), which won the Pulitzer Prize. He also wrote the plays *Van Zorn* (1914) and *The Porcupine* (1915).

Lilla Price Savino (1883–1939) spent most of her life in Virginia and North Carolina, where she lived with her husband, the shoemaker Frank Saverio Savino. Aside from eight letters to the editor, she published two poems in *Weird Tales:* "The Grave" (June 1926) and "The Haunted Castle" (April 1928).

Ann K. Schwader's most recent poetry collection, *Unquiet Stars,* appeared in 2021 from Weird House Press, placing third in the 2022 Elgin Awards for full-length collection. Ann is a two-time Bram Stoker Award Finalist and has received both short and long form Rhysling Awards. She was 2019's Science Fiction & Fantasy Poetry Association Grand Master. A Wyoming native, she lives and writes in suburban Colorado.

John Shirley is the author of numerous novels and books of short stories. He won the Bram Stoker Award for his story collection *Black Butterflies: A Flock on the Dark Side.* His novels include *Demons, City Come A-Walkin', A Splendid Chaos, Crawlers, Dracula in Love, Cellars, High, Gunmetal Mountain, Stormland, BioShock: Rapture,* and *Suborbital 7.* He is also a scriptwriter and was co-writer of *The Crow.*

Anna Taborska writes horror stories and screenplays, with tales appearing in more than forty anthologies and three single-author collections: *Bloody Britain* (Shadow Publishing, 2020), *Shadowcats* (Black Shuck Books, 2019), and *For Those Who Dream Monsters* (Mortbury Press, 2013, 2020). She has been nominated for a British Fantasy Award three times and for a Bram Stoker Award five times, and has won the Dracula Society's Children of the Night Award. Anna has also directed five films.

Providence native Jonathan Thomas has persisted in writing weird fiction amidst (or despite) such diverse livelihoods as postal clerk, artist's model, copyeditor, and percussionist. His publishing history includes *Stories from the Big Black House* (Radio Void Press), *Midnight Call, Tempting Providence, Thirteen Conjurations, Dreams of Ys, Naked Revenants, Avenging Angela and Other Uncanny Encounters* (all from Hippocampus Press), *The Color over Occam* (Arcane Wisdom), *Der Finstere Abgrund der Zeit* (Edition Bärenklau), and *Malign Providence* (Centipede Press).

DJ Tyrer is the person behind *Atlantean Publishing*, editor of *View from Atlantis*, and has been published in *The Rhysling Anthology 2016, Dwarf Stars 2022, Speculations II and III, Gargoylicon*, and *Vampiricon*, and issues of *Enchanted Conversation, The Horrorzine, Journ-E, Lovecraftiana, Scifaikuest, Sirens Call, Spectral Realms, Star*Line*, and *Tigershark*.

Kyla Lee Ward is a Sydney-based author, actor, and artist. Reviewers have accused her of being "gothic and esoteric," "weird and exhilarating," and of "giving me a nightmare." Her writing has garnered her Australian Shadows and Aurealis Awards, and she has placed in the Rhyslings and received multiple Stoker and Ditmar nominations. Her most recent release is the novella *Those That Pursue Us Yet* from Independent Legions Publishing, who also released her collection of dark and fantastic fiction, *This Attraction Now Open Till Late.*

John Greenleaf Whittier (1807–1892) was an American poet and fervent abolitionist. Both these aspects of his life and work are infused with his Quaker faith. Among his notable poetry volumes are *Voices of Freedom* (1846), *Maud Miller* (1856), and *Snow-Bound* (1866). He also wrote a short treatise on *The Supernaturalism of New England* (1847).

Acknowledgments

"All Hallows Harvest" by Michael Potts. Original to this volume. Copyright © 2024 by Michael Potts. Printed by permission of the author.

"At the Home of Poe" by Frank Belknap Long. First published in the *United Amateur* (May 1922).

"Beach Shanty" by Katherine Kerestman. First published in *Haunted House and Other Strange Tales*, (Hippocampus Press, 2024).Reprinted by permission of the author.

"the cellar" by Lori R. Lopez. Original to this volume. Copyright © 2024 by Lori R. Lopez. Printed by permission of the author.

"The Dark House" by Edwin Arlington Robinson. First published in Robinson's *The Man against the Sky* (Macmillan, 1916).

"Dark House of Hunger" by D. L. Myers. First published in *Spectral Realms* (Summer 2016). Reprinted by permission of the author.

"The Darkness of Building 727" by Ngo Binh Anh Khoa. Original to this volume. Copyright © 2024 by Ngo Binh Anh Khoa. Printed by permission of the author.

"Empty Bottles" by John Shirley. Original to this volume.

Copyright © 2024 by John Shirley. Printed by permission of the author.

"An Empty House at Night" by Cristel Hastings. First published in *Weird Tales* (April 1935).

"Endless" by Anna Taborska. Original to this volume. Copyright © 2024 by Anna Taborska. Printed by permission of the author.

"The Ghost House" by Robert Frost. First published in Frost's *A Boy's Will* (Nutt, 1913).

"The Haunted Castle" by Lilla Price Savino. First published in *Weird Tales* (April 1928).

"Haunted House" by Katherine Kerestman. First published in *Haunted House and Other Strange Tales*, (Hippocampus Press, 2024). Reprinted by permission of the author.

"The Haunted House" by Cristel Hastings. First published in *Weird Tales* (May 1929).

"The Haunted House" by John Greenleaf Whittier. First published in Whittier's *Legends of New-England* (Hanmer & Phelps, 1831).

"The Haunted House in Kensington" by Jessie Adelaide Middleton. In Middleton's *The Grey Ghost Book* (Eveleigh Nash, 1912).

"Haunted Houses" by Im Bang. In Im Bang and Yi Ryuk's *Korean Folk Tales: Imps, Ghosts and Fairies,* tr. James S. Gale (Dent/Dutton, 1913).

"The Haunted Palace" by Edgar Allan Poe. First published in *American Museum of Science, Literature and the Arts* (April 1839). Included in Poe's "The Fall of the House of Usher" (*Burton's Gentleman's Magazine,* September 1839).

"A Haven for the Homeless" by Frank Coffman. First published in Coffman's *A Coven's Hornbook & Other Poems* (Mind's Eye Publications, 2019). Reprinted by permission of the author.

"House" by Rebecca Fraser. First published in *Spectral Realms* (Summer 2022). Reprinted by permission of the author.

"The House" by H. P. Lovecraft. First published in *National Enquirer* (11 December 1919).

"The House at Black Tooth Pond" by Stephen Mark Rainey. Original to this volume. Copyright © 2024 by Stephen Mark Rainey. Printed by permission of the author.

"The House in the Arena" by William Hope Hodgson. Chapter 3 of Hodgson's *The House on the Borderland* (Chapman & Hall, 1908).

"The House of Terror" by A. E. W. Mason. First published in Mason's *The Four Corners of the World* (Scribner, 1917).

"House of the Lost" by Ian Futter. Original to this volume. Copyright © 2024 by Ian Futter. Printed by permission of the author.

"The Inn" by Guy de Maupassant. In Maupassant's *The Horla and Other Stories,* translated by Storm Jameson (Knopf, 1925). First published in French as "L'Auberge," *Les Lettres et les Arts* (1 September 1886).

"Kubla Khan" by Samuel Taylor Coleridge. Written 1798. First published in Coleridge's *Christabel; Kubla Khan; The Pains of Sleep* (John Murray, 1816).

"Letter to Licinius Sura" by Pliny the Younger. In *Masterpieces of Mystery,* ed. Joseph Lewis French (Doubleday, Page, 1920). No translator given.

"A Life in Rocks" by Jonathan Thomas. Original to this volume. Copyright © 2024 by Jonathan Thomas. Printed by permission of the author.

"The Midnight Hour" by Algernon Blackwood. First published in *Queen* (24 November 1948).

"Misery Cottage" by H. A. Manhood. First published in Manhood's *Nightseed and Other Tales* (Jonathan Cape, 1928).

"Napier Court" by Ramsey Campbell. First published in *Dark Things,* ed. August Derleth (Arkham House, 1971). In Campbell's *Dark Companions* (Macmillan, 1982). Copyright © 1971 by Ramsey Campbell. Reprinted by permission of the author.

"A Night in an Old Castle" by G. P. R. James. First published in *Harper's New Monthly Magazine* (November 1854).

"Papered Over" by Ann K. Schwader. Original to this volume. Copyright © 2024 by Ann K. Schwader. Printed by permission of the author.

"The Red Ensign" by Tony LaMalfa. Original to this volume. Copyright © 2024 by Tony LaMalfa. Printed by permission of the author.